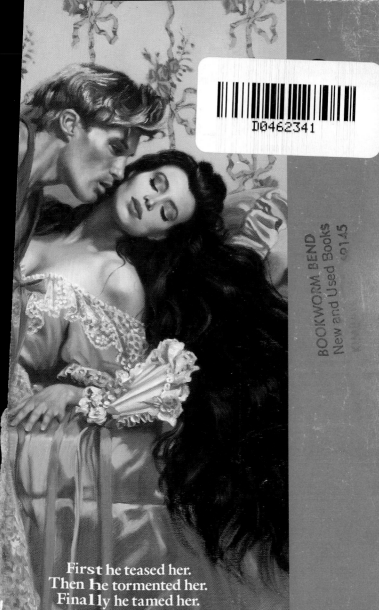

First he teased her.
Then he tormented her.
Finally he tamed her.

"YOU WANT ME, LADY.
EVERY BIT AS MUCH AS I WANT YOU."

"You're an animal!" Jennifer cried.

He grabbed her by the arms and pulled her against him. "Animal I may be, but the mating instinct is running just as hot in your hypocritical little veins as it is in mine. I want you. So badly, I can't think straight. But that doesn't make me any different from any other man. I want you. And you want me just as much. The only real difference is that I admit it."

"Take your hands off me!"

"Why? Do I bother you? Does my touch disturb you? Does it make you feel, Jennifer? Does it make you want things you're afraid to admit? Things you do without?"

"It irritates me, that's all. I don't like it. It bothers me."

"It wouldn't if I didn't disturb you, if I didn't make you feel. You react to me, baby, and that's something you can't deny. And *that,* angel, is what bothers you." He rubbed the pad of his thumb across the fullness of her lower lip, his eyes burning into hers. "I'd like to bother you," he said softly. "I'd like to bother you and keep on bothering you until you scream."

Also by Elaine Coffman

IF MY LOVE COULD HOLD YOU
MY ENEMY, MY LOVE
ANGEL IN MARBLE

ESCAPE
NOT
MY LOVE

ELAINE COFFMAN

A DELL BOOK

Published by
Dell Publishing
a division of
Bantam Doubleday Dell Publishing Group, Inc.
666 Fifth Avenue
New York, New York 10103

ISBN: 0-440-20529-8

Printed in the United States of America

Published simultaneously in Canada

March 1990

10   9   8   7   6   5

OPM

For my mother, Edde Baucum,
who bought me my first book

PART I

There's a divinity that shapes our ends,
Rough-hew them how we will—

Shakespeare, *Hamlet*

1

Weatherford, Texas
1882

When Randolph Baxter opened the door, the sun was rising over the henhouse and General Lee—Rand's prized old English black-breasted red game rooster—was sitting on the back fence preening. Seeing the door open, General Lee ruffled his breast feathers, then stretched his neck, letting go with a loud crow. He was just flapping his wings and readying himself for another majestic blast when Rand stepped off the porch.

"Go do your squawking somewhere else," Rand said, picking up a couple of rocks and throwing them at the rooster. General Lee squawked, his mighty attempt to fly ending with an absurdly awkward landing that left the air teeming with feathers that slowly floated to the ground.

"I came outside to get a little peace and quiet, and I aim to see I get it," Rand said, not feeling the least bit sorry about scolding the old rooster. Normally General Lee and his pompous ways didn't bother Rand, but this morning was different. This morning all hell was breaking loose inside the house, and Randolph had reached his limit.

He crossed the yard and went behind an old toolshed,

prying away a loose board and pulling out a pouch of tobacco and stuffing it in his shirt pocket. Two tabby cats, one yellow and one gray, wandered around the corner of the shed, pausing to watch. Rand ignored the cats as he meandered on down toward the creek to sit a spell and have himself a smoke while he contemplated. The cats followed. As he walked, Rand was talking to himself—not really asking himself any questions, mind you, but just laying everything out in front of him, like a woman would pin a pattern to a length of fabric before she started to cut.

"On the one hand," he would say, then he would mumble a few words, then pause, scratching his chin while he thought things through. Apparently satisfied, he would start up again, taking a few more steps before he would say, "But on the other hand," then he would pause again, his hand going to his chin. Over and over it went, starts and stops, until Castor and Pollux, the barn cats, lost interest and turned away. Presently Rand mumbled something about the whole thing not making any sense, then continued down the path.

The grass was still damp and the air carried the heavy sweetness of woodbine and the early spring roses that rambled along the fence. All in all, it was as splendid a spring morning as one could wish for, and Randolph Baxter had many blessings to count: a beautiful and loving wife, a fine spread, a good crop of spring calves, and more money in the First National Bank of Fort Worth than he could shake a stick at.

But it wasn't his blessings that Rand was thinking of this fine morning as he hunkered over his cigarette, it was sin. Or, more rightly, the sins of his fathers, because he was convinced he had some ancestor or other to blame for all his tribulations—those trying experiences in his life that severely tested and strained his powers of endurance. Rand was a fair man, and he believed in giving credit where credit was due or placing the blame where it rightly belonged . . . and after years of soul-searching he came to blame some forefather with stirring up a little of God's wrath—and credited this ancestor with having had enough sense to die before he could be punished for it. And that left Rand to pay for someone else's mistakes.

Why else had he been blessed with nine daughters, he wondered as he filled a blanket—a Texas term for rolling a cigarette. He wasn't begrudging God the nine daughters so much as the fact that there hadn't been one son to sort of balance things out. Nine daughters . . . it took a rich man to raise nine daughters—and a patient one at that. Why, the house alone had to be huge to contain all those bedrooms, and the rooms themselves had to be cavernous just to accommodate all those doodads women had a fondness for, not to mention all those infernal petticoats. No, it just didn't seem right. He was paying for someone else's sins, sure as shootin'.

But he couldn't think of any sin dastardly enough that would require nine daughters to wipe the slate clean. He prayed he could hold up until he was all daughtered out and the last one was married. Rand frowned, thinking of his youngest daughter, Jenny—the one who was now causing all the trouble and worry. That one might be around for a while.

He watched a lazy old mud cat making circles in the water as he thought about his little Jennifer—perhaps a twenty-one-year-old woman couldn't really be considered little anymore—but his mind kept going back to her, the way she was when she was knee-high to a grasshopper and one of the dearest things in life to him.

And she was still one of the dearest things in his life, but now she was grown and had a mind of her own. And it wasn't always in line with Rand's way of thinking. He flipped his smoke into the creek and closed his eyes, recalling a delicate little face and an abundance of long hair as thick and straight and black as an Indian's, and skin as fair and white as lamb's-lettuce when it bloomed. And her eyes! He wondered how anyone could ever forget Jennifer's eyes

—those remarkable, odd-colored eyes of hers. The color of cornflowers, they were, looking more lavender than blue, and so big that they didn't seem to belong on such a tiny face.

No one had ever been able to figure out, exactly, just where those eyes had come from, and how it was that one so small could have eyes that seemed to speak with such expression, you weren't sure if you were privy to her thoughts or simply gaining a little insight to your own.

He remembered the way she had looked early one morning when he'd just come out of the house—she couldn't have been more than five—waiting for him on the front steps, a little bisque doll in starched blue calico sitting primly with her hands folded upon her white apron, her face radiant as she turned the full light of her eyes upon him.

"Good morning, Papa. Where are you going?"

And Rand had answered that he was going "down to the creek for a spell." He shook his head, remembering the way Jenny popped up like a cork and followed him down the steps. "I'll come with you," she had said. Rand, wanting to sneak a smoke, had just opened his mouth to send her on her way when Jenny thrust her hands into her apron pockets and said, "But you don't need to go to the shed for your makings 'cause I have them right here," and pulled his tobacco pouch out of her pocket.

Rand never did find out how Jenny had discovered his hiding place. It was just another one of those mysteries she held in the shining depths of her eyes. But it had become a ritual after that: Jenny waiting for him every morning and slipping her soft little hand into his, the tobacco pouch in her pocket, as they ambled on down to the creek, him telling her how he never did want her to grow up, and Jenny promising him she never would.

But she had grown up and gone away to college, and Rand had never experienced pain like that before. Even now he would sometimes forget that she was a woman grown, out of college, and on her own, and he would find himself coming out of the house in the early morning, looking at that spot on the first step as if he expected to find her waiting there.

But Jenny was gone and Rand felt the pain of it wedge its way into his consciousness. Jenny. His little girl. His ninth daughter.

And he had been through nine kinds of hell since she had sent that telegram last week from Brownsville:

SCHOOL TERM ENDED. STOP. OFF TO MEXICO. STOP. NO SCHOOL THERE. STOP. WILL ESTABLISH. STOP. BE BACK WHEN DONE. STOP.

Rand had fired off a telegram of his own:

OVER MY DEAD BODY. STOP. YOUR MOTHER DISTRAUGHT. STOP. NEED YOU HERE. STOP. WITHIN TWO WEEKS. STOP. EXPECT COMPLIANCE. STOP.

And he had received this answer back:

TELEGRAM NOT DELIVERED. STOP. MISS BAXTER IN MEXICO. STOP.

Rand decided to wire Jennifer's Aunt Winny, who lived near his daughter in Brownsville, and who thankfully was not his sister but his wife Susanna's. He sent the following message:

NEED YOUR HELP. STOP. JENNY IN MEXICO. STOP. SEND LOCATION. STOP. WANT HER HOME.

This was the reply:

JENNY GROWN WOMAN. STOP. MAKES OWN DECISIONS. STOP. MIND YOUR OWN BUSINESS. STOP. I'LL MIND MINE. STOP.

And that had made Rand furious. "If I ever lay eyes on that scrawny-necked, carrot-headed, shrew of a sister of yours I'll throttle her with my bare hands," he'd said when he'd returned home and showed the telegram to Susanna.

Susanna had immediately started crying, and Rand felt like a fool for making it harder on her. Susanna was as iron-willed, determined, and independent as any woman he'd ever seen, but when it came to their daughters, she was as soft as goose down. And all this business about Jenny's going off to Mexico had her off her feed and nervous as all get-out. And that made it harder on Rand, who was worried enough about Jenny, without adding his concern about Susanna to the pile. Well he knew the kinds of things that could happen to an American woman going into Mexico alone, and one as rich and beautiful as his Jenny would bring every *pistolero* and *bandido* out of hiding to jump at the chance to kidnap her and hold her for ransom, slaking his lust during the interim.

Randolph Baxter was worried sick about his beautiful, headstrong daughter, but for his family's sake he kept it to himself. If Susanna ever got wind that Rand was as concerned about Jenny's well-being as he was, she would have to be placed under a doctor's care. Rand had almost lost Susanna years ago, when their baby daughter died. The next time he might not be so lucky. Whatever it took, no matter how much he was bleeding on the inside, he would never let Susanna know the situation was as grave as it was.

An hour or so later Rand wedged the pouch of tobacco back behind the loose board, tapping it into place, and headed toward the barn. He had just finished exercising his horse, Shiloh, and feeding his hounds and was standing in front of the barn talking to one of the hands when he saw a hack coming down the road in a powerful hurry, hitting every pothole and leaving a trail of dust that settled over the new green sprouts in the cornfield. Rand paused, scratching his chin and watching the hack pull up in front of the gate. Then more trouble descended—four women, wagging and clucking, until the front door opened and Susanna let out a loud wail and flew down the steps, followed by three more wailing women coming out of the house behind her.

While Susanna rushed down the walk and enfolded the four women in her arms, Rand just stood there, watching his wife of thirty-five years and seven of his nine daughters making a spectacle of themselves in the front yard. It was times like this that made Rand just a little happy that Heddy, his eighth daughter, had run off with that penniless cowhand last winter. At least she was in Colorado, and not likely to come all that distance just to join her mother and sisters in making fools of themselves in the front yard. As far as Rand was concerned, all this carrying on about the latest calamity in Jenny's life was about as helpful as throwing a saddle on a dead horse.

Knowing there wasn't any way around it, Rand braced himself and headed toward the house. When he paused at the parlor door, his eldest, Abbey, was speaking rather thickly to her mother through a mouthful of sponge cake. Rand might have known it would be Abbey. She was a wrangler by nature, with the demeanor of an army sergeant; always electing herself straw boss and herding everyone together and shouting orders.

"When did Papa get word that Jenny went to Mexico?" he heard her ask.

Susanna was anxiously twisting the gold wedding band on her finger, her flaming red curls poking from her lace-and-ribbon cap. "Just last week. And I sent those telegrams to you girls straightaway."

Rand was watching Abbey as she cranked up again, wondering how long it would be before she said she was "speechless." Of course, she never was, but it seemed to be a favorite expression of hers.

"Jenny never mentioned going to Mexico in any of her letters, never gave any indication she was developing any interest in starting a school there?" asked Abbey.

"No," said Susanna.

"She didn't? Well, I don't have to tell you, I am speechless. Simply speechless."

"If only you would stay that way," said Rand, ambling on into the room. "I've never seen anyone that could talk in such a steady stream." He looked at Susanna. "We should've named her Flo."

"Papa," Faith said, "remember what the Good Book says about casting stones."

"Faith, just because you married a minister doesn't mean you have to preach like one. Abbey talks too much, and that's a fact . . . you couldn't get a word in edgewise around her if you folded it."

Susanna was frowning at him. "I wish you wouldn't go on about Abbey like that. If anyone heard you, they'd think she didn't have a lick of sense. You know yourself that Dr. Brewmeister said verbosity was a sign of intelligence. And the fact that she speaks four languages proves it."

"Yes, and she can't hold her tongue in any of them."

"Ridicule and anger is not the way to store up treasures in heaven," said Faith.

"I've got more treasure stored than I'll ever need, plus a bonus for raising nine daughters."

"Humph!" snorted Abbey. "More than you'll need, my eye! You don't have enough to make the down payment on a harp."

Susanna intervened once more. "Abbey, stop arguing with your father. You can't both have the last word."

"The only thing that could have the last word around him is an echo," Abbey said with a sour pucker.

Rand looked around the room. It was beyond him just why Susanna wanted to be surrounded by all her daughters at a time like this, when their presence, in his opinion, only compounded the problem. All they wanted to do was talk about the horrors that could befall Jenny. And that would worry Susanna into an early grave. He had to find some distraction or do something to lighten the mood a little.

And that in itself was hard, for every time Rand thought about Jenny, his own heart twisted painfully and he got something in his eye.

"Do you think she was kidnapped?" Abbey was asking her mother.

"I would rather you didn't mention kidnapping to me just yet, I don't believe I want to think about that right now." A crease was tucked between Susanna's brow, her lips tightly held as she wondered just how things had gotten so far off-track with this youngest daughter of hers. She simply didn't know what to think of Jenny anymore. Jennifer had always been just a little smarter, a little quicker, a little prettier, and a little more headstrong than the eight sisters preceding her.

She had always been just a little more trouble too.

Ignoring her mother's distracted look, Abbey said, "Jenny has disappeared. It seems to me that this is the perfect time to mention kidnapping. Surely you haven't ruled it out as a possibility."

Rand's eyes narrowed with disapproval. "Here now, don't be bringing up something else for your mother to worry about," he said, rounding on Abbey. His words had some effect, for a somber silence settled over the room. Susanna closed her eyes, remembering Jenny's telegram, wondering if it could have been sent by someone else, someone who had kidnapped her and wanted to throw them off the track until they had her hidden safely away. But then she remembered the way the telegram had been worded—exactly the way Jenny would have said something like that. And that was probably because Jenny *had* said it. And her mother was sure of it. Besides, Susanna's sister, Winny, had always adored Jenny, often saying Jenny was the child she'd never had.

If Jenny had disappeared suddenly, Winny would have notified them. By her telling Rand to mind his own business, she was saying she knew all about Jenny's plans to start a school in Mexico. Not only knew—if Susanna knew her sister at all, Winny probably approved . . . whole-heartedly. Sometimes Jennifer acted more like she was Winny's daughter than her own, at least judging from the out-of-the-ordinary kinds of things she did.

"No," Susanna said emphatically. Jenny went into Mexico of her own free will. She was not kidnapped."

Abbey dusted the crumbs out of the rocking chair and sat down. "Mother, did you wire Heddy?"

"Yes, of course, but Walt wired us back saying Heddy was going to have a baby come fall, so of course she couldn't make the trip."

"A baby! I'm simply speechless."

Rand started to respond to that but saw Abbey had her eye on him like she was about to fire some question at him. "Papa, what have you done about Jenny's situation?" she asked.

"Jennifer got herself into this mess. She can get herself out," Rand said, pouring himself a cup of coffee and going for the sugar bowl. Then he noticed how his words had affected Susanna. "Della, help your mother sponge that coffee off her dress. Susanna, stop your caterwauling. You know I can't stand to see you cry. No, I wasn't serious. Of course I'll help her. Yes, I remember she's the baby . . . and how sick she was that winter we lost little Irene." *And how you came near to dying with influenza and grief yourself.* . . . "I also remember she's a grown woman, twenty-one years old . . . and that she can cause more trouble than a Comanche war party."

"Something she got from your side of the family," Susanna interjected.

"It wasn't me that put those fool ideas in her head. I tried my damnedest to get her to go to TCU, like all the other girls. Mt. Holyoke, my eye! We were yoked, all right, but I'm not sure how holy it was. And before you ask how I can talk like this, I'll just remind you that our prissy Miss Jennifer Leigh should've bounced her bustle back home after she finished college, gotten married, and had herself a couple of kids, instead of going on down to Brownsville to live with that rattle-headed sister of yours and starting up that damn near worthless school . . . trying to teach a bunch of bean eaters to read in a language they can't even speak. That's our Jenny—forever putting carts before horses. Always has to have a cause, our little Jenny does. Can't meet some respectable man and get married like the other girls did. Come to think upon it, Jenny never would do anything any of the other girls did. Always had to have it her way, forever going just a little beyond what would be considered normal."

"Randolph Baxter, how can you talk like that about your own daughter?" Susanna wailed.

"Because it's true! The girl has a mind like a teakettle— always steamed up about something."

Rand saw Susanna purse her lips as if she'd taken a bite out of a lemon, and cross her arms over her chest, as she did whenever she was in a sulk, and that just egged him on. "Whatever has happened with Jenny, you can bet your bottom dollar your crazy sister had something to do with it," he said.

"Winny is not crazy," Susanna shouted. "You only say that because she's my sister."

"My love, I say that simply because it's a fact. The old biddy is crazy as a loon."

"She's eccentric, Randolph. There's a difference."

"She may be eccentric, but she's still crazy, and I might as well point out here that . . ." Rand paused, catching himself just in time. He had been about to say he held Winny responsible if anything happened to Jenny, a comment Susanna would have collapsed at the merest mention of. Smoothly Rand changed his words to ". . . I hold Winny personally responsible for half the foolish notions Jennifer gets into that lovely head of hers . . . this sashay into Mexico included."

"Randolph Baxter, how can you possibly blame Winny?"

"Did Winny act the least bit concerned after I sent her that telegram?"

Susanna looked a little put out. "No."

"Did she tell us where Jennifer was?"

"No."

"Did she tell us not to worry, that Jennifer was perfectly safe?"

"No."

"Did she reassure us in any way?"

"No."

"Do you think Winny knew Jennifer was planning this trip into Mexico?"

"Yes."

"Do you think Winny approved, that if she hadn't she would have stopped Jennifer herself or wired us?"

"Yes."

"Do you think Winny knows exactly where Jennifer is and precisely how to contact her?"

"Probably."

"Do you think Winny is worried about Jenny, or concerned that something might go wrong?"

"No."

"Do you still wonder how I can possibly blame Winny?"

"No, but she's still my sister."

"A fact I have often questioned," Rand said, about to continue in this vein when Esther cut in.

"Mother, I don't think you should have trusted Aunt Winny to keep an eye on Jenny."

"Right," said Clara. "Who's going to keep an eye on Aunt Winny while she's supposedly keeping an eye on Jennifer?"

"Any woman who gets herself thrown out of a court of law—four times!—for disrupting a trial, shouting obscenities at the judge, and dumping his water glass over his head when she didn't agree with the verdict isn't competent to look after anyone, herself included," Della put in.

"I personally don't understand how Jenny can spend five minutes in the same room with Aunt Winny," Gwen said.

"Neither do I," Rand replied. "Neither do I."

"Please," Abbey said. "You were having this same argument about Aunt Winny before I even knew what crazy and eccentric meant . . . and that's been for at least twenty-five years. As far as I'm concerned, Aunt Winny may be the only sane person in this entire family. At least she had enough sense not to get married and pass the idiocy in this family on to future generations."

There appeared to be a great deal of wisdom in those words, Rand thought, but Beth must've disagreed because she spoke up. "Well, Jennifer isn't married, and look what a pickle she's in . . . hauled off to God knows where. Now, let's get some direction and discuss this sensibly."

"Beth is right, said Della. "Papa, just what have you done?"

"Besides ridicule and poke fun at me," Abbey added.

"Anyone who did that would be a pure fool," Rand said.

Faith gasped. "It's in the Scriptures that anyone who calls another a fool is in danger of hellfire."

"Then Papa ought to be getting awfully warm," Gwen said, laughing.

"Humph! You couldn't warm him up if you cremated him," Abbey said.

"Papa, I asked you what you've done," said Beth.

"Well, let's see. I've tallied all my accounts and exercised Shiloh, and fed the hounds—"

"Papa, will you be serious? I'm talking about our little Jenny."

Rand's expression turned penitent. "I know you are, Puss, and I'm not trying to make light of a serious situation. But with all the facts laid out before me, there are two things that keep reassuring me that things may not be as bad as they seem."

"And what are they?" Beth asked.

"Your Aunt Winny's attitude, which we have already

discussed, but I will have to say that I do believe that Winny loves Jennifer more than she does all of us put together, and for that reason alone she would have contacted us if she thought Jenny was in danger."

"If she's competent enough to form a sound judgment," Abbey said.

"That's one of the negatives," Rand said.

"What's the second reason you mentioned?" Gwen asked.

"I guess I have to say I still have a little faith in Jenny's judgment. Even if she acts the part at times, Jenny's no fool . . . that is, she's no marblehead," Rand replied, his eyes going over to Faith, who smiled and nodded. "The worst part of all of this is the unknown. It's pure, living hell not knowing just what it is that Jennifer is up to and where she is."

"Well, then, we need to set about finding her. Have you done anything about that?" Abbey asked, looking at Rand. "Are you going to find her?"

Rand looked thoughtful. "It's a difficult thing to know how to handle. On the one hand, Jenny is a grown woman, and has always been independent. How do we respect that, yet ease our own minds a little? You know how she has her own ideas about the way things should be, and resents like hell any interference, interruption, or distraction from what she's about."

"And this is a good time to point out that part of the reason Jennifer has always been so headstrong and independent has been your fault," Susanna said.

And Rand had to admit she was right. He had to accept some of the blame for Jenny's wildness. He had spoiled the little imp. Unable to bring himself to call to task a child as utterly adorable as Jenny had been, Rand had to admit he had allowed her to roam the countryside, swim naked as a sunfish in the water trough, and observe a lot more of Mother Nature at work than he probably should have. He guessed it was simply because he had always felt just a little sorry for someone as exceptional as his little Jenny, having to be born a female at a time when that carried a certain penalty with it. He had wanted to give her sure footing. He had no idea she would take off like she'd been fired from a cannon.

Another glance told Rand his brood was still waiting for his answer. "I spent all day Friday with the sheriff in Fort Worth, and we decided the best thing to do was to hire the best gun we could find to locate Jennifer."

"And then what?" Abbey asked. "Shoot her?"

"I was thinking about extrication."

"Why don't you just go after her yourself?"

"Because I don't know where to start looking."

Susanna looked at Abbey. "What your father is trying to say," she said, "is that he couldn't track a bleeding buffalo through eight feet of snow."

"Finding Jenny may be a hell of a lot easier than convincing her to come home," Rand said. "I've never had much luck getting Jenny to see anything my way."

"Maybe not, but you've sure had more success than anyone else I can think of," Della said.

"Have you located someone for the job?" Beth asked.

"Yes," said Rand.

"Has he already started looking for her?"

"He's coming here first so I can fill him in on the details, give him the telegram, and show him a picture of Jenny."

"When will he be here?" Gwen asked.

"I'm hoping this week; certainly no later than next Friday."

"He's not wanted by the law, is he?" Della asked in a quiet voice.

Rand laughed. "No," he said.

"What's so funny about asking if he's wanted by the law?" Clara asked.

"Because he *is* the law . . . a United States deputy marshal."

"How did you find him?" Gwen asked.

"Through an old friend of mine, a fellow I went through college with named Parker. He's a judge now, in Fort Smith, Arkansas . . . Indian territory. I wired Isaac when Sheriff Busbee couldn't think of anyone he knew personally to recommend or whom he would trust to bring Jenny back."

"Do you know anything about this deputy?"

"Nothing more than what Isaac said in his telegram. Said he comes from a fine Southern family . . . graduated from the naval academy. Had quite a promising career as a naval officer, from what I understand."

"Had?" Della asked.

"How is it that a naval officer is hiring himself out as a gunslinger?" Abbey wanted to know. "And where did he get his reputation with a gun?"

"Lord! I don't know everything about the man. My information came by wire and is sketchy at best. I would imagine he resigned his commission."

"You don't know why?" asked Gwen.

"No. Maybe he got fed up with politics or discovered he gets seasick. Hell! I'm not writing a book about him. As long as Isaac says he's the best he's ever seen and faster than greased lightning with a gun, it's good enough for me."

"Is he married?"

"I don't know. I would be inclined to think not. Most lawmen aren't. A man like that, courting death on a daily basis, doesn't need a woman at home weighing on his mind, holding him back, interfering with his decisions."

"Couldn't he get here sooner?" asked Beth.

"No. Isaac did say he'd send him as soon as he returned . . . something about him tracking Belle and Sam Starr."

"He must be good if he's going after Belle Starr," Abbey said.

"Does this gunslinger have a name?" asked Faith, scooting to the edge of her chair.

"Jay Culhane."

"I went to finishing school with a Julia Culhane from Atlanta," Susanna said. "I wonder if it's the same family. Do you know if he's from the Atlanta Culhanes?"

"How in the hell should I know?" Rand said. "Honestly, Susanna, sometimes you can ask the most irrelevant questions."

"Irrelevant to you, perhaps, but I was wondering about his family background. After all, this man is going to spend weeks traveling alone with Jennifer, and we both know what kind of effect Jenny has upon men."

"Yes," said Rand. "She intimidates the hell out of half of them. The other half would like to throttle her."

"Jenny is an exceptionally beautiful woman," Susanna said.

"And a lonely lawman like that is in a perfect situation to be influenced by a woman's dedicated love," said Della.

"Influenced by a woman's dedicated love, my eye!" Rand snorted. "A woman's love is about as dedicated as the morning dew. It's just as apt to fall on a horse turd as a rose."

Nobly Susanna refrained from adding that she had passed up many a rose to marry the notorious Randolph Franklin Baxter III.

"Oh, wonderful, now we have something else to worry about—an unknown gunslinger with a reputation going after our sister. . . . "I just don't know which is worse," Clara said skeptically. "Not knowing where Jenny is or worrying about a man like that going after her."

"We could hire someone else," Faith offered after a few minutes.

"We'll do nothing of the sort," contested Susanna, springing to her feet and drumming her nails on the piano. At least we won't do anything until this Mr. Culhane arrives."

"I can't see what difference that would make," said Gwen.

"It probably won't make any difference at all," Susanna

said, and then she added, "But I find it's much better to be looked over than to be overlooked."

"Good God," Rand said, "are we hiring a man to find Jenny or buying a horse? You don't have to count his teeth. Why pick the man to pieces? He is experienced at this sort of thing, spends his life finding people who don't want to be found. And he's deadly with a gun. Sheriff Busbee said he'd heard Culhane could shoot the tapes off a woman's drawers at fifty paces."

"That's what we're afraid of," said Della.

"Look," Rand said, "I told you he comes highly recommended by an old friend of mine. A man I've known for a long time. A man I trust. If you can come up with something better, I'd like to hear what it is."

"There's no reason to get all out of snuff, Papa," Abbey said. "We're just thinking about what would be best for Jenny."

"And you think I'm not?" Rand shouted, forgetting his determination to keep things on a light note. "I've got more damn worries about Jenny than I can count on both hands, but being concerned about what might happen to her in the hands of a U.S. deputy marshal sure as hell isn't one of them. And I'll tell you something else. I'll stop worrying about her the minute this man gets his hands on her. I almost feel sorry for him! He may be a gunslinger. He may be hard as nails. He may know how to handle a woman as mean as a snake . . . a woman like Belle Starr. But I'll wager half this ranch and every penny I've got in the bank in Fort Worth that he's never, ever come across the likes of Jenny. The poor fool will earn every penny I'm giving him before it's all over."

Rand stopped and stared at his wife as she said, "There is no point in remaining in the same room with a man who would rather vent his spleen than sensibly discuss something as serious as the disappearance of his daughter." Then she turned and walked regally from the room.

A puzzled frown gathered on Rand's face. He was trying

to understand his wife. He had lived with her for over half
his life, loving and living, raising nine daughters, but sometimes he felt like he didn't know her at all. His horse he
knew. And his hounds too. But Susanna? It was a sad thing
to admit—that a man was better acquainted with his horse
and dogs than he was with his wife.

He turned his daughters, "And for your information," he
said to them, "I hope and pray this man teaches that sister
of yours a lesson she won't ever forget."

Then Rand watched in silence as seven of his daughters
rose as dramatically as their mother and filed out of the
room in a correspondingly imperial manner.

2

∽∽

For five years he had traveled alone. A lone-riding man in a lonesome land, he possessed nothing but the mouse-colored horse that moved slow and surefooted beneath him, the worn Smith & Wesson Schofield strapped at his hip and the long Marlin rifle that hung, California-style, from his saddle horn. A man on the move didn't need much in the way of trappings, just a few items rolled in the bedroll strapped behind the cantle, the rest of his meager belongings tucked in the saddlebags: a change of clothes; a yellow slicker; a pair of stovepipe mule-ear boots; a few rounds of ammo; a Mexican blanket with a hole cut out of the center; a straightedge razor; soap; and a few cans of beans, tomatoes, and peaches. Bare necessities.

For five years he had lived like this, never staying in one place long enough to make friends, just long enough to make a few women happy. And then, as quickly as he had come, he was gone. They never knew where he had come from. They never had time to ask where he was going. Most of them never even knew his name.

He was a big man, tall and straight as a telegraph pole, lean as a coyote after a long, hard winter. But his lankiness was deceptive. Tough, rawboned, and rangy, with keen senses and a quick wit, he stalked his prey with the sinuous sureness of a jaguarundi. And like the coyote, he was friendless, respected by his enemies, and possessed an uncanny knack for survival. This, coupled with his lean, muscular body, made him ideally suited for a predatory existence. He was a brooding man and wary; a man who believed in nothing but his horse, his guns, the laws of nature, and the deceptiveness of women.

His face was hard-boned and expressionless; his eyes were cold, a clear, penetrating blue but not cruel. His clothes were faded and well worn, yet like the man that wore them, it was apparent they were not of common quality but had been made of superior cloth, superb in cut and selected with pride—a remnant of another time.

He rarely thought of his past. He never looked toward the future. He lived one day at a time, riding down a twisted stretch of road that had no end, no final destination, freezing his backside in winter, choking on alkali dust in the summer. For five years he had followed this road, hiring out his gun to track down a ruthless killer, a renegade Indian, or an outlaw gang, and then, against his better judgment, he had done something that surprised even him. He had allowed himself to be blackmailed into letting another woman into his life.

He had been in Fort Smith, Arkansas, just having come in from Indian territory—the Nation, as the Cherokee called it—after Sam and Belle Starr had been arrested for horse stealing. On his way out of town Jay stopped by Judge Isaac Parker's office to pick up his pay. Six cents a mile didn't seem like much for trailing an outlaw. But it kept beans in his belly; kept his mind off other things. That's the way it was with them—the hired guns, the deputies that endangered themselves to bring in desperate killers alive. There were over two hundred of them now, men with no future and a whole lot of past—deputy marshals that trailed countless outlaws through seventy-four thousand square miles—not to mention riding herd on sodden peddlers selling illegal whiskey to the Indians, hardened gunfighters, scalp-gathering renegades, mass murders who had gone berserk. And Parker wanted them alive, which meant they had to be brought five hundred miles over a hostile trail to Fort Smith. Small wonder that sixty-five deputy marshals had already been killed, or some of the deputies had gone bad, like Grat and Bob Dalton. Men like Grat and Bob made it hard for a good deputy like their brother, Frank, who was brave and honest as the day was long. At times it seemed like the law was on the wrong side, making it even harder on the deputies. If a deputy killed his prisoner, even if he was attempting to escape, he forfeited his fees and expenses, and worse, if no one claimed the body, the deputy was out sixty bucks for the burial. No, it didn't seem right, but then, that was the way of things.

Jay found Isaac in his office, standing in front of a cloudy mirror, trimming his whiskers. His hair was parted on the right, neatly combed, his face clean-shaven, except for the mustache and goatee. His clothes were dark and somber—a wide-lapeled suit, tie, a vest with a gold pocket watch, fob showing—altogether fitting for a hanging judge. But Parker was fair. Even the Indians admired his impartiality. He had stern policies, but that was something the territory needed after Judge Story, who'd resigned in order to avoid impeachment for bribery.

Isaac caught Jay's reflection in the mirror and said, "You heading out after the Dalton boys?"

Jay nodded.

"I don't understand why a man like yourself will risk his fool neck in the Nation for five hundred dollars a year. You could at least get a job as a federal marshal." Isaac dusted the whiskers off his lapel, then put the scissors away.

"No thanks," Jay said. "Deputy marshals have all the fun."

"You'll keep on until you get yourself killed. It's just a matter of time. You know that, don't you? With your background, your education, you could be so much more."

"That's what I hear about a Missouri senator who became a hanging judge," Jay said, just a little curious about Parker's past. But Parker just smiled that smile that said he knew what Jay was thinking and that he could just go right on thinking it. Jay saw this was pointless. "I'll just collect my pay, and then I'll be moving on out. The Daltons have three days on me as it is."

Isaac handed him his pay. There was a telegram with it. "What's this?" Jay asked, turning the folded piece of paper over in his hand but not opening it. He looked at Parker. "You read it?"

Isaac grinned his slow grin. "Yes, I read it. A rancher in Texas wants you to find his daughter."

"I'm not interested," Jay said.

"Didn't think you would be. Started to wire the man and tell him that."

"Started to?" Jay removed his hat, laying it crown down on Parker's desk. "What stopped you?"

"Five thousand dollars."

Jay shrugged, tucking the telegram into his shirt pocket. "Still not interested."

"Why the hell not?" Parker asked.

"What would I do with five thousand dollars?"

"Settle down. Buy yourself a nice spread somewhere. Get married. Raise a family."

Jay felt like he'd choked on a jalapeño pepper. "I had all that once. And once was enough."

"It could be different this time, Jay."

"Could it?" He shrugged. "We'll never know, though. Will we?"

"She's just a kid, Jay. Twenty-one years old."

"Twenty-one isn't exactly a kid . . . especially when it's a woman." Jay blinked against the ghost of Milly, which swirled like a vapor behind his eyes. Milly had been twenty-one when he'd married her.

"Yes . . . yes, I've slept with your brother . . . and not just once. Don't look so shocked, Jay. Pierce has been my lover for years. The first time was only three months after

our wedding. It didn't take me long to realize I'd married the wrong brother. It was wrong between us, Jay, from the very beginning. I was too inexperienced. I didn't know what it could be like. It wasn't you. It wasn't me. It was us. You could never inflame my senses as Pierce did, never turn my knees to jelly with just a look. . . ."

Milly had been twenty-one then. The first time she'd deceived him.

"There's reason to suspect the girl's been taken into Mexico."

"Then that complicates things, doesn't it?" Jay said.

"You know that country, Jay." Isaac said.

"Yes, and I know women. I don't want a damn thing to do with either one of them." He picked up his hat, running his fingers along the creases in the crown. "Send someone else, Parker," Jay said.

"There's no one else available."

"What about Whittaker?"

"After the Youngers."

"Thornton?"

"Trailing Jim Moore."

"Chris Madsen?"

"He's working with Fannin. Blue Duck and his bunch are stirring up trouble again."

"Shit!"

Isaac laughed.

There was no trace of humor on Jay's face. "You won't give up, will you?"

Isaac shook his head and grinned. "That's why they call me the Hanging Judge."

Jay was feeling restless. Trapped. Cornered. He didn't like the way things were going. He wanted to feel his horse beneath him, the wind in his face. He wanted to put some miles between himself and civilization. He couldn't take being connected with a community for long. First thing you knew, it would begin to feel comfortable. Feeling comfortable was a good way to get a bullet in your back. Out there, he had to forget what his life had been before, had to keep his mind clear. His life depended on it. Outlaws had one good trait—consistency. Once they went bad, they stayed that way. No lawman was fool enough to trust an outlaw. You knew what they were, knew it was either you or them. And that kind of evened things up a bit. But, hell! A woman . . . the only thing consistent about a woman was her inconsistency. A woman simply couldn't be trusted. Any man that went traipsing across the country with a woman in tow was a fool. A damn fool.

Parker sighed, the humor leaving his face. "I'm taking you off the Dalton job. I want you to go after the girl. Her father is an old friend of mine. I owe him a favor."

"No," said Jay.

"You're one of the best, Jay, but you thwart me in this, and I'll see you don't work again. It's this job or nothing." Isaac paused, waiting for Jay's reaction.

"Shit," Jay said. "Shit!"

"What about the girl, Jay?"

Jay didn't answer right away. He just stood there, his arms folded across his chest, staring at the blank wall, the muscle in his jaw working. "You're a stupid son of a bitch . . . sending a man like me after a twenty-one-year-old woman."

"And why is that?"

"You know how I feel about women. Aren't you afraid I'll harm her?"

"That's the least of my worries."

"I've done it before."

"Done what?"

"I roughed up that Slater woman."

Isaac smiled. "Is that what you call it? Roughed up?" He shook his head. "One slap?"

"She was a woman, wasn't she? And I slapped her. More than once."

"And saved her ungrateful life by doing it."

"Listen, Parker, I'll—"

But Parker held up his hand. "No. You listen. You're the only man for this job. My mind is made up. I like you, Jay. And more than that, I respect the hell out of you. But I mean what I say. You go after the girl. Find her. Bring her back home."

"And if I don't?"

"I'll see you never wear another badge as long as you live."

Jay looked angry enough to kill, but Parker had faced men who did more than look that way. "What's it to be, Jay?"

Jay turned and drove his fist against the wall, then brought both hands up to brace himself as he leaned forward, his head slumped between his shoulders. He stayed that way, the muscles tightly bunched along his shoulders, not saying anything for a long time. Then, finally, he said, "I'll take the job."

"Good."

He turned toward Parker. "I'll go after the girl. Beyond that, I'm not making any promises."

"I'm not asking for any. Your word's good enough for me. If you say you'll go after her, I know you'll do your best."

"You're a trusting bastard, aren't you? What if I disappoint you?" Jay asked.

Isaac smiled. "You won't. There comes a time, Jay, when you can't go it alone. Sooner or later you have to trust someone."

But Jay didn't agree. "A man has to be what he is," he said. "Once the brand is burned in place, there's no changing it. You have to wear it the way it's branded for the rest of your life. We've all got our brands, Isaac. You've got yours. I've got mine." Jay walked outside and untied his horse.

"You're a crazy bastard," Isaac said, following him as far as the door. "Maybe that's why I picked you."

Jay swung into the saddle. Isaac was probably right. He

was a crazy bastard. By taking the Baxter job, he was getting involved with a woman who would surely bring out the worst in him; a woman who would resurrect painful remembrances that were best forgotten. He pulled his hat low over his eyes, nodding at Parker, then spurred the gelding into a full gallop, knowing even as he did that the memory once so painfully etched upon his heart would be waiting for him at the end of the line. Just as it always was.

Jay had been traveling for days. Earlier that morning he had crossed into Texas. Behind him lay the Red River, and back, beyond that, Indian territory. He had made good time, for traveling went faster across this immense, grassy expanse of rolling land, where nothing but a few clumps of scattered trees broke the endless ennui that comes with hours spent in the saddle riding across never-ending terrain that screamed monotony. Here the land rolled, like a fat woman's thighs, going on forever. There were no more rivers to ford, no heavily wooded areas to slow him down, no mountains to cross, no renegade Comanche to be on the lookout for. He was traveling light and fast, pushing the sturdy horse beneath him to hold a steady lope. If this pace held, he would reach Decatur before nightfall. One more day should put him in Weatherford.

Jay Culhane breasted a steeply rising hill and reined in the grulla near a motte of scrub oak, then checked the sky. It was a little past three by the sun. Dismounting, he kicked an abandoned snakeskin that had looped itself over the toe of his boot, then, removing his hat, he tipped his canteen, pouring a generous portion of the water over his face. A scissortail flew overhead, its pink undersides flashing, then landed on a branch nearby, the sudden movement ignored by his horse as he lowered his head and snorted, giving himself a good shake. The gelding nudged Jay, pawing the ground, the bit ringing against his teeth as he tossed his head.

Jay laughed. "Okay, Brady. It's your turn, old man." He

poured the rest of the water in the crown of his hat and offered it to his horse. Then he unfolded a piece of paper, his eyes squinting against the brightness of the sun reflecting off the white surface, then slowly traveling over the words as if he were looking for something hidden there, something unsaid yet visible.

The telegram gave few answers and raised a lot of questions. What in the hell was a young, gently bred woman doing in a rough border town several hundred miles from her home and family in the first place? And this business about crossing the border into Mexico—more than likely the girl had up and run off with some smooth-talking drifter. Someone should've dusted the young woman's butt with a willow stick a long time ago. He folded the piece of paper and tucked it back into his shirt pocket. His face was grim, with the slightest curl of a smile. Maybe he'd come across a willow stick somewhere along the way.

A minute later he was back in the saddle, disappearing over the next rise. Five hours of steady riding put him in Decatur. A bath, a good steak, a bottle of rotgut whiskey, and a pair of warm and willing thighs eased the burden of retrospection that had dogged him all day. But even then, sleep was slow to come. He kept thinking about a young woman he had never met. A woman he would hunt like a criminal. Only she was no criminal, but a refined woman. A lady. The whore next to him stirred in her sleep. He had never tracked a lady before. It had been a long time since he had slept with one. He looked at the whore, the coarse features of her face, the short, stubby fingers, and tried to remember Milly. Beautiful Milly. Long flaxen hair falling across his chest like a curtain of silk; her naked skin, warm and smooth like fresh cream. Long, tapered fingers. Teasing green eyes—turning dark and smoldering when heated with passion. Beautiful, lying, deceitful Milly. Yes, it had been a long time since he'd had a lady.

And he planned to keep it that way.

It was late the following afternoon when Jay circled a

small water-filled sink and rode onto Baxter land. Evidently Randolph Baxter went first-class, judging from the condition of his spread, the Box R. The cattle were fat. The grass was good. Whoever Jennifer Baxter was, she had a rich papa. The place had that well-groomed look of prosperity.

But the house was a monstrosity. Perched upon a grassy rise, it looked somewhat like a cross between French mansard and Queen Anne styles, and someone had seen that it displayed about every possible embellishment known to man: pineapple finials, scallops, fish scales, gables with balconies, porches and a seven-sided bay window, elaborate spools and spindles, intricate moldings, pillars, festooned and laced bargeboards. Even the paint suffered from indecision. Before him sat a harmonious rainbow of colors. Everything from purple to plum and four shades of lavender to greens, grays, three shades of terra cotta, blue, and five shades of rose—a painted lady if he'd ever seen one.

Jay had seen a hundred homes of this ilk throughout the South. But he had never seen anything quite like the one that sat before him like a grand old duchess with her eccentric love of the flamboyant and too much face paint. He wondered what kind of people would live in a house like this. He wondered what kind of man Randolph Baxter was. And he wondered what in the name of hell he had gotten himself into. A little pressure from his knees urged the grulla forward.

He rode into the front yard, dismounted, and tied Brady to the hitching post. A few minutes later he found himself facing a stiff-lipped, honest-to-God English butler.

"Have you a card I may present, sir?"

For a moment Jay just stared at him. Then he shook his head, trying to remember how long it had been since he'd presented a calling card. Not since he'd left the refined drawing rooms of Savannah. "Just tell Baxter that Jay Culhane is here to see him. He'll know why."

"I will give *Mr.* Baxter the message. This way, Mr. Culhane, if you please."

Jay stepped into a dark hallway, dimly lit by a chandelier. He wondered if he should have removed his spurs as he crossed the parquet floor and followed the butler into a different world.

"You may wait here, in the front parlor. I will locate Mr. Baxter directly."

"Thanks." Jay said, then watched him leave after a curt bow. Jay looked around the opulent room, which was filled with homey clutter. The Gaveau piano was identical to one that had belonged to his mother, and for a brief moment he had a vision of Jessamine Culhane sitting there in a swirl of taffeta skirts and smelling of rose water. But Jessamine had been dead almost four years now. A broken heart is what his father called it before dying a year later of the same affliction. And Jay knew he was the son of a bitch who'd killed his parents by breaking his beloved mother's heart. Him. The one his mother adored, the apple of her eye, the child of her heart. And he had been denied the final farewell, unable to attend her funeral because he'd been lying half submerged in the freezing waters of Snake Creek near Fort Hall, Idaho, with a Shoshone arrow through his thigh the day she was buried. Of all the regrets that ripped at him, this was the most villainous. But even as the thoughts bled from old wounds, he could see Jessamine's violet eyes smiling down at him, could almost feel the gentle caress of her hand upon his cheek. The forgiveness was there. He knew that. But he could not reach out and accept it—so bent was he upon the road to self-destruction. He closed his eyes against the pleading look in his mother's eyes and shut the door on another tender memory. When he opened his eyes, he focused on the fainting couch for just a moment, before slowly taking in the rest of the room.

As they had on the exterior, the Baxters had taken the easy way out that a surplus of money provides. Instead of deciding exactly what it was that they wanted, they opted for it all: filling, borders, friezes, wainscoting, crown ornaments, girandoles, ornately carved furniture, tapestried upholstery, thick carpets—everything dripping with excess and covered with memorabilia. He walked over to the piano and studied the assortment of silver-framed tintypes arranged there. Was Jennifer Leigh Baxter among them?

"Jennifer is the young woman holding the fan in the large photograph to your right."

Jay looked to see who the rich baritone voice belonged to, then he turned and picked up the photograph. "How old was she when this was taken?"

"That was taken last August . . . on her twenty-first birthday."

A flash of Milly, sitting in the vine-covered swing under a huge, sweeping oak, her laughter floating over him as he stood behind her . . . Milly on her twenty-first birthday.

Jay looked at the man. Did he wonder why he stared at his daughter's picture like he was a brick shy of a full load. He glanced at the girl's picture again. "She's a lovely young woman." An understatement. The girl was beautiful, exquisite . . . strikingly so. Jay looked at her picture once more, because he couldn't seem to help himself. Even in the pale sepia tones of the tintype he could see the purity of her skin, the perfectly straight nose, and . . . dear God, that mouth. As soft and innocent as a child's, with a slight pout that screamed "Kiss me!" Her eyes were huge and round, looking at him with velvety softness. A man could lose himself in those eyes.

But he wouldn't.

The girl was nothing more than a job to him. A job he was forced to take. He felt the surge of immense anger toward her, anger for being stupid enough to go into Mexico in the first place; anger for being the reason he was pushed into something he wanted no part of. Yet in spite of his anger toward her, something about the girl reached out to him. Was it her eyes? He felt the pounding frustration at not knowing their exact hue.

But he would.

He would know that and more. He would know everything about her—every mole, every childhood scar, the exact tint of her skin where the sun never touched. The fierce attraction burned through him and he knew that it would be best for both of them if he walked out on this job right now. The girl would be more than a job to him. He had known it the moment he'd looked at her face. Was that why her eyes were so wide and round? Because she knew it too? It was ordained and irrevocable. Sometime. Somewhere. Somehow. He would take her to his bed.

It had been a long time since he'd had a real lady. Too long.

To break the spell Jay turned the frame over.

"What are you doing?"

"I'm removing the picture."

"My wife will have apoplexy."

"Would she rather have the photograph or the girl?"

"Take the photograph. I can get another one made. Jenny I can't replace." Rand crossed the room. "I'm Randolph Baxter," he said. His hand came out.

Jay's handshake was firm and brief. "Jay Culhane."

"Have a seat, Mr. Culhane. "I'm sure you have some questions, things you'd like to know about Jenny and her disappearance."

Jay settled back in his chair, accepting a small glass of Mrs. Baxter's homemade strawberry wine. His eyes returned to the piano, but this time the woman he visualized sitting at the bench was not Jessamine Culhane. This woman was younger . . . yet her eyes were like his mother's, the color of violets. But her hair, not brown like Jessamine's, was black. Rich. Glossy. Full of life.

As Baxter talked on, Jay wondered if his eyes communicated just how fruitless all of this was. Nothing Baxter would tell him about the girl would do him any good. It was all viewed through a father's eyes, distorted and faintly colored. He didn't really care that the girl was a schoolteacher living near her old-maid aunt in Brownsville. He wanted to know why a twenty-one-year-old girl, fresh out

of a fashionable women's college in the East, would choose
that kind of life for herself. And more importantly, why she
would venture into Mexico alone.

"I guess to answer that question you'd have to understand the women of this family," Rand said. "I've been
married to one of them for over half of my life, and I raised
the rest of them. But I still don't understand them."

"What made her pick Brownsville? Her aunt?"

"Yes. Jennifer could never do any wrong in Winny's eyes.
She invited Jennifer to visit her after she graduated. The
next thing we knew, Jennifer sent us a wire telling us she
had been hired to teach school there. I was against it, but
Susanna went ahead and boxed up Jenny's things, freighted
them all the way to Brownsville for her. She's been there
ever since."

"Does your daughter do this sort of independent thing
often?"

"I wish I could say no, but Jenny has always seen things
she thought needed doing where most people saw nothing
wrong. And once she found a spark, it was do or die."

Which meant she had a talent for sticking her nose where
it didn't belong and getting herself into trouble, Jay was
willing to bet. "You don't think there's a chance she just
sent the telegram to cover up for something else?"

"Like what?"

"Running off with a man?"

Rand didn't have to think on that one. "No. Not Jenny.
She isn't the type." Rand laughed. "I had one daughter
who did that just last year, so I know the type I'm talking
about. But Jenny is different. As far as men are concerned,
she is as innocent as they come."

Jay didn't believe that for a moment. Any woman who
looked the way Jennifer Baxter did wouldn't reach sixteen
with her maidenhead intact. "She may not be so innocent
by the time she comes back from Mexico, if that's truly
where she's gone. I assume you know the kinds of danger
she could get into down there?"

"I know," Rand said with a worried look. "That's why I hired you. I want Jenny brought back home . . . here to Weatherford. I don't care why she's there, or how big a fuss she makes about staying there. Whatever it takes, you bring her home. I'll not have Susanna worried any longer than necessary."

"Oh, I'll bring your daughter home, Mr. Baxter, if I have to hog-tie her to do it."

Rand laughed. "You don't know how true that may be. I'll warn you now, Jenny will try everything. Pleading. Reasoning. Anger. Tricks."

"And old reliable tears."

"That's the one thing she won't try. If you make Jenny cry, you've done something no one else could do. There've been a few times she's come close, but she's never broken down. I haven't seen her cry since she was a little girl." Rand grinned. "But she'll give you a run for your money in any other way she thinks is possible."

"I'm used to trouble, Mr. Baxter. I can handle that."

Baxter's expression turned serious. "I just want my daughter, Culhane. Find her . . . please. As soon as possible." Rand sighed. "I don't want my daughter punished or abused. I just want her home. I want my life back to normal."

"If she's in Mexico . . . and still alive, I'll find her and bring her home." Jay looked at the photograph in his hand. The young woman Baxter described wasn't, in any way, real to Jay. She was nothing but a sepia tintype, stiff and frozen into position. But the woman seared on his brain . . . she was real. Warm. Spirited. Alive. He had no idea where Jennifer Leigh Baxter had gone. Or why, really.

But he would find her.

And when he did, he would take that fan out of her hand, then slip that soft, lacy dress off those white, white shoulders and down, past her hips, to pool at her feet. He folded the picture in half and put it in his pocket.

Jay stood. "I'll be shoving off now. Thanks for the information. I'll wire you when I head into Mexico."

Rand followed him. "Please," he said, "do stay. My wife has planned for you to dine with us and stay the night."

Jay hesitated.

"My wife is having a very difficult time with this, Culhane. She's worried sick about Jenny. She's anxious about the kind of man I'm sending after her. She wanted to meet you. It would ease things up a bit for her if you'd stay."

Jay nodded. "I'll stay to dinner, then. But I'll be heading out after that. I'd like to get a few miles in before I sleep."

As he said he would, Jay stayed for dinner. Later, when he thought back on it, he decided that dining with the Baxters was a lot like going to a circus, where everything was contained under a big top but inside there were so many sideshows going on, you were both delighted and bewildered, yet at the same time left feeling just a little reverent. ·

Mrs. Baxter was the first to arrive for dinner, wearing black.

"My dear," Rand asked, "has someone died? Are you in mourning?"

"Yes," she answered, pressing her kerchief to her nose. "I shall wear black until our little Jenny is back." She crossed the room, extending her hand to Jay. "You must be Mr. Culhane. I'm Susanna Baxter, and I can't tell you how grateful I am that you are going after our Jennifer, although I do hope you will hurry, Mr. Culhane. As you can see, black is not my color."

"A woman as lovely as you would look good in any color, I would imagine."

"Why, thank you, Mr. Culhane."

"Where are our daughters?" Rand asked.

"On their way down, Rand. Give them time. You, of all men, should know how women are." Susanna turned to Jay. "You know, I went to school with a Julia Culhane who was from Atlanta. Would you be any relation to her, by chance?"

"My father had a cousin named Julia who was from Atlanta. She moved away after her marriage. She lives in Philadelphia now, or did, the last I heard."

"Oh. So you no longer have any relatives in Atlanta?"

"My father's Uncle Brice has been dead for several years and some of the family has moved away, but a few of them still live around Atlanta."

"And you, Mr. Culhane? Are you from Atlanta as well?"

"No, ma'am."

"Well, I swan!" she said with a musical laugh. "If it's not Atlanta, it must be close. I'm sure I heard a little touch of the South in your voice."

Jay couldn't help but smile. "I'm from Savannah, ma'am."

"Oh," Susanna said, clapping her hands together. "Oh, how utterly lovely. Savannah," she said wistfully, "such a delightful city. My dear brother lives in Charleston . . . actually, his place is between Charleston and Savannah. Do you know any of the Claibornes in that area?"

"I know of them . . . quite a distinguished family. I've met several of them socially, but I don't know any of them very well."

By the time dinner was served, all seven of the Baxters' visiting daughters were present; all seven of them beautiful, inconceivable, and quite unbelievable, if not theatrical.

Somehow the conversation drifted around to marriage, and Jay learned that Jennifer was the only Baxter daughter who was unmarried. From there the discussion went from one event to the next, story after story, all of them dealing with Jennifer. Clara, sitting next to her twin sister, Della, began talking about the day Jenny put the burr under Della's saddle.

"And if she hadn't done that, I wouldn't have been thrown," Della said.

"And if she hadn't been thrown, we never would have met the Schultz brothers," added Clara.

"And if you'd never met the Schultz boys, you wouldn't have married two of them. What in the name of hell is going on here? I've never heard such an accumulation of sentimental slop in all my life!" Rand roared, disregarding Susanna's admonishment to tone it down or he would rupture something that was best left unruptured.

"Provoke not your children to wrath," Faith reminded him.

"Oh, I beg your pardon," Rand said. "But as Scripture says, 'A man with nine daughters is cursed.' "

Faith looked at her father, raising a brow Jay could only call skeptical. "Now, where does it say that, Papa?"

"Maybe those aren't the exact words, but it does say something about a man with too many daughters."

"You have it all wrong," Faith said. "It says children are like arrows in the hand of a mighty man, and happy is he that hath his quiver full."

"Happy, huh?" Rand said, mulling things over. "Does it, by chance, say when all of this happiness is supposed to happen?"

"Well, I am speechless," Abbey said. "Honestly, Papa, to hear you talk, one would think you were anything but happy about having *any* children."

At the opposite end of the table Esther laughed, then clapped her hand over her mouth when she saw Jay was staring at her. Her face turned bright red and she looked down. Jay continued to stare at her for a minute. He knew it was rude to stare, but he just couldn't seem to help it. She was the only Baxter he'd met who didn't have much to say. In fact, she looked like she would prefer to blend in with the wallpaper.

"Esther is terribly shy," Abbey said.

Rand sighed and looked heavenward. "I'm not trying to sound like sour grapes, you understand. . . . After all, *you* saw fit to bless me with nine daughters, so there must have been a reason. Now, I know there isn't anything particularly bad about having nine daughters. But there isn't anything particularly good about it, either. And I know I'm not the only man with daughters . . . and that somebody had to take them. But would it have hurt anything to give me nine quiet ones?"

"You've got one quiet one, Papa," Faith said. "Count your blessings."

"One out of nine isn't all bad," Susanna reminded him.

Rand nodded and smiled at his wife, losing himself in thought. When his attention drifted back to those seated around him, they were still talking about Jennifer. Catching his confused expression, Susanna explained how she thought it would be nice to have the evening meal in Jennifer's honor.

And Randolph Baxter saw nothing wrong with that.

And then she added that they had decided to tell whatever incident they were reminded of when they thought about Jenny.

"Good God!" Rand said. "It's about as cheerful as a wake in here." Then, looking at Susanna, he said, "Madam, your daughter is off on another wild-goose chase. She is not dead!" And with that Rand pushed his chair back and stood.

Susanna watched him stomp across the room. "Randolph Baxter," she said, "where on earth are you going?"

"To get my Gilbert & Parson's Hygienic Whiskey, Mrs. Baxter," he said. He winked at Jay. "And if you know what's good for you, Culhane, you'll join me."

"Hygienic whiskey?" Susanna repeated. "Whatever for?"

"Headache," Rand replied, "because that's what *I'm* reminded of when I think of Jenny."

Jay shared a glass of brandy with Rand, but when Rand invited him to stay the night, Jay declined once again. There were too many things here that reminded him of home and the family he'd once had. He was anxious to get away from all these people. Anxious to be alone, to sort through the information he'd been given and plan where he went from here.

Later that night, when he camped out on the open prairie, Jay opened his saddlebags, looking for the picture of Jennifer Baxter. He found it—and a curiously shaped object wrapped in brown paper and tied with string. A note was attached.

Directions for use: Take three healthy gulps four times a day. It will make Jenny easier to swallow.

Jay opened the package. Inside he found a bottle of Gilbert & Parson's Hygienic Whiskey.

For a long time he remained there, squatting on his haunches before the fire, the bottle of whiskey in one hand, the picture of Jennifer Baxter in the other. A pain lodged in his gut.

It will make Jenny easier to swallow. . . .

But the sultry-eyed young beauty was much too easy to swallow as it was.

3

Jay pulled the grulla up at the outskirts of Brownsville. Any other time he wouldn't have given a plug nickel to be anywhere near Brownsville, but since he'd been on the move for over three weeks, eating trail dust and living on black coffee, canned peaches, and beans, he was mighty relieved to see Brownsville baking in the hot afternoon sun just ahead. He was dog-assed tired, sorely in need of a few things—namely a warm bath, a close shave, a hot meal, and a loose woman. But even as the thought formed, he knew he'd have to forgo all that. The most important thing right now was finding Jennifer Baxter's aunt . . . "her crazy aunt," as Rand Baxter had said. According to what Rand had written in the packet of information he'd given Jay, the old-maid aunt lived on a small ranch that lay along the the Texas border, formed by the Rio Grande. Jay glanced at the sun. He still had a couple of hours before sundown. Yes, the warm bath would have to wait. And so would the loose woman.

Once he located Miss Claiborne's small ranch and rode up the road toward her house, he was thinking it looked exactly as he expected. Miss Winny Claiborne, however, did not. Jay had anticipated a tiny, bespectacled woman with old-fashioned clothes, ideas, and eccentric taste in furnishings—probably a dozen or so cats, a whistling teakettle, an old organ that wouldn't play, and the smell of creeping age filling her house.

What he found was a tall, skinny woman with carrot-red hair and freckles, with a disposition about as friendly as a stepped-on rattlesnake. He kept his eye on the Winchester she was holding loosely in her hands. She was dressed in the latest fashion, which was so out of place in this part of the world that Jay could only stare at her for a moment.

"I assume you had a reason for knocking on my door right at suppertime. If it wouldn't strain your faculties, would you mind telling me what it was?" Before Jay could reply, she looked him over, her mean little eyes squinting as they scrutinized him from head to foot, then she said, "What in the name of hell's wrong with your hair? You got lice?"

"Not unless I've picked some up since this morning."

"Well, why don't you cut it? Thought you were a damn girl when I first saw you ride up . . . or a goddamn Comanche. Your hair must be a foot long. Don't they have barbershops where you come from?"

"They do, but I just haven't had the time to go."

"Get a haircut," she said. "You look like a chrysanthemum."

"Yes, ma'am," Jay said, trying to keep a straight face.

Not one to let anything slip by, she added, "A shave wouldn't hurt you none, either."

"I'll keep that in mind."

She narrowed her eyes at him. "I don't need any hired help."

"I'm not looking for work."

"I don't give charity to anyone healthy enough to work, either."

"I don't blame you."

She was still giving him the once-over. "And I'm not looking for a reason to stand here in the door staring at a pure fool. State your business or dust the road. I ain't got time to dicker."

Jay stared at the woman, almost blinded by the effect of the sun on all that carroty hair. "Miss Claiborne? Miss Winny Claiborne?"

"Since the day I was born."

"I'm Jay Culhane."

"Well, somebody had to be, I suppose. Might as well be you."

"I beg your pardon?"

"I didn't mince my words, young feller." She tilted her head to one side, like a chicken eying a caterpillar. "I said, somebody had to be," she repeated, turning up the volume.

Jay grinned. "Yes, ma'am, I caught that. I just missed your meaning. Somebody had to be what?"

"I thought you said your name was Jay Culhane."

"I did. It is."

"Well, then, I guess somebody was bound to be named Jay Culhane sooner or later . . . there are just so many names to go around, you know."

"True, but—"

She waved the Winchester at him. "Just tell me what you want. I'm sure you didn't ride all the way out here just to hear the sound of your name coming from my mouth."

"No. I was sent here by Mr. Baxter . . . Randolph Baxter."

"That old coot still alive?"

Jay nodded.

"I'm surprised someone hasn't shot him by now." Her sharp eyes went over Jay again. "Well, what's the old buzzard up to now?" She shut one eye and looked at him, as if trying to size him up, judging for herself his trustworthiness. "He still married to that boneheaded sister of mine?"

"I believe he mentioned his wife was your sister."

"Humph! Susanna never did have a lick of sense when it came to judging men or horses. She'd soon as saddle an ass as a thoroughbred."

Jay repressed a smile. "I understand you know their youngest daughter quite well."

"Only one in the whole damn bunch with a lick of sense, if you ask me."

"It's about Jennifer that I've come. It seems—"

A spark of interest flared in her eyes. "Jenny? Has something happened to her?"

"I don't know. I was hoping you could give me a little information about her."

"You mean her own parents don't know enough about her to tell you? They had to send you hightailing it all the way down to the valley to find out about their own daughter?"

"I'm looking for information about her disappearance."

"Disappearance? Has Jenny disappeared?"

"I thought Baxter said he sent you a telegram and you sent him a reply. You mean you weren't aware your niece has been missing for over a month?"

"Sonny, he did send me a telegram. And I sent him one back. Just like you said." She was looking a little put out now. "Of course I knew she'd been gone for over a month. But I didn't know she was missing."

"It's the same thing."

"More the fool you . . . it isn't the same thing at all. Missing implies you don't know where something is. Gone simply means they are no longer at the place they are normally found."

"Do you know where Jennifer is?"

"More than likely."

"I'd be most obliged if you'd tell me, then."

"Oh, I've no doubt about that."

"Well?"

"A deep subject."

"Miss Claiborne, keeping valuable information from Jennifer's parents about her whereabouts is a serious offense. Obstructing her rescue is a serious offense. Refusing to give information to a United States deputy marshal is stupid."

"And why is that?"

"The girl might have been kidnapped."

"Kidnapped? Hogwash!"

"Whatever you wish to call it. But the Baxters are concerned about their daughter's disappearance and want her found."

"I don't think Jenny feels the same way. Besides, she sent that fool Baxter a telegram explaining why she was going to Mexico. I was with her when she sent it. It explained everything as plain as the nose on your face."

"Just the same, her parents want her found and brought back home, Miss Claiborne."

"I don't doubt that, but you'll have to find her in order to do that."

"That's why I'm here. I was hoping you could give me a little more information than the Baxters did. Can you tell me where, exactly, Jennifer is?"

"Mexico."

"Mexico is a big place."

"Smart one, aren't you?"

Jay groaned. "Miss Claiborne, would you mind telling me where exactly in Mexico I might find Jenny?"

"Well, Mr. Fancypants, you'll just have to find that one out for yourself."

Jay was beginning to realize this torch-headed woman wasn't going to give him the time of day. It would be dark before long. His temper was mounting. His belly was grumbling. He was ready to call it quits for the day. With a sigh of exasperation Jay put the hat he'd been holding at his side back on his head. "If you'll just direct me to Jennifer's house, I'll be on my way."

"Why go there? I thought you said she was gone."

"I did. She is."

"Seems like a dumb-fool time to go visiting, if you ask me . . . when you know there ain't nobody at home."

"I'm not paying a social call. I'd like to see if there's

anything that might help me locate Jennifer Baxter's whereabouts. You do know where she lives, don't you?"

Winny released a cackle. "Sonny, don't you go trying to trip me up. That one is as old as the hills. I know where she lives." She paused once again, pursing her lips together in thought. "I don't suppose it would hurt none to tell you . . . you'll find out, anyway, when you get to town. That sheriff we've got has a tongue that hangs out like a pump handle."

"I sure appreciate your saving me the time of going to see the sheriff, then."

"There's wisdom in those words. The sheriff's a bigger bullet-head than Rand Baxter . . . if that's possible."

"A peculiarity a lot of men seem to have."

Winny tilted her head to one side and propped her rifle up against the house. "Go back down the road a piece. About two miles back you'll pass an old house being used to store hay. At the next crossroad turn left. Jennifer's house is the first on the right, about a mile down that road. You can't miss it. But I'll warn you now, not to go poking your nose where it doesn't belong, rummaging through her things. She's a very private person and mighty particular. She won't take too kindly to some rawboned, whisker face snooping around her place of abode, prowling through her belongings, letting the lice jump out of his hair."

"I'll certainly keep that in mind, Miss Claiborne . . . and I don't have lice."

Winny cackled. "You don't have good sense, either, thinking you're going to bring Jennifer back here against her will." She laughed again and slapped her knee. "Wish I could go along to see that. You're fixing to meet your match."

"I've heard she's quite a little pill."

"Yes, I guess Jenny is a pill to everyone she meets, but she's always been like tonic to me."

"You care a great deal for her, don't you?"

"Like she was my own. And I wouldn't hesitate to cut

the gizzard out of any son of a bachelor that harmed a hair on her head. You best remember that, because Jenny won't come back with you. Not willingly."

"I'll remember, but, willing or not, I'll bring her back. And it makes little difference to me whether she wants to come or not. Good day, Miss Claiborne. Thanks for your help."

Going to Jennifer Baxter's was a big mistake. Too many reminders of the girl lay everywhere, and Jay didn't need any more reminders. The seductive-eyed little witch had strayed like a haunting melody into his memory, aching like a sadness. One he couldn't seem to shake.

Her house was small, neat, and white-framed; its green shutters sorely in need of a couple of coats of paint; the flowers in the front flower bed needing a little water. He picked the lock on the back door and walked down the hall to the bedroom, a pain of longing twisting his gut as he held the coal-oil lantern aloft, the light warming the room with the same soft, golden tones found early of a morning. He had stepped out of wind-baked reality and entered a different world.

Everywhere he looked, it spoke of a woman—soft, feminine—with collections of ornately topped scent bottles, silver-backed hairbrushes, pearl and jet hat pins, lace-trimmed fans, a straw hat tossed in the seat of a lacquered and gilded chair, all deliciously underpinned by the fragrance of a woman. His eyes went to the brass bed, where softly cascading folds of lace draped, held with lavender ribbon and garlands of flowers. Everywhere he looked was fairy-tale whimsy: ribbons and roses in soft, luscious colors, so utterly feminine, yet just a little off-center considering the kinds of things he had been told about her. He had expected cold, bare, even harsh surroundings, certainly nothing that spoke of femininity. He had found just the opposite. What kind of a woman was the real Jennifer Baxter?

He grinned. For one thing, she wasn't overly tidy.

Her bed was unmade, a tangle of white, starched sheets and scattered, lace-trimmed pillows. Something soft and filmy had been dropped on the rug next to it. Compelled by the sudden leap of his imagination, he picked it up, the lingering smell of ripe, mellow roses filling him with longing and a stab of loneliness. He rubbed the soft fabric through his fingers, looking at the creamy color and imagining how the dark-haired beauty would look in it. With a groan Jay tossed the gown on the bed and walked to her dressing table and the collection of silver-framed miniatures, cut-glass and silver-capped containers, powder boxes with ostrich puffs, a silver comb, mirror and brush, and a pair of white gloves. He picked up the gloves. Jennifer had small hands.

He was about to turn away when he noticed a small black-lacquered box. Knowing it probably contained her jewelry, he opened it, anyway. Once again he found the opposite of what he had expected. Oddly enough, it was filled with newspaper clippings . . . all about various marches and demonstrations concerning women's rights, the killing of buffalo, the removal of Indians from tribal lands to reservations, the fur industry, trapping, and whaling. Jay frowned, sifting the clippings through his hands. A strange collection for such a feminine young woman. Perhaps she had collected these to use while writing a paper in college. But why would she save them? And leave them in her jewelry box? He tossed the clippings back, shutting the lid. He would know the answer to that question when he located Jennifer Baxter.

If he hadn't caught one of his spurs on her hooked rug and tripped, he would have missed it. After stumbling, he unhooked the rowel on his spur, seeing he had knocked over the small trash can next to her desk. As he picked up the scattered bits of paper he noticed numerous torn pieces, all the same coarse, brown paper, the penmanship primitive and crudely written in Spanish. Why were these torn when none of the others were? Jay turned the lamp up, thankful he had placed it on the desk before he tripped.

Pulling out the chair, he sat down, spreading the small, torn bits of paper before him. For over an hour he worked on the puzzle, fitting the jagged edges together. When he finally finished, the message didn't make much sense. But two words did jump out at him: Agua Dulce. He knew that place. It was a small town in Mexico, one he remembered seeing on the map he had been studying earlier.

Agua Dulce. It wasn't much of a lead. In fact, it might not be any lead at all. But it was the only thing Jay had to go on.

He rode into town, stopping by the telegraph office to send Rand Baxter the wire he had promised. Then he purchased the few supplies he'd be needing at the general store. His next stop was the blacksmith's, where he purchased a sturdy buckskin for Jennifer. After loading his supplies he grabbed a bite to eat.

An hour later Jay crossed the Rio Grande into Mexico.

Three weeks later he rode into Agua Dulce. It was a small, dusty adobe village, just like a hundred other little dusty towns scattered about—a cantina, a church, the peon version of a blacksmith's, and one small store. But there on the outskirts of town was something that made this town different from so many others. A schoolhouse. A brand-spanking-new schoolhouse.

About a mile farther down the road was a small adobe house, of the same vintage as the school. Would this be where Jennifer lived? Finding out would be easy enough. The school sat off by itself. The only other structure nearby was a crumbling adobe building, which Jay rode behind without being seen. He tied Brady and the buckskin, then made his way toward the one-room school.

The windows were open and he could hear voices. When he looked inside, he saw a Mexican girl standing next to a woman, both of them with their backs to him. The woman had to be Jennifer Baxter. Her hair was done up in back, but he could tell it was as black as sin. She was dressed in a simple but stylish blouse and skirt. She spoke rapid Spanish, the girl listening and occasionally commenting or nodding. He saw her write something down and hand it to the girl. They both laughed, and Jay felt frustrated as hell. Why doesn't she turn around? *Come on, sweetheart. Turn around for me. Turn around and let me see that angel face of yours. Let me see the exact color of those eyes.*

But she didn't turn, and Jay heard himself curse. He continued to watch her, thinking he'd never seen such a tiny wasp waist in his life.

Not pressing his luck, he slipped back to the building where he'd left the horses, picking a spot to watch the school. Some time later the girl left, walking toward town on foot, but the woman remained inside. He watched for a long time, almost to the point of falling asleep, when he heard the sound that flashed across his drowsy mind. Coming down the road was a burro pulling a small cart. The cart was driven by an old, gray-haired Mexican dressed all in white, peon fashion. The old man stopped in front of the school and the woman came out a few minutes later, her back still to him. Turn around, dammit! he thought, then looked startled when she turned and glanced back at the school. Without a doubt, even from this distance, he could see she was the most exquisitely beautiful woman he had ever laid eyes upon. Yes, even from this distance he knew her, knew who she was. Jennifer. Jenny.

She climbed into the cart. Jay watched them until they were far enough away for him to follow, keeping low behind the crumbling walls of the building and the outlying adobe wall. He watched the cart pull up in front of the house and Jennifer climb out. The old man waited until she entered the house, and then he touched his hat respectfully and left. Up until this moment Jay wasn't completely convinced that the girl hadn't been kidnapped. And if she had, and was being held against her will, why was she not under guard? But then he looked at the country around him.

Miles and miles of inhospitable alkali desert, and once she left the village and their well, she would be days from the nearest water hole. Even if she left, Jennifer would have no place to go—not without a horse or donkey, and, more importantly, not without a good supply of food and water. If she had been kidnapped, Jennifer Baxter wasn't under guard for one simple reason: One wasn't needed. The surrounding desert encased her like prison walls.

Still, Jay was inclined to agree with her father. Perhaps Jennifer Baxter had been telling the truth when she said she was starting a school in Mexico. She was certainly working in that school when he'd found her. And she didn't exactly look like she'd been forced to be there—or unhappy about it, either. She must have come to Agua Dulce of her own free will. But why? Why would a woman that beautiful waste her life out here? He looked back at the house where Jennifer lived. Whatever the reason that drew Jennifer out here—school, a taste for adventure, or just plain stupidity—it had nothing to do with kidnapping. He'd stake his life on that.

Jay waited a while longer. The wind was getting up, the sand swirling around his feet and getting in his eyes. He could feel the stiffness creeping into his joints as he waited for the dark cover of night. And even then, once it had grown dark, he waited a little while longer, watching the shadows of her moving across her windows as she walked about the small house. In his mind Jay could imagine all sorts of things she was doing. Some of them were perfectly ordinary—eating dinner, cleaning up the dishes, grading papers, even a little light housekeeping. But the visions of her letting down her hair and removing her clothes for bed . . . He groaned, remembering all too well the kind of things Jennifer slept in.

Cursing his physical weakness, Jay left his refuge behind the crumbling building and made his way toward Jennifer's house, which was of adobe, but built in a style he had seen numerous times in East Texas, with two doors that opened onto the front porch. There were lights on in both rooms, so he watched the house for a few minutes, trying to decide which room she might be in. He had just started toward the house when the light went off in one of the rooms. When he reached the back porch, he chose the door on the right where the light was on and, after trying it, found it locked.

He stepped back, the wind beating against him as he rushed forward and gave the door one mighty kick, looking up with a satisfied grunt when the wind finished the job for him, driving the door inward to slam against the wall with a loud *crash!*

"Son of a bitch!" Jay said. "Son . . . of . . . aaaa . . . biiitch!"

For just inside the door was Jennifer Leigh Baxter in the flesh, every splendid, glorious inch of it, wearing nothing but a thin, silky, one-piece bloomer combination that hit her high on the thighs. His eyes dropped lower, to where a pair of silk stockings covered the best-looking legs he had ever seen. And Jay Culhane had seen plenty. He let loose with another expletive, just as she looked up quickly, her face partially obscured behind a long, dark cloak of hair.

Huge violet eyes rimmed with long, dark lashes, too stunned to register any emotion, stared back at him. The jolt of those eyes was something he hadn't counted on. He kicked the door shut behind him, and for a moment he just stood there, looking at her in the same stunned manner in which she was looking at him.

Jennifer Baxter stood there in the soft glow of a bedside lamp, searching for her lost breath, unable to believe what had just happened. Out of the wind had stepped the most handsomely arrogant and ruthless man she had ever seen. A depth of perception she had never known rushed through her in a single instant as her eyes moved over him. A long, hard body. Sleek and wary. Frozen in readiness. His features were perfectly honed and chiseled; his face registering surprise. A sudden awareness pierced her. Masterful, sensual, devastatingly male, the slow grin spreading across his face sent her a warning. The realization struck her with a force that drove the air from her lungs. The taunting smile was slowly giving way to one that was far less innocent. She understood now, the meaning of the expression handsome as sin.

"You've obviously made a mistake. Would you be so kind as to leave? And close the door behind you."

"Keep looking at me like that, long legs, and I won't be going anywhere."

He was looking at her with the sharpness of an eagle, making Jennifer suddenly aware of what it was that he was looking at. She yanked her dressing gown from the bed and clutched it in front of her, her eyes dark and smoldering with anger. "You've gotten your filthy eyes full. Now get out of here."

"Like hell I will," he said, then gave a strange and bitter laugh that seemed to penetrate the thin fabric she clutched to cover her near nakedness. Those smoky-blue eyes were still roaming over her body slowly, and she calculated what might happen if she were to bolt around him and try for the door, running half naked and barefoot into the night.

"Get out!"

"Not on your sweet life," he said, which was true, for Jay Culhane couldn't have moved if someone had dusted his behind with gunpowder. All he could think of was this exquisitely beautiful woman, with the longest legs imaginable and wearing the sexiest silk stockings. Then he remembered all the hell she had put him through trying to find her . . . but his mind kept flashing back to what she had looked like, standing before him half naked in those goddamn stockings. He wanted to see her that way again. He wanted to see her in nothing at all, save those silk stockings. He couldn't even begin to imagine what they would feel like wrapped around his waist, but by God, he wanted to.

"I said get out! Are you hard of hearing?"

"Not of hearing, no," he said, his smile just a little wicked.

"This is a private residence and you are trespassing. Now get out of here before I scream."

"Scream, then. I won't stop you."

"Why are you here? What do you want?"

He almost laughed at that one. "Why, I've come to see you, of course."

"All right! You've seen me . . . more than you should have. Now leave."

"Only if you come with me."

The impact of that softly spoken phrase stunned her. "Come with you?" she repeated. "Why?"

"Come here and I'll show you."

"I'll just bet you would." Goose bumps rippled across her, yet she wasn't really cold. Her face warmed beneath his hard scrutiny, which reeked of proficiency and practice. She was both frightened and strangely dizzy with something she could only liken to dangerous excitement. "I'm not coming anywhere near you. So you might as well leave."

"Then I'll come to you." Her extraordinary eyes seemed to absorb light as she glared at him.

"If you know what's good for you, you'll get out of here." She was feeling his heat, reaching across the room to touch her like a blistering brand. He smiled then, using the tip of his thumb to push his hat back on his head, and the effect of it jolted her. He took a step forward.

She took a step backward. "Listen, I don't know who you are, or what you're doing here, but I'm obviously not who you want."

"Oh, but you are, angel eyes. You're exactly what I've been looking for."

Jennifer was trembling now, her self-control slipping badly. "Blast you!" she said. "Whatever the reason you're here, I want you to leave. Now!"

"Wrong response. Try again."

Jennifer took a deep breath. Threats and orders didn't seem to be working too well with this man. She would have to try something else. "You obviously have me confused with someone else." The fool had that wicked smile pasted across his face again. She tried another approach. "I'm trying to tell you that you've made a mistake."

"Ahhh, sweetheart, you sure as hell don't look like a mistake."

"But I am, I tell you. I don't know you. You don't know me—"

"No, I don't. But I will."

"Blast and double blast!" she said. "Will you stop this nonsense and leave?"

"You might as well give up. The more you talk, the more I'm convinced I should stay awhile. His eyes moved around the room, resting on a small rocking chair. In three long strides he moved to the chair and dropped into it.

"Just what do you think you're doing? You can't come barging in here like you own the place."

"Can't I." He grinned. "I'm already here, sweetheart. And here I intend to stay. At least for a while."

"And just how long might that be?"

"Until the entertainment's over."

"What entertainment?"

"Your performance."

"What performance? What are you talking about? I'm a teacher. I don't perform."

"You're fixing to."

He rocked back as far as the chair would go, thrusting his long, lanky legs out before him, content to look his fill, finding suddenly that he was in no hurry—no hurry at all. Little Jennifer Baxter could take all night . . . at least that was what he was counting on.

"What do you mean, I'm fixing to?" This man was dangerous, in more ways than one. He was incredibly handsome, wicked—at times almost charming—and could probably kill at the slightest provocation, as well as do a few other unmentionable things with no provocation at all. Her breath was coming in quick little gasps as she watched him draw the pistol from his gun belt and point it at her.

"Drop the wrapper."

"What?"

"You heard me. Drop the wrapper."

"You're insane."

No, he thought, *but I will be if she doesn't drop that damn wrapper, and quick.* He didn't say anything; he simply waved the pistol at her.

"I won't do it," she said defiantly. "You can't make me."

He laughed. "Oh, I can make you . . . without ever leaving this chair."

"How? By shooting me?"

"Perceptive, aren't you?"

"Is this some kind of joke?"

His expression was tight, the line of his jaw hard, just like his voice. "Lady, I've never been more serious in my life. As to my being insane . . . maybe I am. But insane or not, I know how to use this pistol," he said, waving the barrel, which was pointing at her. "Now drop the wrapper."

"You can go straight to—"

"I've already been there and back," he drawled, releasing his legs and allowing the rocker to swing him forward with a snap. Jennifer took a step backward, coming against the edge of the bed. He cocked the pistol. Dryness clutched at her throat. Should she risk it? Would she dare to call his bluff? If she did, she might find he couldn't shoot a woman. But what if he could?

"The choice is yours, angel eyes. Remove the wrapper or I'll do it for you."

He saw the narrowing of her eyes, the glint of pure hatred flickering in their depths. Then, with a haughty lift of her chin, she stared at him, and for a flicker of a moment defiance flashed hotly in those eyes of hers, which were a smoldering deep purple now. Then the look began to dim and fade. He saw her lower lip quiver, and for a brief second he thought she might cry, but she took a deep breath, gaining control. She never took her eyes from him as with deliberate slowness she lowered the wrapper to her waist. And then, with a deep breath, her body erect and proud, she released the fabric and then let it fall to the floor.

His eyes went to the dusky circles of her breasts, faintly visible through the fine, sheer fabric of that one-piece undergarment she was wearing—and it was sexier than hell. Hot, licking flames twisted his guts, shooting shafts of fire into his groin. Desire, white-hot and blistering, reared its ugly head—something he had felt numerous times, but never before had he been unable to find the means to temper it. For a moment Jay couldn't breathe, so dazzled was he by the onyx-haired beauty standing before him in almost nothing. Her skin looked as white and fresh as this morning's milk, and he looked at every supple inch of a body that was fine-boned and gracefully slender.

Although she wasn't a large woman, her breasts were full and generous and perfectly shaped. The quick, breathy way she drew in each breath, frantic and rapid, made them rise and fall like temptation before him. He fought the urge to leap from the chair and grab her with every bit of the aggression he felt. The girl was far lovelier than he had imagined or ever could have hoped. She might have hair as black as sin, but everything else about her was pure heaven. But the look in her eyes was anything but angelic. There was no doubt the girl was scared, but there was defiance in those odd-colored eyes of hers—defiance, determination, and strength.

Jennifer Baxter might be a young woman, but he had his work cut out for him, he could see that.

Still, it puzzled him to find he had scared her into thinking he would really shoot her. But it surprised him more to see that she never—not once—took her eyes from him. Any virgin would've looked away, or cringed or cried or closed her eyes. Jennifer did none of these things. Because she did not look away modestly, Jennifer Baxter branded herself as a woman who had known the touch of a man, the heat of a naked body against her own—a woman who had lost her maidenhead. His curiosity peaked, Jay decided to see just how brazen Miss Jenny really was, and just how far she would really go.

"Now, the rest."

The anger flared again, deeper in her eyes this time, more intense now, but as before, she kept it under control. For a long moment she just stood there, looking at him with the same angry defiance she had shown him a moment ago, then, when he thought she wouldn't, Jennifer began to unfasten her buttons—the task, Jay thought, was maddeningly slow. He studied the way the thin, shimmering silk adorned her body, the seductive way it showed him just enough to tease his imagination. He had never seen a woman wear something as scandalous as this. Was it the latest fashion? He was accustomed to seeing a woman in a chemise and bloomers, not this wanton, one-piece thing that hit her so high on the leg, he couldn't keep his eyes from going higher to the place where they joined, and the shadowy reminder of what lay between. He watched, enchanted. He imagined her wanting him, her warmth closing around him. He watched, holding his breath as she drew the last button through, pulling the pink ribbon at the top apart, then untying it with a jerk.

He felt his mouth go dry, the breath he had been holding rushing outward suddenly, like a ragged sigh. With each breath she took, the thin, cream-colored fabric drew apart, exposing the high, round globes of her breasts to view, then, like a tease, hid them once more when she exhaled. Encouraging her with another wave of his pistol, Jay felt the quickening response of his body as Jennifer turned away from him so that he only saw her from the side. She dropped one shoulder. Obviously she had hoped to deny him by turning away and letting him see her from only the side, but by so doing, she had given him a much more seductive pose—and the Lord alone knew that she was seductive enough as it was. Jay could only think of one word to describe the way he felt around her. Flammable.

He waved the pistol. "Now the rest of it."

She lowered the fabric over the other shoulder before parting it and letting it fall down her slender arms, then slowly sliding it over her slender nakedness to the floor, then stepping out of it. With two fingers she held the silk undergarment in front of her. Then she released it, her eyes never leaving his. With a dry swallow Jay watched it float to the floor. Then his eyes traveled upward. *Dear Mary, Joseph, and Jesus!* There was nothing more exquisite, more beautiful, more indescribable than a woman who looked like this—all milky-white skin, lavender eyes, the blackest hair imaginable—and wearing nothing, by God, but a pair of silk stockings.

Jay had never seen a woman this young behave so boldly —not even in a brothel. Evidently, disrobing in front of a man didn't disturb her too much. And since it didn't Jay wasn't about to stop.

"Now turn around. Slowly."

He saw the shininess of her eyes, and if the girl had been an innocent he would have called it tears of embarrassment or even shame, but on this saucy piece . . . he decided she simply didn't like being told what to do. Some devil or the other in him wanted to taunt her more, to see how far she would bend before she snapped and lost control. "If you know what's good for you, you'll turn around, angel eyes. Now!" Then, more softly, "Do it, girl. I want you facing me."

A flush heated her cheeks and he heard her gasp of out-rage, but she was a good one at self-control, at keeping a passive look on her face—something he was finding damn hard to keep his eyes and concentration on, pretty as it was, because she had the most beautiful breasts and unbelievable legs he had ever laid eyes upon. And Jay Culhane was a man who had been with many, many women—women whose job it was to entice and please a man.

"You want me to help?" He made a move to rise from the chair but checked the movement, lowering himself back to the chair when she turned, her eyes angry and sharp.

He grinned. "Just a little more, so the lamplight hits your sweet little body just right. A little more. Ahhhh, perfect. Sweet, sweet perfection." He laughed. "Now," he said hoarsely, "toss your hair back over your shoulders. I don't want any part of you to stay hidden."

She didn't move.

"Do it!" he shouted.

"You bastard!" she said, tossing her head, her long, thick hair swinging up, then back, then down, behind her shoulder.

"St. Sebastian!" Jay said, springing to his feet as raw desire shot deep into the center of his belly. With tormented hunger he looked at her, soft and downy, arousing the proof of his manhood. Perfect was too plain a word for what stood before him. Flawless. Unsurpassed. Exquisite. Delectable. Luscious. Nothing in his vocabulary would describe her fairness. Jay felt his reaction to what his eyes devoured. It rose hard and hot in his groin, a stabbing, physical pain.

For a long time he just sat there, looking his fill. "Come here," he said, his voice tight.

"You can go straight to hell."

"I said, come here." He pronounced his words purposefully, keeping his face impassive, his voice biting and cold.

"In a pig's eye!"

Then suddenly the hard-tempered lines around his mouth seemed to relax as he rose from the chair. "Very well," he said. "Consider your bluff called." He began walking toward her with long, graceful strides, moving slow and silent. He stopped mere inches from her and she tried to swallow away the lump of panic in her throat as he watched her through critically slitted eyes.

Dear God, this man could send her reeling back across the bed with one slap of his arm. And she knew all too well the danger of being anywhere near a bed with a man who looked like he did. She didn't trust him. She had to get away from here. She had to think of something. Those graceful hands of his, those same hands that had caressed the polished steel of his pistol and cocked the trigger . . . No. She couldn't let him touch her. She wouldn't let him put those hands anywhere near her.

But she stood stone-faced, showing no emotion, when he lifted the pistol and rubbed the side of it against her cheek, touching her with nothing but cold, hard metal. The heavy-lidded eyes regarding her thoughtfully turned liquid with heat. He lowered the gun, bringing the long barrel over the top of her breast, then dropping beneath and lifting. He heard her breathing quicken; watched the frantic movement of blood pulsing against the shallow indention of her throat.

"You aren't afraid of me," he said. "Why?"

She stared right at him, unashamed and proud, which only served to further fan the flames that already raged within him. "Is it because you know what I'm thinking, what I want to do to you?" She closed her eyes rather than answer him, hearing his soft chuckle.

Slowly his hand traveled down to caress the sensitive skin at the back of her neck and she felt the impact of it like the jolt of an electrical charge. Her bones felt liquid and soft. She really didn't understand the way she was feeling, what was happening to her body. She only knew she hated this man with every fiber of her being. She hated his arrogance, his cocksure attitude, the way he humiliated her, thinking she had nothing on her mind but this hateful attempt at seduction. *Easy,* she told herself. *Take it slow and easy. Let him think he has you all soft and buttery in his hands.*

"You're awfully quiet," he said. "Do you always respond this way?"

She opened her eyes, keeping her look passive. "You won't let me go, and I won't beg, so I have nothing to say."

"You don't have to say anything, you know. Your body says it far more eloquently than words ever could," he said with a serious, languid quality. His hand lifted a strand of black hair, drawing it over her shoulder and letting it fall to curl around the coral-blushed tip of her breast. As he began to toy with that lock of hair Jennifer felt the warm, magnetic pull of his body. Her head began to throb, and her ears filled with a strange buzzing. The flesh beneath his fingers quivered. The moment hung suspended in a golden drop of amber, freezing her in a wash of erotic sensation, a moment when she felt no emotional response, save the slow-rising flush that crept up her neck and brought a blush of sweet color to her pale face.

His heated gaze devoured her, but for a moment Jay didn't move, feeling as if he were under some kind of spell cast by this purple-eyed beauty. Lantern light adorned her skin, giving it the texture of rich cream, touching the softly rounded contours of ripe, youthful flesh and dusting it with gold. His eyes dropped to her breasts, judging their heaviness, seeing the faint tracery of blue veins. Was it possible? Could they be as heavy and firm as they looked, and yet so soft? She was like nothing he had ever seen: not in the flesh, nor in a statue, nor in a painting. She was so beautiful, he ached. His eyes went lower, across the faint ribbing of her midriff and the softly rounded belly before stopping at the dark center of her thighs. When he glanced at her, he saw that her delicate coloring burned a deeper rose. The girl wasn't indifferent, no matter how hard she tried to convince him.

Slowly he lifted his hand and trailed the tip of one finger and touched the splash of newborn scarlet on her cheek, following the line of her jaw to her throat, then across, from her collarbone to the fullness of her breast, and down, circling the peaked point, feeling the sudden lurch of his body, the painful tightening in his groin at the contraction of her nipple, which he identified correctly as a response.

"You may not want me to touch you, angel eyes, but

your body sure as hell does." His eyes came up to her face for a moment, then dropped back to her breasts. You're a beautiful and desirable woman, Jennifer Leigh. As fine as porcelain," he whispered, before his fingers threaded through her silky hair and he pulled her against him and kissed her hard.

He had only meant to kiss her then let her go, to brand her with his masterful touch, to show her he could. Later there would be no doubt in his mind as to who, exactly, was in charge here. But once his mouth covered hers, he was lost. His hands began to move over her, caressing the curved shoulders, going down the slim column of her back, squeezing the rounded firmness of her buttocks, and pressing her against him. For a brief moment he broke the kiss, nibbling the softness of her throat and neck, whispering, "You're a lot of woman for any man, Jennifer Baxter. A lot of woman."

"And you're a dead man, whoever you are," she answered, her hand going for the heavy crucifix that stood on the table next to her. Bringing it up swiftly, she crashed it against the side of Jay's head just as he looked up.

4

$\mathcal{S}$he stood over him, the crucifix still in her hand, her eyes going over him with a deliberate slowness she never would have dared had he been conscious. She nudged his leg with her toe, getting no response. She had never seen this man before. She had no idea who he was. But she knew one thing: Whoever he was, he was in no condition to finish what he had started.

"You aren't so cocky now, are you?" she said, her eyes still looking their fill.

She had called him cocky, but she knew what she had seen earlier was no flash assurance, no swaggering confidence, but magnificent harmony between beauty of form, sharpness of mind, and physical perfection. Rangy and hungry as a wolf in the wild, he had looked at her in such a sultry way that everything within her seemed to swell and thicken. She had been looked at before. Many times. But never like this man had looked at her. He had a way of cutting right through polite interest, genuine curiosity, or even the nobler forms of seduction, slicing through those subtle layers to the erotic core, where emotions lay in their purest form: earthy, aroused, animal-sharp, and dangerous.

She shuddered, feeling the dryness suck at her throat, the almost painful pounding of the accelerated beat of her heart as she remembered what had transpired between them, what had almost happened. Who was this long-haired Viking lying like a golden god of war on her bedroom floor?

She nudged him again, and when he still did not respond, she dressed quickly and left the room.

A cold splash of water across his face brought Jay to coughing consciousness. He opened his eyes, seeing that Jennifer Baxter was fully clothed. He blinked and opened them again. She was still clothed. Had he dreamed he had her standing naked before him? No. Not even a dream could be that perfect. Then the fog in his head cleared and he saw they were not alone. Seven Mexicans surrounded him, everything from pitchforks to machetes aimed at him. A quick glance back to Jennifer told him she was in complete control now, but in her eyes he could read no hint of what was about to happen next. She turned away from him and spoke softly in rapid Spanish to the men, too low for him to hear exactly what she said. He wondered if she had ordered them to castrate him, for the seven men began to laugh. Soon it was no laughing matter, when Jay found himself trussed like a goat at a barbecue and hauled outside, his body thrown uncomfortably over his horse, facedown. Several painful miles from town they stopped, pulling Jay from Brady's back—none too gently.

A few minutes later the men rode away, Jay's horse in tow. But Jay wasn't with them. As the sun slowly began to peek over the Sierras in the distance, it cast its warming rays on the chilled and naked body of Jay Culhane. It took him some time, but he managed to work his hands free and then untie his feet. Naked as a scraped hog, he began to walk, finding strength swelling along with the delicious thought about what he would do to Miss Jennifer Leigh Baxter when he found her.

And find her he would.

But first he had to find some clothes before the sun got too hot, or he was going to have one hell of a sunburn in places the sun had never touched. Some time later Jay was hiding behind the low adobe wall around a small hut, waiting for the plump Mexican woman to finish hanging out her laundry. When she finished, she picked up the woven basket and called her children to follow. Jay watched them file into the house, followed by a scrawny dog. A few minutes later the woman opened the door and the dog came sailing through. The door slammed. Jay waited a few more minutes to be sure the woman was going to stay inside, then he vaulted over the wall and made his way to the clothesline. The dog lifted his head as Jay passed but did little more than watch for a minute before losing interest and turning away.

Jay was just stepping into a pair of pants when the door opened and the woman came outside to dump a dishpan of water. Seeing Jay, she began to curse him violently, in Spanish, and Jay, one leg in the pants, began to hop, feeling the cold shock of water followed by the thump of the dishpan as it struck him on the back. Hanging on to the pants as well as the rest of the clothes he had snitched, Jay hurdled the low adobe wall and took off like the devil was after him. Behind him, he could hear the woman still shrieking, but now her voice was being edged aside by the pealing laughter of children. Even in his haste to depart, Jay couldn't help smiling at the thought of what he looked like from behind, his white buttocks flashing in the sunlight as he hotfooted it out of sight. And then, as he had done so many times that morning, he thought about all the things he was going to do to get even with that purple-eyed temptress who had him running bare-assed naked across the hot desert sand. He almost began to feel sorry for Jennifer Baxter.

But not too sorry.

Some time later he was still breathless, but at least dressed, even if it was peon-fashion, in a baggy white pair of pants and a loose-fitting shirt. The pants fit okay, but they were way too short, falling just a little below his knees. Knowing he looked as foolish as he felt, Jay began to walk.

It was almost dark when he saw the baked adobe walls of the village ahead. He still found it hard to believe that he had actually let a tiny slip of a girl get the best of him. Him! A man who had come up against the likes of the Daltons and Youngers . . . hell! Even Belle Starr. He was the last man on earth anyone would suspect of losing his head over a pretty face. She might have a face that was as gentle as a moonbeam, but she was meaner than an acre of snakes.

Jay circled around the village, checking the lean-to shelters and stables behind the small adobe houses, looking for his horses, finding nothing but chickens, goats, and a few donkeys. It was well past suppertime now, and the streets of the dusty village were deserted, the smell of food reaching him and reminding him how hungry he was. He couldn't even remember the last time he'd eaten. Two days ago? Three?

A few minutes later he was fighting the blowing sand as he circled around the crude building that contained the primitive tools used by the village blacksmith. He saw a pony and a donkey in the corral out back, but no sign of Brady and the buckskin. He paused, wondering where they could have taken his horses. There was no other place to look. They had to be inside, so he removed the brace from the door and stepped into the darkness, lighting a lantern.

Just as he thought, Brady was there, in a stall, his saddle and tack hanging nearby. Jay found his clothes were tossed over the saddle, his boots on the floor. For once he was thankful for his height and big feet. They were probably all that saved his clothes from being confiscated by some small Mexican.

Once he was back in his own clothes, he searched for his other horse. He found the buckskin in another stall, the last he looked in. When Jay walked toward him, he saw he was favoring his hind leg. Running his hand along the buckskin's back and down his hip, Jay crouched and studied the hind leg. Five or six deep slices were cut diagonally across the leg from about five inches above the hoof to the flank.

Someone had packed the cuts with axle grease, but even then Jay recognized the damage done by a lariat. Evidently someone had roped the buckskin and he'd become entangled in the rope. Jay had seen it happen too many times not to know how easily a horse would spook and how he would tear his own flesh to shreds when tangled in a rope or barbed wire, in order to get free. The wounds would heal, but it would be a long time. Jay cursed softly, giving the buckskin a slap on the rump to move him out of the way of the door. A quick check of the place turned up only one other horse, a small, ornery-looking pony with a nasty disposition that almost snapped his ear off when Jay tried to check his soundness. He eyed the questionable creature, thinking that this nasty-tempered equine was a perfect match for the Baxter girl. Jay grinned, picturing her perched on a horse that was way beneath her dignity. Perfect. He saddled both horses, then set out to find her.

Moments later he was leading the two horses and fighting the sand once more. He sought cover behind the same crumbling building near Jennifer's house, where he would wait until dark. When it was time, Jay made his way to her place. Just like the night before, the house was dark, except for a faint light coming from the corner room, the room Jay knew was Jennifer's bedroom. Crossing the wooden porch with the grace of a desert fox, Jay paused in front of the door. Then, for the second time in two days, he kicked open the door to Jennifer's bedroom.

Startled, Jennifer looked up to see that the stranger had returned, standing in her doorway, just as he had done the night before, stepping out of the windy darkness, the sand pouring around him, chilling the room and leaving a layer of dust upon everything. She pulled the bed covers higher, under her neck, tossing the book she was reading aside. There was no denying the reality of what she was seeing. The man was back and, if possible, looking larger and meaner than he did before.

"It was my impression," he said sarcastically, "that a

woman, however educated, is legally under the control and supervision of her father until she takes a husband. You," he said, stabbing a finger at her, "are not married, I take it?"

Jennifer shook her head.

"In that case you will obey the bidding of your father. And the first edict is to get out of that bed and get dressed," he said. "You're coming with me."

"You have made only one mistake. *You* aren't my father."

"True, but he sent me after you."

"My father?" she said with a puzzled frown. "My father sent you? You know him?"

"Believe me, I would never, even in my most drunken stupor, have ever considered a job like this on my own. Of course I know your father!" he shouted. "Now get dressed."

"Well, that explains what you're doing here, but it doesn't change anything. I'm not going anywhere, except to sleep."

Jay stared at her, her long black hair spread across the pillow behind her, her eyes huge and daring him to push her further. She didn't much look like she was in a negotiating mood, and he didn't have all night. There was something downright nerve-racking about taking on a job to rescue a woman who didn't want to be rescued. But that didn't matter much right now. The important thing was, they had to be well away from here by morning, before the Mexicans discovered she was gone. The small pony was sturdy but temperamental, and way too small to be very fast.

"Look, Miss Baxter, I don't have the time or the patience to stand here debating the issue. Get out of bed and get dressed, or come as you are. It makes little difference to me. But you are coming, rest assured. You can get dressed and ride, or you can go tied over the saddle in your nightie. The choice is yours."

"Who are you?"

"My name isn't important. What is important is that your father sent me to find you and bring you home."

She looked angry again. "Well, you can tell my father you found me."

"Look, lady, I'm being paid to bring you home, and that means taking you back with me."

"But I don't want to go home!"

Jay shook his head. "You're a strange one. I've never met a woman before who would even consider giving up a life of luxury for one of hardship and deprivation."

"I haven't given it up . . . at least not permanently. And I'm not deprived!"

His eyes went around the room. It was clean but bare. He looked at her. "This isn't exactly a den of luxury you're living in. Why are you here?"

"You won't understand."

"Try me," he said.

She sighed, locking her fingers together in front of her. "These people . . . they need so much. They have no schools, no medical supplies . . ."

"You're crazy."

"No, I'm concerned about my fellowman."

"That may well be, but I'm concerned about your father. He wants you home."

"Home? You mean Weatherford?"

Jay nodded.

"But why?"

"They're worried about you. That shouldn't be so difficult for an educated woman like you to understand. Your mother is worried sick. Your sisters—"

"My sisters?" Jennifer groaned, her hand coming up to her forehead. "Don't tell me they've notified all my sisters!"

"All but one, I think."

"Is Abbey there?"

"I told you, they're all there . . . except the one that married the drifter."

"Heddy," Jenny said. "No wonder mother is worried. If Abbey's there, she'll keep things stirred up indefinitely. She can go on firing longer than a Gatling gun."

If he didn't know how deceitful she and all women were, he could almost believe her attempt at humor was honest. "Look, you can tell me all this on the trail." Jay moved to the chest at the end of the bed and opened it. Ruffling through it, he pulled out a long skirt and blouse and tossed them on the bed. A soft leather jacket followed. After that, a pair of small boots. He eyed the clothing he'd just placed on the bed. "Not exactly what I would have preferred, but it'll do. Now get dressed."

"I told you I wasn't going back. I have work to do here and it isn't finished. You can wire them that I'm all right."

"You can wire them yourself."

"I did! Didn't they tell you?"

"They told me, but they're still concerned."

"I don't understand why. If they received my wire—"

"An ugly woman has no business going off by herself to a place like Mexico. A woman that looks like you do should have her head examined."

"Listen—"

"No, you listen. Don't you have any idea about the kinds of things that could happen to you? The kind of men that roam these badlands? The kinds of things they could do to you?"

"Yes," she screamed at him. "I have a very good idea. I would imagine they're exactly the same kinds of things you tried to do. Mexicans . . . gringos . . . it makes little difference. You're all the same. Lechers, every mother's son of you. Some choice I have—you or them. What difference does it make?"

"You don't believe that for a minute. You couldn't."

"Couldn't I?"

"It doesn't matter, anyway. You're coming with me, and that's final."

"I told you once—"

"Don't you give a damn about your family? Doesn't it bother you that they're worried about you? Don't you care at all?"

He could tell he'd hit a tender spot with that one. "Of course I care," she said. "I wouldn't have sent them a wire if I was as callous as you make me out to be. I simply want to live my own life, that's all. You don't understand my family, Mr. . . . whatever your name is."

"Culhane. Jay Culhane."

She leaned her head back with a sigh and closed her eyes, her hand coming up to massage the bridge of her nose. Then she opened them, looking at him like she was getting just a little tired of all this discussion. "Mr. Culhane, if my family had their way, I'd still be at home wearing a pinafore, pigtails, and a milk mustache. They won't let me grow up. They still see a child every time they look at me."

Jay looked her over and whistled. "Legs, I think of a lot of things when I look at you, but a child isn't one of them."

"Stop calling me Legs!" she shouted. Then, more softly, but with obvious sarcasm, "I know where your mind spends its time, Mr. Culhane."

Jay grinned. "You do? And where might that be?"

"Wallowing in filth, just like a pig."

"I'm going to be wallowing in that damn bed with you in another minute if you aren't out of it."

"Look," she said, her voice almost pleading. "I know my family. If it hadn't been this, they would've found another reason to get me home. I did the right thing. I wired them of my plans and told them when I'd be back. I wasn't kidnapped. I didn't run off with some drifter like Heddy did. I haven't lost my mind. I haven't been raped"—she narrowed her eyes at him—"yet. I came here to do a job, and it isn't finished. So there's no way in heaven I'm going to leave now. You just tell my father that. Tell him I came here to help these people. That I came here of my own free will. That I'm here by choice."

"I don't care if you rode over here on a broom. I was

hired to take you back home, and by God, that's what I'm going to do. Now get dressed."

"You can't come in here ordering me around."

"I can and I am. Now gather anything you'll be needing, but do it quickly. I don't want to spend any more time here than I have to."

"Wait a minute. Let me explain. There is so much that can be done for these people. They need me. They're depending on me. I gave them my word. Don't you understand? I can't go back on that."

"It's either your word or mine. We can't both win. Now get dressed."

"What I'm doing here is important to me. I'm not leaving until it's finished."

Stubborn. Bossy. The list of grievances he was compiling against her was growing. Jay let out a ragged breath, pushing his hat back on his head. "What kind of job?"

"They have asked me to help them start a school, and that's why I'm here."

"Looks to me like you've already started the school."

"I have, but I've just started training a teacher."

"I can't help that. I don't care what brought you here, or how much work you have left."

"Please. Just tell my father I wasn't ready to go."

"You can tell him that yourself." Jay crossed the room. "Now, Miss Baxter, I'm going to give you exactly five minutes to put something on that you can ride in, and to pack a change of clothes."

"I told you, I'm not going anywhere."

Jay reached for her, yanking the blanket she clutched and flinging it across the bed to the floor. He had intended to jerk her to her feet, but when he looked at her lying there in that soft white gown, her hair billowing around her—those damn bewitching eyes of hers and their funny, flowery color—huge, and making him think about things he had no business thinking about right now, he felt his body, of its own volition, responding to her. And his breathing—

it was becoming damn difficult to control. "You have a
choice. You can get dressed and get your sweet little fanny
on that pony outside, or I'll join you in bed."

"You wouldn't dare."

He laughed. "Oh, sweetheart, I'd dare that and a helluva
lot more." He began to unbutton his shirt. Jennifer crossed
her arms over her chest and waited. He was bluffing. She
was sure of it. He removed his shirt and tossed it in the
chair, his hands dropping to his gun belt.

Awareness pierced her at the sight of the hard male
chest, the play of smooth muscle, the flowing curve of
strong male shoulders. He had to be bluffing. If he worked
for her father, he had to be. "I'll tell my father if you lay a
hand on me."

He laughed again. "If you don't get out of that bed, you
can tell your father I laid a lot more than my hand on you."
He pulled the leather tie-down that went around his leg. It
gave with a snap. The finality of that sound sent Jennifer
scooting to the far side of the bed.

The gun belt joined the shirt on the chair. Jennifer
looked at his face and decided that compassion was a foreign word to this man. He didn't look mean or cruel, exactly—he just looked as if he didn't care. Rape or afternoon
tea, there would be little difference in the emotion registered on that impassive face. Truly the man was a barbar-
ian. She swallowed painfully when he looked at her, and as
if he could smell her fear, he smiled wickedly, his hands
going to the buttons on his pants.

One . . .

Two . . .

Three . . .

Four . . .

Four buttons. A four-button man. What was it the girls
in school laughed about? Something about a four-button
man was better than a two-button one, because the more
buttons a man had, the bigger his . . .

Jennifer looked quickly away.

She heard him move across the room and she held her breath. She heard him stop and knew he must be near the other side of the bed. She squeezed her eyes shut. She wasn't going to look at him. She wouldn't. She wouldn't. She wouldn't.

And she wasn't going to get out of bed, either.

She felt the bed sag under his weight, and Jennifer sprang forward like she'd been shot. But she wasn't fast enough, forgetting to consider his quick reflexes. A powerful hand flashed out to grab her arm, jerking her back. Before she hit the bed, he was on her. Frightened, wild, and furious, she clawed at him, raking the side of his face with her nails. He cursed softly, grabbing her hands and twisting them beneath her. She arched her body beneath him, bucking, trying to throw him off, but he nuzzled her throat and whispered in a raw, throaty tone, "Keep doing that and I may not be able to wait until I get your clothes off."

Jennifer went still, her teeth gritting against the irritation of his husky chuckle, her mind planning her next move.

"You learn fast, little girl. Let's see what else we can teach you." He pulled the ribbon that circled her head and gathered the shiny weight of her hair in one hand and drew it away from the embroidered bodice of her thin batiste nightdress, spreading it across the pillow next to her. Then, bringing both her hands over her head, he bound them together with the ribbon, tying the other end of it to the bed. He rolled to one side, his powerful thigh thrust over her legs to hold them immobile. Then he began to slip the buttons of her gown through the loops, and Jennifer squirmed, pulling against the ribbon until it cut into her wrists. He tightened his hold on her hair until the pain of it burned her eyes. "Lie still," he commanded. "I won't hurt you."

"You're hurting me now."

He eased the grip on her hair, his breath fluttering across her bared breasts as he lowered his head and whispered, "I only want to touch you. Nothing more."

"Oh, is that all?" she said with heavy sarcasm. "I can't tell you how relieved I am." Then she squeezed her eyes shut, turning her head as far away from him as the pressure on her hair would allow. She heard the fabric of her gown rip, then felt it flutter softly across her body and down, over her hips, past her legs. She held her breath, knowing what would come next, and yet not really knowing at all.

"You're absolutely the most beautiful thing I've ever seen."

She opened her eyes and looked at him. "I am not a *thing,* and I've *absolutely* never despised anyone as much as I do you. I hope my father kills you for this."

He lowered his head, circling her nose with his, teasing, laughing at her with his mocking eyes. "He might try. He might even succeed . . . if he's fast enough."

"It can't be fast enough to suit me."

He simply laughed, the sound of it dying in his throat as he looked at her. She was panting with fury, deep purple eyes smoldering with rage, midnight-black hair wild and scattered beneath her. With no warning Jay felt his loins leap to life with a desire so intense, it stopped his breath. With a lusting intensity he had never before felt, he wanted her, wanted to take her, to tame her, to make her his. His mouth covered hers, warm and firm, moving with such skill, it took every ounce of her will to resist. He pulled away from her. "If you find me as repulsive as all that, I suggest you give me your word that you'll get dressed and come with me. And that you won't give me any more trouble."

"I'll come," she said, her voice sounding shaky and uncertain, "but the only promise I'll make is to give you trouble every chance I get."

"Wrong answer," he said. "Let's see if we can persuade you a little."

"Rape me, you mean."

He studied her eyes, wide with anticipation, seeing both fear and defiance. "There are worse things to bear than rape," he said thoughtfully. "Have you any idea, sweet little girl, just what I am going to do to you?"

Let him wonder. She wouldn't satisfy his cruel mind by answering.

"So serene. So composed. Let's see just how much in control you are, sweetheart, just how long that composure will last before it slips and breaks, leaving you writhing in my hands, begging me for ease."

"The only thing I'll ever beg for is your bloody head on a silver platter."

"You stubborn, spoiled little witch! I'll bend you to my bidding if I have to break you to do it." He covered her breast with his hand, and she began thrashing beneath him. Nothing, save the pressure of his forearm across her windpipe, quieted her. She lay tied and pinned beneath him, her body heaving to fight for each breath. He raised himself up, knowing she knew he was looking at her nakedness, his hand still covering her breast.

She kept her eyes closed, denying him the thrill of reading any emotion they might register. She jerked when she felt his hand drift between her breasts and circle her stomach—so lightly, it whispered across her like a feather. Her body coiled, rigid and tense from the anxiety of it, from the stress of not knowing what was going to happen to her, what he would do next.

His hands were everywhere, yet so light that she could never be sure if it was his hands he touched her with or a flower petal, or perhaps a silken cord. As his hands moved over her, touching her, he whispered odd, disjointed phrases that penetrated her mind like a drugging smoke.

"You'll never get away with this. My father will kill you."

"Your father, of all men, will understand my reasoning. It's your own fault, you know. Nothing else seems to bring you to heel, although I can't truthfully say I'm sorry about that particular turn of events. Always happy to volunteer my services."

She decided she would say no more. It was useless, anyway. Every time she resisted, she felt him increase the pressure on her hair. Her wrists were hurting from the bite of the ribbon cutting into her skin. And for no reason. She was his. His captive for as long as he desired. She was only fighting against herself, losing her strength. Perhaps if she didn't fight, didn't resist, he would lose interest and let her go. But she began to feel him touching her again, with the same feather-light strokes, maddeningly slow, hovering somewhere between pleasure and pain, and her mind screamed against the torture of it.

His touch roamed at will, over her breasts, across her throat, and down her arms, circling the flat plains of her belly. Slow. Agonizing. She sucked in her breath, feeling the heat of humiliation warm her body as his touch moved down both legs, then dropping to the inside of her thigh. She bit her lip against the desire to scream or to beg him to stop, trying to close her legs against him, feeling them held apart by the overpowering strength of his legs pushing between hers. With the same deliberate touch he stroked lazy circles up her thighs, going higher and higher, until he reached their junction. Then he stopped. Her body tensed, her nerves screaming, she waited, fighting herself, wanting to resist, hating him more with each ragged breath she drew.

Then he touched her. There.

The sensation of it shot through her like the jagged edge of flying glass, and her body tried to coil and draw up in reflex. Again and again he repeated the motion until she twisted against the sweet, curling pleasure that started low in her belly and slowly consumed her. Her body felt as if it were flowing out and away from her, drawing closer to the man who did this defiling thing to her; the one who found pleasure in her shame.

The intimacy of it shattered her. He had no right. No right to share such a tender and long-guarded secret. No right to tutor her body until it ached for a closer unity, begging for the ultimate bonding with him.

Through a blinding daze of desire he saw that her eyes were open now, shame and humiliation swimming in their purple depths. "You were right," she said. "There are worse things than rape."

Her words sliced into him and he recoiled from the impact. He pulled away from her, his head going back, as if he were in pain. Then she saw the flash of a blade as he sliced at the ribbon that bound her. "Forgive me," he said hoarsely, gathering her to him. "But now you know. I will stop at nothing—absolutely nothing—to have your obedience. Both our lives may depend upon it."

He rolled away from her and came to his feet beside the bed. It was the first time she noticed he had not removed his pants as she had thought. He was looking at her strangely. The expression in his eyes was not exactly lust, nor could she call it anger. There was an element of sadness to it, perhaps even remorse. But she knew the kind of man he was—one void of any of the more noble emotions.

"Get dressed," he said harshly. "I don't have time to convince you further."

"Thank God for small blessings," she said as she rolled from the bed, bringing the sheet with her, gathering her clothes, which had fallen to the floor as she circled the bed. His eyes followed her every move. She clutched the clothes to her chest, giving him a withering look. "You could turn your head."

"I did that once. Remember?"

"That was your fault. I'm not accustomed to being ogled when I'm as bare as a peeled onion. Besides, you got the best end of the deal."

"How do you figure that?"

"You just got whacked over the head. I was the one humiliated and naked."

"You weren't alone."

He knew by the startled way she looked at him that she

didn't know the Mexicans had stripped him. "Your friends took my clothes when they left me in the middle of nowhere."

It suddenly occurred to her just how comical he must have looked out there—how embarrassing it was to stomp around the desert naked. And how did he get back into town and retrieve his clothes without being seen? She kept her face perfectly straight. "Evidently they didn't take them far enough, since you seem to have found them with relative ease."

"I spent the better part of a full day in my birthday suit," he said, a lazy, knee-weakening smile spreading across his tanned face. "You should have seen me stealing laundry off some poor peon's line and hurdling the fence like a javelin when she came after me."

"At least you found something to wear," she said, feeling more uncomfortable around this new side of him she was seeing than she did the old one. His easy smile, the teasing light in his eyes—the man was a charmer, and that meant beware.

"Yes, I did find something to wear, but I have a feeling I looked more ridiculous in a pair of fairy-size pants that fit me like nickers than I did wearing nothing. I was covered, but I felt like a fool."

It surprised her that this arrogant man would, or even could, admit to having any feelings at all, let alone his surprising admission that he had felt like a fool. For the briefest moment she forgot all the things that had occurred between them, the multiple reasons she had for despising him. For just a flash of time he was nothing more than an incredibly handsome man raking his hands through his wheat-colored hair, a curving smile softening his hard, molded features, amazing her with what a touch of humor could do to erase the chill of sardonic indifference that she had seen all too often on his face. When she realized she had been distracted, staring in a dazed way into those mesmerizing eyes of his, she saw that he regarded her thoughtfully.

If she had been more experienced, or even more alert, she would have recognized the sensuality behind the slow, lazy smile he turned on her. "When you look at me like that, I question my sanity in letting you go. You're the most damnably seductive woman I've ever encountered. Every movement, every gesture . . . that raw silkiness of your voice arouses even my jaded senses . . ." He sighed and shook his head. "Such an exquisite way to receive an invitation."

"Every time you see a woman that's the least bit pretty, you see a temptation. Is that how you justify yourself?"

The old Jay was back now. "I never justify anything."

"Not even forcing a woman to go with you? How convenient. You don't have to probe the depths of that murky mind of yours to find even a transparent reason for humiliating me as you did."

"My God! It isn't the end of the world to be seen naked."

"It is for me! I'm unaccustomed to such things . . . not being contaminated by a life of debauchery." She pointed toward the door. "Now get out of here if you want me to get dressed."

"Since I've already contaminated you, there's no need for modesty, is there? I've seen everything you have to offer."

"I wasn't offering you anything."

"Ah, sweetheart, but you will," he said with smug confidence. "You will."

"The only thing I'm going to give you is a hard time. Trouble, and more trouble. So much of it, you'll wish you'd never heard of me."

Jay tossed her a straw hat that hung on the back of a chair. "You've already made me wish that, Jenny Leigh."

"Don't call me that! Only my family and friends call me Jenny."

He crossed the room in a flash and caught her firmly by the arms, pulling her hard against him. "And that's exactly what I'm going to be to you for the next few weeks, little girl. Your family and your friend. I'm all you've got out there, the only thing standing between you and certain death. You may not want to admit it, but I'm as necessary to you as breathing." She struggled, panicking, afraid of what he might try. He hauled her roughly back to him, holding her indecently close. "Cross me and you will never make it across the desert."

Then, as quickly as he had captured her, he let her go. "Get dressed."

She turned her back, struggling to pull her clothes on while holding the sheet together. "For the love of God!" he said, his hands coming out to grab the sheet, holding it up between them, almost laughing from the absurdity of it. The bedside lamp behind her silhouetted her body perfectly. She did not speak, but he could feel her anger; as real to him as her scent. As he watched her jerk her clothes on, his anger dissipated. He began thinking how this young, violet-eyed woman, in a very short period of time, had his insides twisting with feelings he hadn't felt in a long, long time.

She was a link to a world he had turned his back on. His past. And he desired her. That made her a dangerous woman. He would have to treat her more harshly than he should, in order to make her hate him. . . .

God help them both if she ever looked at him with anything but hatred or anger in those sultry purple eyes of hers.

God help them both.

PART II

Every path has its puddle.

English proverb

5

≈ ≈

Of all the confrontations awaiting a young woman at the hands of a cynical gunslinger, the least expected would be with a horse.

A horse? An understatement. Jennifer looked at the two animals Jay was leading toward her. One of them was a horse. The other wretch she wasn't sure about. Shaggy-haired, ugly, and small, it looked like a cross between a moose and a sheepdog. She watched him ready the animals with a puzzled frown, then said, "What is that?" pointing at the pitiful creature.

"Your horse."

The frown deepened. "Are you sure it's a horse?"

"Reasonably sure." He made a noise that sounded like a chuckle, but coming from him she wasn't sure it was so. The controlled demeanor of this man made her think that chuckling or smiling wasn't something he took lightly or performed frequently. "Regardless of the way it looks, it has everything you'll be needing—four legs and a saddle—so shut up and get mounted."

"Where'd you find it? The Mongolian steppe?" She circled the creature, noticing that its eyes were following her. Whatever the beast was, it didn't like her. Jenny was sure of that. "Is it a stud?"

Jay paused, looking over the top of his saddle at her, his folded arms resting against the rump of his horse, a slow, lazy smile stretching his mouth. "What difference does that make? It's a horse. That should suffice."

That smile irritated the daylights out of her. "I asked you a simple, direct question, Mr. Culhane. Is it too much to ask for a simple, direct answer?"

"You want it simple and direct? Then check it out and see for yourself. It's simple enough to tell the difference." He stopped, a quarter of a smile lingering about his mouth like it was trying to decide if it wanted to stay or go. "Is that direct enough for you? You do know how to tell the difference, don't you?"

"I'm an educated woman, Mr. Culhane."

"You also come from a family of women." His grin was mocking. "Of course, there were probably some swimming holes in the area that provided you with a good peek at any naked boys who happened to be taking a swim."

"I didn't have to resort to that. We had animals around."

Jay's arched brows lifted in mock horror. He could picture little Jenny Baxter snooping around the barnyard, sexing every barn cat and knitting her brow in vexation as she contemplated a couple of dragonflies flying double. Come to think of it, Jay couldn't remember ever seeing a dragonfly that wasn't double-decked. His gaze drifted back to Jennifer, who was looking like she was waiting for him. "Look, if it's that important to you, find out for yourself," he advised, and began rummaging in his saddlebags. "I've got more important things to do."

"All right, I will," she said. "But if he kicks me in the head while I'm about it, you'll have come a long way for nothing."

"Shit," Jay said. "Shit." But he walked around his horse, his hand on Brady's rump as he did. He approached the small pony. "Lady, you're more damn trouble than you're worth," he said, but his hand slid along the pony's ribs and down to its belly as he leaned over and looked in the proper spot. "It's a stud. Satisfied?"

"No. I'd prefer a mare, but I guess that explains it."

"Explains what?"

"Why he doesn't like me."

"How in the hell do you know that? You haven't even been introduced. How do you know he doesn't like you? You don't make any sense. Hellfire! There aren't any horses that I know of that actually like people. They tolerate us, that's all."

"I still don't think he likes me."

"Studs don't have time to be nice to little girls; they have their minds on something else."

"Horses or humans, males always have their fancy fixed on one thing," she said curtly, and looked at him. He was appraising her steadily with those deep blue eyes of his. His lazy smile was infuriating.

His eyes traveled over her as if he were suddenly seeing her for the first time. "You seem to know a lot about the nature of men. Then you should know it's the nature of things to perform the role they were created for. *Consummate,* if you will. To ignore that would be like a fish not allowed to swim."

"And that includes men and women, I suppose."

" 'Women are silver dishes into which we put golden apples,' " he said.

"A rather eloquent way of defining it for a rough, uneducated man, but the thought it conveys is on your level of crudity."

"Goethe will have to take credit for the eloquence. The crudity, as you said, is mine." He paused a moment as if considering something. "As for the education, is that supposed to make all that nonsense that comes out of your mouth wisdom?"

"Education . . . oh, never mind. It's something you wouldn't understand, anyway."

His hard blue gaze struck her like a slap. "I measure a

man by the depth of his understanding and the capacity of
his heart, not by the skin of a sheep."

"A what?"

"Sheepskin. A diploma, if you will."

"How do you know about that?"

"Education, Miss Baxter. I seem to remember receiving
one, in spite of my crudity." His voice was low now, without inflection, and somehow more powerful because of it,
serving as a reminder that she had wrongly accused him of
being uneducated, as if that alone made her superior to
him. It wasn't so much the challenge in his words as the
twinge of guilt they caused. Belittlement in any form was
unlike her, and it angered her to think this man could provoke her to the point of callousness.

"Where did you study?"

"I studied. That should suffice." His words, although
soft-spoken, carried a warning.

"But . . ."

"My personal life is none of your business."

"No," she said hotly, "it certainly isn't. But I'll tell
you—" She stopped suddenly, an idea forming in her mind.

"You'll tell me what?"

"Nothing. It wasn't important." She watched him shrug,
giving his attention to his saddle once more. She turned
toward her house.

"Where do you think you're going?"

"To close the windows. There's no point in letting the
house fill with sand."

"Five minutes" was all he said.

The moment she entered the house, she hurried straight
through, going toward the kitchen and out the back door.
Once she was outside, Jennifer broke into a dead run, heading for a small adobe hut that was used to store grain.
When she reached it, she jerked the door shut behind her
and leaned against it with gasping relief, allowing her eyes
to adjust to the dim interior. Across from her, five or six
bins were filled with shelled corn, each looking to be about

five feet square and three or four feet deep—more than enough room for her to lie down and cover herself with corn. But she had to act fast. Five minutes he had given her —she had used two of those at most—so she wasted no time in crawling over the boarded end panel and into the deep bed of corn.

Crawling on all fours across several feet of corn isn't as easy as it looks, she soon discovered, as her arms sank in almost to her shoulders. And the corn was dusty, small bits of chaff rising all around her, a great amount of it filling her nose and lungs. She tried holding her breath as she extracted first one arm, then the other, but she found herself sinking farther and farther. She was just deciding it was time to stretch out and cover herself with corn when the door rattled once and then swung inward, propelled by a decisive force that now filled the doorway like an ominous threat as his voice boomed.

"What in the hell are you doing?" Angrily Jay stepped inside and reached for her, just as Jennifer rolled. Seeing he was going to have to go after her, Jay swore and lunged. Jennifer kicked at him, her foot catching him square in the chest. He grunted and let loose with another hair-curling expletive and grabbed her, this time his fingers digging into her arms. "We don't have time to play hide-and-seek," he said gruffly.

"You gave me five minutes!" Jennifer shouted as she tried to twist and pull away. But he caught her around the waist.

"I lied," he answered, panting from the effort. She fought him, wildly twisting and stirring up more chaff than either of their lungs could tolerate. Jay collapsed across her, both of them coughing and gasping for breath.

"Will you be still before we both suffocate!" he shouted, and when Jennifer fought him again, he wrenched her arms around her, holding them behind her back with one hand, the other coming behind her neck to pull her face against him, between his throat and the collar of his shirt. He held her securely, both of them gasping for breath, Jennifer with her cheek against his throat, Jay with his face buried in her long, silky hair. His shirt acting as a filter, Jennifer was able to draw clean air into her lungs and felt the panic of being suffocated gradually subside as her breathing returned to normal.

But with the easing of one fear a new one was born. "Let me up," she moaned in dismay, feeling Jay's thighs pressing her own trembling limbs into the corn, his reaction to their proximity already blatantly obvious and growing more so by the minute.

"Be still, then," he commanded, knowing what caused her discomfort. "You're only making it worse."

Jennifer froze, afraid even to breathe, as if that one insignificant movement might cause the smoldering spark in his eyes to burst into flame.

Jay loomed above her, his hand pulling the long strands of her hair, which lay tangled over her face like satin ribbons. He stared into Jennifer's startled purple eyes, forgetting for a moment that he was supposed to be angry with her. "We seem to have a slight problem here. Wiggling or not, the effect seems to be the same," he said, his voice drifting off to nothing.

By this time, Jennifer was too distracted to speak. All she could do was stare into his face, which was so close, seeing, even in the dimness, every detail. She felt a spiraling warmth spread low in her belly at his soft, lazy smile, which was both inviting and quite disturbing. The unfamiliar warmth that ran through her totally disrupted her thoughts and ruffled her composure. She turned her face away, betraying herself as she did.

His hand came out to drag her gaze back, and her eyes, suddenly huge, searched his. The black ring around his irises seemed larger, making the blue of his eyes more intense as they bored into hers. "I'll have your word," he said. "No more stupid attempts to escape. You'll only be digging your own grave."

She said nothing, and his hand tightened around her

throat. Yet, strange as it was, she wasn't afraid he would harm her. "Next time," he said softly, "I just might let you go. And the desert isn't a pretty place to die." He shook her by the shoulders. "Your word!" he demanded.

"I can't give you my word," she said, meeting his demonic stare with a distressful thump of her heart. She moistened her lips, wondering if she should just give him her word and save herself a lot of trouble that was sure to follow. But taking the easy way out was not her way. She had no intention of giving her word, not because she was determined to get away from him—for her father had sent him, and Jennifer respected Rand too much to defy him—but because she knew herself too well. If Jay pushed her too much, she might, in a fit of anger, break her promise, and that was something Jennifer never did. Better to not give her word than to run the risk of going back on it.

"So that's the way it's to be, then?" His eyes traveled over her face with such a blistering gaze that she questioned her boldness in flinging her defiance in his face—especially when that face was so disturbingly close.

"If you ever pull a stunt like this again, I'll strip you naked and make you ride that way."

"That's why I can't give you my word. If you'd treat me with a little respect . . ." She saw the way he was looking at her. "I'm not a child! I'm a grown woman. Why can't you treat me like one?"

"By God! If that's what all this is about, I can solve that easily enough." His look softened. "So you want to be treated like a woman, do you? Let me ease myself between your sweet legs . . . I promise that will leave you feeling like one."

His heated look made her blush, and still he looked at her for a long time. Then, with an oath, he rolled away from her. Before she knew he was gone, he was out of the grain bin, reaching for her. "Give me your hand."

She looked at his extended hand and then at him, but she made no move to do as he had asked. He sighed. "You go for the last drop, don't you?" Then, not really expecting she would reply, he shook his head, his eyes steady upon her. "All right, then. If you can't give me your word, would it pain you too much to call a truce?"

Jennifer's frown gradually softened, replaced by a curving smile. "Temporarily," she said. "Only temporarily." And she gave him her hand.

Jay studied her fine-boned face, her head held at an obstinate tilt, and couldn't help wondering at her grit. He had never met a woman like her—none quite as beautiful, and certainly none as determined and opinionated—and it disturbed him. And more disturbing yet, she was proving capable of disrupting his thoughts when he needed to keep his mind on something—*anything* besides her.

They were almost to the horses when Jennifer balked.

"Now what?" he said, pausing to rest his hands on his hips and thinking this had to be the shortest truce in history.

"I may be forced to go with you against my will, but I absolutely refuse to ride that," she said, pointing at the pony.

Jay groaned. "Aren't you ever quiet? We don't have time to go shopping. He's the best I could do under the circumstances. Your machete-carrying friends aren't going to sleep all night."

"No, they won't. And they'll come after me when they find me gone."

He laughed. "Armed with rakes and hoes, they're no threat to me. Besides, they don't have any horses."

"It's a poor village. The *bandidos'* frequent raids keep them that way." She paused. "If they're no threat to you, why are you so concerned about getting away before they wake up?"

He shrugged. "Even a debaucher like me hates to kill innocent people."

"That's the first indication I've seen that you might be human."

"Good God, woman! You'd debate the north wind. This is my horse," he said. "And that one," he said, stabbing his finger toward the questionable beast, "is yours. Don't question it. Don't think about it. And for God's sake, don't analyze it to death." He saw she was priming her pump and said, "And don't say another word. It beats walking, and you're too damn critical."

"Don't look a gift horse in the mouth."

"Exactly," he said. "Now, if you would be so kind as to put your sweet little fanny in that saddle, we'll be on our way."

She purposefully ignored his crudity and said simply, "How?"

He paused, looking at her as if he didn't understand, then he shook his head. "For starters, you climb on top."

"I'm not an imbecile."

Any other time Jay would have pursued that vein, but he had neither the time nor the patience to do it now. "Don't tell me you can't ride . . . a rancher's daughter?" Hell's bells! Had Rand Baxter never taught her how? "No one ever taught you?" he asked, his voice carrying a hint of disbelief.

"My mother has always been terrified of horses. She never liked for us to be around them."

"I thought every child knew how to wheedle a pony out of their parents."

"Oh, I did. And Papa got me one."

"And you learned to ride?"

"I . . . a little. I saw a cowhand dragged to death when I was ten," she said. "And a few months later my best friend was killed when her horse spooked and ran away with her. A low branch caught her in the throat."

"You're afraid of them, then?"

"I don't know if *afraid* is the right word. Perhaps *respect* would be more appropriate. I just don't care much for riding horses. I never have. They're beautiful animals, but I don't trust them."

He looked at the pony and then at her. "Then the two of you should have a lot in common."

"Regardless of that, I'm an inexperienced rider. It never caused any problems for me before, since we always used the buggy."

"Well, we don't have a buggy now, so you're going to have to ride. Now, let's get mounted up."

Jennifer looked at the pony, unable to hide her apprehension. Taking a deep breath, she said, "All right. Just give me a minute. I've ridden a little, but never like that."

Jay looked at the pony, his eyes checking out the saddle and bridle. Everything looked normal to him. "Like what?"

"With a saddle like that. I have never ridden astride."

"Unfortunately you have asked for the one thing we don't have. Time. You'll have to ride and learn at the same time."

"You don't seem to understand—"

The hard directness she was growing accustomed to was back in his voice now. "Lady, you're the one who doesn't understand. You are trying my patience. I don't give a damn how you affix your person onto that horse, as long as you do it. You can glue your fanny to the saddle, for all I care."

"But . . ."

He came toward her, stopping just inches away. "Get on that horse," he said, his hands clamping on her arms and turning her toward the saddle. "Now!" He gave her a boost up, then turned away, mounting his own horse. Then he turned and looked back. "Je-*suss!*" he swore, "What in the hell are you doing sitting like that?"

She glared at him, her mouth set and hard. She was still on the horse, but she was sitting to the side, trying to hook her leg around the saddle horn as if it were a sidesaddle. By this time the pony was looking real put out with the whole thing, getting more ornery by the minute. He snorted, shaking his head. It was obvious to Jay he wasn't going to take much more of her damn silliness. If she didn't get herself in the saddle the right way and fast, she was going to find herself tossed on her backside. "You can't ride like that," he said. "No matter how much you try, it won't ever be a sidesaddle. You're just irritating the horse." St. Sebastian! He had never in all his born days seen a woman this stubborn. There wasn't an ounce of compromise in her whole body, and concession was like a foreign word to her.

"But you just told me . . ." She sighed, not bothering to hide her exasperation. "I'm on the horse, am I not? 'Get mounted up'—those were your instructions, I believe."

"Fine," he said. "It's your backside that'll get the blisters, not mine." Jay nudged Brady in the flanks and started off, keeping the first few steps slow, giving her time to settle into position beside him. After a few feet he stopped, turning Brady around just in time to see the pony crow-hop and Jennifer slide to the ground. "You're going to have to face it, Miss Baxter. Sooner or later, like it or not, you're going to have to ride astride."

"When I want your advice, I'll ask for it."

"How in the name of heaven did you get to Mexico if you can't ride a horse?"

"I came in a wagon—and I told you, I *can* ride. I just don't like to. And if I must, I prefer a real horse with a real saddle." She turned, picking up the reins to mount again, then looked back at him. "And furthermore, finding myself denied all of the above, I would think it perfectly reasonable to expect a little compassion on your part. I am doing my best, Mr. Culhane. I am trying. You can either ride off and leave me here as I've requested, or you can dig through that thick skull of yours and find an ounce of patience, giving me a moment to get the hang of this. And if neither of those suits your fancy, then I guess you'll just have to shoot me."

And furthermore? A reluctant smile twitched at the corner of Jay's mouth as he watched her have a go at it, one hand firmly gripping the saddle horn, the other holding the cantle. She and the pony were eye to eye, going in a circle, the pony doing everything to discourage her, but Jenny was hanging on. Her tenacious spirit covered a wide range of things, it seemed.

Finally she got one foot in the stirrup and lifted herself up, only to find she couldn't elevate herself any farther. She dropped back to the ground, hopping along beside the pony on one foot, the other still in the stirrup. Jay cursed and rode toward her. Fool woman was going to be dragged to death if she didn't get her foot out of the stirrup.

Her foot came out then, and she eyed him, letting him know that she had no qualms about biting the hand that fed her. "I'm getting the hang of it," she snapped. "Just give me a minute or two."

Fine, he thought. *Fine. I'll just let her work it out by herself, and if she blisters her backside and breaks her fool neck, that will be her business as well.* He cursed again and rode out of the way, giving her plenty of room, knowing her stubborn pride would get her in the saddle if nothing else did. After a few minutes she lit out.

Jennifer was definitely mounted, but Jay had never seen anyone ride like she was, unless they were dead. She was still struggling with her skirts, the pony, the saddle, her body flung across the seat like a dead man. Her hair had come down and it was obviously tangled with her hand in the stirrup.

"Jesus!" Jay swore again, reining Brady alongside her. "Let's face it," he said, "you're going to have to straddle him." Then, without giving her a chance to argue, he leaned forward and gripped her arm, pulling her hair along with it. Jennifer let out a loud *"Ouch!"* as Jay pulled her off the horse and dropped her on her feet. He dismounted, dropping Brady's rein to the ground in front of him. In three short strides Jay was before her, drawing his knife. As the knife came toward her, Jennifer pressed back against the pony, squeezing her eyes shut. She had done it this time. She had pushed him beyond his limit. If he didn't kill her, he would probably cut her tongue out. She squeezed her eyes tighter and held her breath.

The next thing she knew, there was a loud ripping sound. Her eyes flew open. Jay was squatting before her, slashing a long rip down the front of her skirt. He turned her around and did the same thing down the back. Then he lifted her in his arms and put her in the saddle, handing her the reins. "Now," he said, "you've got all day to get the hang of it."

Several hours later Jennifer was shifting painfully in the saddle, her tender thighs and backside already suffering saddle sores from the pounding her flesh was taking as it rubbed against the seat and cantle with each jarring step the pony took. She eyed the smooth-gaited gelding Jay was riding.

"Doesn't this poor excuse for a horse know how to do anything but bounce up and down?" she said to Jay's back.

Jay pulled up and turned to look at her. "The pony is doing fine. You're the one that's bouncing all over the place. Keep your rear in the center of the saddle. You're hitting every spot between the cantle and the fork. If you keep that up, you're going to have a blistered butt."

He rested one arm across his saddle horn as he regarded her impassively. His hat was hanging down his back, secured by the leather thongs that lay snug against his throat. The moon was full and bright between the clouds, penetrating the shafts of his hair like sunlight, lifting the color so that it glinted silver against the darkness. Yet his face was as inscrutable as it had been earlier, when she'd tried to convince him she did not ride well. He obviously was a proud, stubborn man.

But her own pride was every bit as stubborn and as uncompromising as his. "Your concern is most gratifying," she said overly sweetly, "but a little late. My butt, as you call it, is already blistered."

Surprise registered in his eyes, but only for a moment before he brought it under control. "Has no one ever taught you that a lady doesn't speak quite so bluntly and that she should never resort to vulgarism?"

"Why not? You do."

"That's different," he said, his eyes flickering over her and resting on the ribbon that she had pulled from somewhere and used to tie back her hair. "I'm a man."

She threw her head back and laughed, "I was taught in school, Mr. Culhane, that vulgarism is vulgarism, without any regard to gender."

"You're not in school now, little girl, so I'd advise you to mind your manners and leave the cursing to me."

She felt the burn of anger flare against her cheeks. "And I'll advise you of a thing or two while we're at it," she said, "I am not a little girl. And I don't like to be called a little girl. I am a grown woman. And I don't take orders from you or anyone else."

He threw a leg over the saddle and slid to the ground, then approached her rapidly, stopping just inches away from her knee. He rested his hand against her thigh, ignoring her gasp of outrage. "Little girl, you'd do well to remember one thing," he said, his voice lazy and low, belying the threat she sensed there. "I'll treat you as you behave. And if you continue to give me nine kinds of hell, I'll give your fanny—blisters and all—a proper warming. Understood?"

Jennifer's eyes grew wider as she stared at him, too astonished to say anything. After a moment she said, "Take your hand off me." When he made no attempt to remove the palm that rested against her thigh, she yanked the reins to guide her horse away from him.

His hand shot out, clamping over the pony's bridle, halting him, just before those same hands lifted and, going securely around her waist, brought Jennifer to the ground.

Without thinking, Jenny drew back her hand. Her eyes met his, finding in the blue depths something that held her. His hand went around her wrist. A glimmer of something akin to amusement came and went. "I wouldn't advise that.

I'm not one of your school pups. Woman or not, you slap me and I'll slap you back." He laughed and shook his head. "Such a ridiculous gesture, anyway, for a woman to use against a man of my size. Can you think of nothing better?"

"I've already proven that I can," she said coolly. "Of course, a *macho hombre* like yourself wouldn't want to remember being bested by a woman."

"Your tongue isn't being backed up by twenty peons now, sweetheart. You'd be wise to cease reminding me of that unpleasant encounter, or I might find myself persuaded to reciprocate that little gesture also. And before you say something smart, I'd advise you to consider just how those blisters of yours would fare if they were bare and flapping against the saddle."

"Is that how you plan to keep me submissive? By trying to scare me? Is that the only way you can bend a woman to your will?"

"When I want to bend a woman to my will," he said slowly, "I'll do more than just remove her clothes."

He was still holding her wrist, but her other hand was free, and raising it, she took a swing at him. Instantly his hand tightened on her wrist, the pain shooting up her arm as he drove her to her knees before him. But still the defiance was there, in her eyes, and she did not look away from him. He did not move but stood deathly still, looking down at her, his eyes cold and full of anger.

She didn't know why she had been so impulsive, why she had pushed him, but somehow she had the feeling that even if she had slapped him, he would not strike her. He would probably shove her away from him, or give her a look of utter disgust, and then walk away, leaving her to mount the pony by herself. But there was, at the same moment, an inkling that he would get even with her. At his own time. In his own way.

"Are we going to stand out here all night like a couple of fence posts, or are we going somewhere?" she asked, lifting her chin to show him she might be on her knees but that she wasn't beneath him. When he didn't respond, she clenched her jaw. Attack was better than surrender any day, as far as she was concerned. "If you would be so kind as to release my arm and put *your fanny* in the saddle, we might accomplish more than we seem to be doing at the present."

"I give the orders around here. And in case you've forgotten, I do the cursing."

She lifted a brow. "Do you? I was under the impression you were a hired hand. You do work for my father, don't you?"

"In a roundabout way."

"Then, in a roundabout way, would you release my arm? I don't like to be mauled by the hired help."

Instantly she found herself hauled to her feet. She was ready to give him a run for his money and was prepared to tell him so—only . . .

Jennifer wasn't as prepared as she thought she was, for she looked up at him at the exact moment the moon passed out of the cover of a cloud, its mellow light striking the handsome planes of his face. She had seen that look before, the night he'd forced her to strip at gunpoint, and she never would forget the hypnotic eyes that had assessed her so boldly.

Jay Culhane might appear to be cool and calm on the outside, but inside he was a tangled mass of nerves and hot desire laced with the compelling urge to throw back his head and laugh. The girl angered him. She intrigued him. She caught his attention and held it. She had the face of an angel, the body of a temptress, a mind sharp as a brass tack, and a way of going about things that was funnier than hell. He couldn't help remembering the way she'd looked when she'd tried to mount the pony. When he'd seen her thrown over the saddle like a sack of potatoes—her shapely derriere rammed in the air higher than her haughty little nose—he felt the stabbing wrench of attraction once more. *Little girl, you can't possibly know what an invitation like that makes me want.*

Standing just a head below him, she had observed his lapse of distraction. Looking down at her, his eyes moving slowly over her face, he saw she was frowning at him as if trying to glean his thoughts. He couldn't help smiling. "You wouldn't guess in a million years," he said, following a hunch that said she wouldn't be able to resist a challenge like that.

"If it's so impossible, I daresay I won't even try. Why don't you just tell me?"

"Because I would rather show a hellcat like you."

It took a moment for that to register. And a moment was all he needed. It happened so quickly, she had no time to react. His hands settled firmly on her waist and pulled her hard against him. Jennifer pushed against him, hearing him say in a harsh voice, "The more you struggle, the longer we're here. I thought we'd already proven that once."

"The only thing we've proven is that you're an animal," she said.

Securing her close to him with one arm, he raised the other to tilt her head up, holding it in place with his powerful hand. Her eyes locked with his. "Don't—"

"That's right," he said as she spoke the word. "Open your mouth for me." Then she felt the firm, warm pressure of his lips moving over hers and her lids dropped like weights. *Aren't you forgetting something, Jennifer? Are you going to let him have his way after the way he's treated you?*

She hadn't forgotten, but something within her was wanting this man to kiss her. For two days she had remembered the way he had kissed her, the feel of his mouth upon hers—even while she had been about to bring the crucifix down upon his head. What would it be like now? Without any thought of escape on her mind, without the fear that she might fail? Disturbed by the strange stirring within her, she couldn't help being curious.

What would it hurt? Why can't I satisfy my curiosity?

Why can't I—just for a moment—let him kiss me as if I wanted it? It was simply something she had to know, like why apples fall down to the ground and why oil rises to the top of water.

The thought vanished when he pulled her more closely against him, his mouth moving over hers with hard-driven force. *You should have left well enough alone, Jennifer.* She should have had her head examined. This man had too much experience, knew too many ways to overpower her. She made a small sound of frustration, desire and will warring within her. She pushed against him, twisting, finding she had no room to move and finding, also, that each time she tried, his lips twisted harder across her mouth, hurting, searching, demanding, relentless.

Too dangerous. . . . This man is too dangerous.

She tried to bite him, but he guessed her intentions and pushed her away from him, just far enough to look down into her face with a mocking gleam in his eyes, his hands holding her firmly by her arms. "You're a vicious little thing, aren't you? Tell me, does your daddy know you go around biting men?"

She shoved furiously at him, knocking him off-balance enough that he had to take a step backward, but he did not release his hold. "Do you know what happens to little girls who bite?" He gave her a shake. "They get their little lily-whites paddled."

"You . . . let go of me! What do you think you're doing? You were hired to protect me, or have you forgotten?"

"No, I haven't forgotten," he said, sounding calm and unmoved. "I'll let you go when you behave yourself and keep still."

He kissed her again, just as hard as the first time. She stopped struggling and he loosened his hold, breaking the kiss. She brought the back of her hand up, glaring at him with disgust as she wiped it across her mouth.

Normally not a man easily provoked, Jay was that, and more. He grabbed her, jerking her close. "It will take more than that to wipe the taste of me away," he said, the anger in his voice melting away as his eyes moved across her face. A finger came up to brush her hair back from her cheek, and for a moment she was mesmerized by the way he was looking at her. "You are unbelievably beautiful, you know." Then he lowered his head. "Kiss me, you little witch. Kiss me and tell me you don't enjoy it." His warm lips trailed across her cheek, his arms like shackles around her, holding her against him in a bone-crushing embrace. His hard mouth slammed over hers with a kiss that was everything he meant it to be—insulting, hard, and violent, just like him. Jenny clamped her mouth shut until his hand came up, gripping her jaw, his thumb forcing her lips apart. Then he insulted her further, his tongue invading to conquer territory she would not yield, until he forced her, by sheer physical strength alone, to surrender.

He might be stronger than her; he might force her to accept the discipline of his thrusting tongue; there was no doubt he could subdue her with his crushing strength. She was no physical match for him, nor in finesse was she his equal. Yet she stood firm in her resistance. No matter what he demanded, regardless of the force he used, anything he got from her he would have to take. She would never give. And she found some small satisfaction in that.

Jay felt her stiff capitulation, knowing that by withholding herself she had won. But it was only the first go-around. He kept seeing the image of her naked before him: the purple eyes dark with anger, the soft whiteness of her skin, the kissable pout of her mouth, the silky weight of her pitch-black hair. With an angry oath his arm went around her, tightening until she gasped for the breath that was forced from her body. "It won't work, you know. You can't keep denying something you want."

"Listen, you monster, the only thing I want is to be left alone." She pushed against his chest. "Let go of me! You don't have to make it so obvious that you enjoy humiliating me like this. Why can't you understand the position you've put me in?"

"Don't be such a silly little fool. Understand the position I've put you in?" he repeated. "How can I, when all I can think about is the position I'd *like* to put you in. You want understanding? Find yourself a goddamn priest."

"You're disgusting!"

"Am I?"

"You are . . . everything you say . . . everything you do is disgusting."

"Is that so? Then see how disgusting you find this."

Purposefully he held her gaze, if for no other reason than to show her just how helpless her feminine strength was against him. Then he lowered his head to hers, his mouth stopping the string of oaths she had ready.

Her mouth was soft and warm, sweet as a honey pot, making him forget who she was, what he was doing here with her. Nothing seemed to matter except the drive that made him ache. Dear God! How he wanted her!

She made a muffled sound into his mouth and twisted her body against his. Her movement alongside that part of him that was already way too sensitive and swollen from wanting her made him groan. One hand twisted in her hair, the other dropping to the small of her back to bring her more fully against the tightness in his loins, then dropping lower to squeeze her buttocks gently.

Jennifer felt the shudder race across his muscular frame as he drew her hard against him, her own passionate response coming from low in her throat.

Jay, who had been fighting a battle royal to contain the explosion that was going on inside of him, heard her distressful sound and recognized it for what it was. He never had had such a hard time of it, trying to hold himself back, to practice self-control that he simply did not possess. Without really knowing it, he had slipped the ribbon from her hair, spilling its inky length across her back, pressing her back against Brady, her shoulders resting against the saddle, his knee coming up to slip between her legs.

If he was unaware of what was happening between them, Jennifer was more so, bombarded as she was with so many new feelings. His knee pressed closer. Higher. Until she was straddling it, riding it as he did Brady. The sweet feel of warm pressure where she wanted it most made her groan, and Jay answered by kissing her deeper, his hands laced through the silky strands of her hair, holding her head to increase the pressure of his mouth as his knee stroked her.

Jennifer didn't know it, but for her first seduction she was getting a pretty good lesson. Not really aware of what was happening or where all this might lead, she was carried along with the rapidly moving current. Jay had intended on kissing her just forcefully enough and seductively enough to scare the drawers off her and send her hopping toward obedience. He had no idea she would respond like this. But what surprised him most was finding himself seduced as well. Now it was his turn to groan, frustrated because he had once again misjudged her. He had been right the first time to peg her as no virgin, because no inexperienced maiden would move beneath his hands as she did, knowing just how to wring the last drop of hesitation from him. And since someone had had her before him, there was no reason in hell why he should put off the inevitable. Trembling with the realization that he had succeeded beyond his wildest imaginings, he broke the kiss, nibbling his way to her ear. "Take off your clothes. I'll get my blanket."

She drew back, breathless, her eyes dazed with desire, her mouth wet and swollen from his kisses. She looked at him strangely, the sharpness of her mind dazed, as well as her senses. "What's wrong with my clothes?"

He felt like throttling her. He gripped her shoulders and gave her a light shake. "Look at me, Jenny." When she didn't respond quickly, he lifted her chin and looked into her eyes. "There isn't anything wrong with your clothes, angel. I simply want you naked."

She drew her brows together, obviously hearing him but puzzled by his words. Then a spark of enlightenment flared in her eyes. "If you think to humble me by making me ride across this desert wearing nothing but your blanket . . . Have you lost your mind?"

"Listen to me, sweetheart. I want you to understand just what's happening here. I'll be doing the riding, not you, and when I do, I want you moving beneath me like you were doing a moment ago when I kissed you, only this time I want you on the blanket and naked beneath me. Don't paint it with cherubs and roses. Don't give it gilded highlights. Don't hear the ring of wedding bells in your ears. Don't give it dimensions it doesn't have. It's desire, pure and simple. I want you, and you've already shown me how badly you want me."

Jennifer went rigid. One glance told her he was primed to go as many rounds as she wanted, and as far as she was concerned, there weren't enough numbers in the universe to count that high. She decided then and there that it was time to gain the upper hand. Lowering her head, she rested it against his chest. Let him think she had surrendered. It was the best way to catch him off-guard. And catch him she would.

He had her now, by God. For the first time since he'd encountered her she was being honest. "Tell me, angel face, just how long has it been since you've had a man between your legs?"

She jerked her head back as if she'd been shot. It was all the break she needed. Before he realized what was happening, she found a way to show him just how angry that comment made her. From out of the darkness came her clenched fist, and she planted a dandy just below his right eye, just as she said, "You filthy bastard. I'd kill myself before I'd lie with a saddle tramp like you. Don't you ever take such liberties with me again!"

If the intense smarting of his eye hadn't restored his reasoning, her caustic words would have. Whatever the thing was that had gripped her in confusion moments ago, it seemed to have left her, apparently to prey upon him, because Jay was now thoroughly confused. Had she punched him and called him names because he had misjudged her again—wrongly thinking her no innocent? Or did she call him a bastard and a saddle tramp because she felt he was beneath her station and the thought of making love to a man beneath her was repugnant to her? Whatever the reason behind it, she had most definitely set out to cool his ardor, and cool his ardor she had. In fact, it was so damn cold right now, it would probably take months to thaw.

Jay tried focusing on her, seeing three Jenny Baxters where there should be only one—and none of them appeared to be upset. Angry, yes. But not upset. And that surprised him. Most women would be terrified at this point, terrified of a man they had just socked in the eye, afraid of what he might do in retaliation. But if anything, Jennifer looked like she was still mad enough to let fly with another one.

He stepped back, raising his hand to rub his eye. Jennifer was looking at him warily. "Don't worry," he said. "I'm not going to hit you."

"I'm not so sure I can say the same thing, but I suppose I should be relieved."

He had the audacity to grin. "Most women would be."

"What most women do doesn't interest me in the least."

He shook his head. "You're a hard one to figure out. So different, I find it difficult to know how to deal with you. You're too complex . . . and very confusing." He searched her face. "Where are your tears?"

"Tears?" She wanted to laugh. "I haven't met the man yet that was worth crying over."

"And if you did meet such a man?"

"I still wouldn't cry. I never cry."

"You're very good at subterfuge, but then, that is to be expected, is it not?"

"I don't know what you're talking about. You made me

angry. You insulted me. And I hit you . . . and justifiably, I might add. It was defense, pure and simple. And there's no subterfuge in that. I would think it quite honest."

"The only thing honest about a woman is her body. Her deception, even her hatred, can take many forms, but unlike the rest of her, her body cannot lie."

"I don't tell lies."

He lifted a finger and placed it over her lips, as if to keep her silent. "And you don't cry either, do you, darling Jenny?" His eyes raked over her and he gave her an evil grin, his knuckles brushing the sunken curve of her cheek. "But you will. Before we're through, I'll have you crying for me . . . in the most delicious places."

She gasped, turning away from him, his arms coming out to scoop her up, walking with her to the horses. "You've wasted enough of my time as it is . . . even if your shrewish ways and caustic words weren't beginning to irritate me."

Once again Jennifer found herself thrust into the saddle. He stood there a moment looking up at her, then he handed her the reins and said, "Remember what I said about keeping yourself to the center of the saddle . . . and move with it, not against it."

"And you remember what I said about keeping your hands off me."

"What changed your mind? You were sure hot for it a moment ago."

She closed her eyes, fighting for control. When she opened them, he couldn't believe what he saw. Hell's bells! She'd done it again. He'd never known a woman that was so difficult to provoke. But this one . . . she seemed all too determined to win. She could write a book on self-control. Never had he seen such iron resolve. She didn't bend. She didn't break. She regrouped. And she never cried.

Distracted and fascinated, he didn't see the open palm coming, but he sure as hell felt it jar his teeth with a crack that boomed like cannon fire. "I thought you'd learned your lesson about such violence," he yelled. "I ought to paddle your behind until you can't sit down for a week."

"You and who else?"

"I'm more than man enough to do the job," he said with a snarl, and yanked her against him, his arms holding her trapped against him. His angry mouth descended in a kiss meant to punish more than arouse. She wasn't aware he had moved his hand until it closed over her breast and squeezed. Then, as quickly as it had come, it was over.

He thrust her away and turned. As angry as she was at him, she couldn't stop herself from admiring how easily he swung into his saddle. But a moment later he spoke, reminding her that she wasn't as in control of things as she thought.

"We'll be on our way," he said curtly. "But before we go, I'll give you one last warning. I've seen how indulgent your father is toward that brood of his. It's obvious you've never been made to watch your step or bridle your tongue." His voice was light, but the look on his face and in those eyes sent a chill across her. "That one fact alone absolved you . . . this time. It won't happen a third time. If you care to try your luck again, I'll show you the way of it."

"I doubt I'd have wanted to slap you again, anyway. I've always thought myself much too clever to resort to repetitive measures," she said, lifting her chin and guiding the pony forward, intending to sweep by him—as dramatically as possible on her undignified mount. But he reached out and, taking hold of the pony's rein, guided her in a wide turn and headed in the other direction.

"I said I didn't like to ride. I didn't say anything about not having a working understanding of the basics. I can guide a horse."

"Don't whine, little girl. You may understand the basics of guidance, but your ability to tell direction leaves something to be desired. You were headed the wrong way."

Once again she assumed her position behind him. After a

few minutes her backside was burning from being jostled about, just as it was before. She scooted forward to the center of the saddle. Her eyes on Jay's hips, she tried to emulate the fluid way his body moved with the horse. He was right. It was much easier this way. But she would never tell him that. The man was far too conceited as it was.

For lack of anything better to do, Jennifer once again considered her plight. Here she was riding across the roughest terrain possible on a ragged pony of questionable breeding that lacked the usual mustang qualities of agility, intelligence, and natural sense while possessing all the undesirable attributes of their cussed nature. She thought about her family, suddenly finding herself homesick and miserable. Sometimes it was hard being your own woman. Sometimes she didn't want to be strong and independent. Sometimes she yearned for a man with whom to share her hardships and joys. Her eyes went back to Jay. It wouldn't be a man like him, of course—a callous, unfeeling ogre.

Two hours later they stopped to rest the horses and have a drink of water. Jennifer barely had time to walk the kinks out of her body before Jay was telling her to mount up. As he had before, the hot-tempered little pony had something to say about that. Her body was still aching and moving awkwardly from the fast pace Jay was keeping, and the pony added to her humiliation. His vicious teeth took a plug out of her leg as she tried to mount. And when she recovered from that and attempted to swing her leg over the saddle, the wild-eyed beast tried bucking, tossing her to the ground, where she landed in an inelegant heap. For a few moments Jennifer stayed where she landed, rubbing her posterior and eyeing the brute in the same manner in which the brute was eyeing her. About the time she had decided to tackle the task once more, she found herself yanked up by the collar like a pesky puppy, and planted, none too gently, on her feet beside the pony. She had just managed to say "I *don't* need any help from you" when a pair of rough hands clamped beneath her fanny and shoved upward. She landed in the saddle with a painful thud. Searching the pony's matted mane for the reins, she flung Jay a look hot enough to heat half the cooking pots in Mexico.

"Sometimes, Miss Baxter, a job can be done in half the time it would take to discuss it." He thrust the reins in her hand, speaking more harshly now. "Okay, cream puff, let's ride."

"But it's still dark."

Something close to a smile lingered around his mouth, lingered but never came to pass. "And it will stay dark for some time yet. But the moon is full and the desert sand is light, making it relatively easy to see . . . or haven't you noticed?"

He stood looking up at her, a mysterious stranger with cold blue eyes and a hard mouth; and suddenly the reality of the situation struck her. She remembered the tiny house that had been her home for the past many weeks, wondering how long it would be before the villagers discovered she was missing. Would they come for her? As if sensing her thoughts, Jay moved to his horse and swung into the saddle abruptly, his horse grunting and sweeping in a wide circle before he pulled Brady up beside her. "What's the matter, little girl? Are you afraid of the dark?"

"No. Of course not. I just like to see where I'm going, that's all."

"Well, if that's all that's bothering you, it'll be daylight in a few hours—then you can see where you've been."

"But we can't see where we're going. What if my horse steps in a hole or something?"

"Fortunately the horse has more sense than you do."

Jennifer cast a dubious look at the frowsy-maned pony, but kept her thoughts to herself—for the time being. Then she looked at the back of the militaristic man riding before her. He might be bigger than her, and stronger, but there would be time enough to get Jay Culhane's goat—in a lot of little ways. Then she kicked the little horse, following after

Jay before he was swallowed completely by the darkness that surrounded them.

Growing up, Jennifer had never experienced the childhood fear of the dark. She'd been unconcerned with it for twenty-one years. But that had all changed. She felt an icy coldness penetrate her leather jacket. Her spine tingled. Her heart thumped. She could feel the gentle nudge of attentiveness. There were probably wolves out there. She swallowed, looking around her. Nights in this part of Mexico were cool and quiet, contributing to the eerie feeling.

The openness of the flats did little to ease her apprehension. Silvered shafts of moonlight dancing between the clouds overhead played tricks with the shadows, while the wind moving through the sparse vegetation unnerved her. Somewhere behind her, a twig snapped. Jennifer gave the pony a nudge in the flanks. Ahead of her, Jay's horse snorted and tossed its head, the bit ringing hollow against its teeth. The loud whir of flapping wings told her something large had just sailed overhead. The darkness was speaking to her.

More alert now, Jennifer was learning to listen. "Listen to them, the children of the night. . . . What music they make!" But then she remembered that the quote was from *Dracula.* She pulled her jacket tighter. Once again her eyes went to the back of the man riding ahead. He didn't seem too concerned about the darkness. She kept her eyes locked on his silhouette. *Stay alert,* she told herself. *Do as he does. Don't let him see your fear.* She was learning.

It seemed to Jennifer that they had traveled beneath the moonlight for a long time. From time to time she was conscious that she was looking to the east, watching for the faintest lift of darkness on the horizon, but stubborn as the heat of day, the blackness was not diluted. The cold had penetrated to the very marrow of her bones, or so it seemed, and she could feel the darkness, more substantial than ever, closing in around her. She looked ahead and saw

Jay had stopped. As she drew closer she saw he was unbuckling the billet end of his stirrup strap.

"How much longer are we going to ride?" she asked.

"Until we get where we're going," he said, passing the strap through the bar buckle.

"I can see this is going to be a long trip, full of stimulating conversation and clever witticism . . . all in all, quite entertaining."

"Duty comes before pleasure," he said. He took a slow drink from his canteen and replaced the lid. "Let's be moving. We have a lot of ground to cover and not much time before daylight."

"I always thought it was wise to take it slow . . . pace yourself and you will live a longer life."

"So will you . . . if you keep that mouth of yours shut." He returned her gaze steadily, his cold eyes never warming as they looked their fill. Without knowing why, she knew she was drawn to him in some strange way; drawn and unable to look away. Perhaps it was his face. There was certainly something about it, something in the hard leanness, the irregular features that taken separately were more ugly than attractive but somehow came together in a compromising blend of lusty male beauty, while at the same time maintaining the raw excitement of the ungentled ruthlessness she had first sensed in him.

"Do you have my features committed to memory?" he asked harshly.

"Not yet, but I will before long. Then I'll give a detailed description to the next sheriff I see and have you hunted down for kidnapping."

Jay laughed. "Sweetheart, I'm a United States deputy marshal. A local sheriff doesn't have jurisdiction over me."

Jennifer looked blankly at him, meeting his inquisitive gaze, wondering what was taking place behind those smoky eyes. Something about the way he was looking at her made her throat feel strangely tight and threw an extra beat in a heart rhythm that was already doing triple time.

"Do you have any more threats you want to cut your teeth on, little tiger cub?"

"Oh, shut up," she said, trying to think of something clever to put him in his place.

Culhane merely laughed, then said, "Tell me, angel eyes, how much longer are you going to struggle with the inevitable? You are bested, you know. Now, why don't you be a good little girl and stop giving me all this trouble?"

He had the look of a hunter about him now, sure and stalking, completely detached. She wouldn't give way to the flutter of nervousness that followed. Something about his presence bothered her—a sense of distance and withdrawal, and self-discipline that had been with him so long, it was almost instinctive. Her own instinct told her a man like him was inaccessible and quite dangerous. It challenged her. It made her want to provoke him, to deal him surprise after surprise, to be a constant annoyance, to do anything to put distance between them and make him regret the day he had made the decision to find her.

"Don't look so glum-faced. Triumph is the right of the strongest." He gave her a taunting smile. "Behave yourself and I'll try not to rub it in."

"Don't ride through the *Arc de Triomphe* yet," she said.

6

$\sim\!\!\! \sim$

Morning came like a timid little girl peeking around a doorway, inching her way through; first a head, followed by a shoulder, a foot softly placed, and then another. By the time the sun had gathered its full strength and burst over the horizon, spilling its golden warmth over her chilled body, Jennifer was too weary to care.

It was early yet, but the Chihuahua Desert, a jumble of forms and dimensions, warmed up rapidly. It defied description, this land of astonishing contrasts. It was as if all the geographical areas of the world converged here, a geological dumping ground. Everywhere she looked was isolation, scarcity, and hardship, yet there was a quiet primeval beauty in this land of limitless views and untouched wildness. Behind them, the shadows of the Sierra Madres melted into the heated waves of a mirage, while ahead lay nothing but sandy wastes that rose gradually to form the high rims of the Chisos, Davis, and Guadalupe, as well as the dozen or so other ranges that lay just across the Rio Grande—a short distance in the mind, an eternity away when traveling on horseback.

She tucked her cold fingers inside her jacket, against the warmth of her body, reminding herself that she had been in lonely, desolate places before and survived. In fact, the life she had chosen for herself could be, at times, quite lonely. And it didn't make the loneliness any easier to take when everyone was always against what she was doing—or so it seemed. It wasn't easy to venture out into new territory. And at times she was afraid and lacking confidence, but whenever she tried going back into the life that she was expected to live, it began to pinch, just like a pair of shoes she had outgrown.

"Tell me something, Miss Baxter."

Jennifer looked up to see Jay Culhane pull up beside her. For a moment their eyes met, his cold and wary, hers nervous and uncertain. "What would you like to know?"

"Why a wealthy, well-bred, educated woman like yourself would choose to throw it all away."

"Just what is it that I have thrown away, Mr. Culhane?"

"A comfortable life, wealth, the opportunity to marry within your class."

"I don't think I've thrown anything away, as you call it. The things you refer to will still be there whenever I want them."

"Possibly, if you don't wait too long. Most women your age are—"

"I know what most women my age are doing, and that doesn't interest me at the moment. God gave me a brain. My parents gave me an education. I want the opportunity to use them . . . or at least try. There are things I want to do. I may succeed. I might fail. But I will have the satisfaction of knowing I tried. I can't spend my life being what other people think I should be."

"Why not? Plenty of other women do it."

"I am not like other women." She watched his face for his reaction, expecting him to say something sarcastic, like, "I've noticed."

But he simply said, "What makes you so different? What do you get out of the kind of life you lead that you couldn't get elsewhere?"

"I'm different because I dare, Mr. Culhane. I take risks that other women are too timid or too afraid to take. It's not that the desire isn't there in a lot of them, for I believe it is. I think most women simply can't break away from the mold."

"Still, it's a strange life for a young woman of your upbringing to lead. Don't you ever get lonely for your family, the kind of life you had before? Aren't you ever afraid?"

Jennifer licked her lips against the dryness and stared out across the desert. "Of course I've known fear. I was scared to go to Brownsville; I was fearful of what could happen to me in Mexico, but I was needed and that gave me strength. That, and prayer," she added.

He looked her over. "You're a beautiful woman," he said. "That will get you a lot further than foolish notions or prayer."

"Relying solely on my physical attributes would get me about as far as the nearest bed, I would imagine."

He regarded her steadily, those deep blue eyes moving slowly over her face. "And would that be so bad?" he asked, the hint of amusement in his voice undisguised.

But Jennifer was anything but amused. "I liked you better when you were sullen and quiet," she said, kicking the pony into a trot and riding ahead of him, angry that she could not go fast enough to outrun the mocking sound of his laughter.

Overhead, the sun was arrogant and proud, throwing mirror flashes of intense heat upon everything below, as Zeus would fling his thunderbolts. The air was still and stifling, and silence itself seemed to cling heavily to the flat, colorless plain. Even the ornery pony seemed to have lost some of his zip, plodding slowly along, heavy-lidded, his head drooping and wet with sweat. To ease the stiffness in her legs, Jennifer slipped her feet from the stirrups and let her legs hang free.

Jay rode ahead of her, sitting easily in the saddle, the reins loose in his hands, his manner calm and comfortable, showing no sign that he had been sitting on a horse all night. She stared at him until her eyes grew weary from the strain. He was a very attractive man, she would have to admit, but something about him frightened her just a little, made her wary, as if he held some sort of power over her. There was nothing about him that was not hard and aloof, as deadly and dangerous as the pistol he wore strapped at his side.

Occasionally he would turn in the saddle, just enough to look over his shoulder to give her the once-over. After a moment of contemplation, appraising her with those brazen eyes of his, he would smile in a mocking manner and shake his head, as if he were having trouble believing what he was seeing. Soon, she would think, soon, you'll be laughing on the other side of your arrogant face, you bastard. Then, without saying a word, he would turn back around and, pressing his spurs into Brady's sides, break into a gallop, leaving her to trail him in a choking cloud of fine dust.

Jennifer would watch him ride off, knowing after he had left her like this several times that he would return once he had scouted the area just ahead. But knowing that he would return didn't help her mood any. She was hot, tired, thirsty, and hungry; her pride had suffered significantly; and she hurt in more places than she could count—but she would never expect, or ask, for any consideration or indulgence from him. Well she could remember his last comment when she had done no more than ask if they could stop for a drink of water.

"Little girls that sleep on satin sheets should think twice before trading all that luxury to go traipsing off to Mexico. I would think you'd be accustomed to hardship by now."

"If I wasn't before, I will be by the time we get where we're going."

"You made your bed, little girl, now it's time to lie in it. You chose to go to Mexico. Don't complain to me if the price is more than you are willing to pay. There's an old saying: He who is afraid of every nettle should not piss in the grass.

She brought the reins down hard upon the sides of the pony, riding up ahead of him, his contemptible laughter rocking across the desert floor. Bastard! He never missed an opportunity to be contemptible, to degrade and humiliate her at every turn. No one had ever treated her this way.

A few minutes later she heard the thunder of Brady's hooves as he eased by her, slowing to a steady walk a few yards ahead. She narrowed her eyes at his arrogant back, not bothering to question just how she knew his back was arrogant. It was simply arrogant—just like the rest of him. Ass! He probably had arrogant feet as well. Finding little satisfaction in narrowing her eyes at his back, she went one step further and mumbled under her breath, *"La zorra nunca se ve la cola,"* still feeling the searing stab of stung pride.

He turned to look at her. "If the barbs you shoot behind my back are going to hit the mark, you're going to have to speak up. He laughed. "I can tell by that sour look on your face that I've just been insulted, but—"

"I said, 'the fox never sees its own tail,' or, more simply put, he who criticizes others never sees his own fault."

He scowled. "I see my own faults, little girl, but unlike you, I do precious little complaining about them. And I refrain from blaming others for what is my own damn fault or my sole responsibility."

Who was this strange man with skin like iron and words as harsh as coal oil? Clamping her jaws together and feeling her spine stiffen with determination, Jennifer knew she was probably no match for the angry and powerful Jay Culhane, but she wasn't going to give up without making her mark.

The grip on her control was slipping, and seeing that it was, Jay said, "Jennifer, it's not my desire to hurt or belittle you. Now, why don't we stop taking jabs at each other before we inflict some real damage."

"Why don't you let me send a telegram to my father. If I let him know what I was doing in Mexico, I'm sure he will let me return. How far is it to the nearest telegraph station?"

"It doesn't matter," he said abruptly, "because I have no intention of letting you send any telegram. I was hired to do a job and I'm going to do it. Your father wants you deposited at his front door, and come hell or high water, that's what I'm going to do."

"Then I'll warn you right now, I'm not going to make this easy for you."

"Go ahead. I welcome the challenge." He laughed. "It wouldn't be anything different, would it? You haven't been exactly the most cooperative woman I've ever been around."

"If I get the opportunity to leave, I will. Whatever I can do to pay you back for all your kindness, I'll do it. You can't go without sleep, Mr. Culhane, and you can't sleep with your eyes open. Sometime, someday, you're going to doze off or let your guard down, and when you do—"

"Make all the threats you like, little girl. When it comes time to bed down, it will be simple enough to handcuff you to me."

"You enjoy this, don't you? If my father knew what a bas—"

"Careful, girl. I'm tired of all this name-calling. You might just push me too far." Jay stared at her. "If you did succeed in getting away from me, you'd be digging your own grave. You'd never find your way out of here. If the desert didn't get you, a roaming band of *bandidos* would. Face it. You may not like me, Jennifer, but you need me."

"Like I need another blister on my backside."

"Adept at finding your way across a desert, are you?"

"Listen, you b—"

"Don't you know any bad words besides *bastard*?" he said, the look in his eyes sending her blood racing. "For an *educated* woman you have a very inadequate vocabulary."

"I could call you a lot worse if I wasn't a lady."

He threw back his head and laughed. "A lady indeed. I think you slip behind that label only when it pleases you."

"I don't really care what—"

"Don't you ever shut up? We've got a long ride ahead of us. Do you intend to badger me with questions the entire way?"

"Unless I can find something more irritating to do."

"Having you anywhere around me is irritating as hell, so rest assured, Miss Baxter, as long as you're breathing, you're doing the job."

"Good."

He kicked his horse and rode up ahead, ending the conversation as abruptly as it had started. On and on they rode, beneath the broiling sun, Jennifer wondering if they would ever stop again to rest, Jay wondering if Jennifer would ever shut up. Looking up, she saw him pull up and stare at the sky overhead, then twist around to look back over his shoulder.

"Get down, Jennifer. Quickly," he said, dismounting and leading Brady toward her. When she was down, he took the reins from her and pulled a pair of hobbles out of his saddlebag. After hobbling the pony he did the same with Brady.

"What are you doing that for? I thought you said we'd ride until it was dark."

"There's a storm coming. We won't be able to ride anywhere until it passes. Get your rebozo out of your bag and take it with your blanket and canteen and head for that small outcropping of rocks over there."

"A rainstorm would be a welcome change," she said, watching him tie some strips of cloth over the horses' eyes, then tying another cloth around their noses like a muzzle. "I don't understand why we can't ride in the rain. We'll get just as wet behind those rocks." She paused. "What are you doing that for?" He didn't answer. Jennifer began eyeing the sky again. "I don't see a single cloud. Are you sure—"

"It's a dust storm, Miss Baxter, and unlike any you've ever experienced, I would imagine. To continue riding would be asinine. We'd only use up precious energy and time riding when we couldn't see where we were going. We don't have enough water to stray miles off course."

Jennifer eyed the sky again. "How can you tell? I don't see a thing."

"Look behind you, on the horizon."

She turned and studied the sky for several minutes. "I don't see anything but mountains."

"Those aren't mountains. "What you're seeing is sand, miles of it, coming this way fast. Now do as I said."

Jennifer took one last look at the jagged brown shape in the distance, thinking it still looked like mountains to her, when it began to change shape. A minute later the color began to get darker and the shape climbed higher, placing the sun behind a hazy filter. Hearing the ring of Jay's spurs, Jennifer turned to see he had hobbled the horses near the outcropping of rocks and was removing his blanket from his saddle.

She grabbed her blanket, canteen, and rebozo and ran for the rocks.

"Wrap your rebozo around your head, bringing it low over your eyes and high enough to cover your mouth and nose," he said gruffly.

She glanced at him to see if he was angry, and he wasn't, but she had never seen him more serious. She held up the rebozo. "You want me to wrap all of this around my face? I'll look like a mummy!"

"You'll also be able to breathe." He took the blanket from her, and when she had wrapped the rebozo as he had instructed, he draped the blanket over her head, dropping it low to cover her face and bringing it around her shoulders, then telling her to hold it together in front.

"I'm smothering in here. I'm hotter than a furnace."

"It'll be worse outside in a few minutes." He grabbed her firmly by the shoulders. "Now listen carefully, Jennifer. No matter what happens, don't pull the cloth from your face. Not until I tell you it's all right to do so. Do you understand?"

She nodded.

"Good girl," he said, giving her a pat on the shoulder. "Now, quickly, sit down, your back to the rocks."

Jennifer did as he said, leaning forward when he told her, so he could secure another blanket behind her. Then he wrapped his head, putting his other blanket over his head and shoulders, just as she had done. When he finished, he dropped down beside her, pulling the third blanket over them both. Jennifer was sweltering.

She was about to ask him how much longer it would be, when she heard a loud roar and began to feel the wind blow over her, the sand pelting the blanket. Darkness seemed to smother the sunlight that had been so prevalent only a moment ago, the world around them growing darker still as the speed of the wind increased. Sand began to filter and swirl beneath the covering of the blanket, and the air was difficult to pull through all the covering she had over her face. The feeling she might suffocate filled her with such tension, she didn't think she could stand it another minute. If it wasn't over soon, she was afraid she would snap under the strain. She kept repeating what Jay had said, but she wanted to throw the blankets off and start running.

She pulled the blanket around her as tightly as she could, clenching her teeth and squeezing her eyes together. She tried to think about home and her family, trying to pull the images up in her mind, but she kept seeing that huge, boiling brown cloud that completely blocked the sun. She kept wondering what it would feel like to suffocate, and then she began to pray, because she didn't want to die like this, out here where no one would ever find her. She squeezed her eyes tighter, feeling her body tremble. *I can't stand this. I can't sit here and be buried alive.*

He must have sensed her panic, for just when she

thought she could stand it no longer, his arm came around her shoulders and he pulled her against him.

"You're getting more air than you think," he shouted against her blanketed ear, Jennifer barely able to hear him over the loud roar. She nodded, turning her face against his shoulder and snuggling as close to him as she could get. She felt the tension drain away, Jay's hand coming under the blanket and resting high on her arm, stroking her absently. She took a deep breath, finding her more relaxed state made it easier to breathe. *At least if I die, I won't die alone,* she thought, feeling strangely comfortable and suddenly drowsy. Then she dropped off to sleep.

She wasn't sure how long she had been sleeping when she heard Jay say, "Mmm. I've never seen a woman that appreciated storms the way you do, angel eyes. Makes me wish this one hadn't come to an end."

Jennifer breathed deeply, rubbing her nose against Jay's chest, feeling his hands stroking her back—her bare back. Her eyes snapped open and her head came up to find herself staring into those devilish blue eyes of his, their noses just inches apart. But it wasn't the proximity of their eyes or even their noses that caused her such embarrassment. When she looked down, she saw she was sitting astride Jay's hips, her legs folded back at the knees, resting on each side of his hips, her groin resting on the hard ridge beneath the buttons on his pants. She shifted her weight, trying to slide off.

"Jesus, baby, do that again," he said, his voice low and husky, "and we'll be here all day." She wasn't sure which upset her more, the embarrassing position she found herself in, his low-spoken words, or the strange sensation she felt low in her belly. She braced her arms against his chest to push herself away, just as Jay slipped his hands down, locking them together as they went around her buttocks, drawing her more tightly against him.

She was ready. He knew she was ready. But he had to keep her this way until he could get his hand free. Silently he cursed the rebozo and blanket wrapped around her face, frustrating his attempts to kiss her. But that was something easily solved. He unwrapped both the rebozo and blanket, pushing them away and seeing her damp, flushed face, the huge eyes luminous and looking at him warily.

"Let me up."

"Not just yet. I find I like you just where you are."

She squirmed in his arms, learning quickly that that was the wrong thing to do. He took the lobe of her ear between his teeth and nipped her. "The problem with you, angel eyes, is you just don't know when you're ahead. You keep talking and prodding and doing all sorts of provocative things with that body of yours, until a man can't help himself."

He kissed her, covering her mouth completely with a kiss that left no doubt in her mind that she had been well and thoroughly kissed. She pounded his chest with her fist, but he only kissed her harder, deeper. She twisted her body, freezing in place when she heard him groan. Then he lifted his mouth from hers. "You see what I mean? You're doing it again. You just don't know when to quit."

"All right!" she said, her breathing fast and erratic. "I'm quitting now."

He chuckled, nibbling her throat. "It's too late now, angel. We left that option tumbled in the dust some time ago."

"Just let me up."

"When I've finally got you where I want you?"

"Why do you want to keep me here, against my will, when you know I can't stand the sight of you?"

"You may not like the sight of me, angel, but you love my touch."

"Liar!"

"You like the things I do to you, the way I make you feel, and you're a hypocrite if you deny it."

"I don't like anything about you."

"Like hell you don't!"

"I hate you!"

"Yeah, but you still want me."

"I don't!"

"You want me. You want me to keep doing all the things I've been doing. You could never be satisfied with a man that wasn't just a little bit stronger than you, angel, because you say you want me to stop, but in reality you're thrilled that I'm man enough to know what you really want, and strong enough to override any protest."

"I—" He kissed her, deeply, stopping any protest before it was uttered. The sand pelted the blanket over them, much lighter now, but she could still hear him groan as he pulled her harder against him and kissed her with more force.

Her breath caught in her throat when she felt his hands go around her, felt the rigid definition of his gender stamp its image firmly against the most intimate part of her. Then his hand came over hers and drew it down between them and pressed it against the shape of him. He moved beneath her, hungry and restless. He pushed her hand against him, harder, and she couldn't think for the heavy sound of his aroused breathing, coming strong and warm against her ear. "Oh, God! Stop this! Let me loose, you ravisher . . . you bastard . . . you—"

He groaned, releasing her hand, dropping his forehead against hers. "Easy, baby. Just be still. Relax. I won't hurt you. Just let me touch you."

He began whispering to her softly, releasing her buttocks and kissing her deeply, bringing his hand around and under her skirt, searching and feeling his way up the soft cotton of her drawers until he reached the unstitched crotch. He pressed his palm against her, holding it still when he heard her indrawn breath. "Easy, baby. Relax."

He slipped his fingers through the opening.

"God!" he said. "Dear God!" And then he groaned, the sound coming from deep in his throat.

"Oh, no, I don't want this. . . . Please—"

"Shhhh," he whispered, nuzzling her throat. He moved

his hand against her, touching her gently, but the shock of it raced across her like a searing flame. Her breath caught and he lowered his mouth to hers, kissing her with the same agonizing rhythm that his hand had established.

She groaned, thinking she was making noises of denial, as if by refusing him she could stop the flood of pleasure and possession that drained her resistance.

Suddenly she stopped pushing against him, her head coming to rest against his shoulder as she whispered in a deep, throaty tone, "Please Jay, I don't want—"

"But you will, baby. You will," he said softly, shifting his position beneath her and sending a shudder across her.

She groaned.

"Jay . . ."

The husky tones of his name as she said it sent an immediate response downward. "Jesus! Do you have any idea what you do to me? What it feels like to hear you say my name that way? How it feels to touch you like this, here, where you're so warm and wet?"

She closed her eyes, her head resting against his shoulder. "Open your eyes and look at me, angel. Don't hide from me. I want you to know what's happening here, who is touching you."

She turned her head away, and his hand shot out to grab her hair, wrenching her face back to his. "Tell me," he said, his breathing ragged, sweat running in rivulets down his face and throat. "Tell me you want me." He kissed her, his hand moving against her in perfect harmony. She clenched her jaw against the pleasure of it, shaking her head. He pulled away from her, twisting his hand in her hair harder. "Tell me you want me, damn you! You said you never tell lies, but you're lying now."

"I hate you," she whispered against his throat. "I hate you . . . and I want you. And that makes me hate myself even more."

He lost himself in the thrill of having her open to him like this, mesmerized by the feeling of touching paradise at last, when she screamed in outrage, catching him completely off-guard, and shoved herself away. "You may have made me want you, you bastard! But you'll never have me. Do you hear me? You'll never have me, because I'll never give in to it. Never. Ever. As long as there's a breath left in my body."

"Never is a long time," he said, his voice shaky.

She rolled away from him, springing to her feet, untangling the trailing blanket and rebozo and flinging it to the ground. When he came to his feet, she was holding a large rock over her head. "You take one step toward me and, so help me God, I'll bash your perverted brains in."

Jay was completely spellbound. He still couldn't believe what had happened, or that she had let him be as intimate with her as he had. Jesus! She was something. He closed his eyes, remembering the way she felt when he had touched her—all warm, wet velvet. Then he opened his eyes. She was still shooting daggers at him with those beautiful eyes of hers. Giving her a mocking smile, Jay looked at her and said, "You may have escaped me, angel eyes, but I still have a lingering memory of you." As he said it, he brought the same loathsome fingers he had used to touch her up to his lips and kissed them, drawing in a deep breath as he did, saying, "Ahh, the essence of Jenny," as he gave her a mocking salute.

She let fly with the rock, Jay easily jumping to one side, the rock falling to the ground. When he looked back at her, he thought he had never seen anything more beautiful in his life. He regretted then that he was not an artist, for he would have given much to have captured her thus. Her hair was wild around her shoulders, the sunlight penetrating each shaft, bringing it to life, fire-struck silver on charcoal-black. With her Gypsy coloring and her animal wariness, she was irresistible. Never, never had he seen anything like her. She was wild and angry and very, very beautiful.

"Gather your belongings while I get the horses. We still have a few hours of daylight."

She mounted without saying a word, but he could tell by the way she sat on her horse and flashed those violet eyes at him that she was more than angry, she was livid.

They rode in silence, and Jay thought he would have found it tranquil and pleasant, but he found it quite the opposite. He hadn't realized how much he had enjoyed her silly chatter, even her angry comments. But now? Now she was too furious to speak. He decided the best thing to do was to remain silent himself and give her time to cool off. Christ! He shouldn't have taken the liberties he had taken with her today, but he was only human, and when he felt her go all warm and limp against him, her breathing even and steady, her sleepy body snuggling closer to him, it had been a natural thing to pull her even closer. He himself wasn't sure just who was responsible for getting her to straddle him as she had. It had just happened. She had turned toward him, warm and sleepy, and he had pulled her in his lap, but somehow, in doing so, she had twisted and it had been so simple to guide her in such a way that she straddled him. Just the memory of it was enough to send a twisting ache down where it was uncomfortable as hell. Damn, but she was a finely wrought piece. He found himself smiling at the irony of it. She had aroused the hell out of him—just as she always did—and now he needed a woman in the worst way. And that's where the problem lay, because there wasn't a woman within three hundred miles of this place, except one exquisite, black-haired schoolteacher, and she was off-limits . . . way off-limits. He couldn't endure much more of this. In seducing her, he hadn't realized he had seduced himself as well. He would have to be more careful. He would have to see that it didn't happen again.

They made camp at twilight, Jay hobbling the horses and giving them a meager ration of grain, then building a fire while Jennifer unpacked the saddlebags.

When he had the fire going, he turned, walking toward the small supply of food Jennifer had grouped on a low, flat rock. Seeing him coming toward her and fearing his intention, Jennifer's eyes went wide and she took a step backward.

"There's no need to fling yourself into the fire. I won't touch you, but I can see you're in need of some food and a little rest."

"What I'm in need of is a great distance between myself and you. I—"

"Look, we're both tired and hungry, and you aren't going to tell me a damn thing I haven't figured out for myself, or heard a hundred times before, so save your strength. You don't look like you have enough left to lift a fork." He turned away from her then, and began pulling things out of his own saddlebags, which were tossed on the ground near the fire.

Jay fried a few strips of salt pork and opened a tin of beans. When he handed her a plate, Jennifer walked away from him, as far as she dared, before sitting down on a low, protruding rock. She sat on that rock like she was a part of it, eating in silence, appalled at the way she was wolfing down her food but too hungry to care. And all the time she was eating, her eyes never left Jay. She couldn't shake the memory of that afternoon, the definition of his body, hard and long against her, the shock of panic, surprise, and pleasure that jolted her like the jagged edge of lightning when he touched her. She balanced her plate on her knees and clamped her hands over her ears, trying to block out the sound of his voice ringing in her ears, *I want to touch you . . . I want to touch you . . . touch you . . . touch you . . . touch you . . .*

She hated the man. The way she felt now, she could kill him without batting an eye. But even killing him wasn't enough. He had violated her, in the most private and humiliating way possible. She would never forgive him. Never. She was going to do everything in her power to make him regret ever coming after her. She would make his life a living hell, and maybe—just maybe—he would let her go.

Jennifer never knew just when her eyes, which had been looking at him with such intense hatred, changed to slow awareness of what a perfect physical specimen he was. His was a body the old masters painted on chapel walls, wearing nothing but the cover of wispy clouds. He was long and lanky, his skin smooth and brown. But beneath that lean exterior were powerful muscles that coiled and uncoiled with each move he made. He was a handsome devil, she would have to admit. But he was crude and cruel, harder than polished steel, and he did something to her. Something strange and forbidden. She didn't have her customary strength to resist when she was around him. This man was dangerous. He was deadly, as far as she was concerned. If he ever knew, ever had an inkling just what his touch and his huskily whispered words did to her, she would never make it home with her maidenhead intact.

It wasn't the idea of losing her innocence as much as who she would be losing it to. He was nothing more than a hired gun, a drifter, a saddle tramp. Here today, gone tomorrow. His kind never attached themselves to any woman for very long. Why was it that the bastards were always the seductive ones? What was it about women that drew them to a man who would turn nasty and uncaring? What was it about men like him that made them so exciting? He was so blasted attractive . . . with his long hair ruffling in the wind and the sparkling gleam of salt crystals on his skin left from his sweat. *I can't be thinking about something as common as sweat and finding even that attractive! What's wrong with me?*

Jennifer couldn't deny the attraction he held for her, the way her stomach would knot with anticipation and something deep inside her yearn for fulfillment. But she wasn't stupid. She knew well enough that an entanglement with a man like him was destined for nothing but pain and would eventually go the way of all Greek tragedies.

"Didn't your mama ever tell you it was impolite to stare?"

"I wasn't staring. If you must know, I was looking right through you," she snapped, just a little angry that he had caught her. He always seemed to be in the right place at the right time, like a predator, a golden hawk sitting patiently on a fence post waiting. . . .

He regarded her steadily, those deep blue eyes moving slowly over her face. Something about him, about the way he appraised her with those brazen eyes of his, sent a shiver across her, made her feel things a lady had no right to feel.

She detested him. She hated his cocky self-assurance, his arrogance, his animal magnetism, the way he made her feel unsure of herself and awkward when she had always been so levelheaded and confident. She looked into the cool blue eyes that never left her face. "Didn't your mother teach you it was improper to stare?"

"She did, but I chose to ignore it." He was as cold-blooded and indifferent as she had supposed him to be. She had been right to label him a bastard. He, with his flashy good looks and winning smile; that hip-thrusting way he had of walking; and the low, husky tones of his voice when he spoke. He knew what he was doing, knew he had that irresistible women-love-outlaws kind of appeal. Yet here he was, looking so alive, so warm and masculine and completely at ease. It wasn't fair, not when she was a bundle of nerves, still feeling humiliated and shy to be around him after what had happened that afternoon. But he looked like the incident had been so commonplace that he had forgotten it as quickly as it had ended. And that angered her too. Before he could say anything, she rose and walked toward the fire, finding she suddenly wasn't hungry anymore and scraping what she didn't eat into the coals, then dropping to her knees to wipe the plate with sand.

When she finished, she stood, moving to one side of the fire, saying nothing, simply standing a few feet from him as if she were waiting for something. Jay poured himself another cup of coffee. He looked cross and irritable, crouching low over the fire, cupping the coffee between his two hands. And even that raised her ire—that she would find even the simple act of his crouching near a fire so remindful of his potent attraction.

She studied him for a moment, thinking how it would have satisfied her beyond measure to pick up that coffeepot and dump the entire thing over his narcissistic head. "I'm going to sleep now," she snapped.

He gave her a slow, knowing smile. "I'll join you in a minute."

"I sleep alone, Culhane. I've been doing it for years."

Without looking at her, he turned the cup around in his hands, studying it. "That was before all your threats of running off into the night. Remember?"

"What are you getting at?"

He looked up. "What I am getting at is, I can't very well handcuff you to me if I'm sleeping in another place."

"But it's pointless. I can't escape from this hellhole alive. You said as much yourself."

"Still, you swore to give it a try or crack my skull."

"I can't believe you would actually handcuff a . . ."

He looked at her in that drowsy way he had of looking at her that made her heart pound and her breath come in irregular little gasps. "Handcuff a what, Miss Baxter?"

"A woman, Mr. Culhane."

"A fact you claim when it suits you and fling in my face when it doesn't."

She clamped her hands on her hips. "Are you going to handcuff me or not?"

The dark cloud over his head was gone, and she could see in his slow grin that he was up to some mischief. "Are you going to be nice and stop giving me trouble?" he asked.

"Are you going to keep your groping hands to yourself?"

"I usually find that easy to do, except when it's stuck in my face."

"You filthy pervert. Is that the only way you can get a

woman? By taking advantage of them? By chaining them to you?"

"No. Like you, they usually offer it to me without my having to lift a finger. Of course, I did make an exception and lift a finger or two this afternoon, didn't I?"

Jennifer's face turned scarlet. She couldn't believe he would actually be so crude as to make any reference to that despicable act. He was watching her with those lazy eyes of his, which were focused on the shape of her body as the wind blew her skirts against her, outlining every curve in detail.

She whirled away from him, grabbing her blanket and walking as far away from the fire as she dared, then dropping to her knees to make her bed.

Jay watched her, finding some amusement in watching her build her nest, feeling his own body respond when she crawled across the blanket to smooth out the corners, her shapely little butt rammed in the air, just like that haughty little nose of hers. He crossed his arms over his chest as he watched her lie down on the narrow blanket and grab one side, pulling it over her. But the blanket was too narrow and there wasn't anything to cover herself with. She scooted over and tried again, this time barely covering one hip. Mumbling something in Spanish that sounded like a curse to Jay, she scrambled to her knees and stared at the blanket. Releasing an exasperated sigh, she came to her feet and walked a few feet away, just beyond the light of the fire, dragging the blanket behind her. Jay could see her silhouetted against the sky. She looked like she was wiggling out of her clothes.

A few minutes later she stomped back to the fire, the blanket wrapped around her hips, her skirt in her hand. Once she had the skirt spread on the ground, she lay down again, wiggling around like she was sitting on hot ashes, struggling to unwind the blanket from her body without revealing any of it. At last she had the blanket over her, where it belonged. With a shake of his head Jay began to unbutton his shirt.

"I suggest you close your eyes and go to sleep, little girl, unless you want to watch me take off my clothes."

With a cry of alarm Jennifer turned away from him, pulling the blanket over her head. She was asleep almost immediately, certainly before Jay was beneath his own blanket. Once there, he found he couldn't go to sleep. He lay awake for a long time, staring at the fire, listening to the sound of her rhythmic breathing, remembering a time earlier that day when her breathing had come hard and fast. "Ah, the sleep of the innocent," he said, his hands tucked beneath his head as he stared at the canopy of stars flung into a sky as inky and black as the girl's silky, long hair.

He was feeling as tired as a pair of old shoes, but he couldn't go to sleep. He closed his eyes. A vividly detailed picture of Jenny rose up before him. Jenny with the huge purple eyes. Jenny with her hair down. Jenny with her clothes off. The smell of starch on fine cotton, coal oil, Castile soap, chalk. The scent of sweet almond oil on warm skin. Hair washed in rainwater. She's only a few feet away, rolled up in a ball, cold, but breathing easy. He could make her as warm as a biscuit. Make her breath come in quick little pants. He wanted to see her in her underthings, to watch her take them off. Skin as white as strained cream, narrow shoulders, little-girl waist, generous flare of hip, milk and almonds and warm, wild honey. He longed to touch her, to see if she was as soft as he remembered, to touch her skin under her clothes where she'd be all soft and warm, to feel the points of her breasts as they lifted, to touch the softness of her belly.

But she would have none of that. Today, by a sheer stroke of luck, he had held her, touched her, but he figured it was because she was frightened and exhausted. Tomorrow she would still be madder than a hornet, and he had a feeling it would be easier to climb a briar than to get close to her again. He closed his eyes, as physically aware of her as he would have been if she had been lying naked next to him.

The sun was just coming up when Jay opened his eyes and looked toward the girl. He hoped she was awake because something mighty peculiar was going on under that blanket of hers. It was obvious Jennifer was under the blanket with it pulled over her head, but Jay wasn't sure just what, exactly, was in there with her. She was wiggling like she had a couple of fighting bobcats in there with her. He hadn't seen so much squirming since he and his brothers had put itching powder in the preacher's robes. A few seconds later he had pulled on his clothes and was standing over her.

"Miss Baxter, what in the name of hell are you doing?"

One corner of the blanket was peeled back and two huge lavender eyes peered up at him. "I am getting dressed, Mr. Culhane."

"Well, that's a damn funny way of going about it. Why don't you stand up? I've never seen anyone put their clothes on in bed."

"I don't exactly have any place to dress. There isn't a tree or bush within a hundred miles."

"Why do you need a bush?"

"To dress behind. You don't expect me to dress right out in the open, do you?"

"You did last night."

"That was different. It was dark last night and you couldn't see anything."

"I saw enough," he said. "And in case you have forgotten, I've seen every tasty inch of you before."

"You always have to bring that up, don't you? Tell me, Culhane . . . do you have a nasty little black book that you write everything down in?"

"No, Miss Baxter, I don't. I have a nasty little mind that remembers it all."

7

"**B**astard!" she said, pushing the last button through, then struggling to her feet, her anger coming on faster than a rapid boil.

Jay walked toward her with a coffeepot. "I assume you can cook."

She shook her head.

He paused, tilting his head and looking at her with surprised disbelief. "You don't know how to cook?"

"I never learned how."

"Why not? I thought that was one of the first things a young woman learned to do."

"I wasn't reared in a conventional family. Some of my sisters learned to cook. Some of us didn't. I was one—"

"Of the ones who didn't," he said, interrupting "I might have known. You can't ride. You can't cook." He was raising his right eyebrow at her now. "I assume you know how to eat?"

"If it's prepared properly."

"Oh, it'll be prepared properly," he said with a snarl, "because you'll be doing the preparing."

"I told you I never learned how to cook."

"It shouldn't be too hard for a woman like you . . . one with *brains.*" He shoved the pot into her hands. "Half a pot of water. No more. Water is precious out here. I'll poke up the fire."

Jennifer stood there with the coffeepot in her hand, watching Jay pick up a small stick and stir a little life into the coals. He continued to ignore her, and she decided it was probably just as well. The last look he'd given her had been as hot as the coals he was now stirring, and she had actually felt intimidated—something she rarely felt.

She turned away and began looking for her canteen. After a few minutes she realized why she couldn't find it. In all her confusion after the dust storm she hadn't remembered it. It was still lying near the rocks behind which she had sheltered herself, more than likely half buried in sand by now. She decided she would wait until Jay was in a better frame of mind before she told him about the canteen. Her father was always in a better mood after he'd eaten—of course, that was after he'd eaten something delightful dished up by the Baxters' cook. Jennifer shuddered to think what kind of mood Jay might be in after he ate anything she prepared. *Should I tell him now?* In spite of her inability to cook, she decided not to mention the canteen. He would discover the loss soon enough. She picked up Jay's canteen and poured water into the coffeepot. Still forming vivid pictures of what he might do to her when he discovered her carelessness, she jumped when Jay spoke harshly.

"That water won't boil until you put it on the fire," he said, moving up beside her and taking the coffeepot, then placing it between two smooth rocks that protruded over the coals. Then he handed her a pouch of coffee. "Here's the Arbuckle. We've enough water for two cups."

Jennifer opened the pouch and closed her eyes, inhaling the rich aroma. Then she dumped the contents into the pot.

"Christ A'mighty! Your head must be emptier than last year's bird's nest. Don't you know anything?" Jay snatched the pouch from her and looked inside. Empty. "Jesus! There was enough coffee in there to last two weeks."

"You said it was enough for two cups."

"I said there was enough *water* for two cups." He turned away from her, cursing under his breath, raking his hand through his hair. He went to his saddlebags and came back with a can of beef. "Do you know how to make biscuits?"

She shook her head.

"Atole?"

"No."

"Corn cakes?"

"Uh-uh."

"Tortillas?"

"I tried them once."

"And?"

"They stuck to my hands. Cook said I put in too much water."

He shook his head. "For such an educated woman, you don't know a whole helluva lot, do you? Here," he said, tossing the can to her. "Open this. I guess we'll have to settle for a beef biscuit."

Jennifer rolled the can around in her hand, looking at it. "What do you want me to open it with? My teeth?"

"They're sharp enough," he said, but his hand went in his pocket and he tossed her a knife. "Try not to cut your fingers off."

Jennifer took the knife and began sawing back and forth on the side of the can, like she was cutting bread. For a moment Jay just stood there watching her, a look of utter disbelief on his face. Then, with an oath, and mumbling something that sounded like "don't know shit from jelly beans," he snatched the knife from her and then the can. "I don't think you've got enough sense to hit the floor if you fell out of bed." He stabbed an *X* on the can of beef and peeled it back from the center. Then he jabbed the knife and came up with a hunk of beef, thrusting it toward her. "Do you have enough gumption to find your mouth?"

"Occasionally I have bursts of intelligence, but it doesn't last very long." She clamped her hands on her hips. "Now, is there anything else about me you want to criticize?"

"Not at the moment, but I'm sure you'll make a mess of something soon enough and I'll have to set it straight."

"Just why is it that everything a woman does has to be done three times better than a man to be called half as good?"

"I wasn't aware that was the case," he said, "but perhaps it's because women have taught us they can't be trusted. It's your nature to be dishonest, so you have to work hard to disprove it."

"You can't judge all women by Eve."

"I don't have to go back that far."

"How far back do you have to go?" She studied him for a moment.

Jay sat hunkered by the fire, across from her, watching her silently and feeling a slow tightening in his loins. The morning sun worshiped her face, refining her delicate features and giving a fresh blush to her coloring. He wanted to move around the fire and take her in his arms, to touch the baby-soft skin, to kiss the frown away from her forehead before moving to that perfectly shaped mouth of hers. But most of all he wanted to touch her again as he had touched her yesterday. He couldn't, of course, and he knew it, so he had to be content with just watching her.

She must have felt his eyes upon her, for she looked at him as if she were trying to organize her thoughts and come up with something logical. Was she thinking about him?

"You're married, aren't you . . . or have been? It must have been very painful for you. And that's made you bitter. I'm sorry for that, but don't expect me to pay the fare for someone else's ride."

"Just like a big, old lovable dog, aren't you? Every time you wag your tail, you knock over a chair," he said, his voice nasty and mocking.

"I'm doing the best I can, under the circumstances. Things would go a lot smoother if you weren't so cynical. I can't change the past, but the future would be much more pleasant if you'd stop condemning me so much and trust me."

"I trust you, Miss Baxter. But I won't turn my back."

"Trust in Allah but tie your camel."

"Exactly." He dumped the pot of coffee into the fire.

"Why'd you do that? I thought you wanted coffee."

"I don't have a chisel." He forked a piece of meat and offered her a bite of it. Jenny started to shove it away, but he was looking nasty enough to let her starve, so she took it in her mouth and chewed once, then gagged. It was too awful to chew a second time, so she swallowed it, wishing she hadn't ruined the coffee.

Jay saddled Brady and hung his saddlebags and canteen on the saddle. He gathered Jennifer's bags and looked around, searching for something. "Where's your canteen?"

Jennifer swallowed, bringing her hands around in front of her, looking down at her toe, making patterns in the sand. "I think I lost it."

"You lost it? LOST IT?"

"I think so."

"Jesus, woman, do you have any idea how precious water is out here? Of all the things you could have lost, water is the absolute worst."

"I know. I didn't do it on purpose. If you hadn't upset me so much during that storm, I would have remembered it."

Jay sighed. "Well, there's nothing to be done about it now," he said. "We can't go back and look for it. We'll have to cut back drastically if mine is going to last us."

He turned away, and she watched him clean the coffee-pot with sand, then hang it on his saddle. He removed a small block of salt from his bags and broke off a few chips in the palm of his hand, extending it toward his horse. From a small tow sack between the cantle and his bedroll, Jay poured a meager ration of oats into his hat and placed it on the ground in front of Brady, giving the pony a small ration as well. Then he unbridled the pony and turned him loose. For a moment the animal stood there looking at him, then turned and walked off, favoring his right front leg.

"Why'd you let him go? So I would have to walk?"

"I let him go because he's lame."

"But he'll probably die."

"What would you have me do, Miss Baxter? Carry him out on my back?"

"I think it's cruel of you to just leave him."

"He's been fed and he's alive. That gives him as much chance as we've got."

He broke off another piece of salt and put it in his mouth, then offered the last piece to her. "No, thank you."

"Take it. You need to replace the salt you've sweated out."

Jenny took the salt chips, watching as Jay walked to the fire and began kicking sand over it. She eyed him. Then she eyed his horse, moving a step closer to the gelding.

Brady lifted his head and watched Jenny approach. When she reached for the canteen and took a drink, his ears went flat. She quickly twisted the lid on and replaced the canteen, and Brady lowered his head to Jay's hat, nuzzling for the last scattered grains. Jennifer reached for the reins and Brady's head came up and around to watch. His ears went flat again as Jenny put her hands on the saddle horn. She made a couple of tries to boost herself into the saddle but without much luck. On the third try she wrapped one hand in the apron straps that secured the bedroll and heaved herself up with all the strength she could muster.

This time she made it, but before she could settle herself in the saddle, Brady took a couple of steps and ducked his head and started stiff-legging it with a few short hops, jumping like a spring lizard in a henhouse. He crow-hopped a few more times, the coffeepot clanging against the saddle, making more noise than a cook banging on an angle iron. By this time Jennifer's body was about as close to a right angle with the horse as it could be, but she still held on for dear life. Brady started worming in a zigzagging motion, his feet hitting the ground first on one side and then on the other, and Jennifer went flying from the saddle, hitting the ground with such force that it knocked the daylights out of her. By the time Jay reached her, she was lying in a little half twist, her knees together and pointing in one direction, her torso turned and facing the opposite way. She was lying so still, Jay thought her back was broken.

He came down on his knees beside her, heard her breath come in quick half pants. She moaned then. *Chomp, chomp, chomp.* She opened her eyes to see Brady standing nearby, chewing the last of his oats as peacefully as you please. She tried to speak, but Jay's fingers fanned over her lips. "For once, keep your mouth shut. Lie still until I get you untangled and straightened out." A moment later he twisted her upper body so she could lie flat on her back. "Does it feel like anything's broken?" he asked roughly.

"No. I'm all right . . . I think."

"You had the wind knocked out of your sails, and for a while your lamps weren't lit. But your color is returning. Does this hurt?" Jay asked, moving her legs so that they lay straight. His words were solicitous, but his tone was harsh and uncaring.

"No."

"You were a fool to try what you did. You'd never make it out of here alive."

"I'm not sure I even care," she said.

He let her stay as she was for a few minutes, then his arm went beneath her head and slowly lifted her to a sitting position. "Feeling light-headed? Your head spinning?"

"I'm not spinning, but everything else is."

He had the irritating manner of being able to look amused without smiling, and it always left her wondering if he was amused and tried to hide it by looking serious, or if he was really irritated and tried to hide that by looking amused. *This* time he was irritated, she was sure of it.

He was still looking at her in that baffled way when he

said, "You're okay." He took a firm grip on her arms. "Here. I'll help you to your feet."

Jennifer glanced at Brady, browsing around for any missed grains of oats, looking as tame and gentle as a house cat. It was hard to believe he was hopping around a few minutes ago like a toadfrog in a tack factory. "I don't think *he* likes me, either."

"Brady's a little bucky first thing in the morning. Spent too many summers in the wild. He was just feeling his oats."

"You mean he does that *every* morning?"

"Regular as clockwork. Starts our day off right. Nothing like a good piece of horseflesh in prime condition with a little of the wildness left in him. Puts a little sunshine in your day."

"I'd rather get mine in the traditional way."

"You will."

His tone was light enough, but there was a cold undercurrent of warning; enough that she felt a prick of unease. Jennifer's eyes flew to his, but Jay had already turned away, moving to his saddle and checking the rigging. He began to scan the outlying area, then paused. "Dear God," he said, "Dear, merciful God." He turned toward her.

The look in his eyes stopped her cold.

"What—"

"My compliments, Miss Baxter. You said you didn't want to go back. Well, you win. You won't go back. In fact, you won't ever leave this desert. And neither will I."

"I don't understand."

"Don't you? Then have a look." He grabbed the cheekpiece on Brady's bridle and led the gelding aside. Jennifer saw the canteen lying a few feet beyond, a damp circle near the open spout where the water had leaked out. With a small cry of despair she ran to the canteen, picking it up.

"Don't bother. There's—"

"It's not all gone," she shouted, still on her knees, her

words muffled and frantic. "See? There's a little left. We can—"

"Share?" With a low growl of anger he came toward her, wrenching her to her feet. "Share?" he repeated, then shaking her like she weighed no more than a rag doll.

"Jay, I . . ." She wasn't sure what she wanted to say—anything to make him think, to remove the murderous look from his eyes.

"I ought to leave you here," he growled. "And I still might. Two of us will never make it, but one would have at least a chance." He shook her. "You need the hide peeled from you for what you've done." He was still shaking her, and her hands came up to clamp over his wrists.

"You aren't going to beat me," she said. *Not as long as I have a breath left in my body.* He took another step and she whirled and ran, her feet digging into the soft sand, falling once, then getting up, ignoring the sand in her mouth and eyes and running again. His arm came out of nowhere to wrap around her waist, and they both went flying to the ground, Jennifer hitting first, then both of them rolling, the air driven out of her lungs from the sudden impact of being crushed between Jay and the ground.

She fought and clawed at him, screaming words of rage, hissing threats at the animal that overpowered her, going for his privates with an upthrust of her knee, recoiling in pain when he blocked the passage of air to her lungs with a forearm pressed against her windpipe. She lay still and he removed his arm, Jennifer feeling the panic subside as she drew in gasping breaths of air. She tried to catch him off-guard, sinking her teeth into his shoulder and twisting beneath him, but it was no use. No matter how much fight she had in her, she had one glaring handicap. She was too small. And he was way too strong.

With an oath he grabbed a handful of her hair and held it down with his knee. "Damn you! I ought to leave your stinking carcass out here for buzzard bait. There's not enough water left for either one of us to make it out of here, let alone my horse. I don't even know why I'm even thinking about trying. It's pointless. We'll never make it . . . two of us on one horse . . . Brady will go before we do." He shook her, roughly and without feeling. "Think about what you've done, you crazy little fool. This time tomorrow, you'll be buzzard bait."

"And that will please you to no end, won't it?" she said, gasping for breath.

"Why shouldn't it? When you tried to steal my horse and my water, you intended to leave me for the buzzards, didn't you?" Jay had a momentary reminder that none of his anger would make any difference now. The girl would pay the price for her stupidity—as he would. He didn't know himself whether losing her life or his own angered him more. He shook her harder, her head slamming into the sand. "Didn't you?"

"That's right!" she screamed. "I didn't give you much thought. It was my own hide I was concerned about."

He jerked back and rolled away from her as if he'd been bitten. He came to his feet, standing over her, his shadow raking across her like angry claws. He was suddenly distracted by the small, smudged face that stared back at him with smoldering violet eyes. He fought back the urge to go to her and wrap his hands in her long black hair and jerk her against him, conquering that rebellious mouth once and for all. It amazed him that he didn't strip her naked and take her right now. Heaven only knew it was small enough compensation for the forfeiture of his life.

He saw in her eyes that she expected him to do just that. And he wanted to, had wanted to from the moment he'd first seen her picture, finding her impossible to resist since that night when he had stepped into her room in a swirl of wind-driven dust. He had wanted her. But he'd held off. Now there was no reason to hold off any longer.

No reason at all.

He would have her.

Here.

Now.

A dying man's last request: to meet his maker with an angel in his arms.

He began removing his belt. Jennifer scrambled to her feet, backing away from him, feeling his cold eyes lock on her. What was he doing? Her eyes dropped back to his belt. Surely he wasn't going to beat her. What would it change?

Slowly he came toward her until he was so close that she could see the sweat beaded on his throat. His gaze held her and she was unable to speak. He dropped the belt, unbuttoned his shirt, and flung it from his body. Then his hands went down to the buttons on his pants and he flipped them open, one by one.

Jennifer's mouth went dry with the realization. No. He wasn't going to beat her. He was going to rape her.

"No," she said, backing away. "Have you lost your senses? You're a United States marshal! They . . . they don't go around raping people."

"I don't plan on raping *people.*"

"Then what are you going to do?"

"I'm going to make love to *you,* angel."

"How can you call it making love when I'm not the least bit willing?"

"You won't feel that way for long."

"I will! I know I will! I won't ever be willing!"

"Then we'll have to find another word for it, won't we? What shall we choose? Fornication? Rutting? Copulation? Mating? Or would you prefer f—"

"No! I don't want to hear it!" she said, clamping her hands over her ears. When he didn't say anything further, she took her hands down. "You will go to any length to humiliate me, won't you? Even if it means using filthy language."

"What filthy language?"

"You know very well *what* filthy language. Did you think I would just stand here and let you say a word like that in front of me?"

"What word? You mean the one just before you slapped your hands over your ears?" He gave her a wicked smile. "The word I was going to say was *forced,* Miss Baxter, as in 'forced union.'" What did you think I intended to say?"

"Jay . . . you can't do this."

"Can't I? I'm afraid you grossly underestimate me. I *can* do it . . . in fact, I do it very well."

She looked around her, frantic for some place to run, to seek cover, to hide. But out here, in this vast, empty nothingness, there was no place to run. Her eyes darting back to his, she saw by the triumphant look on his face that he had realized that long before she had. "Jay . . ."

"Come now, surely you aren't going to play the quaking virgin. Aren't you just a little curious, angel? Wouldn't you like to find out what it would be like with me?"

"No."

"I think you're lying, baby. I think you're curious as hell."

"Even if I was, that doesn't mean I'd give in. Civilized people don't go around giving in to every whim, every urge that comes along."

"Why not? What's to stop them?"

"Morals."

"I haven't any."

"Human kindness."

"Mine doesn't extend that far."

"Conviction."

"That's what prompted me in the first place."

"Religion."

"The Bible is full of what we're about."

"It's full of murder, too, but that doesn't make it right."

"It's doesn't have to be right, angel. It only has to be good."

With his pants open, his shirt gone, he loomed over her like an angry, threatening cloud. "It's the end of the line, Jenny. Take your clothes off."

Her eyes smoldered, and for a moment she was afraid she

would lose the small amount of self-control she had managed to keep. "You're just trying to frighten me. You can't really mean it. You wouldn't dare," she said. "Not even you could be that heartless."

"Oh, I dare, all right. As for heartless . . . you are exactly right. Mine was ripped out a long time ago."

She was tired. She didn't want to fight anymore. But then she remembered she didn't want to be raped, either.

"Didn't you understand me, angel eyes? I said, take your clothes off. All of them. I want you mother-naked with your legs spread."

"I don't understand you. What will it prove in the end? What can you possibly hope to gain? Why would you want someone who didn't want you?"

He lunged for her, clamping his hands on her arms, and jerked her against his hard body, his eyes glittering. "I don't want you trying to understand me."

"Then leave me alone!" she said, infuriated by the ease with which he could make the decision to treat her as if she had no rights, as if she were something less significant than a human being. "You've done nothing but force me since the day we met. I'm tired of being forced, and I'm tired of being pushed. Things have gone your way long enough. I may not have any choice about dying out here, but I don't have to submit to this."

"Don't you?" He jerked her closer, his hands braced behind her head, bringing her mouth hard against his, and he kissed her roughly, driving the breath from her until she swayed against him and her knees buckled from the dizzying impact of it. He pulled back. "You'll accept anything I decide to do to you because you don't have any choice."

She wrenched away from him, twisting and ducking under his arms. Then she ran. He caught her before she reached the horse, his arm circling her waist and drawing her back against him, pinning her arms behind her, his hands coming up to pull her blouse from her skirt. Holding her immobile, he hooked his foot behind her ankles and pushed her back, lowering her until she lay beneath him.

He had her where he wanted her, and now that he did, the pleasure seemed to drain away with the anger and the raging lust. He looked down at her, wanting her still—yet wanting her to want him back. She confused him. Everything she represented he had turned out of his life years ago. Still he wanted her.

She was his captive now, tangled beneath him like a snarling black cat, but in truth, she was half angel, half courtesan, with her seductive purple eyes and sultry mouth on a face a cherub would envy. He watched as she looked at him, then squeezed her eyes tight as he slowly unbuttoned her blouse and chemise. He stroked a finger between her breasts and down to her belly. She turned her head away, her fists clenching at her sides. He had never been so aware of a woman's body beneath him.

And Jennifer had never been more aware of the smooth, powerful play of muscles that coiled and uncoiled in the flat, hard planes of a man's belly. His eyes were burning into her like brands, and she arched wildly beneath him, clawing his shoulders and arms in an effort to dislodge him. His body was moving rhythmically against her, and she was fighting two battles now: one to throw his weight from her, another to keep her own body from matching the tempo of his.

Their eyes locked, and for a moment he was looking at her as if there were something he wanted to say to her, something soft and gentle, to soothe the pain of the bitterness that had been between them only moments ago. She stopped struggling as his hand came up to push the tangled strands of hair back from her forehead, lingering to gently trace the shape of her face, then down the bridge of her nose and across her swollen lips.

He thought her incredibly lovely lying beneath him, slim as a willow, her inky black hair spread like a cape around her, those magnificent flower-colored eyes turned upon him

—eyes that had been his undoing from the very beginning. Something tightened in his gut and began to coil and twist, until he thought he would go mad with desire for her. He lowered his mouth to accept her surrender, but at the moment when he would have joined with her and touched those lips he so craved, she turned her head away, and his kiss was laid upon her cheek; a moment gone forever like a flower tossed into a river and floating out of sight.

He pushed his hands into the silky tangle of her hair, and gave a tormented cry. He groaned painfully, and she sensed he was warring with his baser instincts, his pure animal arousal, and some higher code of humanity. Her hands lifted and hovered over the long golden hair at his nape, desire for him urging her to take him in her arms and draw him to her. But her hatred was such that she could not. Her arms fell away without ever touching him, leaving her with a terrible sadness and a hollow sense of loss. Her chest felt crushed from the sorrow it bore, her heart thudding painfully in her breast, the instinctive urge to cry burning her eyes like fire. *I won't cry,* she told herself. *I won't.*

With a frustrated oath he raised himself on his elbows, staring down into her face, drawing a finger across her lips to trace her mouth. "I knew you would take me to heaven, but I didn't know it would be this way." He smiled at her, a mixture of sadness and regret, and the beauty of it almost took her breath away. "I suppose it isn't such a bad way to go," he said, "to meet your maker with an angel in your arms."

He was looking down at her, his smoky blue eyes wide in puzzlement—or was it disbelief? But then the look was gone, shuttered so quickly, she wondered if she had really seen it at all. "Let me up, Jay."

He shook his head, not in a negative way but more like he was warring with himself. "I don't know if I can. There's something about you—what, I don't know or even understand. You have something powerful about you. Maybe you give off a scent, like a flower, or a bitch in heat.

But it's there—a potency—a thing that draws me, makes me go a little crazy when I'm around you."

"That doesn't give you a right to my body."

"No. It probably doesn't," he said. "No more than my coming after you gave you a right to end my life."

"I don't think. . ." Her voice broke. "I'm going to die for what I did, and I think that is enough. . . . I don't think I deserve to be raped as well."

He looked at her strangely, as if he didn't know who she was. Abruptly, without saying a word, he rolled from her and came to his feet. "Cover yourself, then." He put on his shirt and buttoned his pants before putting on his belt, never taking his eyes from her until she had dressed, then he walked toward her.

Exhausted and silent, she offered no resistance as he dragged her to her feet. She stood where he left her, her eyes fixed blankly on the endless waste that stretched before them, as if trying to come to terms with the inevitable.

Jay went to his saddle, removed his saddlebags, and then turned toward Jennifer. She was watching him now, her eyes flicking back and forth between his horse and the saddlebags in his hand. "What are you doing?"

"Lightening Brady's load as much as I can." He slung the saddlebags over his shoulder and began walking toward her.

"Where are you going with those?"

"I'm bringing them to you, angel eyes. A minute ago you were all hot to light out on your own, taking my possessions with you. I intend to see that you aren't disappointed."

"I don't understand."

"You wanted to be the first out of camp this morning. I'm giving you the opportunity, that's all." He stopped in front of her, removing the saddlebags from his shoulder and dropping them across hers.

"You can start anytime you like," he said. "You will go ahead of me. Every time you balk, curse, give me the slightest bit of trouble, or do the least thing to slow us down, I will lighten Brady's load even more by giving something he now carries to you." He turned and mounted Brady, then with a mocking gesture, he waved his arm out in front of him, saying, "Anytime you're ready, Miss Baxter."

"If you think I'm going to walk while you cool your heels and ride, you've got another thought coming."

His eyes darkened. "You will start right now or I'll ride off and leave you here . . . as you intended to leave me. Which is it to be?"

"Which way do I go?"

He heard the break in her voice, but when he looked, her eyes were angry and clear, free of tears. Yet she had sounded so young, so hopeless, he almost relented. But before he softened, he said, "For a few hours the sun will be in front of us and you can follow it. After that, head toward that highest peak in the distance."

"And when it gets dark? What do I follow then? Surely you aren't going to let me off so easy. Why let me rest at all? Why not make me walk all night as well?"

"Because Brady needs the rest."

Hot color spread across her face. "Seeing to your horse's needs before mine, is that it?"

"You're very perceptive. Now, do you want to lead the way, or shall I give you something more to carry?"

Jennifer began walking toward the sun, her carriage proud and her head held high. He watched her for a minute, then nudged Brady into a walk. She was so mad that she didn't think about being uncomfortable for a long time, the first miles eaten away before she had exhausted her memory with a long list of grievances she had against him. Then the anger slowly gave way to the intense thirst she was feeling, the numbness in her legs, the tight, digging ache between her shoulders.

She had no concept of how long she had walked, but her throat was now far beyond dry, and ahead, the desert teased and shimmered like a silver lake. She glanced up, finding that the sun was directly overhead. The heat seemed to be dissolving her bones and confusing her sense of direction. Her knees would give way and she would stumble, then rising to her feet once more, she would begin walking, knowing she was weaving instead of walking in a straight line but unable to do anything about it.

She had to get her mind off her physical discomfort, had to think about something else to keep from going insane. So once again her thoughts went back to Jay Culhane, wondering if his overpowering strength would eventually wear her down and she would end up being nothing more than his whore. At last she had her mind cranking again. Before long, the crank was going so fast that she began to feel the slow, simmering surge of anger. And in a way that was good, because she couldn't be spitting mad at Jay Culhane and think about dying at the same time.

She wondered if he was following her, but she wouldn't turn around, not wanting to give him the satisfaction of knowing she cared one way or the other. Truly the man was the worst kind of bastard, and he had no right to treat her this way. He was being paid to bring her home safely, wasn't he? Paid, and paid well. Paid by her own father. *Paid!* It wasn't right. Her father wouldn't stand for it. *And I'm not going to put up with it, either.* And with that Jenny plopped down in the dirt.

A few minutes later she heard Jay coming up behind her, feeling the instant relief from the sun when he blocked its melting rays with his broad shoulders. She tilted her head back to look at him, realizing he had not been riding Brady but leading him.

"I don't remember telling you to stop."

"I don't remember hearing you, either."

"On your feet, little girl, or I'll make it harder for you."

She gave him a disgusted look. "You couldn't possibly."

He smiled. "Oh, I could, and I will. Believe me. Now, on your feet."

"And if I refuse?"

"We'll start with the blankets."

"Start with anything you like. You can't make me carry anything."

"So you'd rather sit down and die right here, without even trying to make it?"

"I said you couldn't make me carry anything. I didn't say I would stop walking."

"Oh, I can make you carry something, all right."

"And how will you do that? Beat me. Leave me behind? Shoot me?"

"I don't have to resort to anything like that," he said, knowing by the sudden flare of interest in her eyes that he had her attention now. "I suppose I forgot to mention that for everything I give you to carry, I will take something away."

"Take something away?" She gave him a questioning look. "I don't understand. What could you possibly take away? You've already stripped me of my rights and dignity. What's left?"

"Your clothing, Miss Baxter. Down to the last shred, if necessary."

She struggled to her feet. "Even you wouldn't be that cruel."

"Try me," he said, reaching up and unstrapping the blankets and then turning to strap them over the saddlebags. "To show you I'm not a totally unfeeling bastard, I'll let you decide what you give me."

"You're insane!" Her temper flared. "You're—"

"And you're wasting precious time. Now give me something, and give it to me now, girl, or so help me, I'll strip you down to nothing but that baby-soft skin of yours."

"I need my clothing," she shrieked. "You know I do! I'll fry in this sun."

"You should have thought about that sooner." He made a move toward her and she backed away.

"All right!" She stopped looking down at herself, trying to decide what she could give him, when he laughed.

"You don't have to bare those beautiful breasts of yours yet." The mocking grin on his face became wider. "You could give me something . . . less conspicuous."

"You—"

"Bastard," he said wearily. "We've established that fact some time ago." Then he held out his hand and snapped his fingers. "Now, if you please."

She didn't please, but she knew the brute would do as he threatened and strip her. Too angry to ask him to turn his head, she dropped the saddlebags to the ground, reaching under her skirt and struggling with her drawers, wishing she'd had the forethought to wear at least ten petticoats instead of none. When they were off, she threw them at his face, Jay catching them easily in one hand and then taunting her by lifting them in the air with a mocking kiss. Her face flamed, and she called him a string of oaths under her breath. Then she picked up the saddlebags and began walking.

"You're going the wrong way."

"I'm taking the scenic route," she said, turning toward the mountains once more. Jay watched her go, hanging her drawers over his saddle horn, then swinging into the saddle.

By the time they reached the sand-packed slopes that gradually gave way to rougher terrain, her eyes were burning from sweat, her lungs aching, her legs numb well past her knees. When the sand gave way to more lava rocks, she stumbled, feeling the burning sting of cuts on her hands and knees as she went sprawling. She lay there for a moment. Hearing Jay coming up behind her, she struggled to her feet once more.

Searching for some distraction from her suffering, she began to curse him under her breath, and finding some small satisfaction in that, she began to curse him in Spanish, calling him every vile name she could think of, no longer content to whisper them to herself but verbalizing with all the musical thunder of a well-seasoned sailor.

She had almost forgotten he was behind her when he said

calmly, "I must commend your consistency, if nothing else. It would appear that every lesson you learn, you learn the hard way. You've had your last drink of water, Miss Baxter. I suggest you economize with your colorful language and save your strength. You're going to need it."

"And you can go straight to hell, you son of *Hades*!" she said, dropping the saddlebags and following them down.

"And will you come with me, fair Persephone?"

"I wouldn't go to a dogfight with you."

He chuckled, tossing his rifle down beside the saddlebags.

"Don't get any ideas. It isn't loaded." She gave him a blank look, but he simply held out his hand and said, "What are you going to give me this time?"

A few minutes later she called him a bastard again and threw her chemise at him, picking up the saddlebags and the bedroll, buttoning her blouse as she went.

All around her the desert shimmered like glass in the distance as the sun rose higher, then slowly began to drop in the sky. Her skin was burned beneath the caked layers of dust, the sweat that oozed from her pores burning the raw cuts on her hands and knees. Mile after mile they went, over terrain that was growing steadily rougher as they gradually left the sandy flats, the mountains in the distance seeming no closer than they had that morning.

In spite of her pain and discomfort, regardless of her suffering, Jennifer had the underlying feeling that he would stop if she fell down and told him she couldn't get up. But she wasn't going to beat him by chicanery. No, she wouldn't give up, and she wouldn't resort to deceit, and she wouldn't let him get the best of her. Besides being angry and humiliated, she was defiant and determined, and this defiance pushed her forward on leaden legs that were too heavy to move.

Some time later she fell again, this time even her thirst for revenge unable to get her back on her feet, even though she tried, time and again, resorting to a half-stumbling, half-crawling action. A sharp, bruising jab to her hipbone and another painful stab at her breast drew a strangled cry from her. She was too numb to care anymore who won. In the end they would both lose. Unaware that although she had given up, her body hadn't, she fought her way to her feet, swaying as she tried to take a step. Her chest hurt from overexertion and dust, and a dizzy wave of darkness threatened. Her lids fluttered and the desert seemed to whirl in circles around her.

When she opened her eyes, she saw a pair of dusty boots, then closed her eyes against the blinding glare of the sun. She tried to tell him she was thirsty, but her mouth was sealed from the dryness. Something cool touched her lips. Cool and damp. Her tongue came out to verify that and came in contact with Jay's finger. He dipped his finger in water a second time and rubbed the moisture across her parched lips.

"Open your mouth," he said roughly.

She did, expecting him to fill it with water. When he shoved a couple of wet pebbles into her mouth, she tried to spit them out. "No!" he said, his hand coming out to clamp over her mouth. "They'll help fight the dryness. Just keep them in your mouth like you would a jelly bean."

"I *chew* jelly beans," she said.

"Somehow I knew you would," he said succinctly. "I wouldn't advise chewing these, however."

The pebbles did help, but Jennifer was too exhausted to really notice. On her feet and walking once again, her aching head dropped lower. She was no longer curious about where she was going. An increasing numbness began in her feet and moved upward, making it possible for her to stumble and fall and feel nothing. Her lungs no longer hurt, or if they did, she no longer felt it. Her head throbbed painfully. She dropped to her knees. *Let him strip me naked and drag me the rest of the way, or leave me to feed the buzzards. I don't care anymore.*

"Then I would say you've learned your lesson."

Jennifer stared blankly at the scuffed boots, then lifted her head, trying to focus on the fathomless eyes that stared back at her. The eyes came closer and she shrank back, her retreat halted when a pair of hands slipped beneath her armpits and lifted her up. Steadied by one arm that held her against his body, she felt herself lifted, carried a few feet, and put in the saddle, Jay mounting behind her.

He gathered the reins in his left hand, his other hand coming around to hug her midriff and pull her in place against him. Something in the back of her mind told Jennifer to balk, to put up resistance to his high-handed ways and not to let her head rest against his chest, but the command to do so was lost somewhere in her nerve network. As Jay urged Brady forward, Jennifer's head thumped against his chest and she closed her eyes.

The desert was painted in dusk's pink-and-golden hues when she opened her eyes again, taking a moment to realize that sometime while she'd slept, Jay had turned her to sit across his lap, both of her feet hanging down the right side of his saddle. Her right shoulder was wedged between his left arm and torso, her cheek resting against the solid firmness that was his shoulder. She shifted slightly, seeing a damp ring outlined in salt where her head had been. Trying to keep her head still, she looked up, seeing a strong chin sprinkled liberally with whiskers. There was a strange combination of smells: man, horse, sweat, and her own scent, all mingled together in fragrant reassurance that she was still alive. But for how long?

She shifted her position, careless of the fact that she was touching him from knee to knee. His hand came up to lift her head, twisting his own to look at her, but he didn't speak for a long time, and neither did she. Strange as it was, she was experiencing the most perfect contentment of the moment, with no thought—not once—of the past or the future, no consideration given to the roles they must both play, the inevitable end to which they would come together. There was something perfect about silence. Something strange in the way you could share silence with another person and, although no words were spoken, come to an understanding of each other that was far stronger than any verbal bonding.

She wondered about this strange man who held her, feeling his lips in her hair. Her heart quickened in response. Her mouth was dry. She had been thirsty for so long. The heat was everywhere, sapping her strength, drawing precious fluids from her body. She thought she heard a bee droning, but it was only a loud buzzing in her ears. Her mind grew foggy. Her eyelids drooped, then fluttered and closed. She drifted off to the blessed release that comes only with sleep.

8

By the time they stopped at
the ruins of an old village near a small canyon of layered
ash embedded with sanidine crystals, Jennifer had had
more than enough time to regret ever trying to steal anything from Jay Culhane. They rode over rocky terrain that
wasn't much to look at, but at least they were out of the
flats and out of the wind. Already the sun had lost some of
its fierceness as night approached, bringing the promise of
blessed relief from the intense heat that drained what precious moisture their bodies retained.

She tried to speak, but her mouth was too parched and,
like her skin, abraded with wind-driven grit. Jay dismounted and reached up to lift her down. But her muscles
were so stiff and sore that when her feet touched the
ground, her knees buckled and she would have dropped to
the ground if he had not held her. He brought the canteen
to her lips. "A couple of small sips for now, no more," he
said. We're precious close to the last of it, but I'll let you
have more in a little while."

She filled her mouth once and swallowed immediately,
but on the second sip she retained the precious fluid for as
long as she could before swallowing it. *So this is the last of
it. How long will we live now? One more day at best, no more*

than two, without water. She felt emotion constrict her throat and she turned her face sharply away.

She felt his hand on her face, gently turning her until he looked full into her eyes. His voice was softer than usual and seductive. "I did not expect it to end like this. And although I regret your involvement, I cannot say that I am sorry. I must admit, I find the thought of going to my death with you in my arms much more pleasant than taking a bullet in the back and dying alone in some isolated ravine."

She tried to turn her head away, but he held her firmly. Her eyes blazed up at him. "What makes you think I want to lie in your arms my last few moments on earth? To die is punishment enough, but to go this way, to bear the brunt of your mockery, to meet my maker with the residue of lust upon my lips . . . it is too much."

He looked down at her, his eyes moving over her slowly, as if he were committing her to memory. "You make it devilish hard for a man, angel eyes."

"I loathe the sight of you. I can be nothing but honest."

"Ah, my sweet innocent, you may uphold your hate for me, but when I look into your eyes, I see the quickening of desire." The lazy tone of his voice should have warned her, but she could only think of his proximity and the illogical way her body responded. He smiled and leaned toward her. "Deny me if you will, but your body will not, for I remember the way it rises to accept the pleasures of my hand."

"Bastard!" Her hand came up to slap him, but he caught both her wrists easily, holding them behind her with one hand. She hated him. But more than that, she hated this weakness in her that made her desire him as much as she loathed him.

"I grow weary of your accusations and your caustic tongue. Mark me well. My mother was well married to my father before she had a child. I am no bastard born, and will not suffer to be called one. Is that clear?"

"I hate the sight of you," she said.

"That I don't doubt. But I will have your answer." He

tightened the pressure on her arms and she cried out at the pain that shot through them.

"Yes," she said, fighting back tears, "it is clear."

He lowered his head and she would have turned away, but his other hand came up to capture her chin. He brushed his cheek against hers, the rough beginnings of a beard harsh against her blistered skin. But in spite of the tenderness of her flesh, a shiver rippled across her and she heard him chuckle. Then his hand dropped lower to release the buttons of her blouse, pulling it apart and baring her to him. He ran one finger down between the valley of her breasts, then across, teasing the sensitive points. She felt them tighten in response and closed her eyes against the mocking sound of his laughter. "Yes, my beauty, you say you hate me, but your body will give no sanction to such a lie."

He released her suddenly. Her knees buckled and she sank to the ground, too weary to care where she rested, as long as she rested.

She could hear him setting up camp, and she wondered why he bothered. By this time tomorrow, it wouldn't matter if they had eaten or rested. It was strange to note that even faced with death, they would go on with their lives as if the certainty did not exist. She caught him looking at her over the back of his horse as he removed his saddle and she rolled over to her stomach with a groan and stretched out on the ground, wincing as she straightened limbs that had been cramped in one position too long. As she drifted off to sleep she was thinking, *I should be up giving that bastard as much trouble as I can.* Yet there was some small satisfaction in thinking him a bastard, even if she could not say as much.

Jay turned to see Jennifer spread like a deer hide staked in the sun to cure. Even in her exhausted, filthy, sunburned state, she was desirable, for he *knew* what lay beneath all that grime and tatters. For a moment he regretted having been so harsh with her; he had no real wish to master her, only to make her see reason, to be honest with herself. *It's for her own good,* he thought. *She will admit her desire for me, as I have admitted mine for her. Until that time she will learn of my strength and I hers.* Then he remembered how little time they had left. His eyes were still on her and he felt a catch in his chest that faded to a strange tugging. *Time. I need more time.* And he cursed softly, knowing time was one of the things he did not have. The other was Jennifer.

He shook his head, feeling a smile lift his lips in spite of the certainty of approaching death. Before him was sprawled the most tenacious pest he had ever met. But she was one hell of a woman, a real fighter. She was like a sailing vessel, where the thrills of high speeds and latent danger merged. Strange that she made his mind go back to think upon his time at sea, when he hadn't thought of that part of his past in such a long, long time.

He looked at the endless stretch of sandy flats that lay behind them, remembering the exhilaration of standing at the helm, the feel of the wheel in his hands, and wondered if Jennifer, too, would be like a great vessel vibrating with the passions of the moment. She was a challenge, this black-haired beauty. Tricky at the helm but lightning-fast downwind.

There was no doubt the girl intrigued him. And although he had little use for women, save the obvious, he knew Jennifer was not like so many others, broad of beam and shallow-drafted. Jennifer was a sailor's dream, lean and deep-drafted, tapering down to the keel.

She heard him coming, his spurs ringing in the dust. Of course, it wouldn't be like him to let her rest, since it was his nature to torment her at every turn. Her eyes were still closed, but she knew he was standing over her, surveying the wreckage. A scuffling sound; her body was touched, then rolled. On her back now, a warm, callused hand followed the contours of her neck and lifted her head, bringing the metallic taste of a canteen against her lips.

Thirsty beyond anything she had ever known, she felt the frantic drive for life-sustaining water as her hands gripped the canteen and she took two big swallows, her eyes open and accusing when he took it away. "Even if there was plenty of water, I couldn't let you drink your fill."

"How lucky for you . . . justification for torture."

"A mockingbird would run out of song before you run out of comments," he said, but she didn't pick up his usual tone of sarcasm. Jennifer opened her mouth, but he cut her off. "You talk too much, angel."

Another hot retort formed on her lips, but this time he used the canteen to block it. "Be quiet, little girl, or I'll take your toys away." Two sips, and once again the canteen was removed.

She watched him replace the lid. "Is that all I get?"

"You're lucky I gave you any at all. This is *my* water, or what's left of it, in case you've forgotten."

With arms weak and trembling, she pushed herself to a sitting position. "Forget? How can I? Every time I move, I remember. I remember being treated like an animal . . . or worse." She watched him as she spoke, noting that her words appeared to have little effect upon him, and that angered her. "I doubt my father intended for you to treat me like this when he hired you. He sent you to find me, not to dole out punishment. My father is a kind man. Even his animals have the right to water and rest."

"You gave up your rights when you tried to steal my horse and lost two canteens of life-sustaining water. Before, you were just a pain in the ass."

"Before? What am I now?"

"Now," he said, "you're my prisoner. And that, little girl, gives me the right to do anything I please with you."

Jay's gaze lingered on her sunburned face, redder now than before, and wondered how she could still look so tempting. He followed the curve of her breasts to the narrow waist and down the length of unbelievably long legs, tucked beneath her. *Trim and sleek as a racing yacht.* Tired as his body was, he found it strange that his desire for her was as fresh and alert as it had ever been. Fatigue, it was his displeasure to note, had little effect upon the instrument of passion.

Passion. It had been so long since he had experienced it. Lust, yes, but little he could call passion. Had his passion been a casualty of such a long winter, when all the budding illusions and sunny dreams of his earlier years had frozen and died? Or was he simply too indifferent to care anymore? Oh, for a while he had pretended to take life seriously—to love, to hate, to trust, to forgive—but in time that, too, had passed. Despair, he had learned, is the reward of hope. Better to cease all anticipation than to fight constant disillusion. Hopes. Dreams. Family. Commitment. He had found something to replace them, and little did it matter to him that the replacement wasn't as noble. He didn't need those things anymore. But he knew his body would betray him with its restless yearning. As it had in the past, as it did now. He was man. She was woman. He would have her, and before too long. Some things were meant to be.

Those damn violet eyes of hers were watching him intently. "I'm not your prisoner, for you haven't won yet."

"You're my prisoner . . . captive . . . hostage . . . my *whore,* if I so choose." Then he turned away from her before she could look at him in a way that would cause him to feel disgusted with himself. He walked back to Brady and put on the hobbles, turning him loose to find what sparse grass he could between creosote bushes that covered the terrain like an orchard.

She scrambled to her feet, feeling wobbly and unstable. "I'll never be your anything," she said, and he turned away. Of course, that angered her. "Why don't you slake your lust on some lower form of life . . . something on your level? Then I won't have to suffer your lecherous looks."

His eyes swept over her with contempt. "You're safe for

now. I've seen cleaner barnyards. As for my baser instincts . . . let's just say you smell like you should be left alone."

That stung, but she tried not to show it as she shouted back at him, "Good! I can't be left alone enough where you're concerned."

Jay walked slowly toward her. She knew his look of indifference was feigned. She had irritated the life out of him since the moment he had first laid eyes upon her. Just her presence infuriated him, and he didn't bother to hide his disgust. She watched him walk, rawboned and lanky. There was something about the way he moved, his bearing, the way he stood at ease that made her think of the military.

It's probably because you feel like you're standing before a firing squad, she told herself, and dismissed the thought from her mind.

He paused in front of her, close enough that she could look into the dark blue of his eyes and feel their pull. Jennifer closed her eyes, feeling the vitality of him reaching out to her. Warm and penetrating. Throbbing with life and virility. Overpowering. Tall as a lodgepole pine, his very presence seemed to dominate her. *We are at cross-purposes, you and I,* she thought.

"If you lay a hand on me, I swear I'll make you regret the day you came after me."

He stood very still, studying her through those piercing eyes of his. "Little girl, if that's all this is about, I can promise you, I *already* regret that." He came closer still, and she scrambled backward.

"I'm warning you. Don't you dare lay a hand—."

"The only hand I'm tempted to lay on you is my palm to your backside. I bet no one has ever blistered your backside."

"Go ahead. Blister it. Every other part of me is blistered. We might as well make it unanimous."

For a moment Jay looked amused. "Why don't you give me your word that you'll behave yourself?"

"You mean be meek and obedient?"

"Among other things," he said. "Do you agree?"

"Go stick your head in a bucket. That's the problem with a male-dominated society now. Women are tired of being burdened with a multitude of negatives in order to preserve male initiative. I, for one, am sick of being told to exercise restraint and abstinence and never give vent to my feelings as a man can."

"You're giving pretty good vent right now."

"And I will continue to do so until I draw my last breath."

A sad look came over him. "That may not be far away." The pain that crossed her face ate at him, and he didn't understand why, exactly, he wanted to make it easier for her. Yet he knew he had to keep her on her feet and fighting. If they had any chance at all, she had to have strength. He smiled, remembering how quickly he had learned she had more fight in her when she was angry. And provoking her to anger was something he found he did quite well. "Careful about waving around your words of female independence. You'll never find a husband like that."

"Who said I was looking?"

"Looking is a woman's favorite pastime."

"*I* am not looking."

"At your age you're close to becoming a spinster, and we both know that in society's eyes there is nothing more pitiful than a spinster."

"I don't give a fig what society thinks . . . or *you*, either, for that matter. In my family, emotional deprivations have always been offset by the relationships between the women."

"I've seen a couple of prime examples of the rapport between the women in your family. A sickness carried by the female line. A warp on the distaff side."

"Family closeness isn't a form of sickness—well, perhaps in *your* family but not in mine. Women aren't like men. We have so much more to hold us together."

"Like what?"

"Religion, for one thing."

"Ahh, yes. Charity duties and prayer meetings."

"It is natural for women to turn to each other, whether they are joined in religious activities or common household tasks. Those are things we can do without intruding upon the male and his overblown sense of propriety."

"It makes one wonder why all women work so hard to get a man if marriage is so distasteful. How much better for us all if they preferred to stay single."

"Either way, a woman loses."

"How so?"

"Because a woman's social existence is almost totally dependent upon marital status. No marriage, no social life. Yet her legal identity ends the moment she says 'I do'. A man swallows a woman the day they wed, and she is slowly digested. *That's* how a man and wife become one. If she's lucky enough to survive him, she is regurgitated into society once more, to pay off her husband's debts and manage as best she can."

"For one so young, you have a pretty grim view of things."

"I don't think it's any more grim than yours. We are both products of our past. Take yours, for instance."

His eyes darkened, and his face wore a threatening expression. "Watch where you step, little girl."

Jennifer merely looked at him sweetly and smiled. She had struck a nerve, but she was tired and thirsty and hungry and sunburned and windblown to a state of near idiocy. She wasn't up to dueling with him. Not now. Dazed and physically exhausted, she hadn't the strength to talk, much less to stand. She began to sway on her feet. Her ears began to ring. A chill pricked at her skin. Her eyelids fluttered and her eyes rolled to the back of her head as she slumped. Jay caught her before she hit the ground.

When she came to and opened her eyes, it was dark. A few feet away a fire blazed, the desert-dry wood crackled and snapped, releasing thin columns of gray smoke in a brilliant shower of orange sparks. Jennifer watched as a tall figure, outlined by the firelight behind him, walked her way: Jay, with his customary long-limbed stride, pausing just before he hunkered down beside her.

"I think I swallowed my pebbles," she said in a scratchy, dry voice.

He chuckled. "Well, they were *little* ones. There's no harm done." He thrust a plate toward her. "Here. Try a little grub."

"Worms?" She looked horrified. "You're eating worms? I'm going to be sick. I don't want any. I don't even want to see them. I'd rather starve. Honest. I'm not hungry. Please. Take them away." She turned her head away.

"Jennifer—"

"No, no, and double, quadruple no. You have carried this torture thing a bit too far. Dying from lack of water is one thing . . . even making me walk the soles off my feet. But expecting me to eat worms goes beyond the bounds of sanity. You can beat me to death, but I won't eat worms. Ever!"

"Jennifer!"

"If you like worms so much, *you* eat them!"

"Will you shut up for a goddamn minute?" She turned her head back so she could see him, catching his sigh of exasperation. He looked at the plate in his hand. "Grub," he said with forced patience, "is a colloquial term for food. I wasn't speaking of grub worms."

"Oh," she said softly. "Grub . . . you mean, like chow?"

"The rations," he said with a rare smile, "not the dog."

She really was a little ashamed of her outburst. Not too ashamed, mind you, but a little. She was always so outspoken and prone to outbursts, a habit that didn't always fit in with the image she had of herself as a mild-natured person. She considered an apology, but that wasn't her nature, either, and besides, there was no way on God's green earth she was going to come anywhere near an apology for anything around him. But it did rankle to think that once again he had gained the upper hand. It wasn't like her to quit until she had finagled it back. But when her eyes happened to light on Culhane's face, he was staring at her in such an odious fashion that she laughed.

Damn, he thought, rising to his feet. Even the sound of her throaty laughter went straight to his groin. And that part of his body didn't need any more encouragement. It was going to be a long night. A very long, hard night.

He pushed the tin plate toward her with the toe of his boot. "Eat," he said.

"No. Really, I can't. I'm too tired. I just want to sleep," she said, and already her eyelids were growing heavy. "It's all right with me if you eat my part." And she drifted off to sleep.

Sometime during the night she was vaguely aware of Jay's hands upon her, peeling away her dirty clothing. A flare of resistance surfaced in the form of a weak "Stop that," but by the time the words were out of her mouth, she couldn't remember, for the life of her, just what it was he was supposed to stop.

"I don't care," she murmured. "I don't care if he rapes me, as long as he's quick and lets me sleep."

She vaguely heard his amused chuckle as he leaned forward, nuzzled near her ear, and whispered, "I am neither quick nor subtle. When I make love to you, sweetheart— and I will—you won't want me to be either one."

"Hmm," Jennifer said, sinking into oblivion as strong hands began to rub her aching muscles.

Jay, watching her eyelids flutter and close, was wondering how in hell she could sleep at a time like this. Just looking at her sent him spinning out of control. And touching her . . . dear God!

His eyes swept over her as she lay sprawled before him, imagining her long legs wrapped around his waist or, better yet, draped over his shoulders. He pushed the blanket away, feeling his throat swell when he saw just how short her shift was, barely reaching mid-thigh. His breathing quickened. His hand moved of its own volition, sweeping down the length of her long, shapely legs, his head lowering to breathe warm, sultry words against her neck. "God, if you only knew what you do to me."

"I know," she said with a husky laugh, "and I want you to keep it under your zipper."

"Brat," he said, nipping her lightly—a teasing bite that quickly turned into aroused kisses that were covering her back and shoulders.

Jennifer was wide awake now and she tried to roll over, but Jay's hand settled on the small of her back, holding her in place. "Don't move," he whispered. "Just open your legs."

The husky tones of his voice slammed into her, sending a jolting tingle down her spine. He was still nuzzling her as his hands began to slide downward, caressing the firm curves of her buttocks, then lower, to the tops of her legs. "Open for me, angel eyes."

His hands were doing the most delicious things, encouraging her far more than his words. She stiffened when his hands slipped between her legs and nudged them gently apart. She gasped when his fingers found her, stroking her with a maddening rhythm. His warm breath and well-placed kisses seemed to be everywhere. There was magic in those fingers of his—some sort of sorcery that made her moan, moving her legs farther apart and sending a sudden flood of warmth downward when he whispered, "St. Sebastian! You must be an angel . . . you feel like heaven."

Jennifer wanted to tell him what he was doing to her felt pretty heavenly as well, but suddenly something gripped her and her body was no longer her own. She whimpered, her breathing mere panting now, as Jay drove her into a crazed frenzy that was unbearable, until she shuddered, a soft, ragged scream followed by a satisfied sigh.

He hadn't made love to her—she knew that much, for she had been around animals enough to know that—but whatever he did had to be awfully close. And if that were the case, a person could die from the real thing. She wondered just how many women Jay Culhane had sent off into blissful sleep with those magic fingers of his, but she was too relaxed and too drowsy to speak. The last thing she remembered was Jay's amused, yet uncomfortable, groan as he kissed her cheek and drew the blanket over her.

When next she opened her eyes, the world was all warm and golden. She fished around for her clothing, using the blanket for cover, as she always did, wiggling into her skirt and blouse.

"Good morning," Jay said.

Her eyes lost their sleepy look. "Did I sleep too long?"

"Long enough. We need to be on our way. If we have any chance at all, we'd better ride before it gets too hot. A double load for two days in this heat with little or no water is too much, even for a horse like Brady."

"Well, tell Brady that all is not lost. I'm quite confident that I'll do something to win your disfavor before the day is out and you'll have me walking again."

He lifted a brow. "Planning more mischief? I wouldn't try it."

Some remarks didn't deserve a reply, and that was one that didn't, so Jennifer ignored him, rising to her feet and folding her blanket. She stood straight, as if she were regally robed and awaiting assistance. Jay stood there, watching, content to let her wait. She was selfish and spoiled, calculating and deceitful—this much he knew. And yet there was a wistfulness about her and a hint of melancholy in those violet eyes that brought unwelcome compassion.

It surprised Jennifer when Jay helped her into the saddle, then picked up Brady's reins and began walking. "Aren't you going to ride?"

"In a little while."

As the day wore on, Jennifer found it was growing more and more difficult to ride sitting behind him and holding her body stiff and erect. More than once she had found herself leaning her face to rest against his broad back, and with a start she would resume her rigid position. Riding behind him like this, Jennifer was growing more aware of Jay as a man and not just as her captor. Whatever he was, he possessed a certain amount of male magnetism that was difficult to ignore and quite unlike anything she had ever dealt with before.

It was mid-afternoon when they stopped. "That's the last of it," Jay said, taking the canteen from Jennifer and replacing the lid.

She looked overhead, the sun a white-hot orb of torture that seemed too stubborn to drop lower in the sky. "How long before we cross the Rio Grande?"

"Too long to make it without water."

"And how long is that?"

"Two days, maybe three."

"How long have we got?" Her voice cracked. "How long can we last without water in this heat?"

"We'll be miserable as hell in a few more hours, but we can last another twelve to fourteen hours, maybe more." He watched her, knowing what her reaction would be and bracing himself for it.

Her lower lip quivered, and for a moment he thought he saw tears in her eyes.

"I suggest you put off crying. It's precious water wasted," he said, but before he finished speaking, she seemed to get a firm grasp on herself.

"I—"

He cuffed her lightly on the chin and said, "I know. You never cry." She smiled at him in a manner he could only call optimistic. And like a general who could muster the flagging courage of a hundred men with a few inspiring words and have them follow him gladly into the battle from which there is no return, she said, "Then let's not waste any more time standing in one spot."

She walked a few steps and turned to look at him. "We've got a lot of territory to cover, Culhane, so let's stop standing around like a couple of fence posts." She slapped her dusty hat against her leg and put it back on her head, then she grinned at him.

She squinted up at the sun. "Well, as long as we're alive, we aren't dead."

"Astounding observation," he said, his words as dry as his throat.

"You know, the Mexicans have a saying: *'Vale mas correr gallina que morir gallo.'* It is better to be a running hen than a dead rooster." Back straight, head held high, she walked to his horse and turned, waiting for him. "Well, Culhane? Do you intend to accept our demise, or are you going to fight it every step of the way?"

Of all the reactions Jay had expected from her, this was not among them. That she would rise to the occasion like this and be offering her strength to him was a complete surprise. He was feeling a little guilty for not being completely honest with her and telling her about the *tinajas,* the natural cisterns that were sometimes found in the rough, rocky country ahead, where rainwater collected and stayed remarkably clean and cool throughout the dry season. But to tell her and then find none would be even more cruel. The girl was taking it on the chin. "Perhaps," he said, hoping to ease her fears and his guilt, "we will be lucky enough to find water in one of the dry arroyos that lead to the Rio Grande. I've heard it's happened before."

If she heard him, she made no mention, and when Jay looked, she was already mounted behind the cantle on Brady's broad rump. He stood looking at her for a moment, thinking she was the kind of woman a man could build something with . . . if she were the kind of woman a man could trust. If he were the kind of man who could trust a woman.

Ahead, the raw backs of mountains were coming into view, hazy and a long way off. But there was no cause for elation. The Rio Grande was still two or three days away. She felt the dryness of the desert in her mouth and looked around her, seeing nothing but a sunbaked slope ahead and a roadrunner, which stood motionless, blending with his surroundings. Her head was beginning to ache, and Jay's back offered some respite from the stiffness in her neck.

She looked away. Nothing really mattered now. They were going to die. It would be dark soon. She doubted they would live through another day. Soon, she thought. Soon it will all be over. A hundred years from now no one would care whether or not little Jennifer Leigh Baxter took liberties with the person of Jay Culhane or not. The whole thing seemed pointless. She pushed the brim of her hat to one side and pressed her face against his back.

She dozed, and when she woke, the first thing Jennifer noticed was the changes in the land around them. The land was becoming rougher, still hot and dry, but they had been climbing gradually into desert brushland dotted with agave, prickly pear, and brush, yet still dominated by silence, endless space, and death.

Brady snorted and Jay reined up, removing his hat and wiping the sweat from his forehead with his sleeve. While his arm was absent from his side, Jennifer peeked around, seeing a jumbled nest of boulders that partially blocked the neck of a narrow canyon. Something was wrong. She sensed Brady felt it, too, for he was acting spooky and ornery, pawing the ground and tossing his head. As Jay leaned forward to rub the gelding's neck, the knotted muscles in his back told her he felt it as well. She pulled away from him, sensing the tension and wariness in his manner and not wanting to be a distraction to him. She was about to ask him what was wrong when she heard the unmistakable sound of horses moving slowly across rocky terrain. Jennifer looked up and suddenly tasted fear.

9

Above them, on the crest of a slope, about fifty yards from the boulders, sat four mounted Mexicans. *"Bandidos,"* Jennifer whispered, looking at the man in front and recognizing the dusty sombrero with its pointed crown, the bandoliers crossed over his chest, the handlebar mustache, the long-shanked spurs with their star-burst rowels. Behind him, like aides-de-camp, were three more *pistoleros.* She had seen *bandidos* of this ilk many times in Brownsville and Agua Dulce, *pistoleros* whose aggressive weaponry kept them in a state of alert preparedness while having a disabling psychological effect on anyone unfortunate enough to encounter them. To these men, hostile encounters between Mexico's abundant ethnic groups and Americans of any caliber were reason enough for terror, violence, and banditry. Time and again they crossed the Rio Grande to rustle cattle and horses and to plunder the border towns and ranches.

The leader, dressed more ornately than the others, rode forward about five yards, then stopped. His horse was a big black, about fifteen hands and blooded, ridden with a fancy Mexican hackamore with a plaited bosal across the nose instead of a bridle. His saddle, as well, was fancy and silver-garnished. And probably stolen.

"Hola! Habla español?" The dark eyes of the leader were watching Jay.

Jay didn't say anything. The Mexican looked annoyed. Well, she could understand that! Silence. It was something Jay did with skill, giving himself the upper hand—it was what made him so blasted superior. Painfully aware of the way the two men were looking at each other, she realized that as strange as it was, the most powerful feelings were often expressed without words.

The Mexican spurred his horse and came closer, stopping about ten yards away, his three companions moving closer as well. The leader was fat with a sagging belly, standing out against his three lean companions. On his face the man wore a smile, but his eyes were dark and shifty. Jennifer felt herself shrink behind the protection of Jay's warm, familiar body.

"You are indeed a fortunate man, *señor,* to have such a *señorita* as you have with you, while I am stuck with the likes of these." He motioned toward the men behind him, then looked back at Jay, amusement dancing in his black eyes. Jennifer shuddered. That was a face that could slit your throat while smiling. "I should like to buy the *señorita* from you, *señor.*"

"The woman is my wife."

The fat one smiled wider. "Then I should like to buy your wife."

"She isn't for sale."

"Everything has its price, *señor.* Even your wife. But let's not discuss it on our horses. Get down, my friend. Let's share a little pulque." He grinned. "Before we share your wife."

Jennifer ignored that last comment. The *bandidos* had pulque and, more likely than not, water. Panic thrummed in her chest. Water she wanted desperately, but at the price they were asking? Jay would figure something else out. He had to. He couldn't take her back to her father if he traded her to this band of men for pulque. *But he isn't too happy*

*about taking you back to your father in the first place. Why
wouldn't he trade you to quench his thirst? You haven't exactly made this a pleasant trip.*

A sharp elbow to the back is what Jay got when he said,
"We'll share a little pulque, then."

"And the woman?"

"First the pulque."

The fat one smiled.

Swallowing a cry of terror, Jennifer wanted to speak in
her defense, but the muscles in her throat constricted and
her words came out in a stale, dry hiss. *"You bastard."*

But if Jay heard her, he didn't let on. The black, greedy
eyes of the *bandido* roamed over Jennifer. She nodded,
knowing her smile was rather pathetic, hoping a pathetic
smile was better than none at all. She was praying he
couldn't see how her lip twitched with uncertainty. Men of
this type thrived on fear, and fear was something she was
feeling in excess. Jay, she couldn't see, but the *pistolero* sat
watching her, making her wonder what he was thinking
behind those black eyes. Already he was toying with her,
waiting at the mouse hole. A sudden thought struck her.
No. Surely not. She dismissed it. But it came back to nag at
her. Could it be? No. Surely this wasn't the infamous
bandido known as El Gato, the cat.

Jay rode forward a few yards, pulling Brady to a stop
against an outcropping of rugged rock. Turning to Jennifer,
he said, "We'll make camp here."

"Here?" she repeated, wondering why he didn't choose a
place in the open, a place less confining. Here they were
trapped against the rocks. At least in the open they would
have a chance. "Why—"

"Don't ask any questions. Just do as I say." His voice
was low, but its tone was iron-hard and controlled, which
was more than Jennifer could say for her own high-pitched
voice.

"But I don't—"

"I know you don't, and there's no time to explain. Just

pretend your tongue has been cut out. If you don't, it may be. Do you understand?"

"Yes," she whispered.

"Don't cross me in this, Jennifer. I'm warning you."

Those last words were said with such omnipotence that Jennifer wouldn't have dared.

Soon she was squatting on a blanket next to Jay, her thirst quenched at last from the water from one of the *pistoleros'* canteens. Jay drank very little water, but he didn't appear to have such qualms about drinking pulque. After what seemed like hours the fire began to die down, yet Jay seemed in complete control. The *pistoleros,* however, were becoming louder and more impatient, no longer bothering to mask their interested looks in her direction. Jay must have sensed this, too, for he draped a blanket around her, his arm going across her shoulders and settling her against him. She hadn't been aware she was cold until she felt the warmth of his body against her. She was grateful he had been considerate enough to cover her with the blanket, offering some protection from the hungry, prowling eyes opposite them. The fat one was still watching her with those feline eyes, his look growing more bold and more possessive with each passing minute.

Jay must have noticed, for she felt him pull her more firmly against him, bringing his hand beneath her chin to tip her head back. He kissed her roughly, a stamp of possession. When the kiss ended, Jennifer came so close to slapping him, but the look he gave her overrode even her anger at his insolent treatment of her. She glanced at the fat one again, seeing his beady eyes upon her. If she was going to be pawed and kissed, better by Culhane than by him.

The fat one smiled. "I wish to speak of the woman now, amigo."

"Then speak," said Jay.

"What will you take for her?"

"She isn't a horse. I don't sell women. She stays with me."

"Do not be so hasty, *mi amigo.* You have yet to hear my offer."

"There is no need. The woman is priceless."

Four pair of eyes were on her. "I can see why you would feel that way; however, I would advise you to find a price, señor." Then to his friends he said, *"El que no toma consejo, no llega a viejo."* The men laughed.

"The person who does not take advice will not live to be old," Jennifer whispered to Jay.

The one Jennifer thought to be El Gato smiled and spoke to her in Spanish. "Do you speak as well as you understand?"

Jennifer nodded, and the fat one's eyes lingered on her. *"Usted tiene cuerpo de tentación y corazón de arrepentimiento,"* he said, which meant, "You have a body that tempts and a heart that evokes repentance."

Jennifer turned her head into Jay's shoulder, feeling the blessed comfort of his warm palm coming up to stroke her back. He kissed the top of her head, then whispered, "You're doing fine. Just keep your head."

Suddenly the *pistoleros* stood, and Jay was on his feet as well, pulling Jennifer up with him. When she was standing, he moved her behind him and she rested her forehead against the hard muscles of his back. She knew what these *bandoleros* were about. And she knew that Jay was all that stood between her and rape or death, or both. Although Jay had come close to raping her a time or two himself, Jennifer knew she stood a much better chance defending her honor with him than she ever would with these *pistoleros.*

"We will be going, amigo. Keep the pulque. We will take the woman." He laughed. "A fair trade, is it not?"

Jay laughed. "Pulque for a woman is always a fair trade."

"You can't mean that!" Jennifer shouted as she reached for Jay's arm, a curse forming on her lips. It was the break the *pistoleros* had been waiting for. Before Jay could push

her away from his gun hand, the four *pistoleros* had drawn
their weapons.

"You were a fool to bring a woman, señor. An even bigger fool to bring a woman with the body of a whore and the
face of an angel."

"Jay?"

"Shut up."

The fat one smiled. "Stand away from the woman, señor." Jennifer watched in horror as Jay stepped to one side,
rubbing his thumb against his palm as if he were itching to
draw his gun. The fat one noticed as well, for he said, "You
would be dead, señor, before your gun cleared leather. No
woman is worth dying for. Not even one as beautiful as this
one."

"You will come with us now, señorita." He motioned for
Jennifer to come with them and she glanced quickly at Jay,
her heart tumbling to her feet when he nodded.

"I have no choice now. You'll have to go with them." His
eyes remained on her, and for the rest of her life she would
remember how proud he held himself even when bested,
how his eyes seemed to reach out and touch her, warming
the very soul of her at a moment when she should have felt
cold and alone.

There were so many things she wanted to tell him, so
many things she had said out of anger, things she hadn't
really meant at all. But she was running out of time; the fat
one was growing impatient. "If you value his life, señorita,
you will come with us now."

"I won't leave him," she said. "If you're going to kill
him, you'll have to kill us both." She took one last look at
him.

He remained silent, his eyes on the soft, flowing curves of
her beautiful sunburned face, the stubborn tilt of her chin.
Now, when he was backed to the wall, unable to defend her
or himself, the girl went all soft and loyal, throwing her lot
in with him. It was her volunteering her loyalty that stirred

him strangely. That, and her bravely flaunted words that she would rather die with him than leave.

"Do as he asks, Jennifer."

Her eyes went to Jay and pleaded silently with him.

"Go on," he said. "Off with you now."

She stepped forward, then paused, turning back to look at him, her eyes shimmering with tears that fell silently down her cheek. He looked at her for a long time without speaking, his eyes so dark that they no longer looked blue.

"You're no bastard," she said softly.

"And you never cry," he said, just as softly.

Jennifer turned away, her knees almost giving way at the husky tones of his voice. Something within her cracked painfully. It couldn't end like this. It couldn't. It wasn't the thought of dying. She had lived with the thought of death hovering over her head for two days now. But to die with Jay—this she had learned to accept. But to die this way . . . Raped. Never knowing what had become of him. It was because of her that he would probably die. She knew men of this ilk. They might say he would go free. But they couldn't be trusted. Jay would be dead before she was out of sight. If only she could go with the knowledge that somewhere he still lived—proud, arrogant, and free, his long hair ruffling in the wind, his laughter ringing across the desert flats. If only she could know this, then she might go without so much regret.

The fat one grabbed her arm, taking her with him, and Jennifer went, no longer feeling any fight within her. They had almost reached the horses when she heard one of the men say, "El Gato, what about the gringo?"

"Kill him."

"Nooooo!" Jennifer screamed. She twisted free and ran the short distance back to him, skirting the fire to reach him. Before she knew he had done it, she was sprawled in the dirt, where Jay had shoved her. She rolled over, too terrified to feel any pain, in time to see Jay hit the dirt and roll through the fire. His body smoldering, his clothes

charred and black, he shot two of the *pistoleros,* one between the eyes, the other just below the ear as he turned to
make a run for it. Rolling to his feet, he aimed at the remaining two.

El Gato's hands were in the air. The other *bandido* threw
his pistol at Jay's feet. "It would seem, amigo, that you will
keep both the pulque and the woman," El Gato said. "I am
your prisoner."

"What you are is a dead man," Jay said, and fired. At
such close range the impact was phenomenal, hurling the
bandido into the darkness. Jennifer was on her elbows now,
watching Jay walk toward the last man. The *bandido* suddenly went to pieces, down on his knees, his hands folded in
prayerful entreaty, jabbering away in terrorized Spanish.
Pleading. But still Jay walked forward. The Mexican, who
looked, with his folded hands, like he was genuflectings
flung himself prostrate to grovel at Jay's feet.

"Por Dios," he kept saying. *"Por Dios."*

"A Dios rogando y con el mazo dando," Jay said.

"Some people pray to God with one hand and slap their
fellowman with the other," Jennifer repeated in a whisper,
her head snapping up to look at Jay as he spoke again, in
perfect, rapid Spanish.

"On your feet, hombre. God has spared you. See if you
can't give some miserable thanks for his generosity."

"Sí. Sí," the *bandido* said, falling to his knees again.

"Don't give thanks to me. Get out of here. Go home. Do
something constructive for your people." The man stopped
whimpering and rose slowly to his feet, then turned toward
the horses. "No," Jay said. *"No caballo. No agua."*

The man broke into a run, stumbled, sprang to his feet,
and started running again, sobbing *"Madre de Dios, Madre
de Dios"* as he ran into the night.

Jay turned toward her, his blue eyes dark and unreadable
as he watched her closely.

"You're angry with me, aren't you? Because I grabbed
your arm. Because that gave them the upper hand."

"Yes," he said. His eyes flickered over her, narrowing perceptibly. "I'm angry enough to murder you," he said. "With my bare hands." He did not move, nor did he take his eyes from her face, but his voice was laced with such cold and bitter anger that she wondered if even murdering her would be enough.

"I was trying to help you," she said in her defense. "Contrary to what you believe, I didn't want you to die." A muscle moved in his cheek, as if she had slapped him, but beyond that, he was as inscrutable as ever. She looked into his eyes and saw such an icy blue hardness. Then, with one swift motion, he reached for her arm and yanked her to her feet. Blood and sand caked her lips and filled her mouth with grit.

"You're going to kill me now, aren't you?" she said, quivering.

He looked like he couldn't believe what he had just heard, then he said, "Don't be so goddamn stupid."

"But you are. I know it. I can see it in your face."

"You can't see shit, and you know it. It's darker than the inside of a whale's belly out here."

"Do it!" she screamed. "Just do it and be done with it."

"What the hell are you talking about? You can cut the dramatics. We aren't trying out for *King Lear.*"

"Kill me, damn you. Don't make me wait like this. At least you let them die quickly."

Anger flared in his eyes. "As you wish."

From out of nowhere a knife appeared, its polished steel sides flashing against the struggling flames of the fire. In one quick move he had his arm around her waist, her back hugged against his chest, the cold blade of the knife pressed against her throat. Jennifer closed her eyes, thinking she was no better than the Mexican who had cowered before Jay's rage.

"Is this what you wanted, little girl?" he murmured against her ear. "Shall I kill you quickly with my knife, or slit your lovely white throat and let you bleed to death slowly?"

Jennifer struggled against him, only to feel the increased pressure of the knife against her throat. She went limp. "Which is it to be, angel eyes?" he growled. "Shall I kill you, as you were trying to kill yourself?"

Jennifer cried out when he wrenched her around to face him, the knife still close to the tender flesh of her throat. With an oath he flung the knife away, his hands going to each side of her face. "So beautiful. So brave. So goddamn stupid. If I ever see you endanger yourself like that again, I'll make you walk all the way to Weatherford buck naked."

He jerked her closer and his mouth came down, taking hers with such violence that her insides wrenched with fear. The following shock of the intimate thrust of his hard groin against her made her realize that even in fear and facing the threat of death, she was all too aware of his magnificent body. His hand slipped to the lower part of her back and pressed her against him. She trembled with a faint swirl of passion mingled with panic that left her weak. Then he tilted her chin and lowered his mouth to hers with such gentleness that it caught her completely off-guard. He moved over her mouth expertly but with such tenderness that it disarmed her. He was angry with her. She had not expected him to be gentle. Yet his touch was the touch of a lover, the caress of a man who wanted to give, not take.

Her confusion was quickly shattered by the sudden realization that she wanted to lie with him like this, wanted to feel his hands on her. She shuddered at the thought, her eyes growing wide with surprise and liquid with desire. Too experienced to miss what was happening to her, Jay brought his mouth down to slant across hers, taking her startled gasp of surprise and kissing her until she moaned deep in her throat and her arms went around his neck, the heat of his body penetrating and leaving her soft and drowsy.

He dropped to the ground with her still in his arms, covering her body with his own. She pushed weakly against him as his hand came up to caress her breast and then she realized that he had unfastened her blouse without her even knowing it. He kissed her throat, her face, her breasts, her mouth, telling her what he was going to do to her, whispering love words, sex words, words of how beautiful she was, how much she pleased him, how he desired her.

Her heart pounded painfully beneath his hand, her breath lodged in her throat. Everywhere he touched her, he left a flushed trail of heat. He kissed her again and she melted against him, whispering his name as his hand came under her skirt and along her leg, finding the place he searched for. She cried out when he touched her there.

"Has it been a long time for you?" he whispered against the damp skin beneath her ear.

Dazed, she looked at him, not comprehending, only conscious of how much she wanted his mouth on hers once more. He kissed her again, more softly this time. "Tell me."

When Jennifer didn't answer, he pulled away from her, cupping her face in his hands. "Look at me, angel face. I need to know. I want you to the point of madness, but if it's been a long time, I'll go slowly, though God knows your body is telling me it can't be quick enough for you."

A pan of cold water in her face couldn't have been more effective. With a strength she didn't have to muster, she caught him and shoved with all her might, rolling from under him as she did, springing to her feet. "You filthy, low-down, good-for-nothing, jumping-to-conclusions bastard!"

Jay groaned, rolling to his back and wearily covering his eyes with his hand. "Not again," he said.

Jennifer was so furious, she kicked him in the shin. "What the hell?" he said, flinging his hand away and nailing her with his hot eyes. She hauled off and kicked him again.

"I can't stand the sight of you!"

"Jesus! I'm getting tired of these trite phrases," he said, rubbing his leg, then coming to his feet, dusting the sand off his clothes. When he finished, he looked at her, her blouse gaping open and giving him a partial view of those same luscious breasts he had touched only moments ago. She was hurt and angry enough to kill—fierce and wild and unbelievably beautiful that way, consumed with raw, primitive rage. And Jay, having a few primitive passions of his own, felt his body throb and harden just looking at her. The ironic humor of it all consumed him.

"I was trying to be considerate," he said. "Obviously you're not accustomed to that."

"What I'm not accustomed to is a man putting his hands on me, or kissing me, or saying to me the kinds of things you were saying to me."

"Just what are you trying to tell me?" he said, tremors of doubt racing through his body.

"How long has it been for you!" she shrieked, flinging the coffeepot at him.

Jay ducked as she said, "I'll tell you how long it's been for me, you bastard." A can of beans came flying toward him and he dodged it as well, a chuckle rumbling to the surface from deep within his belly.

"It's been forever! Do you understand that? No one, I repeat, *no one,* has ever touched me as you have." Another can of beans. A can of tomatoes. "I have only been kissed twice in my whole life, and neither of those made me feel . . . like . . . yours . . ." Her words dwindled down to nothing and she froze, her arm drawn back, ready to let fly with a can of peaches. Realizing what she had almost revealed, her eyes flew to Jay, praying he had been too busy protecting himself to hear. But he had heard, all right. The biggest earsplitting grin she had ever seen covered his face.

"Neither of those kisses made you feel like what?" he said, the humor leaving his face as he started toward her.

Jennifer saw him coming and dropped the can of peaches, her fortitude crumbling. It was just too much. She had been mistreated and tortured, living with the threat of death for two days, pushing her body beyond endurance, going without water, coming dangerously close to being raped—twice. She had seen men killed. She had been mauled, had her chastity questioned, her body explored, her education broadened—beyond her wildest imagination —not to mention the humiliation of being laughed at. And now she had revealed something to him that she never should have divulged.

"Ohh!" she said, stamping her foot. Horrified, she wished she were at home so she could run to her room and slam the door in his face. But there was no place to hide, and the brute's laughter was still ringing in her ears. In desperation she clapped her hands over her face and dropped to the ground, her skirt billowing around her.

Jay crossed the distance between them, coming down beside her, enfolding her in his arms. "There now," he said. "It's all right. You've been through a lot. It's all right to cry."

Jennifer's head snapped up and she scrambled away from him and to her feet. "I'm not crying," she said, taking angry swipes at her eyes. "I told you, I never cry."

"Right. You never cry and you've never been kissed, and you've never had a man make love to you—at least not one that knew what he was doing. No wonder you behave the way you do. That's the problem. My girl, you need the right kind of loving badly. You've been surrounded by a bunch of doddering, drooling fools who lacked either the drive or the knowledge, or else they were too afraid of you to give you what you needed. A man like that is worse than having no man at all, and before this trip is over I'll show you the truth of it. No wonder you're so unbearably rebellious and headstrong. You need to be loved long and hard, and by someone who knows what they're about."

"And *you,* of course, just happen to be a man who knows what he's about," she said, doing her best to keep the lid on her temper but sounding as hateful and sarcastic as she possibly could.

"Of course," he said. "Although I would have thought that you would have figured that out by now, since we've—"

"Shut up!" she yelled. "Just shut up. It doesn't take much of a man to lord it over a helpless woman."

"Helpless? Sweetheart, I'd place my money on you any old day of the week."

"You have the strangest way of paying a lady a compliment."

"Not really," he said calmly. "I wasn't paying you one."

Jennifer gritted her teeth in silence, hearing him chuckle in that husky way he had. "If I'm so odious, why do you keep trying to seduce me every time I turn around?"

"Because I recognize you for what you are, and I even admire you for it—for your stubborn strength, your indomitable Gypsy spirit, the resilience of your constitution, your almost asinine belief in yourself, your lack of fear, your salty tongue, your aim with a tomato can, and the pragmatic way you go about everything. Except when you let that temper of yours get the best of you, which must be a legacy from that redheaded mother of yours."

"Don't think you can insult my mother—"

"Be quiet, Jennifer," he said in a matter-of-fact way. "I'm not making fun of you or your mother. Believe me, I admire you. I suppose it's because I have . . . or had . . . many of those same qualities when I was your age. Will you stop tapping your fingers and listen? I don't find you odious at all—quite the contrary. I find you extremely seductive and very desirable, and that's probably why I find it difficult to keep my hands off you . . . that and the fact that I can't ever remember being around a woman that tied me in as many knots as you do, or being around one as much as I'm around you without making love to her."

Jennifer looked at him as if she couldn't believe her ears. "Are you trying to tell me you're in love with me after a few short days? You're either insane or quite the most flamboyant liar I've ever come across."

"No. I'm not a liar or insane. And I'm certainly not in love with you. I want you, Jennifer. Badly. And I intend to have you before this journey comes to an end."

"Wonderful," she said, throwing up her hands and talking to the sky. "Now I have to sleep with one eye open, wondering when you're going to pounce."

He shook his head. "I had a more romantic encounter in mind than some sort of sexual leapfrog, if that's what you envision."

"I'm not envisioning anything. I can't think of anything less appealing than being tortured all night by a man with more hands than a deck of cards."

"I'm not trying to torture you or extract a pound of flesh. I want you. It's that simple. I want you, but I also respect you."

"Oh, how lovely! You respect me? And is that supposed to make me leap into your bed? Tell me, would you respect me as much after the fact?" She crossed her arms and shot him an angry look. "Respect? Hogwash! I respect a boa constrictor, Culhane, but I wouldn't want to sleep with one."

"I have never asked this of another woman, but I am asking you to be my woman."

"Your woman?" She pondered that for a minute. "Is that the same as a wife but without the benefit of marriage?"

"If you wish to put it that way, yes."

"A mistress, in other words?"

"Not exactly. A mistress would imply a long-term situation, setting you up in a house, providing for you financially. We have, at best, a few short weeks."

"I see. Sort of a cheaper, poor man's version of a mistress. A traveling companion. A bed warmer."

"Those all sound very one-sided. I would hope you would receive as much benefit from this arrangement as I would."

"And what would that be, besides calluses on my backside and raw elbows?" She was too angry now even to be embarrassed by her frankness.

He threw back his head and laughed. "That's one of the things I adore about you. You are painfully honest and horribly direct. I've never met a woman like you. You believe in calling a spade a spade."

"And I believe in calling a bastard a bastard. And *you* are a bastard of the first water! You are a cad, Culhane; the worst kind of pervert, a lecher, a throwback in time, a prehistoric lizard, a cannibalistic swine—and without a doubt you have the most swelled head of any man I have ever had the displeasure of meeting. Furthermore, I realize that I am at a terrible disadvantage. We are in the middle of this godforsaken desert, so I can't very well order you out of my house and off my property; neither can I retire to my room and refuse to come out until you leave. But I'm giving you fair warning: If you so much as touch me again, I will have you arrested for rape at the first sign of civilization we come across, and I will personally request that they hang you until those vulgar eyes of yours pop right out of your head."

"Goodness," he said, smothering a chuckle. "I had best be watching my step from here on out."

"If you don't want that personality of yours tied in more knots than a pig's tail, you'd better," she said, coming to her feet and turning away from him to move to the saddle, from which she removed her blanket.

Jay ignored her for a while, giving her some time to herself, time to settle down, while he poked up the fire, tossing a couple of twisted roots into the flames that would ignite quickly. Ignition was instant, and the dry, pulpy wood burst into flame.

After some time Jennifer moved near the fire, picking up a stick and poking at the coals. Jay tossed her a piece of jerky. She caught it, laying it in her lap, then picked up the stick, poking at the fire once more.

"Jay—"

"Jennifer, be quiet."

"But I want—"

"Why can't a woman learn to keep her mouth shut?"

"We can, but I don't think that's the problem. You have a thing about women, don't you?"

He had the audacity to leer at her. "Don't most men?"

"You know what I mean. You don't care for women. I want to know why."

"Shut up, Miss Baxter."

"Has there been a woman in your past? One who—"

"You can shut up of your own accord, or I'll do it for you."

"Your mother is a woman. Or have you forgotten?"

"My mother is dead."

"I . . . I'm sorry. What about sisters?"

Silence again.

"Brothers? A father?"

"No tengo madre, ni padre, ni perro que me ladre," he said, turning away from her and staring off into the blackness. "I have neither a mother, nor a father, nor a dog to bark for me. Now, will you shut the hell up?"

10

"Ain't fittin' to roll with a pig."

Not until Jennifer tossed the stick aside did his low, ominous voice cut through the darkness. "What did you say?"

"I said, 'ain't fittin' to roll with a pig.'"

"I assume one of us is the 'pig,' as you so eloquently put it."

"Yes, and it isn't me."

"I had a feeling that would be the direction you would take," he said tightly. "Care to explain?"

She looked at him, sitting there looking as calm as a dead fish. But she knew that underneath all that calm silence he was deeply angry with her, as he always was whenever she poked around in his past. She sighed, thinking she was feeling a little too tired to go many more rounds with him. She picked the stick back up and began drawing circles in the dirt. "It's just an expression I picked up from Aunt Winny."

"That doesn't surprise me in the least. It sounds exactly like something she would say."

"You've met Aunt Winny?"

"I have."

"You went to Brownsville?"

"I did."

Irritation poked at her. "Can you express yourself with something besides two-word answers?"

"I can."

"One of these days I'm going to get used to your idiosyncrasies . . . that peculiar way your personality is constructed. Then it won't be so easy to bait me."

"You won't be around me long enough to do that."

She snapped the stick in two. She wasn't sure why, but something about his words, the finality of them, stung and made her feel just a twinge of sadness, which was ridiculous. She didn't even like the man. And more than likely he didn't like her, either. "You don't like me, do you?"

"Not particularly."

"Yet you said you wanted me."

"Yes, I did."

"Did? Is that in the past tense?"

"Correction. I wanted you then." He looked at her, the penetrating power of his eyes slicing to the core of her. "I want you now."

Her voice was shaky and unsteady. "Don't . . . don't you find that odd?"

"No. Should I?"

"I would think so. How can you want someone you don't particularly like?"

"The two aren't connected."

"They have to be connected somewhere. They're both a part of you."

"One is a preference. The other is . . . visceral."

The fire popped, throwing a shower of glowing orange sparks. Jennifer jumped at the sound, but Jay sat with his dark blond head slightly bent as he leaned forward, his elbows resting on his knees, his eyes fixed on a point in the darkness beyond the perimeter of the fire. Something about him touched her, like a heart-quickening song that seemed to vibrate with sadness and a wild, reckless sort of passion. The warm glow fell high on his cheekbones, casting the hollows beneath in deep shadow. Rich, golden light seemed to catch and hold the straight line of his nose, the strong thrust of his squared chin, then dance away to flirt with the burnished tones of his hair, darting in and out, as a dancer would spin, touching it here, shying away from it there.

He was so damn good-looking.

But he was a beast.

He appeared relaxed, yet she knew him better now, knew the tight control, the guarded awareness, the tension and anger that could be released in a twinkling to flare into explosive action.

She simply couldn't help staring at him, the word *visceral* drumming repeatedly in her head—a word that dealt with crude, earthy emotions and deep sensation. A word very much like him. The man she saw—hard, rawboned . . . visceral—was nothing like the man she heard through his speech—educated, eloquent, multidimensional with substance and depth, with a commanding vocabulary at his disposal.

She sighed and tossed the two broken pieces of the stick into the fire, like a token of surrender. She was so blasted tired.

When she looked up, he was watching her, a near grin curled across his lips, more heartbreaking because it gave only a hint of what the real thing could be like. "All questioned out?"

"Small wonder."

"Why is that?"

"I would think it would be as plain as an old shoe."

"And if it isn't?"

She shrugged. "It's difficult to carry on a conversation with you. You aren't known for overly long answers. You don't like to talk about yourself. You can't talk about me without ridicule and anger. You don't even make an effort to contribute in the area of generalities."

"Not even a sense of humor, huh?"

"Absolutely not. You don't joke, Culhane. You poke."

He stiffened at that. "Talk won't get you across the border."

"Neither will silence. I'm not asking for formal discourse, just a little conversation between two human beings. Basic communication," she had said quickly.

"We have nothing to talk about, little girl."

"How do you know that? Perhaps if you weren't so closed, if you tried . . ."

"We have nothing in common. As the saying goes, 'You can't speak of ocean to a well frog, the creature of a narrower sphere. You can't speak of ice to a summer insect, the creature of a season.' "

She had gone instantly quiet beneath his stare, no longer feeling the need to talk. That he would even know there were ancient Chinese philosophers would have surprised her a few days ago. That he had ever read the writings of one she still found astounding. That he could quote, word for word, left her feeling inarticulate and suddenly voiceless. He was like a bucket of water around her, always dousing her spirits and putting out her verbal fire.

She stood up and dusted the ashes from her skirt.

"Turning in?"

"Yes."

"Aren't you hungry?"

"I'm starved, Culhane, but not for anything you've got in your saddlebags."

"There's not room for much variety."

"Oh, I wouldn't say that. I think the variety is quite interesting. There's tomatoes and jerky, or beans and jerky, and when you tire of that, you can have peaches and jerky. There's only one problem as I see it."

"Which is?"

"The jerky is as tough as a bootstrap. The tomatoes have enough acid to eat their way out of the can. The beans are as hard as buckshot. And the peaches taste like mush."

He had the audacity to laugh. Gazing at him now, his clothes charred and blackened with soot, his hair ruffled and uncombed, she felt oddly enamored. There was something nostalgic about him, and she wondered if that was because there was something in his past he'd done and regretted, or something he should have done and didn't. She was inclined to think there probably wasn't. Of all the things that struck her about Culhane, experience was high on the list. She watched him roll lazily to his feet and move to his saddlebags. A minute later he offered her a can of tomatoes and a piece of jerky. She declined the former and took the latter. Returning to her blanket by the fire, she gnawed on the tough piece of meat, watching him fork tomatoes out of the can.

"Finish up," he said curtly, tossing the tomato can into the fire. "I want to be out of here before daylight." He turned away, walking toward the horses and fading from sight.

Jennifer took advantage of his absence and stretched out on her blanket, pulling one corner of it up over her shoulders. She wanted to be asleep before he returned. She was too exhausted to endure any more of the mental fencing he seemed to enjoy. When she was rested and primed, he was a formidable foe. In her present state she felt as effective as a July snow. And that was an uncomfortable situation to be in. She hadn't forgotten the way he looked at her, or the throaty sound of his voice when he'd said, "I want you now."

She heard him return and began chewing her lip nervously as she heard him approach. When he drew closer, she feigned sleep. The footfalls stopped. She knew he was standing over her. "Jennifer," he said, nudging her gently with the toe of his boot.

But Jennifer didn't respond. It seemed he stood over her forever. Then, when she thought he would never leave, he said something she couldn't hear and turned away.

He had moved away from her—back to his own blanket, she guessed. A muffled grunt. Boots dropped with a soft thump into the sand. A sudden gasp of surprise, or was it pain? The soft whisper of clothing leaving a body. What was he doing? Stripping himself naked? Jennifer swallowed, curiosity chasing her exhaustion away. She did her best imitation of an exhausted woman heavily drugged with sleep and turned over. For a few minutes she lay absolutely still, her eyes held tightly closed. Then, cautiously, one eye opened to a narrow slit. She could see him through the fire —Vulcan, rising from the flames, naked and beautiful and alone.

Never before had she thought of a man as soft and beautiful, nor vulnerable, for those were things she normally attributed to women. But there was a certain frailty to men. A susceptibility to being hurt, of which she had been unaware. He could hurt. And he could be wounded.

A piece of wood popped. A shower of sparks rose in the air. The fire burned brighter, bathing his naked body in the color of fine claret. It was then that she noticed he was bent over some task, giving attention to his left thigh. Opening her eyes wider, she could see him move to the other leg. What was he doing? And then she remembered he had rolled through the fire.

Rising up on one elbow, Jennifer looked at him more closely. Even from where she was, she could see that his skin was inflamed in many places—some of them impossible for him to reach. Was that why he had come to her, calling her name and nudging her with his toe? To see if she was awake so she might help?

He paused and lifted his head, like a wary animal might do if sensing danger. Slowly he turned toward her. "If you're easily offended, I suggest you go back to sleep."

"I've tended burns before."

"But not, I trust, on a naked man."

"I don't find the human body offensive."

"Desirable, then?"

"Illness and injury render such notions foolish and out of place," she said, getting up and coming around the fire toward him.

"Where do you think you're going?"

She ignored him. Approaching from the side, she took the wet strip of cloth from his hand. "What are you putting on them?"

"Pulque."

"Pulque?"

"Would you rather I waste the water?"

"Don't you have a medicine bag or anything?"

"A pitiful amount of laudanum."

She thought for a moment. "Do you have any oil or grease?"

"A little gun oil."

"Where would I find it . . . and the laudanum?"

"In my saddlebag."

Jennifer had often helped Susanna make liniment for burns from limewater, linseed oil, and laudanum. She thought for a moment, then mixed a little pulque, gun oil, and laudanum in a cup and saturated the cloth strips. Walking back to Jay, she could see that he was too tall for her to do justice to the burns high on his shoulders. "Is there any way you could lie down so I can get to you better?"

He sat down next to her and she dropped to her knees beside her. With that wicked smile he said, "Is it my body or my burns you wish to minister to?"

She picked up the shirt from which he had torn the strips and dropped it between his legs. "Burns I have done before. As for the other, I am inexperienced."

"You've lived in Brownsville for over a year, part of that time in Mexico, alone and unchaperoned. You expect me to believe you're untouched?"

"I was a schoolteacher, Mr. Culhane, not a whore. And I don't give a fig what you believe."

He grunted. She probably didn't give a fig. She was a most unconventional woman, with her independent ideas that women should be equal with men, telling him that a woman had more to glean from life than watching saucepans, changing diapers, and darning her husband's socks.

She began to wipe the ashes from a few minor burns on his neck. "You have such gentle hands for a firebrand. Where did you learn your nursing skills?"

"I was the youngest in a family of nine women, remember? If there was anything I lacked, it wasn't instruction."

"And if there's anything you abhor, it's instruction."

"I don't recoil at instruction, Culhane. It's orders that I find offensive."

"You remind me a lot of your aunt."

"Thank you."

"It wasn't meant as a compliment."

"But I chose to take it as one. My aunt is an unusual breed of woman. I admire her very much."

"Your father said she was as crazy as a bullbat."

Jennifer laughed. "You don't understand the relationship between my father and my aunt."

"Does anyone?"

"Papa and Aunt Winny do. I actually think they get a lot of pleasure out of all that verbal cannon fire that goes on between them. Of course, it wasn't always that way. They hated each other at first."

"Just like us?"

"No. We *still* hate each other."

"And they don't?"

"No. But they did in the beginning. Papa had courted Aunt Winny a few times before he met Mama."

"Ahh! The spurned lover."

"I don't think it was ever quite that serious, and from what I hear, they fought like cats and dogs the whole time he courted her. She thought Mama had lost her mind when she married him. But over the years they've developed a strange sort of respect for each other. They're as verbal as ever, but the regard is there."

"I bet the two of them together is a sight for sore eyes."

"You should see the whole family together."

"I'm not sure I could take that, except in small doses."

"We can't, either. That's why we only get together once every couple of years or so."

"I can understand that. Your family is a bit overpowering at first. And then there's the business of so many daughters."

"All nine of us." She stopped dabbing at his blister. "Did you pay attention to the names?"

He gave her a strange look. "Not enough to remember more than one or two."

"They're in alphabetical order. Abbey is the oldest, then Beth, Clara—Della and Esther are twins—then Faith, Gwen, Heddy, and me."

"What happened to *I*?"

"That was Irene. She died when she was little." Jenny sat back. "I think that takes care of the front. If you'll turn around, I'll see to your back."

She turned her head away while he changed positions.

"You can look now. I'm decent."

When she turned her head, she saw he was lying on his stomach, his shirt draped over his well-muscled buttocks. There were only a few burns, and none of them bad, so it didn't take her long. When she finished, she climbed to her feet and turned away.

"Where are you going?"

"Where I can have a little privacy." She turned away from him, thankful for a few minutes in the darkness, away from him, even if it was to relieve herself. A few minutes later she was wrestling with her skirts, trying to uncover enough to get the job done while keeping everything necessary covered. Men, she decided, had a definite advantage in that department.

He was sitting on the blanket drinking pulque when she returned.

"You'd better take it easy with that stuff," she said. "You've had quite a bit tonight, and it's potent."

"An expert on my drinking habits, are you?"

"No. Just observant."

He turned his head toward her, taking another deliberate swallow before putting the pulque down. "Does my drinking offend you?"

"No."

"Does it cause you pain?"

"No."

"Then shut up."

His bitter words stung. Ordinarily she would have lashed back at him, but for some reason she didn't. She couldn't stop thinking it strange that they had come so close to having a real conversation for once, and now he was his usual surly self. Was that what irritated him? That he had let his control slip and acted human? Whatever the reason, she was too tired to give it any more thought. Jay's problems were Jay's problems. She had enough of her own to be concerned about. She turned away and walked toward her blanket.

"Jennifer!" his voice boomed across the silence at her.

She didn't reply.

"Jennifer!" he said again, louder this time.

She kept walking.

"God damn you! Answer me!"

She stopped and turned. "What do you want now?"

"Come here."

"Why?"

"I want you to have a drink with me."

"I don't drink."

"Come here, Jennifer."

She turned on her heel and walked away. She had just put one foot on her blanket when he came up quickly behind her and spun her around. She stumbled against him and felt iron-hard hands snap tightly around her arms. "Leave me alone, Culhane. I'm tired."

"Do you think you're too good, too refined, to have a drink with me?"

"I told you, I'm tired and I don't drink."

"You don't cry. You don't whore. You don't drink. That's a lot of don'ts. Tell me something you *do* do."

"I *do* a lot of things. I just prefer not to do any of them with you."

He swept her into his arms and turned quickly, carrying her to his blanket, on which he lowered her on her back, his strong legs coming over her as he straddled her. She closed her eyes, refusing to look at him. *Maybe if I ignore him . . . if I refuse to fight him . . . maybe he will leave me alone.*

"Look at me, angel eyes."

Jennifer kept her eyes closed, jerking with a startled scream when his hand came out to rip her blouse apart. Her eyes flew open and she looked at him with such loathing and disbelief that it stunned him. With a curse he grabbed the pulque in one hand, his other hand diving behind her head, his fingers twisting tightly into her hair as he jerked her up to a half-sitting position. He brought the pulque to her lips. "Drink it," he said.

She shook her head, the edge of the pottery jar cutting her lip, but still she kept her teeth clenched tightly. He wrenched her hair tighter, until tears of pain slipped from her eyes. "Drink it, damn you, or so help me, I'll twist your haughty neck off your shoulders."

Her eyes flashed daggers at him. "I wouldn't drink with you if you drowned me in it, you bastard!"

He tipped the jar, the pulque sloshing against her mouth, some of it running into her nose, the rest of it running in a wide stream down her throat and across her chest, soaking into her chemise. He looked down at her, her breasts heaving beneath the transparent chemise as she coughed and fought for breath. He tipped the jar again, and Jennifer felt herself strangling.

She went crazy, fighting like a wild thing beneath him, lunging for his face with her hands. He blocked her thrust with his forearm, wincing when her nails dug into his burns. He threw the jar over her head and Jennifer took advantage of that one break to shove with all her might and to roll from under him. She scrambled to her feet, catching the glint of his knife, which was lying across the cup she had used to bathe his burns. Snatching the knife, she took a watchful stance, her eyes wide and alert, the knife drawn back in her fist over her shoulder.

Jay came to his feet, his body instinctively dropping to a wary crouch. She didn't know the first thing about using a knife, holding it haft-up over her shoulder, instead of down low, blade up, ready to drive deep into a man's gut and rip upward. Still, her rage and instinct could make up for considerable skill. Slowly he circled her, knowing she would soon tire, if nothing else, from the amount of energy she was using to keep her body tightly coiled and ready to spring. Like a coyote teasing a snake, he taunted her, faking a lunge, then twisting away with a laugh when she struck at him. He teased her without mercy, circling and closing the distance between them.

"What are you waiting for, angel," he said softly. "You've got the knife." Then he shouted, *"Use it!"*

She jerked at the impact of his words, his mocking laugh licking at her like flames. "Watch what you're doing. Keep your eye on your opponent at all times. Don't let me distract you, even for a moment. You're getting tired, aren't you? You're going to have to use the knife or put it down. You can't hold it forever."

In spite of his attempt to rattle her, she surprised him by staying relatively calm. The firelight gleamed on her wet chest and throat, the thin, soaked fabric of her chemise plastered against her breasts. She was like a wild, trapped thing; magnificent, cornered, wary. He lunged at her, then twisted away. Startled, she jumped back, almost losing her balance.

"Strike now, angel. Strike or yield."

He watched her lick her lips, her eyes wide and full of uncertainty. "Here, I'll make it easier for you." He stopped moving, pulling himself up, out of his crouch, his chest an easy target for her. "Come on. What are you waiting for? You've got a taste for blood, and I'm willing. Don't tell me you haven't the stomach for it. Haven't you seen the way the peons butcher a goat? It's a little bloody and a little slimy, but that's what you're after, isn't it?"

He lunged at her again and she stabbed at him, his hand locking powerfully around her wrist and crushing down upon the fragile bones. "Drop the knife, girl, or I'll break your wrist." He increased the pressure and she winced, the knife clattering to the rocks beneath them. In an instant Jay kicked the knife away, twisting her arm and dragging her against him. She fought, trying to wrench free. Her knee came up between them, her aim a little off but close enough to cause him a moment of pain. He cursed her, then leaned forward, upending her and tossing her over his shoulder, carrying her a few feet to the blanket and dropping her. She lay stunned, gasping for breath, just for a moment, but it was long enough for him to see her dusky-tipped breasts. She saw the look in his eyes and tried to get up, but Jay came down on top of her.

She began fighting him in earnest now, striking, clawing, biting, but he wasn't conscious of anything, save the breasts crushed softly beneath his hands and the mouth that cursed the day he was born. Desire for her snapped like a tightly strung wire, and he lowered his head to her, taking her curses into his mouth.

"Let me love you," he whispered hoarsely.

"Damn you, *no!*" she said, gasping for breath. "Not like this . . . dear God! Not like this."

Dazed with desire and wretchedness, he lifted his head and looked at her. "Why?" he asked hoarsely. "Why do you deny what we both want?"

"Because I'm filthy," she screamed at him, pummeling his chest with her fists. "Because you're drunk, damn you, and you probably wouldn't even remember it tomorrow. Because you want me, but you don't give a damn about me. Because I know I won't ever be the same if you do." She was still pounding his chest, but it wasn't the pitiful blows struck in anguish and anger that made him decide to release her. It was the sight of her, small and half naked, fighting him with the last ounce of strength she could muster. He rolled away from her and came to his feet, turning away.

And he would have left her then. If he hadn't looked back at her one last time and seen her curled on her side in a tight ball, the wrenching sounds of her abject despair tearing into him as her knife never could have done. He dropped beside her.

"Jenny?" His hand came out, warm upon her shoulder and she drew herself up tighter. He gathered her into his arms and she pounded at him with so little strength, he hardly felt it. "Don't! Don't do this to me! Don't! Just leave me alone," she cried against his chest.

"Shh. I'm not going to hurt you." He drew her closer to him, stretching out beside her, holding her close, touching only her head as he stroked her hair. "It's all right. Don't cry. Nothing is going to happen. Close your eyes, angel. Close your eyes and sleep."

Jennifer lay rigid, waiting for him to begin his assault upon her. But he continued to do nothing more than hold her and stroke the hair that lay across her arm. Gradually the stiff tension gave way to trembling, but she was too numb to know if it was from exhaustion, the sudden release of tension, or the lower temperatures of the desert at night. Perhaps it was all three.

Jay felt her trembling, heard her deep breathing. Releasing her, he slipped away, gathering the other blanket, and returned, slipping down beside her and drawing the blanket over them both as he drew her into his arms. Gradually her trembling subsided and her body relaxed and curled against him, one small hand spread across his chest. He picked her hand up, drawing it from beneath the blanket, and looked at it. How could anything this small hold a knife as she had? He kissed her palm, replaced her hand upon his chest, and followed her into sleep.

The fire had burned down completely when he felt her jerk in her sleep, the incoherent words she spoke muffled against his chest. She lifted her head, her eyes wide and staring, and he knew she wasn't really seeing anything. He slipped his hand behind her head and drew her against him. "Go to sleep, angel. Everything will be all right."

He felt the flutter of her breath across his bare chest as she breathed deeply in her sleep. And the deep, satisfied sound of his sigh hovered for a moment before being carried away by the stirring winds of a star-dusted night.

11

A week later they saw their
first glimpse of civilization.

The town was like a hundred other Mexican towns: poor;
sun-scalded and dry; a study in monotony save for the pale,
cerulean sky that in keeping with the theme of scarcity
spared not one white cloud and the scalloped arch of the
mission where the priest doled out prayers and penitence.
In the distance the rugged peaks of desolate mountains rose
high over the desert flats, while limestone bluffs gave way to
the thorny tangle that ran along the river to provide a home
for white-winged doves, black bears, bobcats, and mountain
cats—animals too smart to come near the missions,
presidios, and flat-roofed towns scattered along both sides
of the Rio Grande, where truculent Comanche had once
roamed. The Indians were gone, trampled like the vanish-
ing prairie grasses, but in the land the savage hostility remained.

Jennifer still rode behind Jays but on her own horse now,
a *bayo coyote*—dun-colored with a black dorsal stripe—the
smallest of the horses ridden by the *pistoleros* Jay had
killed. The other horses, a blue roan and two bays, followed
Jay, strung together by a lead rope he had fashioned from a
lariat. He had treated the horses well, but Jennifer could

not stop thinking about the three bodies that were no more than skeletons, for the vultures had come early.

As they approached the first adobe hut an Indian woman was grinding maize that had been steeped in limewater into a smooth paste on a grinding stone called a *metate*. Beside her smoked a mesquite fire with a large earthenware griddle on which the maize, shaped and flattened into tortillas, cooked. Squatting in the dirt around her were six or seven children, clean but gaunt and hungry-looking—most of them crying. Two of the smallest were pulling on the woman in a frantic way, their dusty faces streaked with tears. In her lap, a baby, no more than a week old, lay naked and squalling, its tender skin already reddened by the sun. A pot of atole bubbled on the side of the fire nearest the woman. As Jennifer pulled up to watch, the woman dipped some into a clay bowl and passed it to her children, along with a lump of brown sugar. Each child drank some of the gruel, then took a bite of the sugar before passing it on.

On one side of the hut stood a scrawny stand of maize, fighting the dry stalks of the previous year's crop for a place in the sun. A young girl gathered shriveled ears of corn. Between the maize and the house, a younger girl carried stones to stack around a hand-dug well to keep the chalky alkaline soil from flaking into the water. Beyond her, another small girl struggled with a basket of laundry bigger than she was. Not making much headway with the basket, the girl turned toward her mother and said something Jennifer could only guess was a request for help. The woman stood, cradling the baby in her arms, and walked—with the slow steps of a woman not long from childbirth—to where a hammock was strung in the shade of the hut. A man Jennifer figured was the woman's husband was deep into his siesta, his sombrero over his face, a bottle cuddled against his chest. The woman paused, asking for help. The man grunted and the woman shook him, repeating what she had said. He lifted his hat. Jennifer was sure the woman was Indian, but there was little doubt her husband was Mexican—well fed and lazy, for his flabby belly reflected none of the gauntness of his wife and children.

The woman said something that must have displeased her husband, for this time he threw the bottle at her. It hit her cheek with a terrible crack, just as his foot came out to kick her away. The woman stumbled, miraculously keeping the baby in her arms. When she got to her feet, a trickle of blood ran down the side of her face.

Jennifer looked at Jay, knowing he would be making his customary inspection of things. The implication of his silence was obvious. He considered what was happening to the Indian woman none of his business, and he would not interfere, no matter how wretched her condition was—and that probably could be extended to include all women.

She caught his eyes upon her, telling her with a look that he expected her to mind her own business too. A man like Jay wasn't concerned with inequality, more than likely putting women in the same class with lunatics, criminals, imbeciles, children, and dogs. His way of thinking was as archaic as the Napoleonic Code: "Woman was given to man so that she could give him children. She is therefore his property, just as a fruit tree is the property of the gardener."

"Aren't you going to do something?" she asked.

"I'll do what needs to be done. You stay out of it, Jennifer. I'm warning you."

Jennifer waited a minute or two. Jay didn't seem to be in any hurry to "do what needs to be done."

Jay could wait if he wanted to.

She couldn't wait any longer.

Jennifer couldn't do anything about the woman's husband, but someone had to help the woman. She was off her horse in a second, going to the jug of water by the fire and dipping a cloth in it, then going to the woman, whose eyes were full of fear as they turned upon Jennifer with a look that was both heartbreaking and frightening. She shrank back, clutching the squalling baby to her breast. Jennifer spoke softly to the woman in Spanish, reaching out with the cloth and wiping the blood from her face. Suddenly the woman grabbed her arm and pushed her away, her eyes full of fear and looking over her shoulder. Jennifer turned around.

The woman's husband staggered from the hammock, his eyes ugly and hostile. The children had all stopped crying, all except the baby, who wailed pitifully. The tension was so thick, Jennifer could taste it in her mouth. The man began to curse and make ugly threats as he advanced. It was all she could do not to cover her ears and run.

Jennifer's nerves were strung tighter as she stared into his face. Instinct told her to run as fast as she could. Yet she stood there, making an effort to control her voice as she began speaking to him, calmly at first, offering help, then losing her control at his belligerence and making angry gestures toward his children and wife as she spoke. But the terrible face that stared at her with the eyes of the damned was not the face of a man to be reasoned or reckoned with.

In slow, liquor-slurred words he told her what he was going to do to the *yanqui gringa*—how he was going to remove and carve her liver to feed the hungry children she was so worried about. He picked up the bottle he had thrown at his wife and slammed it against the adobe hut, then turned toward Jennifer with the jagged remains in his hand.

Jennifer's father had given her many warnings during her short life about thinking a thing through before she involved herself, but the words had never before seemed so wise.

A scream seemed to solidify in her throat when the man said, "When I finish with you, Yanqui woman, you will think twice before you shove your face in another's business."

For a drunkard the man moved surprisingly fast, leaping forward, his arm swinging in a wide arc, the ragged edge of the bottle grazing Jennifer's cheek. She screamed, crossed her arms protectively over her face, and felt herself scrambling backward until she struck something and screamed again, blind panic taking over as viselike arms encircled her.

"Get behind me . . . now." She felt herself being pushed away, Jay stepping around her.

Her reaction was instinctive, wrenching herself away from Jay just as he pushed her out of his path, doing a half circle around him, stopping in time to see him yank a blue rebozo from a bush upon which it had been spread to dry. In a blur of motion he wrapped the rebozo around his left forearm, and when Jennifer realized what he was doing, she brought the back of her hand up to stifle a scream that fought its way to her throat as the man lunged.

Jay's reaction was automatic. His left arm, wrapped in the blue rebozo, came up to meet the jagged edges of the bottle, buying him a little time. The next time the man was quicker, striking swiftly with a thick grunt, jabbing the bottle at Jay's throat. Jay deflected the blow with his shoulder, the bottle clawing like a talon across his biceps, three furrows that filled with blood. Again the bottle came like an angry glass bullet, ripping into the blue fabric, gouging into the flesh of his arm. Jay staggered backward, off-balance, by some miracle maintaining his footing. His fist smashed into the man's nose. Warm blood covered his hand. That blow would have downed most men, but not the Mexican. For a moment he looked dazed as he and Jay looked at each other, sweat and dirt and blood poulticed like a medicated mass to mangled flesh. The Mexican charged again, and Jay was ready, bringing his wrapped arm up. The fabric tore and the jagged glass ripped and drew blood. On and on they fought—lunge, parry, attack, retreat—across the hard-packed yard, crashing through the parched stalks of the previous year's corn, around the corner of the hut, and out of sight.

Frantic, Jennifer looked for something to use as a

weapon. Finding nothing, she ran around the corner just in time to catch a glimpse of Jay as he backed over the basket of laundry and fell. The Mexican stood over him, nothing but an overturned basket of laundry separating them, triumph glittering in his eyes. Then he sprang with explosive force, just as Jay rolled. The Mexican cleared the tumbled mound of laundry, but his foot, clumsy and burdened by his weight, hooked on the handle of the basket, throwing him off-balance. He fell in a sprawl, legs splayed, arms twisted at odd angles, one pinned under his body. Powdery puffs of dust rolled from beneath him like tumbleweeds driven before a storm. The Mexican lay grotesquely still, a prisoner beneath the heavy press of his own weight.

Jennifer's eyes flew to Jay, who rose to his knees. He wiped a thin trickle of blood from the corner of his mouth and came to his feet. His eyes flicked over Jennifer. "You okay?"

Jennifer nodded. "I should be asking you that."

"I'm all right. Bone-tired but breathing." He unwound the rebozo. Already his arm was purpling and bleeding from a dozen places. On one side of his shirt a spot of blood was spreading; there were two bright spots on his thigh, like the puncture marks of a monstrous snake.

Jay looked down at himself, his lips parted in a pained grimace. "I don't think I have enough blood left for a mosquito." She looked at him just as he looked up and their eyes locked. He had been through a great deal for her, and Jennifer did not know how to thank him without sounding apologetic. She was sorry for involving him, risking his life, for the pain that had been inflicted upon him, but she was not sorry for acting upon what she believed in.

"It's my fault that you're hurt." Her words were so softly spoken that Jay wasn't certain he'd even heard her speak.

"Let's get out of here," he said gruffly. "I don't think I could last another round if he wakes up in a fighting mood." He looked down at the Mexican, still lying where he fell. Jennifer looked at Jay, catching the odd expression on his face. With his foot Jay nudged the Mexican, then pushed him, and the Mexican rolled over, a strange gurgling sound coming from his throat, one arm flinging itself away from his body, the other releasing its death grip on the bottle and twisting grotesquely to rest on his chest. Jennifer looked at the neck of the bottle protruding from the man's throat like the hilt of a knife.

So much blood. A sickish-sweet odor reached her, and Jennifer knew it was her own voice she heard running ahead of the wind, a pitiful, hysterical wail that took her stamina. She felt herself go wobbly in the knees.

"Don't go weak and helpless on me now," Jay said, grabbing her by the arm, his fingers strong and biting into her flesh. She stared at him with pleading eyes.

"The man is dead." His voice held none of the violent tremors that shook her. "And I hope you're fixed for high riding," he said, jerking her along, heading toward the horses. The woman, standing with her children now, was looking down at the still, sprawled body of her husband. Jay paused beside the woman, speaking softly to her in Spanish. "I'm sorry. Your husband is dead."

She turned her eyes upon Jay, and those eyes struck him like the unknowing eyes of an animal being led to slaughter. He felt the slow, beleaguered weight of accountability. How could he explain he had not meant for this to happen, that it was all because the pampered and spoiled daughter of a wealthy rancher had nothing better to do than to leap before she looked. Jay looked off into the distance. They would have to leave town. There would be no soft bed for him in this town that night. Nothing but more hard ground and cold beans. Maybe it was just as well. Staying under a roof too long made a man crazy.

Jay was so lost in his own silence, at first he didn't notice that the woman was speaking. *"Mi esposo es muerto y no le hace conmigo!"*—"My husband is dead and I don't care." She glanced down at her husband, then at her children, and said, in Spanish, "The fat old lion doesn't roar as loud as he did."

The children laughed, and Jennifer watched, spellbound, as one tiny little girl, no more than four years old, stepped forward, approached Jay, then stopped in front of him. She didn't speak but simply stood there, looking at him as if he were some sort of vision. Jay smiled at her, a smile so brilliant and tender that Jennifer wished above everything that he had once bestowed such a gift upon her. Then he dropped down to his haunches and whispered something to the child, and the little girl nodded. Jay reached out and took her in his arms, coming to his feet.

The woman smiled and looked at Jay, a flare of bold sagacity in her black eyes, and Jennifer saw a sudden depth of feeling leap between them: the Indian woman with her children and her poverty; the hired gun with his well-oiled gun belt and his silence.

Shifting the little girl to his back, Jay carried her to where Brady was standing and let her unstrap his saddle-bag. Then he dug deep, fished out a bag of pesos, and went to the woman, offering them to her as he said, "There's enough here to see you and the children through a few months."

The woman shook her head. "You have helped enough, señor. Keep your money," she said.

Jay opened the woman's hand and placed the bag into it, then closed her fingers over it. "I'm sorry we can't stay to help." His eyes went to the sprawled Mexican lying in the dirt. "We need to be on our way."

"I will not give you away, señor. Go in peace."

Jay nodded, lowering the little girl to the ground in front of him. "Do you need anything?"

"No, gracias. You are very kind." She looked at Jennifer and then toward their horses. "Vaya con Dios."

Jay stood there for a moment, looking at the woman, blood running down his arm, his hat held respectfully in his hand, and Jennifer felt a searing pain in her heart. Of all the things she had expected of Jay, this concern, this tenderness, this compassion . . . it didn't fit the man who had killed three *bandidos* so recently, and yet, in a way it did, for he seemed so natural, as if this kind of empathy and understanding were very much a part of him. The picture of him squatting in the dirt before the child . . . holding her in his arms . . . the little girl riding on his shoulders to his horse . . . Jennifer felt torn between admiration and jealousy.

What would it be like to have him treat her like that?

As they headed for their horses and mounted, Jennifer couldn't take her eyes off him. Once he was in the saddle, he turned to look at her, those deep blue eyes fixed on her with an odd expression she couldn't quite fathom.

"You were kind and very generous with that woman," she said. "And the child as well."

"I'm not a beast, Jennifer. I have a few humane qualities left that haven't been completely destroyed. If you would stop making assumptions about me and passing judgment, you might discover that." He turned Brady up the road.

Jennifer followed, saying, "I didn't mean to imply—"

"I'm sure you didn't. How could you? You don't know me well enough to imply anything."

Suddenly her world seemed to spin off course. He was right. She didn't know him well, and never would, for soon he would have her back home and go on his way. She realized how lonely his life must be, how hard he tried to show his indifference. She suddenly felt very shallow for not seeing the depth to this man before now. A sense of melancholy threatened to overwhelm her. She looked back at him, returning his measuring stare.

"I've been wrong about you. No cold, unfeeling gunslinger would have treated that woman as you did."

His eyes were steady upon her. "I appreciate the thought, but I'm afraid I'll have to disagree with you. You had me pegged right from the start. I'm a son of a bitch, through and through."

"I don't think you are. It's what you want me to think. That's why you go out of your way to prove . . ." Her words faded away as the intensity of his gaze seemed to reach out and touch her. The mellow sun struck his hair, as if trying to lift its precious golden color . . . and his eyes! They had never been so clear. She had always seen him as handsome, even at her most angry. And there had never been a doubt about his intense kind of masculinity. But now she was seeing him as if for the first time, and she felt dazzled by it. She desired him, and had never seen him in this light before. The impact of it almost knocked her from her horse.

"You shouldn't look at a man like that unless you want to encourage him, angel eyes." His disturbing eyes rested upon her mouth for a moment, then lowered to her breasts. Seeing her color rise, he laughed. Jerking his hat low over his eyes, he kicked Brady and yelled, "Let's make a few tracks!"

They rode hard and fast, not stopping until they had covered many miles and the horses were too winded to go any farther. Jay pulled up and let the horses blow. She saw that he had already dismounted and was walking toward her. "Give me a piece of your skirt."

He was still bleeding from his wounds, none of them mortally deep, but one or two she thought were deep enough for stitches. She dismounted, ripped a six-inch border away from the bottom of her skirt, and handed it to Jay. He took the fabric strip but did not move, simply looking down at her for a long time.

Truth was, Jay was thinking, that Jennifer was just too damn appealing for her own good—or his, either, for that matter. Just touching her with his eyes made him ache all over. And he wanted to do more than just touch her. He wanted to make sweet, sweet love to her for a week without stopping. He wanted to watch her face, to see the soft, wide-eyed expression in her eyes when he did. He could spend the rest of his life looking at those eyes. He realized what he had just thought. Jennifer had disturbed him more than he realized. It wouldn't do to have her softening toward him. He had let his guard down earlier for just a minute. He couldn't let it happen again. He felt the gnawing frustration of wanting her, at the same time knowing he had to keep the fine edge of her temper turned toward him. His breath caught in his throat when he realized just how badly he wanted her in his bed, then felt a surge of irritation that he couldn't control his thoughts any more than this. He was allowing himself to become too soft where she was concerned. And she was responding to it. He hadn't meant to become so distracted by her. There was no room for distractions in his life. It was a good way to get himself killed.

"What are you thinking?"

"Why do you ask?"

She laughed nervously. "I . . . I'm not sure. The way you were looking at me, I suppose."

"And how was that?"

"Like you were seeing me but not seeing me."

"I saw you."

"But part of you seemed to be elsewhere, as if you . . ."

"As if I what? What else were you going to say, Jennifer?"

"Nothing, Jay. Absolutely nothing."

"Bullshit!"

"I can do without your crude expressions."

"Yes, you probably can. You seem to be very good at doing without."

"What is that supposed to mean?"

"You can be so honest about so many things. Why can't you be honest with yourself? Honest about what you really want."

"In what way am I being so dishonest with myself, as you put it?"

"Denial, angel eyes. Denial."

"You don't know what you're talking about."

"But *you* do, don't you? You know exactly what I'm talking about."

"I don't."

"Don't you think I see the way your eyes go over me? The way your body reacts when I touch you? You want me, lady. Every bit as much as I want you."

"You're an animal."

He grabbed her by the arms and jerked her against him. "Animal I may be, but the mating instinct is running just as hot in your hypocritical little veins as it is in mine. I want you. So badly, I can't think straight. But that doesn't make me any different from any other man. I want you. And you want me just as much. The only real difference is, I admit it."

"Take your hands off me!"

"Why? Do I bother you? Does my touch disturb you? Does it make you feel, Jennifer? Does it make you want things you're afraid to admit? Things you do without?"

"It irritates me, that's all. I don't like it. It bothers me."

"It wouldn't if I didn't disturb you, if I didn't make you feel. You react to me, baby, and that's something you can't deny. And *that,* angel, is what bothers you." He rubbed the pad of his thumb across the fullness of her lower lip, his eyes burning into hers. "I'd like to bother you," he said softly. "I'd like to bother you and keep on bothering you until you screamed." He looked down at her lip, which he was still stroking. "So kissable. So goddamn desirable." He lowered his head to hers, speaking against her mouth. "Someday you're going to realize what you're feeling, darling Jenny. And when you do, you're going to be woman enough to admit you want me."

Darling Jenny? He called me darling Jenny? Oh, Lord, the spirit is willing, but the flesh is weak. Please help me, because if you don't, I'm in big trouble. The next thing she knew, she was surrounded by the warm, male scent of him, her hips nestled in the cradle of his. *Warm. He's so warm, everywhere . . . his skin . . . his mouth . . . even the*

*words he whispers. . . . How did I never notice it before?
How did I ever think him cold? Warm. So very warm. So
warm and . . . hard.*

"God," he whispered, his mouth seeming to be everywhere at once and driving her to distraction. "You kiss like
an angel. You must have been kissed by them to be this
sweet, to look like you do. Were you? Hmm? Were you
kissed by angels, darling Jenny? You must have been.
That's where you got those eyes." He groaned and buried
his hands in her hair. His words died away as his mouth
slanted over hers.

He wasn't cold and harsh now. His mouth was as warm
and wet and hungry as it had been a dozen other times
when he had kissed her. But this time it was different. So
very different. His mouth moved over hers gently, coaxing,
teaching her of his hunger. His words were soft and warmly
whispered. His kisses were warm and gently offered. But
his body, dearest God, his body . . . Everywhere he
touched her, he was hot, and hard, and it felt so right.

Was it the slow, seeping realization of where they were
and what they were about? Or the sight of the blood from
his arm on the side of her face, reminding him that they
were still on the run? Or could it have simply been the old
conditioning creeping out of the shadows of his subcon-
scious to remind him that the last time he had allowed
himself to care, to follow a woman like a hound after a
bitch in heat, that he had paid far too great a price in the
end?

With an animallike groan he pushed her away from him,
holding her at arm's length, wanting to ram his fist through
a wall, to kiss her swollen mouth until it bled, to drive
himself into her until she begged him never to stop . . .
anything to ease the frenzied rage fed by so much frustration.

He started to turn away, but her hand touched him
lightly on the arm. "What is it?" she said softly. "What's
wrong, Jay?" Her touch seared him like a white-hot iron.

She watched as he threw his head back and closed his eyes, the sweat-glossed skin on his throat stretched until the cords stood out, his breathing fast and deep and erratic. The anguished expression on his face told her he was fighting his own devils now, devils that really had nothing to do with her. And yet, in some mysterious way she knew she was involved—more than she had realized until that moment. "Talk to me. What's wrong?"

He opened his eyes, his face showing so much inner struggle. Then, slowly, his eyes began to clear, his breathing slowed, and the tension began to ease from his face. "We can't stay here. I don't know what I was thinking." He looked back in the direction from which they had just come. "We need a few more miles between us and what we've done before we stop."

"It was my—"

"Dammit! Not now, Jennifer," he said harshly. "You should have considered the repercussions when we rode into town, not now, when it's too late."

"Jay—"

His hand whipped out to grab her wrist. "Don't step out of character now and apologize."

"I wasn't going to apologize," Jennifer threw back at him. She pulled back from him as far as she could go. His fingers hardened their grip, squeezing like a vise. "You saved my life back there. I was going to say thank you."

"Don't. I don't need or want your thanks."

"No. You don't want or need anything, do you? You're not human, Culhane. You're a damn machine!"

She felt his gaze as it traveled slowly down her body, then, humiliating her further, as it traveled slowly upward again—but the look itself was cold, detached.

"Don't worry. For a moment I thought you were capable of feeling. I won't make that mistake again." She jerked her hand back and turned away from him.

"Jennifer . . ." he said, his hand stretching toward her. She looked back at him, seeing that the harsh lines around his mouth had softened, catching an almost tender look of regret, but it was too late to stop the flow of angry words building within her. "Now what? Did you forget to say something? Did you let an opportunity to inflict more pain pass by? Another jab, perhaps? Another crude comment? Or, like the animal you are, were you planning to go straight for the jugular vein?"

His hand fell away to his side.

Jennifer saw and knew it would be a long time before a man like him, a man held by pride, would reach out to her again. *Dammit! It isn't fair. What do you want from me? Why can't I understand you? Who has done this to you? Who has made you shy away from all human contact? What is there in your past that still has the power to destroy you? Why are you so blasted afraid to show you might care?* The anguish she was feeling made her snap at him. "What are you staring at? It's not like you don't know what I look like."

"Am I staring?" he said softly.

" 'Devouring' would be more like it. And I'm sick of you looking at me like I'm a bone about to be tossed to a starving dog."

"Don't worry, little girl. You're safe for now. I like my food washed before I eat it."

"You viper!"

They stood silently, the air tense between them—Jay, his look taunting, waiting to see her lose control; Jennifer, lifting her head, her jaws clenched in total defiance, showing him he could wait until the cows came home. She wanted nothing more than to get away from him, wanted nothing more than to throw herself against him and feel his strong arms wrap around her. *I love him . . . I hate him . . . I'm going crazy.* She felt herself filling with despair.

She didn't understand him anymore. That shouldn't surprise her, because she didn't understand herself, either. Something was happening here, the bedrock beneath them was shifting, throwing them together—something neither of them wanted. Things were changing between them, and Jennifer didn't have the faintest idea what had prompted the change, or, for that matter, what the change was or an inkling of how to handle it. She just wasn't sure of herself anymore. Before, it had been easy. They were always angry, at each other's throats, so there was a simple answer. Stay mad all the time. But now . . .

Thinking back, she could see a gradual easing—in spite of all the friction between them—into a sort of uneasy awareness. The longer she was around Jay, the more she learned about him, the more she liked him . . . and, yes, as he had said, desired him. Earlier that day as he'd fought the Mexican, when she saw his concern for the woman and her children, something in her heart had opened toward him.

Buried deep inside this hard, angry, cynical man there was tenderness. But how did one go about peeling back the layers of pain and disappointment and sadness to find the gentle man crushed beneath the weight of his past? And was she even sure she wanted to? What if she didn't like what lay beneath?

She simply could not picture Jay Culhane tender and loving and gentle, no more than she could picture a mountain lion being a house cat. Until she came to grips with this softer side of Culhane and all these perplexing new feelings, she could not hope to fight him and win—or even hold her own. But she could ignore him. She could go, like the fox to her lair and nurse her wounds, building up her strength.

The sound of Jay calling to her to mount up pulled her back to what they were about. She returned to her horse, riding along beside him in complete silence. They rode for miles without speaking, except for the few times Jay offered her his canteen.

"You want a sip of this before I put it away?"

"Yes." She took the canteen and drank thirstily, wiping her mouth with the back of her hand before screwing the cap back in place. When she looked up to hand the canteen back to him, he was watching her, his hand coming up quickly to pull the brim down on his hat as he looked away.

She thrust the canteen toward him. "Thank you."

He took it, looping it over his saddle horn. "You're welcome."

Late that afternoon they came upon a small adobe hut with a lean-to shelter and the first source of fresh water they'd come across since leaving Agua Dulce—a well.

"Wait here. I'll have a look around." He handed her Brady's reins and the lead rope for the other horses.

Jennifer waited, swatting occasionally at a horsefly that couldn't seem to decide if it wanted to bite her or her horse. A few minutes later Jay came around the side of the building. "The place is deserted, but it hasn't been for too long. There's a parched garden out back with a few tough ears of corn and a dehydrated assortment of vegetables. But the well is good, and there's enough feed in the lean-to to give a good ration to the horses. They're sorely in need of a little feed and a day or two of rest." He took the lead rope and Brady's reins from her. "I'll put the horses out back."

"We're going to stay here, then?"

"Doesn't a bath and a roof over your head sound good to you?"

Jennifer dismounted and walked toward the house, stepping onto the porch. "I'd like to see what I'm going to be bathing in, as well as the condition of the house before I answer that." She stepped inside. When she came out a few minutes later, Jay had put Brady and the packhorses away and was standing by the well, washing the worst of the cuts on his arm.

He turned toward her. "Everything okay?"

"Like you said, it's baths and a roof over our heads." She turned away from him, returning to her horse and loosening the cinch on her saddle.

"Go on inside. I'll put your horse away."

"If you had wanted to put my horse away, you would have done it when you put the others up."

"Dammit! I left him here because I thought you might like to get some things out of your saddlebags."

"You could have brought the saddlebags inside. I notice you have yours."

"Jennifer . . ." He dropped the bucket back into the well. The rope uncoiled with a whir, the bucket hitting the water with a resounding splash. "Goddammit! If you'll wait a minute, I'll do that."

"I can do it myself" is what she said.

Go to hell! is what she really wanted to say, but she bit back the retort that flared like lit gunpowder. Without saying a word, she grabbed the horn and the cantle and yanked, just as the gelding lowered his head and shook himself, making the saddle come off a lot quicker than she had planned. The force of it coming down at her—faster than she had expected—hit her like a heavy weight. For a moment she staggered under the weight and surprise of it and, admittedly, was teetering a bit but holding her own— at least until Jay shouted at her.

"Damn your stubborn hide. Why can't you let anyone help you?" He was still standing by the well but turned toward her now as he spoke, holding her framed in his unsettling gaze. Seeing him looking at her like he was, she lost her concentration and the saddle shifted. Wobbling beneath its heavy weight, Jennifer soon toppled into the dirt, the saddle coming down on top. With a mighty shove she scrambled from beneath it, coming up with Jay—who started in her direction—in her line of vision.

"Stay where you are! I don't need your help."

He stopped. "Why do you always have to be so stubborn?"

"Why can't you just leave me alone?" she shouted across the yard at him.

"Why are you so irritable?" he shouted back.

"I am not irritable!"

"Then why are you snapping at me?"

"I am not snapping!"

"Jennifer, you *are* snapping," he said more softly. Why?"

"You should know exactly why I'm snapping at you!"

"But I don't. I haven't the faintest idea what I've done."

"Hah!"

He looked at her for a minute. "Jennifer, I don't think I've done anything to cause you to act like this."

"Well, if you haven't, you will soon enough. A leopard can't change his spots, Culhane. And as far as spots go, you're covered with them!"

She was having a hard time of it, and he knew he was partly responsible, although he wasn't any more certain about the recent turn of events than she was. The past week or so had been hard as hell on him. And today, since that incident with the Mexican, she had been acting even stranger. It was bad enough that he was feeling all sorts of strange things churning around inside him, without Jennifer feeling the same way. Earlier, she had been unwavering. Volatile and explosive, yes. But unwavering. Now she was as mercurial as hell, and at times her behavior was downright erratic. It didn't make sense. Jennifer was an intelligent, determined woman with her head screwed on straight—at least it had been until recently. If he didn't know better, he'd swear she was pregnant.

"Jennifer?" he said softly.

"What?" she snapped back.

"Come here."

"Why?"

"I want to talk to you."

"Talk? You? A man who doesn't know the first thing about conversation? You want to talk? You don't know what you're saying, Culhane. You haven't put more than five words together the entire time I've known you."

"Does that mean you don't want to talk?"

"Yes!"

"Not even if I promise to put six or seven words together?"

"Stop trying to humor me. I don't want to talk!"

"Why?"

"We don't have anything to talk about."

This conservation was beginning to sound a lot like one they'd had before. "If you come over here, you might be surprised to learn we have a *great deal* to talk about."

"If I came over there and you said more than two words, I'd be surprised, all right."

"Then why don't you come over here?"

"Because I'm not in the mood for any more of your surprises."

"Is that the only reason?"

"Because I don't feel like it."

"That's not a very good reason, Jennifer. Surely you can do better than that."

"Because I wouldn't trust you as far as I could throw a snake. Is that better?" She caught a strand of her hair back out of her face and tucked it behind her ear. Then she crossed her arms and looked at him warily. "You've got something up your sleeve, Culhane."

He laughed. "There's nothing up my sleeve, save a bandage on my arm. That's about all I have room for, angel eyes."

"Don't you dare joke with me."

That one surprised him. "Why not?"

"You don't have a sense of humor."

So did that one. "I don't?"

"No, Culhane, you don't. A joke coming from you is about as fitting as socks on a rooster."

"That bad, huh?"

"Or worse."

"And here I've been thinking I had a sense of humor for years."

"You may have had one for years, but you lost it somewhere along the way. You certainly don't have one now. Take my word for it."

He was amused that she could hound him for weeks about his silence and lack of communication, only to throw all attempts to talk to her back in his face when he came around to her way of thinking. He sensed in her a yearning to belong, a passion to be recognized, a hungering to love and be loved, to give and protect with all the fierce loyalty she possessed. He didn't want to be the one to meet her needs, and just thinking about it made him as uncomfortable as the devil. But he wasn't entirely satisfied to let her slip quietly through his fingers, either—to find what she wanted and deserved with someone else just didn't sit too well with him.

It was a known fact: Women couldn't be trusted.

And that meant Jennifer couldn't be trusted. Hadn't her own family said as much?

For now he would enjoy her. But she was not a permanent fixture. He had no room for anything with roots in his life. He had a hunch Jennifer was a woman who would put down deep roots, the kind that grew through the walls of wells and buckled sidewalks. The kind you couldn't get rid of, once they were planted. But it didn't matter, not really. Because if the truth were known, she probably had no desire to be around him five more minutes than she had to.

He rolled his sleeve down and put the bandages away. Then he started toward her.

She gave him such a venomous look that he stopped— the finest edge of amusement in his bearing—and folded his arms as if prepared to wait this one out.

"Don't you dare come near me!"

"Why not?"

"Because." Jay had a fleeting glimpse of what she must have looked like as a child. Utterly adorable. But she wasn't a child now. She was more woman than he knew how to handle.

"Because why?"

She shrugged, looking thoroughly confused. "I don't know. Just because. Because I'm angry at you. Because you don't like me. Because I don't like you, either. Because you like to provoke me at every turn. Because you take the greatest pleasure in humiliating me. Because I don't like who I am when I'm around you. Because you make me do and say such stupid things and then laugh at me when I do . . . just like you're doing now."

He clamped his jaw together to keep from laughing. "Goodness! That's an awful lot of becauses to work on. Do you think we could work on just one of them for now?"

"I don't want to work on any of them," she snapped. "Now get away and leave me alone."

"Why is that, do you suppose?"

She felt like growling at him. *Grrrrr!* He was the most irritating, exasperating person she'd ever met. He just wouldn't leave well enough alone. "Because I don't want to."

"Why not?"

"Don't be so blasted stupid! Do you honestly think I'm that dumb? That I think it would do any good?"

"Why wouldn't it?"

"Because it just wouldn't." She stopped, narrowing her eyes at him suspiciously. "I know you, Culhane. You'll do anything you have to do to come out on top."

"Oh, I don't know. Occasionally I've been known to let the woman on top."

"Ohh!" she said, stamping her foot, angry enough to bash his head in. "See? That's what I'm talking about. You will do *anything* to best me! You always have to win." A blush stained her cheeks. She had almost said he didn't play fair. He would have had all sorts of fun with that one.

"So that's it? It isn't so much the fact that I win. It's just that you don't like to lose. Not that I blame you. I'm not overly fond of losing, either."

"Humph! How would you know?"

"I've had my losses."

That brought her up straight. "I'll just bet you have. How many times? One? Two? Do you have any idea what it's like to lose *all* the time? To be defeated before you even start? Sometimes," she said, fighting the quiver in her lower lip, "it isn't any fun being a woman."

"No," he said softly, walking to her and stopping close enough to reach out and touch her. "I don't suppose it is. But it isn't always fun being a man, either."

That sent her back into her slump. She sighed. "Here we go again."

"If I promise to give you a few victories now and then, do you think we could at least reach a compromise? Sign a peace treaty?"

"Oh, sure, let's reach a compromise, as long as you get what you want," she said angrily, shoving against his chest. Then she lifted those winsome lavender eyes, giving him the sort of look that makes a man forget all the reasons he had for staying angry.

"Jenny . . ."

Jenny. Jenny. Jenny. What will I do with you? His life heretofore had been normal, if not happy; a sort of latent period in which he began to feel the weaker sex no longer held any power over him; a time when he felt a primitive superiority over the one thing he held in such contempt: women. But then, just about the time the relentless need for a woman's softness dwindled to nothing more than a biological drive, he began to feel the tugging draw of an old flame flickering—a latent force stirring to life—the old insanity. Slamming into his life course with full-spread sails came a woman, and something inside him snapped. From the instant he first saw her, a curling fire swept through his loins, a fuse awaiting the shock of flint. From that moment he'd been sold into that greatest slavery, a kind of torment from which there is no release. Except satiety. It was something he'd never wanted. He understood nothing about it, except that he dwelled in Eden when he was with her, and it pained him to think there would come a time when he was not.

12

❧❧

"I might have known."

Jay stepped across the porch and poked his head through the doorway. Jennifer was standing in the middle of the room, her hands clapped on her hips, surveying the bare cupboards and sparse furnishings, and looking thoroughly put out. Jay's eyes followed hers around the room, and seeing nothing to warrant her sour look, he pushed back his hat and scratched his head. "Now what?"

"When there's finally enough water to take a bath, there isn't anything to take a bath in."

"I'm sure we can find something."

She glared at him. "The only thing I've found that would even *hold* water is this," she said, angrily shoving a small clay pot across the small table toward him. "I couldn't even wash my hands in that!"

She looked so angry and dejected, he found it impossible to hold back the urge to smile. "Don't give up the ship yet."

"Don't be so nautical." She looked at him, feeling even more irritated because he could go through the same grueling weeks of travel she had and stand there looking so heartbreakingly attractive. Oh, yes, this one could be a real charmer when he tried. Thankfully he was too busy being such an overbearing brute to realize just how devastating he really could be. "Why don't you go find a horse to beat and leave me alone?"

"It's more fun picking on you. Horses don't talk back."

"If keeping my mouth shut is all it would take to get you off my back, I'd gladly remain silent for the duration."

"I'll admit the idea has its merits," he told her. "Impossible. But full of merit."

"I'm no different from any other woman with two arms, two legs, and an adequate vocabulary."

"I'm not going to climb in the same cage with you on that one."

"Why are you always so antagonistic?"

"Am I?"

"You are."

He shrugged. "It's something to do."

"So is standing there looking stupid."

Jay didn't say anything for a while, content to stand there for a minute looking at her—looking stupid, he guessed. He had never met a woman who would stand up to him as this woman did. Somewhere along the line her struggle for dignity had rescued her from the snobbish emotions that consumed most women. The expected, the mundane—they had no place in her life. She was a warrior, a Valkyrie whose daily dragon slaying gave her a special vibrancy few humans possessed. She apparently responded to stronger stimuli than her counterparts. One week of her life was filled with enough excitement to see the average thespian through a ten-act play.

"I want to tell you something, Culhane."

Jay crossed his arms over his chest and leaned against the wall. From the look of things, this was going to be a long one. "Okay. Shoot."

"I know you think I'm a weak-in-the-knees kind of woman," she said. "And you hate weakness of any kind, don't you? No! Don't answer that. Not until I've had my say."

She glanced at him and he nodded, looking a mite uncomfortable, as if he expected her to raise hell and put a chunk under it. But he didn't say anything.

"You see, I've figured you out. To keep my powder dry and my hammer cocked, you egg me on, using insults and sarcasm to take verbal jabs at me just to keep my dander up. You know that makes me madder than a hornet, and we both know that if a hornet is anything, it isn't defenseless."

"What would I have to gain by doing that?"

"Nothing, except you'd rather have me up and fighting than acting like a slug."

"And that's bad?"

"Not if you enjoy being a manipulating reprobate. I know you think your callous treatment makes me carry my own weight so I'm less of a burden to you."

"You're a pain in the ass, Jennifer. I never said you were a burden."

She wouldn't have believed that if she'd seen it written in Hebrew on a clay tablet. "Don't hedge. I know what I'm talking about. It's taken me awhile, but I've got you all figured out now. You think because I'm a woman that I'm stupid and foolish and weaker than you are."

"You *are* weaker than me," he said. "My height alone gives me the advantage."

"I'm not an idiot! I was speaking of mental weakness. Any man that judges one woman by what he's observed in another is a fool."

"You don't have to lay it on with a trowel, Jennifer. I can follow that bee to the beehive." Jay could tell by the way her eyes widened in surprise that something he'd said really surprised her.

"I'll have to admit, I didn't expect you to agree with me so easily."

"I said I understood what you were saying, angel eyes. I never said I was agreeing with you."

"Well, are you?"

"No, I'm not."

"Bastard!"

His laughter was infuriating. "Your acerbic tongue is far worse than my manipulating."

"I don't remember anyone declaring you free and clear of an acerbic tongue," she said rather rudely. "Perhaps that's why you are so quick to spot it in someone else."

He laughed again, wondering why he didn't feel his usual urge to throttle her. Maybe it was because he was suddenly discovering it was such a challenge to find out what went on inside that lovely head of hers. He studied her face while she watched him, her eyes alert, her head tilted to one side.

He pushed away from the wall.

"Where are you going?"

"Outside, to wash my *acerbic* tongue."

"What about my bath?"

"Don't fret. We'll think of something. As a last resort, I could always lower you down into the well with a rope," he said, ducking through the door just as the clay pot sailed through and shattered on the porch.

She felt like crying. She didn't, of course. Instead she looked around the depressing room, wondering why she had bothered to spend at least two hours cleaning it when it didn't look any better than it had when she'd started. Well, it looked somewhat better. But not much. At least the floor was swept and the blankets folded on the rope bed. And outside, Jay's coffeepot was filled with a few hard kernels of corn, a meager strip or two of jerky, and the paltry selection of dehydrated vegetables the garden had to offer. Tough as everything was, it could boil until doomsday and never become soft enough to eat.

"The horse trough."

The boom of Jay's voice startled her, and Jennifer turned around to see that the pest was back, standing in the doorway once again. "Is it safe to come in now?" he asked.

"I guess," she said, glancing around the room. There doesn't seem to be anything else to throw."

"In that case, since you're all out of ammunition . . ." He stepped into the room.

"Why did you say 'horse trough'?"

His eyes traveled over her. "I think it's just about the right size."

"The horse trough?"

He nodded.

"For what?"

"For you to bathe in."

"Bathe in a horse trough? Me?" Her hands were back on her hips again. He could hear the sound of her foot tapping clear over where he was standing. "You are suggesting that I bathe in a horse trough? In the middle of the corral? In broad daylight? Have you lost your mind?"

"I don't think so."

"Have you ever seen what a horse trough looks like? They're full of slime!"

"This one isn't. It's been empty too long. I just filled it up."

"I can't bathe in a horse trough."

"I thought you wanted a bath."

"I would give my eyeteeth for a bath right now."

"Then you should really consider the horse trough."

"And where will you be while I'm sitting in a horse trough in the middle of nowhere . . . in broad daylight?"

"Around."

"With your eye pasted to every crack in the wall, more than likely."

"Why would I do that?"

"To get your eyes full."

"I can do that easily enough without gluing my eyes to every crack in the wall. *You* should remember that," he added.

The instant surge of color to her cheeks told him she hadn't forgotten that first night any more than he had. He found her embarrassment confusing, yet it amused him. He was expecting a hot retort.

He got one soon enough.

"Forget the bath," she snapped, snatching her hat off the table and stomping outside.

After having her first hot meal in weeks, Jennifer's mood improved—somewhat. Seeing she wasn't in exactly what he'd call a good mood, Jay picked up his saddlebags and headed for the door.

"Sneaking off?"

"No. Were you hoping that I would?"

"I couldn't be that lucky. Where are you going?"

"To take a bath."

"In the trough?"

"Do you have a better idea?"

"No."

"The water is cool and clean. I'm hot and dirty. I don't intend to pass up an opportunity like this."

He left, and Jennifer sat down at the table, her chin resting in her hands as she thought about what Jay had said. *Cool and clean. Dear Lord! What I wouldn't give to be cool and clean.* You can. Use the horse trough. *Get your mind on something else, Jennifer.*

She eyed the bed, wondering which one of them was going to get it for the night and who was going to get the floor. She looked at the floor. It was too close to the bed, and she didn't trust Jay Culhane. Maybe he would agree to sleep outside.

She lifted her hair up off her neck, wondering if it looked as bad as it felt. She didn't want to think about the last time she had washed it. She felt so hot and sticky and dirty—and there was Jay Culhane cooling off in the horse trough. She came to her feet. She wouldn't drive herself crazy thinking about that.

Opening the door, she hoped the evening coolness would come rushing in. When it didn't, she stepped outside. She heard a splash and looked around in time to see Jay step, bare-assed naked, into the horse trough. And he didn't seem to be in any hurry to sit down. He just stood there looking at her with that overconfident grin on his face. She wasn't even aware she was staring until she heard him shout, "If you're going to stare like that, you might as well come closer so you can get a good look."

Jennifer gasped.

"Close your mouth, angel. You'll get flies in it."

With a horrified squeal Jennifer whirled around. "Going inside to find a crack?" he yelled. She ran past the door, slamming it behind her, the mocking sound of his laughter penetrating the solid wooden door.

The more she thought about him scrubbing the grime from his body and washing his hair, the more she realized she wouldn't be able to stand being around him if he was clean and she wasn't. Or, more correctly, he wouldn't be able to stand being around her. She'd have to stay downwind of him for the rest of the trip. It would give him one more opportunity to lord it over her, just one more way he could use to ridicule her and claim his male superiority. She wouldn't stand for it. She would have a bath come hell or high water. By this time she was so hot and cross, she wouldn't have cared if the entire city of Fort Worth was standing outside. She wanted a bath, and by Jessie, she was going to have one.

She was just gathering the things she would need when he opened the door. Jennifer turned around, her eyes sweeping over him, noticing the change in his appearance. Looking at him now, she had never felt so dirty or so ugly. His face had been scraped free of all its whiskers, and his hair was shining and lying in damp, softly curled layers around his head. He was wearing a pair of buckskin pants and no shirt. And he looked handsome and virile and . . . She couldn't stand it. It was all she could do to keep from asking him if he felt as good as he looked.

"Are you going somewhere?" he asked, his eyes sweeping over her in much the same manner she had allowed hers to sweep over him.

She looked down at the bundle in her arms. "I've decided to take a bath."

"In the trough?"

"Yes."

"A wise decision. I hope you feel as good when you're finished as I do." Her face flushed and she looked away as he walked to the bed and dropped his saddlebags down on the floor beside it. "I'll drain the trough and draw you some fresh water."

"No," she said, a little louder than she had intended. When his eyes narrowed, she hastily said, "I can do it. You're my guide, not my nursemaid. I don't expect you to do everything for me."

"I won't," he said flatly. Then he smiled. "Your guide? Is that what I am? A guide?"

"I . . . I wasn't sure what I should call you. 'Guide' seemed appropriate enough. You are guiding me to Weatherford. I certainly couldn't find my way alone."

He walked toward the door, stopping for just a moment beside her, his hand coming up to cup her cheek. "I'll draw the water." When she opened her mouth to protest, he placed a finger over her lips. "I want to do it. Okay?"

She nodded, then watched him leave. Half an hour later he returned. "I didn't mean to take so long. The horses kept coming to the trough for water, so I had to pen them in the lean-to. You'd better hurry if you're going to bathe before dark. You don't have much time."

"I *planned* to bathe in the dark."

"You're joking!"

"No, Culhane, I'm not."

"Jennifer, you can't bathe in the dark."

"Why?"

"I just don't like the idea of you being out there where I can't see you."

"Pervert!"

He laughed. "That's not what I meant. I wasn't planning on spying on you, but now that you mention it—"

"I didn't mention it. You did."

"Regardless, you didn't have any qualms about spying on me, so what's the difference?"

"I did not spy on you! I was in open sight all the time."

"Well, whatever you want to call it, I still don't like the idea of you being out there alone in the dark."

"Don't you think for one minute that I'm going to ask you to join me."

He ignored that. "You don't know who might be prowling around out there at night. Remember the *bandidos?*"

"You're within shouting distance, Culhane. If anything happens, I'll call you."

"Men like that won't give you the chance to call out."

"I don't want to discuss it anymore. You're just trying to scare me. I've already made up my mind."

"And I said—"

"I'm not asking your permission. I don't feel comfortable bathing outside. At least if it's dark, I won't feel . . ."

"Naked?"

"On public display."

"How can you feel on public display when there isn't another human being within a hundred miles of this place?"

"I thought you were worried about someone slipping up on me?"

"I give up," he said, shaking his head.

"That's just as well, because my mind is made up. Now, if you'll occupy yourself inside until I get back, I'll take my bath."

"Jennifer, I'm warning you," he said rather gruffly. "Wait until morning. I don't want you going out there now."

"That's your problem, Culhane," she said sweetly, giving his clean-shaven jaw a pat as she walked by. Jay stared at her in furious amazement. This wasn't the way things were supposed to be going. Somewhere along the line, things had gotten way off track. He scowled just as she stopped at the door and said, "Do you have soap?"

Jay didn't say anything. He simply turned and dug through his saddlebags until he found the soap. He held it up and waved it at her. "Soap!"

She came toward him, holding out her hand, but Jay promptly hid the soap behind him. "Culhane, I want to take a bath."

"That's a grand idea," he said, his eyes checking her out. "You look as if you could use one."

"Will you give me the soap, blast you?"

He stepped closer, looked down at her, then lifted his head and gazed up at the ceiling as if he were considering it. "All right, I'll give it to you."

"Thank you very much," she said, reaching for it again.

"Only if you pay a forfeit," he said, the soap going behind him again.

She crossed her arms and glared at him. "I can imagine just *what* forefit you had in mind."

"A forefit for the soap. Those are my terms . . . my only terms. Take it or leave it."

"Jay . . ."

"Take it or leave it," he repeated. He smiled innocently, his face the picture of sweetness, but she had seen that glint of mischief in those devilish blue eyes before. He wouldn't give her the soap without the forfeit.

"All right. What is it?"

"A kiss."

She frowned. *"One* kiss?"

"Unless you're volunteering more. I'm an agreeable man."

"You're about as agreeable as a caged tiger."

Jay said nothing.

"You can have the kiss—*one* kiss—and I get the soap. Is that clear?"

"Clear as branch water."

"Well? What are you waiting for? Give me the kiss and the soap so I can go."

"*You* are supposed to kiss me—"

"Culhane . . ."

"I'm the one with the soap. Remember?"

Wearing her most exasperated look, she walked to him and pecked him on the cheek.

"You call that a kiss?"

"Of course it was a kiss."

"No, it wasn't a kiss. That was a smack. I want a kiss. A real, honest-to-goodness kiss with plenty of—"

Jennifer grabbed his face between her hands and yanked him forward, covering his mouth before he could give vent to the colorful description she knew was following. *Uh-oh! That was a mistake, Jennifer. A big mistake. A very big mistake.*

The moment, her lips touched his, Jay took over, kissing her with knee-weakening thoroughness. If one were to have only one kiss, this would be about it, she thought, wondering if he could hear the blood singing in her veins. It occurred to her that this kiss was going on a little longer than any kiss should, but she simply couldn't bring herself to end it. After all, a bargain was a bargain. And she wasn't about to have Jay Culhane taunting her about ending a kiss before the forfeit was paid. She would kiss him until he ended it . . . if it took all night. She knew what Culhane was doing. He was kissing her so thoroughly, hoping she would terminate it so that he could claim another forfeit. She was on to him now. She had lost too many rounds to his subterfuge. She wasn't about to lose this one.

In the end, it was Jennifer who won out. Not that she outlasted Jay but because Jay realized that if he didn't end it and give her that damn bar of soap, he was going to end up letting his lust overrule his common sense. He broke away from her, his breathing hard and fast, his voice shaky as he handed her the soap. "Take it and go, Jennifer. Now!"

She reached for the soap, and as she did, a wicked little

gleam lit up her eyes. "You lost that one, you know. You got the kiss and I got the soap. But the sun has gone down. Now I'll have to take my bath in the dark."

He grinned at her. "You would have, anyway, you little witch. And you know it."

"True, but it does give me a certain satisfaction to know I outfoxed you."

"You didn't outfox me, Jennifer. You just primed my pump."

Her eyes grew round and she looked downward to validate his words. He was right. His pump looked awfully primed, even from where she stood. With a gasp she whirled and ran through the doorway, just as Jay exploded with laughter.

While Jennifer was taking her bath Jay sat on the bed, his back braced against the wall, his long legs stretched out in front of him, his hands crossed behind his head. He was thinking about Jennifer. He was getting hard, a condition that was getting to be a pretty common state of affairs whenever he was around her.

"Christ!" he said, wondering just how much more of this he could stand; this constant wanting her without being able to do anything about it. It was eating him alive. That was something new for him—to want a woman and not be able to have her. Even the refined ladies of Savannah had welcomed him with open arms and drawn drapes. But this violet-eyed temptress thumbed her nose at him, leaving him wound tighter than an eight-day clock. Something had to happen—and happen fast. He was carrying an awfully big charge with a mighty small fuse.

He rolled over with a groan when the sound of Jennifer's voice floated through the open doorway. He couldn't make out exactly what song she was singing, but it did little to ease his condition.

The moon was high in the sky, and the flats around her were silent and cool. Jennifer shivered as her clothes fell from her body and the cool breeze danced across her skin.

She looked at the water, shimmering in the moonlight, and felt a shudder of delight. She glanced back at the house, seeing the rectangle of light that stretched through the open doorway, but Jay wasn't in sight. She stepped over the edge of the trough and into the water. She hadn't expected it to be quite this cold, and the shock of it made her gasp loudly in protest. She stood in the trough for just a moment, until her feet and legs adjusted to the temperature, then she slowly lowered her body into the water.

Jay heard Jennifer squeal, and knowing she had just stepped into the water and wasn't wearing a stitch, he groaned, feeling that part of him that had just begun to relax grow tense and swell. He was hard again. He closed his eyes and tried to go to sleep, but that didn't seem to work, either. In fact, nothing seemed to be working except that part of him that throbbed painfully each time Jennifer splashed.

It was going to be a long night.

The first thing that amazed Jennifer was just how fast her body cooled off, and how quickly the refreshing coolness began to grow cold and change to chilling discomfort. By the time she had soaped her body twice and started to lather her hair, she was shivering. She scrubbed it and rinsed it once, then lathered it again. She ducked her head under the water a second time, holding her breath and running her hands through the long strands to separate the tangles and rinse out the soap. When her head broke water, she was gasping for breath.

She was twisting her hair into a rope to squeeze out the water when she heard a brushing sound on the tin roof that covered the lean-to where the horses were. She glanced up, just in time to see a section of rope about three feet long slide off the roof and into the trough with her. Instinctively she reached forward to throw it out of the trough, when the rope whipped into an *S* shape and then twisted into a figure eight. The word *snake* exploded inside her head, but it wasn't the word she screamed.

"Jay!"

She began slapping at the water, trying to drive the thrashing snake back far enough so she could get up and over the side of the trough without being bitten. By the time Jay had sprung from the bed, she was screaming hysterically, but he wasn't sure what was wrong. He had seen there wasn't anyone around her as he streaked across the porch. As he hurdled the fencing around the corral, he was able to understand only two of the jumbled words that Jennifer was screaming in such a state of frenzy. Over and over he heard it, his heart pounding in his throat: "Snake! Jay! Snake!"

She had made it to her knees when she felt his arms go around her and pluck her from the trough as if she were no heavier than a leaf. She locked her arms around his neck, still chanting the words like a litany. She was shaking and shivering uncontrollably by the time he carried her across the porch and inside. He lowered her to the floor and forced her arms away from him. She looked at him as if he'd slapped her, her body twisting to get close to him. But Jay held her away from him, turning her slowly, his eyes scanning her body as a mother would do with her newborn, only he wasn't counting toes. He was looking for puncture marks.

Finding no evidence that she had been bitten, he picked her up and carried her to the bed. But when he tried to put her down again so he could get a blanket to wrap around her, she clamped her arms tighter around his neck, whispering hoarsely through chattering teeth. "No, Jay. No."

"It's all right, love. It's all right now. I've got you." With Jennifer still in his arms, he picked up the blanket and returned to the bed, sitting down with her in his lap. "Jennifer?" he whispered. "Listen to me. Were you bitten anywhere? Jennifer?"

It was no use. She wasn't responding to anything he said, but she sure as hell was hanging on to him. "Easy, sweetheart," he said, pulling away from her just enough to see her face. He cupped her cheeks between his hands, looking down at her closed eyes. "Jennifer, look at me," he said. "Open your eyes and look at me." He shook her gently and her eyes fluttered open. For a moment she appeared to be having trouble focusing, then the fog cleared. "Are you hurt? Do you feel any pain?" She shook her head. "Are you sure you weren't bitten anywhere?"

"I'm all right," she whispered, her arms coming up to lock around his neck, her next words muffled against the warmth of his strong neck. "Don't leave me alone in the dark."

He kissed her head, tucking the blanket around her. "I won't, angel. I won't." She curled tightly against him, one arm still clenched around his neck, the other gripping his arm. For a long time he sat that way, whispering soft words, kissing her face, one arm holding the blanket against her, the other beneath the blanket stroking her from her thigh to her softly rounded hip.

Gradually her breathing eased, the shivering only intermittent now. Jay could feel just how smooth and silky her skin was, how round and firm the breasts pressed against his naked chest were. He was on fire everywhere she touched him, but her skin was like cool satin, every inch of her round and feminine and soft, except her nipples, which were rock hard. And so was he. He had been aroused for a solid week. And it had taken every ounce of strength he possessed to keep himself off her. What little residue of self-restraint he had managed to retain was expended with the energy released when he raced to her side. Not a thimbleful remained. Jay was like an old, cracked pitcher. One touch and he would shatter.

He felt her stir, and his body stiffened.

"Jay?"

"Hmm?"

"You were right. I shouldn't have bathed in the dark."

"It was my fault. I shouldn't have let you."

"I won't do it again."

"You've got that right." He pulled back, holding her at arm's length, looking at her beautiful, clean face. "Are you okay?"

She nodded. "A little shaky, with a whole new appreciation for light." She paused. "The snake slid off the roof and fell in the water with me. I didn't know they could climb."

"The serpent tempted Eve from a tree, remember?"

"What was he doing on the roof at night?"

"More than likely he was living in the lean-to. When I put the horses in there, he probably went up one of the posts. I would guess he found the roof was too slick and too slanted for him to crawl across."

"So he slid into the trough with me."

His hand went around her neck, his thumb stroking her soft, damp skin. "Not intentionally, I'm sure. Snakes don't care for water."

"What about cottonmouths?"

"It's too dry around here for any kind of water snake."

"Do you think it was poisonous?"

"It could have been. I don't know. But you're lucky you weren't bitten." He dropped his head back to rest against the wall. "Jesus! I'll never forget the sight of that snake thrashing around in there with you. It scared the hell out of me. I thought you'd been bitten at least a dozen times." He opened his eyes and looked down into hers, his hands gripping her shoulders firmly.

"Jay . . . you're hurting me."

He eased the pressure. "I ought to beat the living daylights out of you for scaring the hell out of me like that. Don't you realize that if that snake had been poisonous and had bitten you, you could be dead right now?"

She leaned forward until her lips brushed his throat. "And if I were dead, Jay," she whispered, "would you miss me?"

"Christ!" he said. "Jesus Christ! I would do more than miss you. It would have been the biggest regret of my life."

Apparently she liked that answer because she sighed and nuzzled him some more. "Why, Jay?"

"Because I would have let the best-looking piece of ass around slip through my fingers."

He heard her gasp, felt her body stiffen, but before she could react further, he locked his arms tightly around her. "I'm joking, angel. Don't get your drawers in a bunch."

"I'm not wearing drawers, Jay. I'm not wearing anything."

Jay groaned. "Don't remind me," he whispered. "It's hard enough."

"I know," she said. "And it's poking me in the hip."

"It serves you right. Fishing for compliments like you were."

"It's the only way I can get around you, Jay. You're not very generous in that department."

"I'll start working on that," he said, kissing her face. "In the meantime there is one area in which I can be most generous."

"I'd rather you practiced on your compliments."

Suddenly he rolled with her in his arms, falling down to lie across the bed, his body pinning hers beneath him. "Wanna start now?" he asked, biting her ear.

"No," she said with a laugh, pushing him away, but not too far.

"Too bad," he said, kissing her eyes. "You've got the funniest-colored eyes I've ever seen. They're like flowers."

"Thank you, I guess."

His hand slid down her throat, lingering a moment at the soft beginning of a swell, then dropping lower to find her breast. He followed with his head. "And you've got the sweetest little breasts . . ."

Jay's being suddenly was filled with the gentle fragrance of her hair, and something primitive and urgent leapt within him, something too strong, too overpowering, and too damn good to stop. He was a man, with a man's desire, and it had been too long since he'd had a woman, and he knew the moment he touched her that just any woman wouldn't do. Jenny. Only Jenny.

"God . . . Jenny . . . love . . . I want you. Too much," he whispered against her breast. "Too damn much." He groaned suddenly, the husky tones of desire in control of even his voice. The heat of the unspoken message stabbed into the center of her, like a key unlocking all her secrets and releasing all the love and passion she felt for this man. His mouth searched and found hers waiting; Jennifer returned his kiss with the same eager passion he gave to her.

"Do you know what it's like to touch you like this?" he asked.

"No, but I know what it feels like when you do. Is it the same thing you're feeling?"

"If it isn't, it should be," he said, his mouth covering her breast. Her body jerked in response.

For now there was only one man and one woman, one common drive pushing them forward. She moaned as his mouth moved over her, leaving a trail of fire everywhere he touched. She wasn't so naïve as to think this thing between them was settled, or that it would be smooth sailing from here on out. Tomorrow was another day. And with the return of day, and the reminder of who they were and what they were about, the old roles would come back into play. Tomorrow the hard, cynical man would take charge of her life. But it wouldn't be the same as it had been before. Now there was a deeper link, a newborn understanding that was steadily growing between them. He had his mission and his past. And she had her independence and her future. But there was tonight. Just for tonight he was hers completely —hers in a way she had never known him. Warm. Gentle. Relaxed. Teasing. And for now very, very aroused.

Her heart picked up a new beat, her breathing strong and deep. Jay's hands moved over her, as if he had known her for a thousand years, known just where to touch her lightly, making her body jerk in response, and just when to coax, and just the right thing to say, and just where to put his hand and drive her wild.

His mouth came back up to hers, his tongue stroking and seeking. She stiffened and pushed against him when his hands drew her thighs apart, his own moving to lie where hers had been. She felt him hard against her, but she couldn't think because of the heat building within her. He kissed her until she was dizzy, his tongue stroking her again and again until she whimpered.

Her body was aching now and she moved restlessly beneath him, her hands stroking his back, then moving lower to grip the smooth, tightly clenched muscles of his buttocks.

"Yes," he groaned into her mouth. "Touch me, Jenny. Touch me like you want me."

Her fingers raked the contours of his back and hips, then came around between them. When he flinched, she jerked her hand away.

"No angel, I want you there. I want you to touch me," he whispered, his words coming hot and sweet against her skin. He gripped her tightly and rolled them both to their side. His hand closed over hers, bringing it down to rest against his hardness. Her hand trembled with uncertainty, and she felt him smile, the soft hoarseness of his voice rippling across her like a cool breeze. "It's all right. You can't hurt me," he said.

"Jay? I don't . . ." She buried her head against the tight muscle of his arm.

"What is it? What's wrong? Does this embarrass you? Would you rather not . . ."

"I'm not embarrassed. Not with you."

He released the breath he was holding. "Then what is it?"

"Show me, Jay. Show me what to do."

"Jesus!" he said softly. "Just talking to you like this is pushing me too near the edge." His hand came out to take hers again. "Put your hand around me," he said. "This way." He closed her fingers around him tightly and began to move her hand in the way that pleasured him.

He kissed her again, the rhythm of his tongue against hers matching that of her hand surrounding him. Then with a shuddering groan he pulled her hand away. "Jennifer, you know what is going to happen if we don't stop . . ."

"I have a pretty rough idea."

"It's going to get a hell of a lot rougher if you don't tell me to leave you alone right now."

"If you want to stop," she whispered, "why don't you?"

"Because," he said into her mouth, "I don't want to stop. But I'm warning you now. If you don't tell me soon, so help me God, I won't be able to in another minute." He saw the tension of indecision pull at her face. She wanted him, he was sure of that—at least her body did. So what held her back? Where did this hesitancy come from? He paused and raised his head, looking at her, remembering the night he had asked her . . . *How long has it been for you* . . . And she had thrown a coffeepot at him. His eyes returned to Jennifer. *Naaah,* he thought. *She couldn't be.* No matter how much she protested or claimed otherwise, there was no way on God's green earth that Jennifer Baxter could be a virgin.

Absolutely no way.

Jennifer saw the flare of lust deep in his eyes, the sharp lines of desire that were etched around his tightly held mouth, and she felt the steady tug of indecision. She wanted him, but something within her remained timid still. Was it because Jay was so blatant and obvious? Was it because the demand of his desire was so potent and without constraint, frightening because of the intensity of it? In truth, it was both reasons that halted Jennifer in sudden confusion, not knowing how to proceed. Scarcely breathing, she waited for him to draw her against him, relaxing her, easing her fears with that way he had of melting her with just a look, weakening her resistance with just one patient kiss, as he had done so many times before.

"I take your silence for submission," he said. He had played his hand with as much forbearance as he could muster, and now what little patience he had managed to scrape together was completely gone. His concern for her timidity and hesitancy had given way before the onslaught of his desire and need for her. That, and the prevailing feeling that she had known the feel of a man between her legs before—and in all likelihood, more than once.

A shocked gasp caught in her throat and her hands came against his chest in a show of resistance. Holding him at arm's length, she said in a breathless whisper, "You are jumping to conclusions. My silence was in a negative form. I don't want . . ."

He silenced her, his fingers coming over her lips. "Sweet Jennifer, you no longer have a vote."

She was immediately aware of just how thin the ice she skated upon was when an almost lecherous smile spread across his mouth. His hand shot out and clamped around her wrist. "It's time," he said, reaching for her other hand, "to settle this thing that exists between us once and for all. You want me and I want you. One of us needs to take the initiative, and I've decided it will be me. The issue is settled and no longer a topic for debate."

The frankness of his words and the realization of his intent turned her protests into a weakening cry of despair. She jumped out of bed, taking the blanket with her, and turned to flee, but his arms came out, first one to block her way, then the other to seal off her retreat. She backed against the wall, his arms braced on either side of her. "You were made for loving," he said huskily, ripping the blanket from her.

Her nudity.

It was her beautiful, primitive nudity that struck him like a blow. The picture of her would be forever etched upon his mind; the way the moonlight penetrated the dark interior of the cabin, touching her with a moonbeam, her dark head with its wild, fierce hair tangled about her, the fair skin that gleamed like polished pearls; the way she stood motionless and lost.

God help him, but he wanted her, even more fiercely than before. For weeks his desire for her had driven him, filling him with burgeoning pressure and stealing his resolve. He had denied it. But no longer.

He took her in his arms, trapping her against him. Her breasts hardened into sensitive points as one hand came up to caress her, igniting every nerve. His mouth came down hard upon hers. She pushed against him in a feeble attempt to escape his passion and the drugging sensation that threatened to disarm her, but he pulled her more firmly against him, his lips slanting across hers, devouring the sweetness of her mouth. He was relentless in his demanding search of the warm depths of her mouth, stroking her with his tongue. Jennifer made a small whimpering sound deep in her throat. And Jay, his blood heated to the intensity of raw animal passion, was excited and filled with the need to express a powerful, unsatisfied craving for her.

A flame, intense and burning, licked up from low in his belly and up to his chest like a wrenching pain. His blood hot, he was anything but the expected haven of safety for her. Digging his hands almost painfully into her hair, he yanked her head back and brought his mouth down on hers with crushing force, his body aflame with the rush of lust that surged within him.

The kiss was too forceful, too filled with his unquenchable thirst, to dominate her, to possess her with an almost violent need. She waited for the kiss to grow more gentle, as it had so many times in the past, wanting to respond to that Jay, to kiss him back with all the pure-hearted passion in her being. But this other Jay, this insatiable and intense man who was filled with a restless and frightening desire, terrified her. She pushed away from him, ducking under his arms and fleeing to the other side of the bed, drawing her arm across her mouth to wipe the insulting kiss from her lips, which still felt the numbness of his brutal assault.

"Stay away from me or—"

"Or what?" he said, advancing slowly. "Or you'll scream?" He unbuckled his belt. "Or you'll scratch my eyes out?" He yanked the belt through the loops with a loud whoosh! And that slapped her in the face with the reality of what was happening. "Or will you love me to death?" His voice was soft with satisfaction.

"Jay . . . I mean it. Don't come any closer."

"Your threats are weak, angel, and my purpose is strong. I'll not be turned away again. I trailed you over half of Mexico, putting up with more shit than I would take from any living creature. I've coddled you and nursed you and taught you to survive. I've backed that tongue of yours with lead, and men lay dead because of it. I've watched you dress in the darkness and seen the way firelight kisses your skin. Early in the morning, before the sun had burned away the mist, I watched you let down your hair and brush it, twisting my guts into tighter knots, each stroke a reminder of what you do to me, of how much I wanted you. You've flirted and made eyes at me and moved your body in ways that make a man remember the feel of a woman thrusting beneath him. You've tempted me, teased me, denied me. You've run as wild as a Gypsy, my girl, but tonight it stops. You need a man to tame your wildness, Jenny. Now. And here."

Jennifer was so shocked, she could only stare at him. A tremor went through her as she stared into his hard blue eyes blazing with emotion. She swallowed hard, then gasped in surprise when her eyes dropped to the four buttons down the front of his pants as he began to unbutton them. The implication of it left her feeling torn. She had resisted his advances for weeks, and although she was not entirely innocent, she was still a virgin—something she could not protect against many more attacks of this nature.

"Jay . . . please. Can't we talk about this?"

"There'll be no more talking. Not for a while. Tonight I'm going to break you to the saddle. I'm going to ride you until you yield or crumble like a biscuit. I'm going to take everything you've offered me, every delightful inch you've used to tease me and drive me to distraction."

"You can't. Not even you would dare something like that." But as she said the words, she knew in her heart that Jay was capable of that and more. Stunned, her eyes were still focused on those buttons, all open now, the pants riding low on his hips. Her defenses were so shattered with the reality of what was happening, she slowly raised her eyes to his face for the few swift passing seconds it took for him to reach her.

Wide-eyed, Jennifer stood mute, not even trying to find the words that would reason with him, knowing in her heart that she wanted this as much as he did. Watching him remove his boots and slide his pants over his slim hips, she felt dizzy with wanting, breathless from what she knew was about to happen. With a low growl he caught her to him, taking her in his arms and turning. Jennifer swallowed the gasp that rose in her throat. It wasn't a gasp of fear or even one of denial, but rather a gasp of sudden awareness. The waiting was over. The bold warmth of his alien hardness hot against her thigh reminded her that her innocence would soon be a thing of the past. The bedropes groaned as he lowered her to the mattress, and followed her down, covering her with his body.

She shuddered, breathless and dizzy from the intensity and force of the hot kisses against her mouth and throat, dropping lower across the soft mounds of her breasts. Without really knowing why, she moved against him in eager response, the swift intake of his breath telling her that she had done something that pleased him, and she stole a quick look at his face above hers. The moonlight gave off just enough light for her to see his eyes were blue-black now, hard with passion. She felt dryness claw at her throat, her body growing warm and embarrassed at the way she

had behaved, remembering how those scalding eyes looked
their fill at her nakedness, then she turned her head away
and closed her eyes as if by doing so he wouldn't be able to
see.

"Don't turn away from me, Jenny. You've nothing to be
ashamed of. Angels pale by comparison." He let his eyes
travel over her once more. "You are beautiful, and yet
beautiful seems too inadequate a word to describe it."

Jennifer tensed and buried her face against his chest
where the hair curled dark against his skin. As the familiar
scent of him reached her, she relaxed, whispering against
his hot flesh. "I think you are beautiful too."

"God," he whispered. "Even the sound of your voice
goes over me like a caress. I'll never have enough of you.
Never." He kissed her possessively, his mouth hot with the
passion of a warrior in battle claiming his prisoner. And
suddenly she felt something within her give and confusion
warred within her, her emotions torn, her mind at battle
with the yearning of her heart and body. She wanted to join
with him, to mate and be one with him, for being something separate and apart brought her only restlessness. He
gave her no peace. Not any longer.

Never again would she be able to look upon his beloved
face without her heart wrenching. Never again would she
hear the sound of his voice without her breath catching in
her throat.

Her whole being shuddered as if suddenly awaking from
a long sleep. She loved him with his pensive silence; she
loved him with his golden throat exposed, his head thrown
back in laughter. She loved his pride and his arrogance, his
self-assuredness. She loved that swaggering walk and the
burnished gold that streaked his hair. She loved that mouth
that could say such delightful things and kiss her in such a
delicious way. She loved those hands that would kill for her
and then touch her possessively. She loved those eyes when
they were light and teasing, and when they gleamed black
with the heat of passion.

She yearned with passionate desire to give herself to him completely, to pour out her very heart's blood to him. But she wanted as much in return. He wanted her and that should have been enough. But it wasn't. She wanted more, so much more from him. Her heart was burdened with it and sang out from the insanity of it all.

She began to draw unto him, nestled like some tiny creature, and the dearness of it set his limbs to trembling and his body caught fire. She clung to him as the flames swept over him. When he kissed her, and her mouth, soft and moist, welcomed him, he felt as if his veins would burst.

His spell was taking firmer hold of her now. She knew he was waiting for her with all the seething potency he possessed. She could feel the powerful, clinging weight of him now, bringing her down to be devoured. She knew then that it wasn't enough for him to possess her body. Her entire being—her freedom, her girlhood, her independence—were all sinking beneath the deathly grip of his raging desire and strong physical will. He wanted her totally and completely, taking what she offered and demanding more.

And Jennifer gave it. Always a giving person, she was even more so when love was involved. Led by blind instinct, she accepted him and relinquished herself to him. Vivid and intense, a warmth flowed through her and she felt herself opening like the beak of a small, hungry bird, taking, accepting, begging for more.

Suddenly Jay pulled away from her, staring down into her face, a frown of puzzlement marring the perfect line of his brow. "Why?" he said tightly. "Why would you come so willingly after denying me for so long? Why now? Why like this?"

"I don't know," she said. "I don't understand my emotions, the response I feel. I know only that when you look at me I get all warm inside and when you touch me your will becomes mine."

He smiled and drew his finger across her lips very gently. She wrinkled her nose as her hand came up to chase his finger away. Who would have thought it? Beautiful. Open. Passionate.

And his.

Everywhere he touched, she burned. Even the slightest flutter of his warm breath across her skin left a smoldering trail of fire. She was all warmth, and hot, hot desire.

"Jay . . ."

"Don't fight me, Jennifer. Not now." Then with a groan, "Dear God, not now." He kissed her throat, moving over the curve of her shoulder. "I can't help what's happening between us any more than you can. I don't know how to fight it anymore. I've done everything I could to keep this from happening. I tried to make you hate me . . . so much that you wouldn't be able to stand the sight of me, let alone my touch. Even tonight, I tried . . . I tried to keep my thoughts and my hands off you. I was whipped before I started. Even before I heard you scream. Before I carried you wet and slick and sweet-smelling in my arms. I'm a man, Jennifer. I ache. I want. I need. I'm not made of iron. I can't fight anymore. I want you. I intend to have you."

"Wait . . ."

"I'm through with waiting. You want me. I've known it longer than you have." When he thought she was going to say something, he said, "I won't let you deny it, Jenny." He kissed her. "Not any longer."

The bittersweet melody of his words lingered in her head, and still she waited for the words of denial to rise in her throat, words hurtful and caustic enough to hurl against him and quench the flame of lust that set his body aflame. But the words would not rise. Not this time. Not for this man.

He loomed above her, weighted, alive, and familiar, and suddenly something within her opened in recognition and it was as if she knew him. With every fiber of her being she understood that this complicated man had been denied so much in his life. She had no knowledge of the facts, but the ruins were there, smoldering still.

He was in position, and she was open and so wet that he couldn't hold back any longer. He pushed into her, squeezing his eyes shut as he felt her tight warmth close around him. God, she felt good.

And then he stopped.

He had reached the barrier.

The one that wasn't supposed to be there.

"Shit," he said hoarsely, the blood pounding against his ears. He dropped his forehead to rest against hers. "Aww, Jenny . . . shit!"

But it was too late now. He couldn't stop. His mouth closed over hers, knowing he was going to hurt her. "Jenny . . ."

Some pagan warmth within her blossomed instinctively at the sound of her name. She felt as if she had been only half alive, as if part of her had lain dormant, waiting for this man to bring his magic and touch her, bringing her to life. Her hands came out to caress the muscles of his biceps, feeling the warmth and power of him drawing her and she shuddered, aware of the pressing heat of him covering her.

Man . . . He was so different from her, so different and new, she wanted to learn every secret, to discover every texture and smell that was a part of him. She buried her face against his shoulder, inhaling the warm, sexy fragrance that was his alone . . . masculine . . . natural . . . and very arousing.

Her body was racing ahead of her now as his hands moved over her, knowing just where to touch and the exact pressure to use, drawing a moan from her parted lips that sounded like a throaty purr. The answering chuckle stirred the desire to a thicker intensity within her, and she wiggled beneath him, trying to get closer. And then he began to make love to her, touching, talking, an overture of little melodies that built to a higher pitch and escalated tempo until she was mindless with both wonder and delight. She was like a starving person seated before a banquet. She wanted to taste it all.

He touched her, inflamed her, showed her things about her body she never knew existed, then he wrapped her in the fierceness of his desire for her, only to leave her whimpering with need. It was nothing like she had imagined, for truly she could have never dreamed such as this. And when the moment came, she knew she never would have enough of him.

His hands went under her buttocks and he lifted her to meet him. "Jenny . . . sweet, sweet Jenny," he whispered against her throat. Everywhere he touched her she was like velvet, hot and wet and sweet. The madness of it consumed him and he drove into her, swift and hard and true. She let out a strangled cry of pain. Her body went rigid. She could not breathe. She had no thought save the intense burning of untouched flesh that had been so violently torn.

He froze, the muscles of his arms trembling as his entire being shuddered.

He was inside her. At last.

All the way inside.

And it felt good. So damn good.

"Jay," he heard her whisper, and he almost lost it just hearing her say his name.

Silence hung over them. "I judged you wrongly, yet even that knowledge isn't enough . . . I can't let you go, Jenny."

He began to move within her, easing himself deeper. "Put your legs around me. Hold me to you, darling Jenny. Let me give you something in return for what I have taken."

Jennifer felt him deep inside her, knowing he had taken nothing, for how could she ever consider it in that way when it had been so freely given? "Love, you're so tight and it's been too long. "I can't get enough of you," he said with a groan. "I don't think I will ever have enough. Lord, Jenny, you were worth waiting for. I've never felt anything so good. He lifted his lips, drawing himself up, then slowly lowering back down. Again. And again. Over and over, until he had shown her the way of it and she matched his perfect rhythm.

"I can't wait any longer. Come with me, Jenny. Come with me now, my wild Gypsy love."

Her eyes flew open and something leapt between them.

"Oh, God," she said in a low, husky whisper, her hands holding him fast against her. "Why did we wait so long?"

This time he did lose it. When he felt her own body jerk and heard her whimper, he smiled and nipped her throat. "You're one hell of a woman," he said, feeling satisfaction like he had never known. And it was true. There wasn't another woman in the world like her. By God, she fought him, and ran like a Gypsy, wild and free, along beside him, and even in this, even when he made love to her, she wasn't about to be outdone. *God! Had it been real?*

Yes. It was too good not to be.

He collapsed on top of her with a groan. He heard her sigh, felt the sweet ruffling of her breath as it fluttered over him. He was too spent, too weak to do much more than nuzzle her neck. He lay that way for a time, and when he rolled over, still holding her against him, he saw that she was asleep. She sighed and moved in her sleep until she was resting comfortably in the cove of his arm, her head on his shoulder, one leg thrown over his.

Right.

That was the only word he could think of to express the way he felt. Right. There was something right about what had happened between them. There was something right about the way she felt, sound asleep and curled against him. There was something right about the peace he was feeling inside. Something right about this woman. And there was something right about keeping her beside him for as long as he could.

He leaned over and kissed her mouth, softly enough that she didn't stir, but hard enough to seal the bargain. He lifted his head and caught the slightest curl of a smile upon her lips. He lowered his head and closed his eyes. There was also something right about the way a man felt when he knew he had satisfied his woman.

But there was something wrong.

And Jay pondered upon it, his mind going back, searching for the cause. Then he remembered. He had wronged her. He had misjudged her. He had thought . . . no, not only thought, but he had treated her as if she were no virgin. He wasn't usually such a bad judge of character. But he had erred, and he wasn't a man to let something like that ride. He would make it up to her. Before things were finished between them, he would find a way.

He was almost asleep when he heard her.

"Jay," she whispered.

"Hmm?"

"You still have the worst sense of humor."

Jennifer's head was lying on Jay's shoulder, her long hair like the wind-whipped tail of a kite across his chest. He smiled, absently running his fingers up and down her arm. "It didn't seem to bother you a minute ago."

"It doesn't bother me now." She kissed his chest. "Close your eyes and rest for a little while."

He raised one eyebrow. "Are you trying to distract me with sleep?"

"No. I'm trying to get you rested up."

"Oh? And why would you suddenly be concerned with my being rested?"

"Because I want you to make love to me again."

Up popped Jay's head. "I'm rested enough for that," he said, still amazed at her incredible lack of guile, her remarkable honesty. Out of curiosity, he asked, "Why?"

"Because I think I almost got the hang of it. One more time and I should have it down pat."

Jay was thinking she had it down pretty good as it was. "You get any better and I'm a dead man."

She rolled over, on top of him. "Then prepare to meet your maker," she said, and kissed him soundly.

He didn't feel much like talking after that.

PART III

These impossible women!
How they get around us!
The poet was right: can't live with them, or without them.

Aristophanes, *Lysistrata*, 411 B.C.

13

⚯

It was either Eve or Cleopatra who had said, "I don't give a fig for snakes."

And by the time Jennifer rode beside Jay through the dusty streets of Matamoros, Mexico, and started across the Rio Grande into Texas, she was the third woman in history to feel that way.

Jay had killed two snakes during the week that had passed since the night one had fallen in the trough with her. The second episode came two days later, when Jay woke up and found a diamondback curled inside the crown of his hat. The shot had awakened her. The next snake Jay blew to kingdom come was one that had frightened Jennifer's horse, causing him to throw her. It knocked the lights out of Jennifer and scared the hell out of Jay.

"I was beginning to think I'd never see Texas again," she said as they splashed through the muddy waters of the Rio Grande. It was easy crossing this time of year; it had been a hot, dry summer and the last trickle of melted snow that fed the headwaters of the Rio Grande in the mountains of Colorado had all but stopped.

In the distance, Brownsville looked like little loaves of bread baking in the afternoon sun, just as it had the day she left. They rode through town, going down a road of deep dust that billowed belly-high to a tall horse. They passed an abandoned wagon bed that lay in a pasture, a mesquite bush growing through the seat—a marker that told Jennifer they were less than a mile from the gate that opened onto Aunt Winny's ranch.

"How much farther?" Jay's voice cut through the throbbing headache she had been fighting all day.

"A couple of miles to Aunt Winny's. Another mile or so to my place."

"We'll put up at your aunt's for a few days." His eyes went to the swollen purple knot on her forehead, then dropped to the scrape on her cheek. "You need to get to bed, and there's no one else living at your place, and with you being unmarried . . . I'm sure the ladies of Brownsville would find it easy to castigate any beautiful, young schoolteacher they found with a man sleeping at her house." She turned to look at him as he rode beside her, the sunlight caressing his golden features, drawing from the depths of his vivid blue eyes the naked emotions that hovered there. "You would not be an exception, I'm afraid."

His words were kindly spoken, but it was a cruel reminder of the condition her reputation was in. He was right, of course. She couldn't let him stay at her house. But his being right did little to allay the bitter taste of reality. "It's so kind of you to be concerned about my reputation at this point in time."

He stared at her, a frown gathering between his eyes. She looked away. "I daresay it would have been more to my benefit had you shown this much concern for my reputation a week ago, although it's a little late for such thoughts now."

"Don't be bitter, Jennifer. It doesn't become you."

"Neither does the word *whore.*"

Jay jerked Brady's reins so hard, the gelding dug in with a squeal and sat back, digging up a choking cloud of dust. At the same instant Jay's hand whipped out to jerk her reins, his jaw tight and clenched as he looked down at her. Once again he had that hint of towering authority about him, that almost regal bearing that always reminded her of the military. He looked hard and brutal, capable of anything at this moment. She flinched and leaned back. "Don't you ever"—his voice slashed at her with the force of a knife —"let me hear you say something like that again."

She stared at him without blinking. "Why not? It's the truth."

He dug his hands into the thick braid of hair at her nape and yanked her dangerously close, his face almost touching hers. "Which? That you're a whore? Or merely that the term is an unflattering one?"

"Either. Both."

He released her, almost throwing her away from him. "To save my life, I don't know why you get ideas like that in your head, or where you find the justification to express them."

"You, of all people, shouldn't have to search too deep for the answer to that."

"One night of pleasure, angel eyes, does not a whore make," he said, urging Brady forward.

Her own horse started forward as the color drained from her face. He saw the change and felt it twist his insides, as if he had struck her. "Is that what it was? Pleasure?"

Jay stared at her in disbelief, his eyes glittering their darkest blue. The taut planes of his bronzed face grew even harder. "And what," he said icily, "would you call it?"

"Being used." As soon as the flippantly tossed words left her mouth, Jennifer knew she hadn't spoken the truth. She could never truthfully accuse Jay of that, regardless of his motives. Pleasure, he had called it, his words having the clarity of truth. For he *had* pleasured her, far beyond anything she had ever hoped to feel. He hadn't used her; she had received as much from their mating as he had. But she was hurt. And if she was going to be honest about that as well, she would have to say it wasn't because Jay had made love to her. It was because he hadn't tried to touch her since.

"I see," he said, and pulled the horses up. For a moment he sat beside her, staring into her face as if he could find something there, some clue as to which direction to go with her. Then, with an oath, his hand locked around the back of her neck, he nearly unseated her a second time as he jerked her forward. "Bitch," he said. "Beautiful little bitch!" He jerked her head closer, bringing his mouth forward to meet hers, the force of his kiss almost painful, the anger in each stroke of his tongue unbearable. Suddenly his other hand came forward, grabbing the front of her blouse and jerking. Two buttons came undone. The next instant he thrust his hand down between her tender flesh and her chemise, enclosing her breast and squeezing it hard. As fast as it had happened, it was over. With a stunned expression and swollen lips, she looked at him.

"That," he said with deadly calm, "is what it feels like to be used. Remember it when you're lying in your prim and proper bed with an itch between your legs and no man to scratch it."

"You filthy animal."

He released her, easing Brady into a faster pace, and rode on ahead, leaving Jennifer to follow, eating his dust with a bruising reminder burning across her lips.

About a mile down the road they met a man coming toward them in a buckboard pulled by two blue-nosed mules. He pulled up when he saw them, looking as if he wanted to chew the fat for a spell. Jennifer wasn't in the mood to talk to anyone, and Jay didn't look like he was in the mood to breathe.

"Hello, there," the man said, looking at Jay, then at Jennifer. "Littleton Mosley, here . . . folks 'round these parts call me Little P." Jennifer looked at Jay. He looked like he was going to be rude and sit this one out, so she introduced both of them.

"You folks coming from town?"

Jennifer said, "Yes. We just passed through. We're going as far as the Claiborne place. Is that where you've been?"

"No siree. I passed by there a while back. But you couldn't hire me to stop."

Jennifer thought that odd but didn't mention it. "Could you tell if there was anyone at home?"

"That hotheaded woman who owns the place was working in the garden when I drove by. You can't miss her. She's wearing a blue bonnet—won't do her much good, though. She's already got so many freckles, there ain't room for any more . . . looks like she chewed tobacco and spit against the wind."

"Sounds like you know her pretty well."

"Ain't nobody in these parts who don't. Name's Winny Claiborne. *'Miss* Claiborne to you,' she always says. Cain't figure out why she's so uppity 'bout being a spinster." He paused, scratching his chin. "If you're goin' to her place, you better watch out. She's got an old billy goat that's meaner than a striped snake, and she's always totin' a rifle."

"Anybody courting her?" Jay asked.

"Hell, no! That woman's so mean, the tide wouldn't take her out."

Jennifer couldn't help laughing, then she said, "Why not?"

"She's skinny as a cake of lye soap after a week's washing."

Jay looked at the grin on Jennifer's face, thinking how pretty she was when she smiled. He wished he'd seen her do it more often. Then he remembered he hadn't given her much to smile about. "You get along with her?"

"That woman is past strange. Nobody gets along with her. She's got a disposition that would curdle milk. And there's that other woman who lives with her. She's strange, too . . . both of them like two old crows."

Jay's eyes were still on Jennifer. Then he looked back at Little P. "Doesn't sound like we should stay very long."

"I wouldn't stay there at all if I was you. I'd hightail it back to town."

"You would, huh?" Jay said.

"Darn tootin', I would! I wouldn't spend more than five minutes with that woman. They couldn't mint money fast enough to pay me to do it."

"I'm afraid we don't have any choice," Jennifer said. "Miss Claiborne is my aunt."

"Shoot me for a billy goat! You don't mean it!"

"I'm afraid so," she said, trying to look serious and finding it extremely difficult.

"Well, it ain't your fault. Nobody gets to pick their kin. I guess I'd better be headin' on out. My old lady will be rasin' five dollars worth of hell if I'm late for supper." He tipped his hat. "Giddyap, there, mules!" he said, making a clicking sound with his tongue.

The mules didn't budge.

He slapped the reins against their backs. "Come on, Haw!" he said. "Git up there, Gee!" He slapped the reins again. But no amount of coaxing would make the mules budge.

"I think you've got a couple of sulling mules on your hands," Jay said.

"Happens all the time. A mule ain't worth havin'. A blue-nosed mule ain't worth shootin'."

"They look like pretty good mules."

"They do, at that—but looks ain't everything. When these two get started in a sull, you couldn't make them move enough to break an egg under their collar." He tied the reins and climbed out. "Happens every time . . . always end up havin' to rook em. You'd think they'd get tired of it after a while," he said, going around to the back of the wagon and picking up a handful of hay. He carried it back to where the doubletree was hitched to the wagon, staring at the hindquarters of the two mules. "Can't rightly remember which mule I rooked last time." He glanced at Jay. "I try to alternate—that way the same mule don't get the hot seat all the time." He scratched his head, eyeing the backsides of the two recalcitrant mules.

"Gee looks a little singed to me," Jay said.

"Think so?" He stepped closer, lifting Gee's tail, then doing the same to Haw. "Looks like you might be right." He lifted Haw's tail slightly and wedged the hay underneath it. Then he took out a match and lit the hay, throwing the match and running for the wagon. "Only bad thing about rooking a mule is," he said, heaving as his stomach led him into the wagon, "you gotta be ready to go when they are." He backed up against the seat and sort of dropped himself into it. He picked up the reins. About that time, Haw warmed up to the idea of leaving and lit out, hell-bent for breakfast.

"Nice visiting with you folks," he yelled over his shoulder. Jennifer and Jay looked at each other and laughed. They waited beside the road until Little P rattled out of sight.

Just as Little P had said, Aunt Winny was in the garden. She was wearing her blue bonnet, bent over her okra, a pair of white gloves on her hands as she went after the okra with a paring knife.

She heard them coming and turned to watch them ride up. She dropped the knife into the basket with the okra and pulled her gloves off, poking them in her pocket. Her eyes traveled over Jennifer, then locked on Jay. "Well, I see you found her."

"Just like I said."

"What took you so long?"

"I had to chase her all over hell and half of Georgia," he said, climbing down and coming around Jennifer's horse to help her down. Jennifer saw him coming and dropped from the saddle under her own steam. When she hit the ground, Winny said, "You look like somebody drug you through a cactus. What the blue blazes happened to your face?" She was talking to Jennifer, but her eyes were on Jay. "You beat her up?" she said to him.

"There was a time or two I considered it," said Jay.

"My horse threw me," Jennifer said.

"Looks like you landed on your face," Aunt Winny replied.

"That's about as close to the truth as you can get."

"That's what you've got feet for, you know . . . so you'll use them."

"She had the wrong end up when she came down to do that," Jay said.

Winny looked at Jay. "You growing a beard or eating a porcupine?"

Jay's hand came up and began rubbing the stubble on his chin. "It's the beginnings of a beard, I hope. I never cared much for porcupine."

"Well, I don't like beards. I ain't too sure I like you."

Jennifer had been looking at her aunt, catching the way her orange hair was frizzed and poking out of her bonnet, here and there like bits of straw under a scarecrow's hat. She glanced at Jay and hastily put in, "Aunt Winny doesn't take to people too fast. It may take her a while to warm up to you."

Winny snorted. "He looks about as easy to warm up to as a corpse. You got your tail over your back about something?"

Jennifer said, "I think he's tired of me."

"Why's that? You been on the warpath again?"

"Daily," Jay said.

"I can do my own talking, if you don't mind!" Jennifer snapped at him.

"Why are you raising a ruckus at him? He looks as miserable as you do."

Jay started to say something, but Aunt Winny rounded on him. "It doesn't take two people to peel a banana, sonny," she said. "I'll do my own dressing-down." She was looking at his whiskers again. "If you're planning on sleeping in my house, that porcupine on your face is going to come off." Her small blue eyes got even smaller. "I see you're still growing hair."

"There aren't many barbershops between here and Agua Dulce."

"I got a pair of sheep shears in the barn."

By this time Jennifer was thinking she'd better get the two of them separated or the subject changed. "We met a friend of yours coming up the road."

"That old fool Little P?"

"Yes," Jennifer said. "That's a strange name . . . Little P . . ."

Winny snorted. "Not if you got little privates."

Jay was crude enough to laugh, and Jennifer hastily said, "He said he passed this way and saw you working in the garden."

"He did. Had the gall to stop and ask me if I had any clabber. So I had to leave what I was doing and fetch him a bowl of clabber. It took four bowls to fill up that big belly of his. 'Course, that made Pearl madder than an ole settin' hen when she saw I'd given away most of her clabber. Hell! I'd've given him Pearl if it would've gotten rid of him any quicker. I don't see how his wife puts up with him—like sleeping with a big ole tub of lard."

"The way he talked I didn't think he ever stopped by here," Jennifer said.

"He stops . . . every time he comes up the road, regular as clockwork . . . going or coming. He just doesn't want anyone to know it. I don't know why he thinks a body would be interested in an old blubber butt like him. He smells worse than a tumble turd. I've got sheep that smell better. About the only thing he does well is eat. Always fast with a spoon and slow with his money."

Winny Claiborne looked at the sky. "Looks like I'd better be getting my okra picked. You two go on up to the house. Pearl is there somewhere . . . following the shade around the house, more than likely. She can help you if you need her." She tilted her head toward Jay. "Put him where you want to . . . *after* he cuts that hair and scrapes his face." She looked back at the sky. "I got work to do." She started to pull on her gloves, then stopped, looking at Jay and then at Jennifer.

"You two going to stand there all night like a couple of fence posts?" Her beady little eyes were still going back and forth between the two of them. Then she shook her head. "You must be in love," she said. "You both act stupid."

Jennifer let out a good laugh when she saw Jay actually look like he couldn't think of anything to say. And she would have sworn his face turned a little red. He looked at the sky and back at Winny. "You expecting a change in the weather?"

"Yep."

"What are you predicting?"

"That it'll get dark." She pulled her gloves on and went back to cutting okra.

Pearl—her real name was Pearly Mae—was in the kitchen swatting flies and drinking a glass of buttermilk with sugar in it. When she saw the buttermilk, Jennifer knew it had two tablespoons of sugar in it, because Pearl always drank buttermilk that way. When the back door slammed shut, Pearl turned around, giving Jay his first look at her. As Jennifer had explained, she was a lot like Winny Claiborne in appearance, and since they were distant cousins of some sort, that didn't seem out of the ordinary.

Like Winny, she was tall but not skinny, and instead of carroty red hair, Pearl's hair was steel-gray and twisted into a knot that looked like it had been tossed up there by accident. Her bearing was regal, her clothes stylish and well kept. And she was the best cook in five counties, which was good because Winny didn't know how to light the stove. Like Winny, Pearl didn't form any snap judgments as to whether she was going to like a body or not. Her favorite expression was "Humph!"

But when they walked into the kitchen, Pearl put down her buttermilk and looked at Jay. "You a salesman?"

"No," said Jay.

"Wouldn't let a salesman in my front door," said Pearl.

"I'm not a salesman."

"And he came in the back door," Jennifer said.

"Humph! You look like a salesman to me."

Jennifer leaned over and whispered, "That's a compliment. I'll tell you about it later."

A few minutes later Winny came in with her okra. She looked at Jennifer and the ragged clothes she had on. "You look like something the cats drug up and the dogs wouldn't take. Go take a bath. I'll go over to your place and get some of your things." She looked at Jay. "And you . . ."

"I'm going to town," Jay said. "I need some clothes."

"What you need is a damn barber! The barbershop is in the hotel," Winny called after him.

Jay got his clothes. He also got a bath, a shave, and a haircut. Jennifer got a bath and some clean clothes. All through supper they kept sneaking looks at each other, taking in the changes in appearance, making assessments and judgments, until Winny laid down her fork and told both of them to take a good, long look at each other.

"Now eat your supper and quit your eyeballing. It'll give a body dyspepsia watching you two drool over each other."

After supper Jay went down to the corral to feed the horses and make a few repairs to the saddles. On his way back, he found Jennifer in the backyard, in a hammock that was strung between two elm trees. She was asleep, a copy of *Jane Eyre* collapsed like a rooftop over her chest. He leaned against the tree and watched her for some time. Then he moved beside her and, dropping to one knee, leaned over her.

A moment later Jennifer felt the lightest touch against her lips. When she opened her eyes, Jay was standing over her. He was so near, yet in many ways still very far away. It was the first time Jay had made anything that even remotely resembled an advance toward her since that night in Mexico. She was just contemplating whether she should slap his face or put her arms around his neck when he lowered his head again.

An unexpected stir of expectation rose inside her. He closed his eyes. His mouth touched hers, gently molding to meet the shape of hers. His lips moved upon hers, almost tentative, soft, without force, warm.

Jennifer wanted more, hoping, expecting him to deepen the kiss, to crush her in his arms. Yet he remained passive, the sensation of being kissed enhanced and frustrating at the same time. He seemed to enjoy kissing her, but he made no move to touch her or even kiss her more forcefully. She was uncertain as to what she should do. If they both remained this passive, she would never feel those strong arms close around her. She raised her hand to the back of his head, pulling him closer. *Jane Eyre* fell to the ground.

There was something thrilling and gratifying about taking charge of the kiss, because she was getting exactly what she wanted; felt just a little wicked because of the memories it stirred of another time she had been in his arms. With a soft groan she opened her mouth, feeling his body stiffen with surprise, then relax as his tongue came forward.

"No man can resist kissing a sleeping beauty," he whispered, his lips warm and firm as the words brushed against her.

"What makes you think I want to see two fools with their lips glued together, fornicating in my own backyard?" Pearl said.

Jay and Jennifer both looked up to see that Pearl had come outside to hang the mop over the clothesline. "We were hardly fornicating," Jay said.

"What were you doing, then?"

"I was whispering something in her mouth."

"And I can well imagine what it was." She stopped under the clothesline. "You lock your bedroom door tonight, Jennifer. You hear?"

They both laughed when Pearl slapped the mop over the clothesline and stomped into the house. "Fornicating in the backyard," she said, going up the steps. "When I was a young girl, no one would have dared."

"You never were young, Pearl. You were born old," Winny said, coming around the side of the house and following Pearl inside. "At least they've got enough sense not to do it in the front yard," she said. Then, with a quick look in their direction, Winny closed the back door.

After Pearl left, Jennifer watched Jay lower himself to the ground and prop himself against the elm tree. He was wearing a faded chambray shirt, the soft blue color against his tan making his eyes seem lighter, more alive. He reached up and, giving Jennifer's hammock a push, listened while she told him about Pearl.

Years ago Pearl had run off with a corset salesman. It happened only a year or two after she had come to live with Winny. He had showed up on their doorstep one Sunday afternoon, and when Pearl opened the door, he said, "Hello, lovely lady. I'd like to introduce you to a new line of—" Pearl had yanked him into the house and closed the door. "Show me what you've got," she'd said.

He must have had a lot, because according to Aunt Winny, Pearl didn't surface for over a week. Winny left trays in front of the bedroom door and always picked them up empty, but when they finally came out, Pearl and the salesman were both looking a little pale and weak. Two days later Pearl, dragging her traveling bag in one hand and her traveling man in the other, climbed into the salesman's wagon and drove off. Three months later Winny opened the front door to see Pearl standing there, her hatbox, her bird cage, her liver tonic, and her traveling bag beside her. "I'm back," Pearl said, and stepped inside.

Winny looked out the door. First in one direction and then in the other. "Where's your corset salesman?"

"Wore out," Pearl said.

It was never mentioned again after that.

When Jennifer finished, Jay kept on pushing the hammock. Overhead, a breeze fluttered the elm leaves, and a locust started to buzz. Jennifer closed her eyes, listening to the sounds around her, the steady creak of the hammock telling her Jay was close by. She drifted off to sleep.

It was almost dark when she opened her eyes and sat up. Jay was still propped against the tree, asleep. She came to her feet quietly, lifting her skirts and walking softly by. His hand came out quickly and locked around her ankle. Her hand came out to steady herself against the tree.

"Did I scare you?"

"No, but you almost sent me tumbling."

He was still holding her ankle, his thumb stroking where a man's thumb had no business being. "I don't think this looks too good," she said. "You've got your hand under my skirt."

"But it's a long way from where it would like to be."

"Don't . . . don't talk like that. Turn me loose. I need to go inside."

"Need or want?"

"Very well, I want to go inside." She tried to leave.

"Wait . . . stay out here a little longer," he said, releasing her leg and coming to his feet.

"Jay, it really would be best if I went in."

She was right. There was nothing to be gained by detaining her, by staying out here with her like this, putting himself through more torture. Yet he could no more stop himself from detaining her, from thinking about the things he wanted to do with her, than he could stop breathing. She was his one weakness, and he couldn't seem to help it. For over a week the memory of that night in Mexico flooded his consciousness and fired his blood, while his common sense told him that this was one beauty he should leave alone.

He looked down into the face that was turned up toward him. God! What a face! Hers was a face that made a man go a little crazy when he saw her. In her eyes was the kind of look a man would do anything for. A king would abdicate a throne for a woman like this; battles were fought, poets made immortal. Jesus! What would it be like to have her love?

"Are you afraid of me?"

"I have reason to be, don't I?"

"It pains me to think so."

"After the fact," she said. "It didn't seem to pain you at the time."

"You think not?"

"I think you enjoyed it. I think you're like a cat, Culhane. You like to play with people, whether you are hungry or not."

"Oh, I'm hungry," he said. "You'd be surprised to know just how hungry I really am." He lifted a hand as if he would touch her. She took a step back, giving herself time to search her mind for direction.

"You may be hungry, but I'm not being served. Not tonight. Not anytime. Not to you."

"I want you, Jennifer."

"Oh? And what am I supposed to do about that? Shall I lift my skirts and let you take me here . . . in the yard . . . backed up to a tree? Or should I leave my door unlocked and await you all perfumed and willing in my bed? Tell me, just what does that imply? Marriage? Is that what you seek?" She laughed, a mocking sound that sliced across him because of its bitterness. "I think not. I think it's just a liaison you're after. Someone to warm your bed until we get to Weatherford."

"I can't offer you marriage."

"And I never thought you would. That makes this conversation pointless, doesn't it?" She turned and reached for her skirts, but his hand came around her arm.

"You let me take you once. What's the harm in it now?" He traded places with her, spinning her around and backing her against the tree. His eyes searched her face. "You can't hide what you feel. Your eyes tell me all I want to know. You still want me. And you know, just as I do, that one night will never be enough."

"Let me go inside, Jay."

"You can go to hell for all I care, but I'll never let you go."

"You don't have any choice. I don't belong to you. I never have."

"Liar!" he said, his mouth covering hers, his body pushing her against the rough bark, forcing her lips open with his kiss. He kissed her harder, deeper, the desperation in his kiss pushing her until she moaned and lifted her arms around his neck. He tore his mouth free, his breathing harsh and rasping. "Damn you," he said. "Damn you for the little liar you are." His hands came around her throat, his thumbs pushing her chin up, forcing her to look at him. "You belong to me, lady, and I'll tell you why. Because I touched you and you opened like a flower beneath me, because you never gave anyone what you gave to me, because I pumped my soul into you and you took it and more, because I'll wring your goddamn lovely neck if you ever let another man touch you like I did." He stopped and looked at her, seeing the pale face, the wide eyes. He dropped his forehead against hers. "Jenny, Jenny, Jenny. You've got me all torn up inside." Then he made a strangled sound and wrapped his arms around her, pulling her to him gently. He held her close, rocking her against him. He didn't try to kiss her. He didn't speak. But his silence, the way he was holding her, the unleashed tension she felt vibrate in his arms told her more than his words or even his kiss ever could have.

"Jay . . ."

"Don't talk right now. Just let me hold you for a minute more, and then . . ." He took a deep breath and his body trembled. "And then I'll let you go."

"But, Jay . . ."

"No. Don't say something you'll want to take back tomorrow. Don't tell me anything you'll regret."

She already regretted loving him, but she could do nothing about it now. "But I want you to know . . ."

"I know," he said. His hands threaded through the hair on each side of her face, tilting her head back so he could see her. His eyes searched hers. "Can you understand what I'm saying, Jennifer? I know. Dear God, I know, and it's eating me up inside."

"Then why . . ."

He sighed, drawing her head and turning it to lie flat against his chest, his chin resting on the top of her head. "I can't deal with all that right now. This is too new. And it goes against everything."

"I don't understand."

"I know you don't. How could you, when I don't understand myself? You're right, though. You're smart to fight me. I'm no good for you. I want you like hell. But even when I want you the most, I could kick myself for it. I'll hurt you, Jenny. In the end I'll hurt you. There's too much garbage in my life."

"Tell me what it is. Sometimes talking about it helps."

"Leave it be, Jennifer."

"But—"

"Leave it," he said harshly, but he took her hand and led her across the yard.

The kitchen was dark; the light coming down the hall was from the front room. Jennifer started down the hall, then stopped and turned around. Jay was standing where she'd left him. "Come on," she whispered.

"You go on. I'll bed down in the barn."

She whirled around and went back, and going around behind him, she pushed him along to walk in front of her. "You've got to pay your dues, Jay."

"Dues, hell! They want to peel my hide. They're worse than two old cannibals. It isn't safe to sleep in the same house with them."

She smothered a laugh. "It's just their way. Once you've passed the test, you'll see."

He stopped, looking at her. "Has anyone?"

"What? Passed the test?"

"Survived," he said with a groan as she began dragging him into the room.

As she thought, Winny and Pearl were in the front room, Pearl sitting on the sofa hemming kitchen towels, Winny at a small game table sorting seed into piles to be dried and put away for next summer's garden.

Jennifer went to the piano bench. Jay had the misfortune to sit in Aunt Winny's collapsible rocker, which unfortunately collapsed. When he hit the floor, the look on his face was so funny, Jennifer couldn't help laughing. Jay scowled at her and heaved himself up, tossing the chair cushion at her as he did. The cushion came sailing toward her and she leaned to catch it, coming too near the end of the bench with all her weight, and it tipped over, dumping her on her fanny with a startled "Oh!"

She sat there in a swirl of yellow gingham, trying to decide the most graceful way to come to her feet when Jay's hand came out, palm up. She gave him her hand and he lifted her to her feet. "That," he said, whispering in her ear as she came up, "is what happens when you laugh at others."

Jennifer sat back down on the piano bench, careful to get in the middle this time.

With a "Humph!" Pearl picked up her hemming and bumped Jennifer off the piano bench. "You two rattle-heads can have the sofa."

So Jennifer and Jay sat on the sofa, and Jay, apparently exhausted from all the travel and bored out of his mind, escaped by going to sleep.

"Has he been drinking?" Winny asked.

"I don't think so," Jennifer said.

"He looks like a drinker to me," Winny said.

"He looks like a carouser to me," Pearl said.

"Well, he's a United States deputy marshal, so you're both wrong," said Jennifer.

"Marshals can be drinkers," Winny said.

"And carousers," Pearl said.

Jennifer looked at Jay, wondering if he was hearing any of this. She was afraid they would start asking questions about the past few weeks and she didn't want to answer them—not with Jay in the room. She looked at Pearl. She looked at Winny. She looked back at Jay.

"Why are you squirming?" Winny asked.

"She's got worms if you ask me. She's too scrawny. Nervous and scrawny . . . it's a dead givaway," Pearl said.

"I don't have worms!" Jennifer looked at Jay. He was still asleep. She lowered her voice. "I'm just tired."

"Go on to bed," Winny said.

"I thought we were going to talk about the *recent* unpleasantness," Pearl said.

"What unpleasantness?" asked Jennifer.

Winny gave Pearl a sour look. "That's Pearl's term for the time you were in Mexico."

"It wasn't unpleasant," Jennifer said.

The glasses on Pearl's nose slipped. "That's what I was afraid of," she said.

"Oh, shut up!" Winny said. "Can't you see she's plumb tuckered out?"

Pearl's eyes roamed over Jay thoroughly. "I can see *why* she's tuckered out. Maybe it's the same reason *he's* looking so tuckered out."

"I'm going to bed," Jennifer said. "I'll take the pink bedroom. We can put Jay in the front bedroom, if that's all right with you."

"You ought to put him in the breeding pens with the other studs," Pearl said, giving him the once-over again. "Still say he looks like a salesman."

The next morning Jennifer decided to go to town with her aunt and Pearl. Jay was chopping wood when she found him. "I'm going to town," she said, coming across the yard toward him.

"I hope you're taking *them* with you."

"I am." She looked at his smooth brown back and felt an

extra thump in her heartbeat. "Why are you chopping wood? There's plenty stacked by the shed."

He stopped chopping and turned to face her, the ax hanging loosely in his hands. Jennifer just stood there looking at him as if it were the most perfectly natural thing in the world for her to do—and in a way it was. Everywhere he was golden, from his hair, which looked much darker soaked with sweat, to the sheen of perspiration on his face, which gave his skin a polished look. His body was dusted with fine golden hair that became a little darker and a little thicker as it spread onto his chest. There was no doubt about it. He was as fine a sample of manhood as could be found anywhere. "I just need something to do . . . some sweaty, physical labor," he said.

"It looks like you've found what you were looking for." She glanced back at the house, seeing the buggy. "There's Aunt Winny with the buggy. I've got to go. It may be almost suppertime before we get back."

"I'll enjoy the peace and quiet," he said, watching her run across the yard, holding the skirts of her proper blue dress in one hand, the other on her head to keep her hat in place.

Jay wasn't anywhere around when they returned. After changing out of their dress clothes into work clothes, Winny went to work in her garden and Pearl went to slop the hogs. Jennifer was piddling around the house.

When Jay opened the back door, Jennifer was standing just inside the door with a hammer in her hand.

"What are you doing with a hammer?"

"I'm going to put a nail up here so Aunt Winny can hang her bonnet on it when she comes in."

"You got a nail?"

She fished around in her pocket and extracted one. It was, she would have to admit, a big one.

"Do you need a nail that big, just to hang a bonnet on? It looks like a railroad spike to me."

She looked at the nail. "I think it is," she said, and laughed.

"What did you do while I was gone?" she asked, holding the nail in place.

"Not much."

"Like what?" She gave the nail a whack, hit it wrong, and it flew across the kitchen.

Jay picked up the nail and came back to her, taking the hammer and driving the nail in. He turned and handed her the hammer. He didn't look like he was in a very good mood. She wasn't sure he was even going to answer her question when suddenly he said, "At three-thirty I read the Montgomery Ward catalog from cover to cover. At four o'clock I tried to take a nap in the hammock, but that blasted goat kept chewing on my boot. At four-thirty I pried what was left of my razor out of that damn billy goat's mouth. At five I drank a glass of warm milk and ate a piece of cold chicken. At five-thirty I played four hands of poker against myself. At six you came home, so I could tell you, *I am not staying in this lunatic asylum one more night!*"

14

He stayed one more night.

In truth, he stayed several nights. As a matter of fact, he stayed a whole week. But Jay wasn't the least bit happy about it—acting as bothered as a rattail horse tied short in fly time. And Jennifer wasn't sure just how much longer she could put him off. The horses were sufficiently rested. The tack was repaired. Her family in Weatherford had been wired days ago. And Jay was ready to leave, and told her so in so many words. But she stalled, wanting just a little more time with him.

"Jennifer," Aunt Winny said, seeing the two of them squared off like Grant and Lee, "for two people to get along, one of them had better be good at taking orders," a comment that drew a startled look from both contenders.

Jay scowled, a look directed solely at Jennifer. "Can you be ready to leave tomorrow morning?"

"Maybe," she replied.

Jay, looking like his nose was out of joint, said, "Let me rephrase that. *Will* you be ready to leave in the morning?"

"*Maybe* . . . and that's final!"

Jennifer knew Jay had been ready to leave a week ago, knew putting it off was making him as sore as an old bear. But in spite of his cranky mood—which Jennifer suspected had only a little to do with Aunt Winny and Pearl—he had been cordial to her. The problem was, Jennifer didn't want Jay to be cordial. Anything but cordial. Arrogant was better than cordial. Overbearing was better than cordial. Angry was better than cordial. Cordial was a strain on the nerves. Cordial was like she wasn't there, something she didn't know how to respond to. He was so meticulously cautious. She never thought to see a man like Jay Culhane behave that way. As they moved into the second week of cordial, Jennifer began to drag.

When Winny walked into the kitchen, Jennifer was sitting at the table, making a list of things she wanted to buy when she went to Fort Worth. "What's the matter with you? Your face looks like a train wreck."

"I don't know. I think I need a liver tonic."

"What you need is a man."

"I'll take the liver tonic."

Winny went to the sink and washed her hands. She dried them on one of the towels Pearl had just hemmed. "You don't need a liver tonic. I've been watching you. You're in love."

"I'm not."

"You are."

"I couldn't be."

"You are."

"I don't want to be."

"You are."

"Damn!" Jennifer said, pounding the table. "Damn! Damn! Damn!" The pencil rolled across the table and fell on the floor.

"You still are," Winny said, and hung the cup towel on the peg. "Beatin' the daylights out of my table won't change nothing."

"Aunt Winny, what makes you think I'm in love?" Jennifer asked, picking up the pencil.

"I'm observant . . . one of those rare people that does more listening than talking."

"How come you knew before I did?"

"I pay attention to the signs."

"What signs?"

"The lovesick signs."

Jennifer was looking skeptical. "What, exactly, are love-sick signs?"

"Just a lot of little things that go on, things that say you're in love. Things that are as plain as milk."

"Can you give me an example?"

"I can give you a lot of examples."

"Give away," Jennifer said.

"When I hand you the furniture polish and you pour two teaspoons of it into the cake batter, you're in love."

"I thought it was vanilla!"

"When the best-looking bachelor in five counties stops by and asks you to take a stroll with him in the moonlight and you say, 'Whatever for?' you're in love."

"I hardly *knew* the man."

"When the minister tells you, 'Jesus was a Jew,' and you answer, 'Only on his mother's side,' you're in love."

"Someone told me that was true."

"When you get out of bed and put your drawers on backward, you're in love."

"It was dark!"

"When you pour the dishwater in the churn and throw out the milk, you're in love."

"They were in identical buckets."

"When you make up my bed with me in it, you're in love."

"I want the liver tonic," said Jennifer.

"You want Culhane."

"I am *not* in love."

"You are, and once more, he's in love with you."

"You don't have to get angry!"

"I'm not angry."

"Then why are you shouting at me?"

"I'm not shouting."

"Just give me the tonic."

"Jennifer Baxter, you're a fool!"

"It runs in the family."

"You're worse than my sister."

"Mama says I'm just like you."

"She does?"

"She does."

"Yes," Winny said. "I suppose you are." She looked at Jennifer, her hands going to her hips. "Well, there is no reason to stand here arguing like a couple of chickens after the same worm . . . not when there are things to be discussed."

Jennifer stood up. "I just came in here for the liver tonic."

"When is the last time you spent some time alone with him?"

Jennifer sat back down. "When Pearl locked us in the storm cellar."

"That was an accident. That doesn't count," said Winny. "When was the last time he touched you?"

"When I poured out his bottle of whiskey and he tried to choke me."

"That doesn't count," said Winny.

"When was the last time you did something together?"

"When we washed the goat."

"That doesn't count," said Winny.

"When was the last time you kissed?"

"I can't remember."

"You need the liver tonic," said Winny, taking it from the cabinet and handing it to Jennifer.

Jennifer swallowed a spoonful of tonic and washed it down with water. She made a horrible face. "Ugghhh! That stuff is wretched. What's it made of? No! Don't tell me." She pushed the stopper back in the bottle and put the bottle away. "You know, I don't understand him. I really don't. I don't understand why he acts like he likes me one minute and hates the sight of me the next."

"It's called sabotage. People end up being their own worst enemies, destroying the things they want the most, things they need."

"That doesn't make sense. Why would he do that?"

"Fear. He's afraid."

"Afraid? Of what?"

"Of succeeding. Of failing."

"You don't make any more sense than he does," Jennifer said hotly, coming to her feet and walking angrily to the window. She could see him now, down by the barn with the blacksmith, who was putting new shoes on Brady. He's so blasted good-looking and so damn stupid, Jennifer thought.

She watched him a moment longer, then turned around. "So . . . how do I handle this? What do I do with a man who's afraid to let himself care?"

"You talk to him."

"Talk?" Jennifer looked at her aunt like they had just met. "Do you know what it's like to try to talk to Culhane? A two-word sentence is a long answer for him."

"If you don't deal with the problem between you, Jennifer, whatever is there will die a slow death, no matter how much love or feeling there is between you. When you don't open up to each other and talk, you slowly poison what you hoped to save."

"If we talked, we'd end up killing it quicker."

"That's the chance you have to take. Are you afraid to take a risk? I'm surprised. You never would have learned to walk if you had been too afraid of falling to ever take a step."

"You don't know how angry he can get, especially when I start asking questions. He doesn't like to talk about himself, especially his past. If I asked him to talk, he'd close up like a clam or tell me it wasn't any of my business . . . or else he would just walk off."

"He's just testing the waters. Pushing you to see just how far he can go. Somewhere in the back of his mind he probably has the feeling that he can't trust you . . . can't trust that you mean what you say. He's got his eye on you. He can't hide the fact that he cares. I honestly believe the man is in love with you. But he's scared. He's asking for proof, not realizing that the more proof he asks for, the more he pushes you, the more he is helping you fail the test. No matter how much you love someone, or they you, you have to face the fact that eventually you will drive the other person away when you continue to put them on trial."

"Wonderful! Neither one of us gets what we want then."

"But in the end he can justify it all by saying, 'I knew she couldn't be trusted.'"

"It sounds like a game of Russian roulette to me."

"Exactly. Sooner or later you're going to pull the trigger and the chamber isn't going to be empty."

"This whole thing is hopeless," Jennifer said, throwing up her hands and coming back to sit in the chair. "I knew better. I should have my head examined. Why am I such a clabberhead? I knew a man like him was nothing but trouble. I knew I couldn't trust him! I knew he—" Jennifer stopped talking to stare at her aunt. Was Aunt Winny crazy or what? Why was she sitting there grinning like a fool?

Winny was grinning and sitting there, calm as a dead fish, a gleam in her eye and a smile on her face. Jennifer was ready to agree with Little P. Her aunt was past strange. "What are you looking at me like that for? Do you know something I don't?" Jennifer asked.

"No. I'm just listening, Jennifer. Listening to what you're saying. You should try it. Why don't you listen to what you just said?"

"Ohh . . . leave me alone. You're just making it worse."

Winnie patted her hand. "I wouldn't want to be in your shoes for all the flax in Flanders," she said, and started from the room.

"Aunt Winny!" Jennifer shouted. "Come back here. I don't know what to do!"

"Talk to him. Get him to talk to you. Show him he can

trust you. You'll have to take it slow. It won't be easy. The closer you get to succeeding, the more he will fight and withdraw. He's a strong man, Jenny, but he's scared. He doesn't want to risk being hurt anymore. It's easier for him to stay where he is—even if he's not happy—because it's familiar and, after all this time, comfortable. You're rocking his boat, Jennifer. He'll do everything he can to get you to stop. Even if he has to throw you over the side."

"You make it sound like I'm pleading for my life."

"Aren't you?" Winny asked, then walked from the room.

Five minutes later Pearl came in with a bucket of milk.

"I don't know why it's so hard to be a woman," Jennifer said.

Pearl put the bucket on the table and looked at her. "Because you have to put up with men," she said.

That afternoon Jennifer was shelling peas with Pearl when she decided to take a stab at establishing some sort of communication between herself and Jay. When she saw him heading out the back door, she called after him, "Have a nice afternoon!"

"I have other plans," he said, and slammed the door.

"Ohh!" Jennifer gritted through her teeth. "He is the most obstinate man I've ever known!"

"You're the one that's obstinate," said Pearl.

"Well, so are you!"

"No. I'm just set in my ways. *You're* obstinate."

"Then what is he?" asked Jennifer.

"He's a beef-witted fool."

He probably was, but that didn't help her much right now. After a moment of speculation Jennifer decided to give it one more try. She went to look for Jay and found him running a curry comb over Brady's broad back. "Jay?"

"Now what?"

"I want to talk to you. Do you mind if I stay for a while?"

"Suit yourself," he said, tossing the curry comb into the feed bin. "You can stay in here if you like . . . if you don't mind being alone." He picked up the reins and led Brady from the barn.

She followed him outside. "Jay Culhane, you may not think I know what you're trying to do, but I do!"

He sighed and turned to face her. "You may not think I know what you're trying to do either, but *I* do. You are as transparent as glass, Jennifer. I can see right through you."

"Well," she said, unable to keep from looking just a little hurt, "you're sure missing a lot," and she turned away.

Jay watched her go, remembering the hurt look on her face. She was angry and upset and it was all his fault. *It's what you wanted, isn't it?* But as he led Brady into the corral, he was thinking that getting what he wanted didn't carry as much satisfaction as it should have. In fact, he didn't feel satisfied at all. He felt like a louse. He didn't like to see her hurt. He didn't like turning her away. He didn't like being cold. He wanted her happy. He wanted her in his arms. He wanted her to feel the heat of his passion. He couldn't go on like this. It was eating him up. It didn't matter that he knew he wasn't good for her, that he would only hurt her in the end. It didn't matter that he was trying to push her away from him for her own good. None of it mattered because he wanted her and he knew without a doubt that Jennifer wanted him just as badly.

Sometime later, when Jay walked into the house, Jennifer was frying pork chops. She put the last chop on the platter and turned away from the stove, almost dropping the plate when she saw him standing in the doorway. He looked at her crisp gray dress, The spotless white apron, the tiny waist, the incredible eyes, and . . . the platter of pork chops.

"I didn't think you knew how to cook," he said, his voice hard.

"I know how to cook *normal* food on a stove with pots and pans."

Remembering the way she botched everything she

cooked on the trail, he was so angry, he forgot why he'd come to find her. "What else did you lie about?"

"I haven't lied about anything!"

He wanted to throttle her. He wanted things right between them. But he couldn't trust her. How many other things had she lied about? He looked at her for a moment, then said something under his breath and turned away.

"Aren't you hungry? Don't you want to eat?" she called after him.

"I'm not hungry."

That did it. Jennifer picked up an empty pot sitting on the cabinet and slammed it down on the table with all her might. It sounded like a cannon had just gone off in the kitchen. Jay jumped as if he'd been shot. Then he turned toward her as she rounded on him. "I've had it with your surly attitude and your snide remarks. You've got your tail over your back about something, and I want to know what it is." For a moment she thought he was going to leave. "Don't you *dare* walk out when I'm talking to you," said Jennifer.

"If I didn't, I wouldn't get anything done. You're always talking, Jennifer."

The fool was looking amused now, and she considered throwing the pot at him. "I don't understand why we can't get along. It seems one of us is always angry. When I try to talk to you, you snarl—"

"And when I try to talk, you look at me like I just filled your mouth with sheep-dip."

"That's because you . . . oh, never mind! I don't think it's possible for us to both be in the mood to communicate at the same time."

That cocky half grin was back, and he was having trouble remembering that he had caught her in another lie. *Well, it was a little lie.* "We've communicated once or twice, I think. The results were, as I recall, dangerous."

"Dangerous?"

"When we both want to communicate, Jenny, when

we're on the same bent, we don't talk . . . we ignite." He was speaking softly now. "I remember what it was like between us. I close my eyes and see your silhouette in stardust. Every time I breathe, I inhale the scent of my soap in your hair. Whenever I look at you, your clothes seem to melt away and I see you as you were then, naked and wet and trembling in my arms." He saw the struggle in her eyes, the nervous movement of her hands. So much hurt and anger. *Why do we keep doing this to each other?* He couldn't change the way things were . . . who she was. Who he was. But he felt like a young boy when he was around her. And he wanted her so much, he ached. He still had a little time with her. Nothing between them could ever be permanent. He would have to be content with that.

He had taught her desire; taught her to want him. And now she was looking just a little lost, like she had been given a new body, alien and strange and new. Things were happening inside her—desires and wants and needs—yearnings she had neither the knowledge nor the experience to control. Her behavior, her actions, her looks were anxious and wavering, full of caprice and a touch of dread. She seemed fragile now, bewildered. She looked away. He gave her a minute, content to look at her in these whimsical surroundings, the plain cupboards with their flamboyant collection of china, the old speckled coffeepot stuffed with flowers she had yanked out by the root. He felt a prick of desire laced with sympathy, striking him hot and then cold. Her very state of incertitude told him she was unaware that she was courting him, for it was obvious she had not the faintest inkling how to initiate what she ached for. He could not help but take advantage of her unease, her lowered guard, to cross the room. She kept her head turned away from him, so that when he looked at her, he saw not her face but her graceful neck, the white, fragile skin, the inky spirals of a few determined tendrils of hair that were so like her in their refusal to cooperate. He lifted his hand and wrote *Kiss me* across her neck.

She sucked in her breath, her shoulders scrunching up to chase his hand away. "Don't do that," she said in a breathless way. "It tickles."

He dropped his head to kiss her where the skin was infinitely soft and fragrant. The hand clasping her waist squeezed tightly. His breath was warm, like fingers curving around her throat. Jennifer trembled at the scorching path left by his fingertips, sliding across her throat to cup her chin and tilt her head up. "You see, I remember a great deal. We're good together, don't you think? The schoolteacher and the gunslinger. I haven't forgotten, angel eyes . . . have you?"

Forget? How could she? The memory of it was burned upon her heart. There would never be anyone like him. Never. How could she ever be content with any other? How could love be so miserable? Why must it be such an explosive merging of love and anger, and jealousy and misunderstanding, and yes, even hate? Why had she chosen to love this volatile, unpredictable lawman who was always turning her ideas and values upside down? And then it came to her. The big question: *Why can't I make him love me?*

He pulled her back against him slowly, his hands coming around her waist and upward to caress her breasts, his breath strong and warm across her sensitive flesh. He turned her in his arms. "Something good happens when I touch you, like this . . ." He kissed her mouth softly. "Like this . . ." One slender finger trailed the line of her collar to the button between her breasts. "And like this . . ." His hand slipped inside to touch where the skin was full and tight.

Too much, he thought. *I want her too much.* So much that he wanted to shove her back against the cupboard and raise her skirts and pump out this thing that weakened him like a drug. So much that he couldn't get her close enough, couldn't touch her in enough places. "Does this embarrass you? Does it make you want to run away?" The husky, fluttering tones of his voice floated over her like the stroke of his hand.

"No," she said, dropping her forehead against his chest. "It makes me . . ."

He drew her head up so that she was looking at him. "Makes you what?"

She closed her eyes. "No," he said, kissing each of them in turn. "Open your eyes. Look at me, angel . . . Jennifer, it makes you what?"

"Want you."

Her words surrounded him in a warm vapor. "I want you too," he whispered. "I want you too damn much. More than I should. So much that I can't think straight when I'm around you."

His breath mingled with hers now. "Come outside with me, Jenny. Let's go down to the barn."

"No, Jay, I can't."

"Yes, you can." He took her hand. "Come on."

"Not now, Jay." He heard the unsteadiness in her words, the hesitation in her breath, the slight tremor that shook her hand he still held. Not now . . . He felt the sense of urgency jerk as if shot, then flow out of him. What was she telling him? Not now . . . not tomorrow . . . not ever.

"Then when?"

She stared at him, her confusion obvious. He knew that she fully intended that it would never happen again between them, that in spite of what she felt, what she wanted, she intended to deny them both the pleasure of it. But understanding her intentions, he found he wasn't discouraged —frustrated, yes, but not discouraged. He would have her again, for there would be a time when her body would rule her mind. They had a long way to go before she would be able to admit what he already knew, but there was a slight joy in knowing that time would come.

As if severed by a bolt of lightning, they sprang apart when Winny walked into the kitchen. She eyed Jay. She eyed Jennifer. Then she eyed the plate of pork chops. "Where did you get those chops?"

"Mr. Mosley dropped them by on his way to town."

She was still eyeing the chops. "Pearl won't eat them."

"Why not?" asked Jennifer.

"She won't eat pork."

"Why won't she?" asked Jennifer.

"She said it makes you stupid."

"Maybe I should stop eating pork," said Jay.

"I don't know why you're worried," Jennifer said. "You're already stupid." He looked at her, seeing she had not recovered as quickly as he—still looking confused—the look now mingling with embarrassment and what he could only call a spark of anger. She removed her apron and slammed it on the table and marched from the room, banging the door behind her.

Jay looked at Winny and rubbed his temples. "I need something for a headache."

Winny looked at Jay. "I've got something for your head, all right, but you're doctoring the wrong place."

Jennifer walked out of the yard, not bothering to close the gate behind her. She walked as far as the barn and stopped. Rapscallion, Aunt Winny's billy goat, was standing in the doorway of the barn, looking at her like he hadn't forgiven her for the bath she and Jay had given him the other day.

She took a step toward him and Rapscallion tossed his head. Sometimes Rap could be very amicable. At other times he was downright mean. Today looked like one of his mean days. She looked at his long white hair, remembering the terrible time Jay had getting Rap tied so they could wash him. It took all four of them to get him in the squeeze pen after they had a rope around his horns and feet. Then it took about four washings to get the coal oil off him. Even now his white hair was yellow in places. She couldn't understand what made billy goats want to eat everything they came in contact with. And she couldn't fathom how this one had managed to devour the top half of a metal can full of coal oil. And what a mess he was, smeared with coal oil, getting it all over the laundry she'd just hung out. Washing him probably had saved his stupid life. But looking at him now, he didn't appear to be too grateful.

She took another step and Rap tossed his head again, shaking it at her like a warning. "Go butt a stump!" Jennifer said, swinging a wide arc around him. "Go on! Get out of here! Shoo!" She clapped her hands and Rap lowered his head. Jennifer grabbed a shovel that was leaning against the barn door, just as Rap charged. When he was almost to her, she jumped to one side and brought the shovel down with all her might. It made a tremendous noise, the repercussion of it vibrating up both her arms. The handle splintered and broke, and Jennifer cried out as she felt the needlelike spears of wood dig into her hands. Rap wasn't fazed.

His head was down and Jennifer knew it was only a matter of time before he took off after her again. He was too close to the barn door for her to dart in there, and it was too far to make it to the backyard. He would mow her down before she ever reached the gate. The fence that penned the nanny goats was the closest and, ultimately, her only choice. Jennifer lit out. And so did Rap. He closed in fast, so she only made it as far as a broken plow, making a couple of circles around it, trying to keep Rap on the opposite side. For a minute or two it looked like a game of tag. Rap on one side of the plow. Jennifer on the other. Then they came to a standstill, watching each other from their opposite sides. When she caught her breath, she eyed the distance between her and the fence. Then she took off again, wincing as she grabbed one of the boards in the fence to pull herself up. She'd made it as far as the third board when she felt something yank her skirt. Looking down, Rap had a mouthful of skirt, chewing away. She tugged on the skirt and Rap sat back, locked in like a pit bull. She couldn't go up. She couldn't go down. And that was how

Jay found her a few minutes later when he came sauntering toward the barn.

"Looks like you've gotten yourself up a tree," he said, stopping a few feet away.

"Help me down, Culhane. Before this masticating mastodon devours my skirt!"

He didn't say anything.

She turned as much as she could, still maintaining her footing. "Are you deaf as well as dumb? Help me down!"

"I'm not sure I want to."

"What are you going to do? Leave me stuck here like a goose on a spit?" She heard him laugh. "It isn't funny, Culhane."

"That depends on your perspective, angel. From where I stand, it's funnier than hell."

"It isn't funny. He tried to run me down. I broke a shovel over his fool head and he still—"

"I know. For a minute there, I wasn't sure you were going to make it."

"You saw? You watched and didn't offer to help?"

"I'm down here, aren't I?"

"You took your sweet time getting here, you—"

"Bastard." He grinned. "If I were you, I'd talk nicer . . . that is, if you want me to help."

"I don't want your help! Just go away," she said, her voice picking up a quiver. "Go on! Get out of here! I don't want anything from you, least of all your help!"

She heard him sigh and turn away, his footsteps fading. She leaned her head against the fence, thinking that if she ever got close enough, she'd yank his gun from his holster and shoot him with it.

A minute later she heard him approach. Then she felt the pressure on her skirt ease and looked to see Jay coming toward Rap with a lariat. Rap had turned now, lowering his head and shaking it at Jay. When he charged, Jay stepped easily to one side and roped his horns as he passed. Then he tied the rope to the fence several feet from Jennifer. By this time she was already coming down. "Stay away from me," she said, seeing him coming toward her.

She felt his arm go around her waist, the breath leaving her body as she was tossed over his shoulder. "Put me down! I don't want your hands on me! I'm warning you! Don't you dare take one more step! Put me down this instant!"

"Jennifer! Shut up!"

"What happened to her?" Pearl said, holding the door open as Jay stepped into the kitchen.

"She and Rap were going round and round," he said, lowering Jennifer to her feet.

"You're so amusing," she said, feeling her hands burn. She held them out, looking at the splinters. "I need to find a needle," she said, walking from the room.

"Jennifer, let me see your hands."

"You've seen all of me you're going to see," she said, her voice carrying down the hall.

"Well, I've sure as hell seen plenty!" he shouted after her.

"Pig!" he heard her say, and a door slammed.

Jennifer found a needle in Aunt Winny's mending basket. She picked out a few of the splinters, but some were too deep, and she never had been very good at doing anything with her left hand, which meant the splinters on her right hand weren't getting much attention. She heard a door close and figured Jay had left. She threaded the needle through the fabric on her bodice and headed for the kitchen. Pearl could help her.

As she approached the kitchen she heard Aunt Winny say, "Maybe you should let someone else take her on to Weatherford . . . or let her go on the stage by herself."

"You couldn't trust her to go five miles. She'd be back in Mexico before dark," Jay said. "I was hired to take her to Weatherford, and by God, I'm taking her there, come hell or high water!"

"I don't know about the high water, but there'll be plenty of the other," Pearl said dryly. Jennifer decided it must have been Aunt Winny coming in, instead of Jay going out, when she'd heard the door close.

"Your mind's made up, then? You're leaving in the morning?" asked Winny.

"Before daybreak."

"I think you should rest a few more days," said Winny.

"If I stay around her much longer, I'll either end up killing her or going stark raving mad," said Jay.

"Or both," said Pearl.

"I hate to see you leave until you've worked things out. I don't like seeing Jennifer upset."

"If I thought it was possible to work things out, believe me, I'd do what I could. I don't know what she wants. I know what she *needs* . . ."

"I know what she needs too," said Winny.

Jay's eyes snapped over to her and a flicker of understanding passed between them. Jay let out a shout of laughter. "Damn, but I'm beginning to wonder why some man never snatched you up," he said.

"I'm the kind of woman that would get sick having to be nice to the same person every day. If it's marriage you're wanting to discuss, why don't you marry her?" asked Winny.

"What?" It came out like a pistol shot, almost staggering Jennifer where she stood in the hallway.

"I don't think it's such a bad idea," said Pearl. "Not one of her great ideas but not a bad one."

"It certainly isn't one of her great ones!" said Jay. "What in the name of all that's holy would I do with a wife?"

"If you don't know the answer to that," Pearl said, "you couldn't be a salesman."

"I told you I wasn't a goddamn salesman! And I'm not an idiot, either. Marry Jennifer! A man would have to have his rafters loose to take on a job like that."

"Are you saying you won't even consider it?" asked Winny.

"That's exactly what I'm saying. She's run in the wild

too long. I don't think there's a man alive that could bring her around. Marriage . . . Jesus! Just hearing her name raises the hackles on my neck." A chair scraped. "I'll sleep in the barn tonight. You see that Jennifer is ready to shove off before daybreak."

The door closed. Jennifer waited a minute and then went into the kitchen. One look at her face and they knew. "You heard," said Winny.

"I heard," answered Jennifer.

"You going with him tomorrow?" asked Pearl.

"Yes."

"Of course she's going," said Winny. "She's got to see this thing through."

"If you want my advice—"

"Hush up, Pearl. If she followed all the advice everyone is giving her, she would be so confused, she wouldn't know sunup from sundown."

The back door opened and Jay stepped inside. His saddlebags were thrown over his shoulder. "I was wondering," he said, "if it would be all right to get enough coffee to last us to the next town. It would save time if we don't have to go back into Brownsville."

Pearl was already moving to the cupboard. "I was planning on packing up a few things for you to take with you. Just leave those bags on the table there and I'll have them ready to go in the morning when you are." She set the coffee grinder on the counter and started digging for the coffee beans. "Why don't you rest your feet while I get these things rustled together?"

Jay gave Jennifer a quick glance and moved to the table. She was thinking this was a good time to dash down to the barn and get a saddlebag—while Jay wasn't there. She looked at Winny and slipped from the room.

It took her a few minutes to find just where Jay had stashed all their gear. But once she located the saddlebag, Jennifer picked up the lantern and made it as far as the door. She had just turned out the lantern and hung it on the peg when Jay stepped inside. Only one lantern was burning in the barn now, one Jay had sitting on a bench at the opposite end, near the tack room. It was light enough to tell it was Jay who startled her but not light enough to see the expression in his eyes.

"What are you doing out here?" he asked.

"Getting a bag to pack." She started around him.

He caught her arm. "What's wrong, Jennifer?"

"Nothing." She looked down at the hand gripping her arm. "Will you release my arm?"

He didn't release her. She was a fetching sight standing in the half-light, all white, white skin and coal-black hair. He felt a moment of frustration because he couldn't see the color of her eyes. He had a feeling they would be dark purple now, and narrowed at him. He smiled, rubbing his thumb on her arm. "Ah, Jenny, you make it so difficult. How can I accept that in a few weeks this will all be over and I'll go on my way? What have you done?"

"I've done nothing."

"Haven't you?" His other hand came up and pulled the pins from her hair, allowing it to tumble down her back. "Haven't you?" He brought a section of it over her shoulder, rubbing the length of it with the back of his fingers. "I think you have," he whispered. I think you've done a great deal." She inhaled sharply when his hand moved over the swell of her breast.

She slapped his hand away. "I'm your charge, Culhane. Not your chattel."

"You're a little hellcat, is what you are—one quarter refined lady, one quarter hellion, one quarter prim schoolteacher . . ." He paused.

"Yes? And what about the rest? One quarter what? What is the rest of it, Jay?"

"The rest is all woman."

"I'm not something that can be sectioned off into quarters like an orange. You don't know anything about me. I'm not sure you even know very much about women."

"I know more about women than you could ever teach me."

"I'm not so sure. Do you know what I think? All this time we've been together, you haven't seen me as I really am. Not once."

"I see you."

"You look at me, Jay, but you don't see me. When you look, you see someone else."

"You're crazy."

"Who was she? Who is this woman you think I am? I see you . . . a lot of times, when you don't think I know you're watching me."

"You're a beautiful, desirable woman and I'm a man. Why the hell wouldn't I look at you? There'd be something wrong with me if I didn't."

"But that's not the way you look at me—not the way a man looks at a woman. You're looking for things . . . signs . . . clues . . . anything to tell you that you had me pegged right from the beginning. You're being unfair with me, Jay. You won't accept me as I am, yet you won't tell me who I'm supposed to be like. No wonder I'm confused."

"Is that what you are? Confused?"

"Among other things."

Jay couldn't kid himself. No matter what she said or did, he still wanted her. He had learned that much about himself. She was like a fever running hot in his blood, yet he held himself in check. He sensed she would resist him, but she had resisted him before. He felt trapped and boxed in. One minute he felt like he was running out of time, that she would be home soon and he would be forced to ride out of her life. At other times he couldn't wait to get shuck of her. He was beginning to think he'd lost his mind. He was standing here with her, his body hard and trembling in readiness, yet he kept thinking that all he really wanted at this very moment was to hold her. To hold her and understand her.

"Yes," he said softly, "I suppose you are confused. God knows I am."

"There's no reason for you to be bewildered. You're the one with all the answers."

"Answers to what?" He knew without asking what she was talking about. She was curious. She had prodded him before.

"Don't insult me! I'm not stupid. You *know* what I'm talking about."

"Yes," he said, releasing a ragged breath. "I guess I do." He looked off for a moment, then his eyes came back to her. "Why is it so important to you? What has my past got to do with anything that happens now? Why do you think it has anything to do with us?"

"Because your past is part of you."

"The past is dead."

"Not *your* past."

"It's dead, and it will stay that way."

"It's not dead. It's very much alive. Dead things have no power. They're inactive. Dead things can't destroy." She put her hand on his arm, felt the muscle leap. "Your past still has a mortgage on you."

It was a moment before Jay said anything. "My past was buried a long time ago. It doesn't bother me now."

"If it doesn't bother you, why can't you talk about it?"

He opened his mouth to answer her, but the words would not come. She stood in the faint light, looking up at him with an expectant look on her face, waiting. There were so many things he wanted to tell her, things he wanted to say. But he couldn't call the words up. She was still looking at him, as if she was waiting to hear what he had to say. The expectant look began to grow weaker and gradually fade.

He saw the disappointment creep across her features and he thought she would turn away. His hands came up, on either side of her head, holding it tightly, and he drew her against him and kissed her.

She pulled back. "It's no good, Jay. There are too many

barriers in the way. You pull me against you with one hand and use the other to push me away. You think everything can be solved by kissing, that passion will drive the monsters out of your mind."

"You didn't complain about my kissing you before."

"That's just it. It was before. This is now, Jay. Things are different now."

"What's different? I haven't changed. You haven't changed. You aren't cold to me . . . you're a long way from being that. My kisses sure as hell lit your fires a few times—and would again, if you didn't block my way."

"You can't keep relighting the same bits of wood. Ashes don't ignite. You've got to add more kindling."

"What do you want from me?"

"Who are you? Why do you long so to belong and deal with everything by turning away? I've seen you face hardship and danger. I know the kind of life you lead. You would stand up against any odds, yet the fear of a few questions turns you to clay."

He didn't say anything. After a moment she turned.

"Wait," he called after her. "We might as well have this out now . . . it'll eat at both of us until we do."

"I'm tired, Jay. I haven't even packed yet. We'll have plenty of time to talk on the way."

"I thought your head was crammed full of questions."

"It is, but they'll keep one more day."

"You've been itching to quiz me for weeks, picking and hammering. Well, now's your chance. Fire away! Ask what you want. You may never get the chance again. Come on! Ask me! Ask me all those questions I'm so afraid of."

She saw that he was prepared for her to dig deep—not only prepared, but hopeful, because the more she dug, the more pain her questions inflicted, the more he could feel justified in hurting her back. She didn't want to dig. She didn't want to cause him pain. She wanted him to see he could talk to her, to see he could tell her anything and she wouldn't feel disgust and turn her back on him. She wanted him to trust her.

"Well? What are you waiting for? Ask me, damn you!"

"All right!" she screamed. "Who is the woman in your past?"

His eyes said he was ready for that one. There wasn't a flicker of surprise. "The woman was my wife," he said, then turned and disappeared into the darkness. Jennifer followed him with her eyes, staring numbly at the last place she had seen him, knowing he was closed to her again. *The woman was my wife. . . .* The news hung like an elusive shadow over her heart.

15

❧ ❧

It was still dark outside when Jay opened the back door and stepped into the kitchen. Jennifer was sitting at the table, drinking a glass of milk and eating a sausage biscuit, looking a little frayed around the edges. And she was feeling a little thrown together, too —not that there was anything wrong with her dark brown riding skirt and tan jacket, but it was just one of those mornings when nothing went together right. Even her hair, which was normally easy to manage, looked wild and unruly. Her Aunt Winny must have thought so, too, for when she walked into the kitchen, she took one look at Jennifer and said, "Did you have trouble getting dressed this morning, or were you in a hurry?"

"Why?" asked Jennifer.

"You look like you threw your clothes in the air and ran under them."

Jay, who was looking as fine as a new-scraped carrot, had the gall to laugh. So far her day wasn't starting off too well.

A hour later Jennifer was sitting on her horse, ready to go. She had already hugged her aunt good-bye, but Jay was standing a few feet away, still talking to Winny and Pearl. He said something and they all laughed, then Jay turned away to mount Brady. As he turned, he pulled the reins out from under his belt where he had them tucked. Winny walked over to Jennifer, putting her hand on her knee.

"You're as quiet as a bird when a hawk flies over," she said. "Don't fight it too hard. Sometimes it's easier to give a man a free hand . . . if only for a little while."

"Why? So he can run it all over you?"

Jay swung into the saddle; checked Brady, who started off; and looked at Jennifer. She was sulled up worse than Little P's mules. He guessed a little rooking wouldn't hurt her, either. "Do you want to kiss and make up?" he asked.

"I don't kiss strange men . . . and you, Culhane, are very strange!" By the time Jennifer rode out of the yard, a good ten yards ahead of Jay, she was looking about as happy as a rooster in an empty henhouse, according to Pearl.

Jay gave the two spinster ladies a rather fond smile and tipped his hat. Winny looked at him, a teasing gleam in her eye. "You're the kind of man I like, Culhane."

"What did I do to deserve a compliment like that?"

"Maybe I just like the way you snap a woman's garter," she said, holding out her hand to give him a shake. "She's feeling lower than a gopher hole right now, so you'll probably have to give her garter another snap or two along the way."

He laughed. "Maybe I won't have to resort to that."

"Humph!" said Pearl. "If you don't, she'll stay madder than a pig on ice with his tail froze in."

"He'll do what needs doing," Winny said, stepping back. She brought her hand up to shield the bright stab of sunlight shining in her eyes. "She's like a daughter to me, you understand. I wouldn't trade her for an acre of pregnant goats."

"I'll look after her," Jay said.

"Then we've said about all there is to say," she said. "If you're ever back down this way . . . well, I'd be mighty put out if you didn't stop by."

"You wouldn't want to get married, would you?" he said in an admiring way.

"I'll do some considering on that, Mr. Culhane. I surely will," she said.

"You do that, Miss Claiborne," he said with a wink. "You do that."

It was obvious over the next few weeks that Jay had his work cut out for him when it came to dealing with Jennifer. As far as molds went, she just didn't fit into any of them. Trying to understand her was about as easy as trying to hear the color red. It just couldn't be done. And Jay found that baffling, if not irritating, because it had been his experience to wedge women into one of four basic groups, like seasons. It was something he had been doing for a long time, something that had worked—that is, until he'd met Jennifer Baxter.

When Jay was a young man in his prime in Savannah, he found himself besieged by women. And along with the women, which of course he welcomed, came a lot of problems, which he didn't. Of course, Jay—and the other young men of similar background and uncanny good looks—knew what made women happy. But like centuries of men before them, they just weren't able to keep them that way. Straining to understand the feminine mysteries of logic, intuition, and reasoning had more than once pulled Jay and his circle of Savannah's young rogues away from a game of pitch or horse racing. They'd gather around the cotton bales being loaded down at the wharves to contemplate and discuss the one subject that was always in the backs of their minds: women.

It was one such afternoon, as fine a sunny April day as one could wish for, that Savannah's prime was gathered around the bales and barrels, discussing just that. An old black man with wiry gray whiskers, and more wisdom than the Book of Solomon written across his face, happened by, giving the young men a whole different view of women.

"Women," he said. "Now, they're a thing apart. And you'll most always find 'em like your four seasons. First of all, there's your early springs—the kind of thing that just happens when you brush up against one in the swimming hole or on a hayride. Takes a lot of agility, your early spring does. Then there's your hot summers. They're the sort that's always primed and on the lookout—you gotta be careful with your hot summers because you get kinda lazy around them and then they sorta sneak up on you. I had one like that once. My regular gal's mammy didn't go for no foolin' 'round. But I almost had her talked into it once, till her mammy chased me out of the barn with a pitchfork. Next thing I knew, there was your hot summer looking as fine as frog hair and willin' as they come. Easy to be consumed by your long, hot summer." He put his pipe hand down to rest on his knee. As I recollect on what came next . . . guess it had to be your late fall. Now, they're the kind that hit you like a two-by-four up-side the head—that's your late fall. Like a weed that suddenly starts to bloom, here comes this pretty little prissy thing that was skinny as a poker, and now look at her. . . . But your late fall is one you don't want to hang around too long. Always has a mammy with a big rolling pin and a pappy with a shotgun. I almost got caught like that once, still got the buckshot in my shoulder to prove it. If you're lucky enough to have one . . . well, your late fall's one you won't forget. I still remember mine. . . . Whenever this ole shoulder starts to aching, I just think on that little miss I had once—Lawd, Lawd! Her skin was the color of coffee and as fine as cream. After your late fall, there's your hard winter. That's the kind to stay away from . . . 'course, no man ever does. It's your hard winter that finally does a man in, ruins him for all the other seasons. Turns a man into the kind of pappy that carries a shotgun, ready to pepper all the young bucks' behinds. 'Course, I've been married to your hard winter for some forty-five years now, and I have to say, it ain't all bad. Ain't nothin finer than your hard winter when she thaws."

As far as Jennifer was concerned, Jay figured after much contemplation that she had to be your hard winter. She certainly had ruined him as far as any other woman was concerned. And Rand Baxter certainly looked like the kind of pappy that carried a shotgun—not only carried it but knew how to shoot it as well. And lastly, he had to admit that there wasn't anything like Jennifer Baxter when she thawed—absolutely nothing. But he'd be damned if she would do him in.

But there were times he wondered about that. She had come mighty close a few times. But that was a woman's nature. As the Bible says, "Man is born unto trouble, as the sparks fly upward." That could probably be applied to women as well. Around Jennifer, it was a thought that carried little comfort to know that simply meant you hadn't seen the last of misfortune, although he had to admit she hadn't been as much trouble on this last leg of the trip as she had on the first. In fact, the worst thing she had done was to tie the packhorse too loose after they broke camp one morning. While Jay was finishing his shave down by the creek, the horse had pulled loose and quietly slipped away.

Jennifer told Jay what had happened when he returned. "Well, there's nothing to be done about it now," he said.

For a moment Jennifer just looked at him, a puzzled expression on her face. "Didn't you hear what I said? The packhorse is gone!"

"I heard you the first time."

"Aren't you going after him?"

"It would take up too much time to track him through all this brush."

"But my clothes . . . all my clothes were in that pack. I don't have anything to wear but this!" She gestured toward her skirt.

"I'll make sure we make camp by water every night so you can wash your things out."

"Oh, well, that really makes me feel better," she said, and then more hotly, "And just what am I supposed to sleep in while they're drying?"

"I remember a time you found my arms sufficient for that."

"Not anymore," she said, and turned away.

At a place called Calf Creek, adversity struck again.

After all the trouble Jennifer seemed to get herself into whenever she was around civilization, Jay decided it would be better to shy away from towns and do their camping on the trail. He picked a nice shady spot on a small creek and helped her unpack their supplies. Jennifer was so content that she couldn't help singing as she bent herself to the task of making biscuits and frying the last of the bacon. When Jay brought the canteens up from the creek, he stopped on the other side of the fire, watching her. "Thought you didn't know how to cook on anything but a *real stove* with *pots and pans,*" he said, tossing her the canteen.

She caught it with one hand and grinned at him. "I'm a fast learner."

"You're an even better liar."

She wasn't going to let him get her dander up. But it was hard. She was just itching to fling some nasty remark back at him. But she was determined to kill him with kindness . . . if it didn't kill her first. She watched him walk to the horses, thinking he was going to unsaddle them, but when Jay gathered the reins, she knew he was leaving. "Where are you going?"

"Deer's plentiful in these parts. Thought I might find us a tender little backstrap, seeing as how you've learned to cook so well." He yanked the reins and rode off, balancing the butt of his rifle on his thigh as he loaded it.

"Jay . . ."

He spurred Brady into a gallop.

"Damn you, Culhane. Come back here!"

"Such talk for a lady," he yelled over his shoulder. His laughter followed him over the next rise.

"You louse!"

For Jennifer it was quite an adjustment to be in harmony with a man who had all the attributes of a gentleman but wasn't one. A gentleman gave a lady the benefit of the doubt and at least *pretended* to believe her, whether she was telling the truth or not. And there were certain rules and codes of behavior a gentleman would always abide by, especially when he was around a lady. But Jay didn't give a fig for codes and rules and found nothing wrong in breaking them, whether he was around ladies or not—and he would talk about the most forbidden subjects in front of them. Just like the night he'd said, "Little girl, you need a man to make love to you in the worst way." Of course, when she'd replied, "In the worst way? Then that must mean you," she wasn't exactly cleaving to ladylike codes, either.

She finished cooking, then went to sit in the flowers that grew down along the creek. Having more sense than to strip naked in the open, Jennifer pulled off her boots and sat at the creek's edge to bathe her legs and feet. Then she gave herself what Rand called a dab bath—that being the kind the birds took when they splashed in a mud puddle—a little dab here and a little dab there. Everything else clean, she washed her hair, deciding to let it just hang in one long braid down her back. She had just turned back to camp when a loud rumble rolled across the creek, and for a moment she thought it was the distant rumble of thunder—until a band of horses galloped over the rise and down toward the water. From where she stood, it looked like about twenty or so horses were being driven by three men. As far as she could tell, their camp wasn't in the path of the running horses, but knowing how unpredictable a horse could be, Jennifer found the nearest tree and placed herself behind the ample trunk.

When they reached the water, the horses stopped, milling around for a few minutes, then moving to the water's edge to drink. Their sides were lathered and their nostrils flared, obviously having been driven at a fast pace for some distance. The three riders, spotting Jay and Jennifer's camp, rode across the creek.

"Hey, Clark! Looks like someone left us some supper," the youngest of the three said.

"Then we'd best not disappoint them, Threader. Hand me a couple of them biscuits. I'll keep a look out for that damn marauding stud." He reached for the biscuits as Threader dismounted and picked up the pan." "Yeooww!" he shrieked, and dropped the pan.

"Hot, ain't it?" Clark said.

"Naah, it just don't take me long to look at a pan of biscuits."

Clark laughed and turned to the other rider. "Beecher, you keep your rifle ready. That son of a bitch shows up again, kill him. I don't give a shit what Old Man Coffer says. Thoroughbred or not, that horse is a crazy killer."

The one named Beecher reached to unsheathe his rifle, but before he could, a pawing, screaming stallion thundered over the rise and galloped down to the creek, nipping at the band of mares. Clark shouted, "Don't shoot now, you'll stampede the mares. Get a lasso. You, too, Threader."

Jennifer peered around the tree to watch. Within minutes the men had dropped their biscuits in the sand and galloped back to the creek, lassos whirling over their heads. Two men roped the stallion around the neck. The third, Beecher, heeled him.

The stallion was magnificent. Even from what little Jennifer knew about horses, she'd seen enough of Rand's prime horseflesh to know this was as good, if not better, than any stud in their breeding barns.

"What should we do with him now?" Threader asked. "Think we could get him back to headquarters all tied up in a nice little bow for Old Man Coffer?"

"I'd rather tie his ass in a knot and the hell with Coffer," said Beecher.

"I ain't taking two steps with that crazy killer," Clark said. "You keep him tight." Clark dismounted and tied his lariat around the trunk of a tree, leaving the other two men to hold the taut line with their horses. "Toss me that whip of yours, Threader."

Threader pulled the leather that held the whip and tossed it. Jennifer flinched when Clark uncoiled it and began to lash the air with a sickening crack. *Jay, please hurry. I'm trying to stay out of trouble . . . but if you don't hurry . . .*

Just then the whip hissed and lashed across the distance, striking the stallion in the hip. The stallion screamed and strained against the ropes that held him. *Please, Jay . . .* Two. Three more times. *I'm sorry . . .*

On the fourth lash Jennifer pulled her rifle from her saddle, and on the fifth crack of the whip she fired a shot.

"What the hell . . ." Clark whirled and grinned slowly, using the butt end of the whip to push the hat back on his head. "Well, I'll be a sorry son of a bitch . . . will you look what just sprang out of this here tree?" He grinned wider. "Are there any more in there who look like you?" When Jennifer didn't reply, he said, "Just be patient, little filly. We'll have this stud whittled down to size in a minute, then we'll see about you and those—" he paused, letting his eyes slide over her—"tasty little biscuits of yours."

He cracked the whip again, and Jennifer fired, blowing it out of his hand. His hand was red with blood when he drew it back. "You two steady that stud until I take care of this little filly here. She's actin' a mite bucky and needs someone to ride the kinks out of her." He dismounted, holding his hands up in the air, walking toward Jennifer. "Got to respect a woman with a gun," he said, then stopped a few feet away. "Now, what seems to be the trouble here?"

"You three release that horse and be on your way."

"He belongs to us."

"That doesn't give you the right to beat him to death."

"So . . . you'll put the gun away if we release the stud?"

"That's right—"

Jennifer didn't have time to say more because Clark kicked his boot into the soft sand, sending it flying into her face. The next thing she knew, she had been slammed against the tree trunk, the rifle wrenched from her. Rubbing her eyes, she tried to see Clark's menacing face. "We're gonna finish up here, and then we're gonna show you something. You know the best place for a woman . . . to keep her out of trouble?"

Jennifer shook her head.

Clark laughed. "Flat on her back. Legs spread." His hand came up to clench around her throat. "You make a mental picture of that, missy, and you hold it, because I can make it bad . . . or I can make it good for you, depending on how much trouble you give me. Got that?"

Jennifer nodded, almost gagging at the sight of his blood on her clothes.

Clark started to turn away but rechecked himself. "A filly what looks like you ain't a loner. Where's your man?"

"Looking for me?" a low voice behind her said.

Jennifer whirled in time to see Jay step out of the brush and brace his rifle on his forearm, taking aim. "You have until I count to three to get mounted. By the time I reach five, you and those two friends of yours had better be across the creek."

Clark said, "Listen—"

"One . . ." Jay cocked the rifle.

Clark ran for his horse. "I won't forget this," he said, mounting. "We got laws to protect us from the likes of you. Won't take a second to send a wire and have a federal marshal breathing down your neck."

"Jay Culhane, United States deputy marshal out of Fort Smith, Arkansas. When you send that wire, tell Isaac Parker I've almost got this job wrapped up, if I don't run into any more of the likes of you. Two . . ."

Clark flinched and said, "Jay Culhane? Ain't you the one who brought in Blue Duck?"

"Two or three times."

"Wasn't Culhane the one who shot Arizona Fats last spring?" asked Threader.

Clark looked from Threader back to Jay. "That *was* you, wasn't it?"

"He should've stayed in Arizona," Jay said. "Three."

"We're going. We're going," Clark said. "Got any objections to us taking our horses?"

"Leave the stud. The mares are yours."

After the men had cleared out, Jay worked his way toward the stallion, talking low as the horse reared and pawed the air, secured now by one lariat tied to the tree—the one that belonged to Clark.

"Jay, can we—"

"No," he said before she had time to finish. Then, more softly, he added, "The stallion isn't coming with us, but I'll not turn him out like this. Get the axle grease out of my bags." As she went to his bags Jennifer smiled to herself when she heard him mumble something about how he was going to explain to Judge Parker that he'd threatened to shoot three cowhands over a rambunctious stallion.

"This horse has been broke to saddle," Jay said, applying the thick, black grease to the open cuts. The stallion snorted and tossed his head but didn't rear.

"How can you tell?"

"See this white mark on his back? A saddle rubbed him, traumatized the spot, turned the hair white."

"For a sailor you know a lot about horses and gunmen."

"I grew up with horses. As far as men go, they're all the same—gunmen, sailors, lawmen." Jay washed his hands in the creek. "Now, if you can stay out of trouble long enough, I'll go back to where I left that deer and finish cleaning it—if the coyotes haven't beat me to the job."

"I can stay out of trouble."

Jay shot her a questioning look, then shook his head and

mounted. "Unless you expect me to eat sand-buttered biscuits, you'd better mix up another batch."

She made more biscuits.

After supper Jay sat on an old faded Indian blanket, cleaning and reloading his rifle and checking his revolver, spinning the cartridge chamber until Jennifer thought she would scream. Then, without a word, he stood, putting his gear away, and walked to the creek and sat down. After staring at it for a long time, he pulled off his boots and shirt. Then he stood to unbutton his pants, giving her an amused look.

"I plan on taking a bath. You can sit there with your mouth open and watch, or you can find something to do."

"Like what?"

"Like opening that package in my saddlebags. There's something for you to wear tomorrow. Not exactly of the caliber you're used to, but cleaner than what you've got on now."

"Something for me? How did you . . ." She frowned, clamping her hands on her hips. "Did you go into town?"

"Get the clothes, Jennifer, or watch my naked backside."

"Don't talk about me being difficult. You are absolutely infuriating!" she said, marching to the saddlebags. "Why did you buy me clothes?" asked Jennifer, resisting the temptation to look back at him.

He called over his shoulder, "We'll be reaching your folks' place soon. I don't want you to go in looking like something I dragged all the way from the valley by the heels."

She opened the package, finding, as Jay had said, something cleaner, but not of the same quality to which she was accustomed. It did touch her, though, that Jay had included a small blue-satin ribbon for her hair, a brush and mirror, and a small bottle of lavender water, along with the skirt and blouse and underthings. He might think her a pain in the neck. He might treat her like he wished he'd never laid eyes on her. But looking at the small collection of feminine trinkets lying on the wrinkled brown paper, Jennifer knew, with a swelling of her heart, that Jay Culhane was many things, but he wasn't indifferent to her. A man who went to this much trouble . . . who bought things like this for a woman . . . a man like that had to care.

When Jay returned, she was sitting on the blanket, holding the blue ribbon in her hand and thinking, *"A length of blue ribbon to tie up my bonny brown hair. . . ."*

"You can turn around now. I'm clothed head to toe. Nothing obscene to frighten you with."

But Jennifer didn't want him to see how much his thoughtfulness had affected her. She didn't want him to know. She was falling in love with him. And the feeling was too new, too uncertain to disclose, much too personal to share. She just wanted to hold it, like a mother does her newborn, to her breast, to stare at the wonder of this beautiful thing that had suddenly sprung to life within her. She couldn't bear his rejection or his teasing, his taunting remarks, his callous disregard of fragile feelings.

She was afraid she would make a fool of herself if she stayed there, so she went down to the creek to change. She rinsed the blood from her clothes and spread them on a bush, then gave herself another bath, all that blood having undone the first. Putting on just her chemise and drawers, she wrapped herself in a blanket and went back to camp, going straight to her own blanket, where she sat down, using the corner of the blanket to towel her hair.

Jay looked up. "You aren't very talkative tonight, are you? And here I always thought that buying a woman a gift wound her up enough to talk your ears off." He moved to his saddle and spread out his blanket. A minute later he was stretched out, his arms folded beneath his head, his eyes closed.

Jennifer couldn't keep her eyes off him. He looked incredibly tall, lying as he was, long and lean and all male. His belly was flat, his arms slender, but she remembered just how strong they were. His face and hands were so brown—it wasn't easy to forget how fair the rest of his body looked in comparison. The memory of it made her look away.

With a mumbled oath he sat up, removing his gun belt. He took something out of his saddlebags, then began cleaning his pistols, silence rising around them like smoke from the fire. She picked up a twig and drew a map of the state of Texas, making a dot for Weatherford and one for Brownsville. Over where Mexico would be, she made a dot for Agua Dulce. Along the Rio Grande she made another dot for El Paso, and another dot to mark the place they were now camped. Home was still a long way off.

As they often did, and of their own accord, her eyes drifted back to him. Like a favorite pastime, she absorbed the details of his body, something she found to be a lot like reading a book for the second time—so many new discoveries, a wealth of fresh disclosures she'd missed the first time around. *I could spend the rest of my life studying him and still never know all his beauty, his secrets.* He was like the craggy summit of a cloud-covered mountain. Strong . . . enduring . . . shrouded in mystery . . . silent . . . the inspiration of a thousand poems, the object of a hundred expeditions, the focal point in a dozen paintings.

He aroused in her a wild sort of tenderness that she supposed was inspired by just looking at him. But she hated his remoteness. She was growing more certain that she did indeed love him. She didn't want to. She didn't want to be obsessed or devoted to him, like a homeless mongrel, comforted by an occasional crumb, an amused look, or an occasional pat on the head.

Jay watched her out of the corner of his eye, knowing she was going all soft and feminine on him, looking like she was near to crying over those damn ribbons. *You poor, dumb shit,* he told himself. *You knew what would happen when you bought all that stuff. You're gonna make a real fool out of yourself in a minute or two.*

He had feelings for her, and he would be lying to say

they didn't run pretty deep. He cared. He didn't think it would come as any surprise to her. She knew him well enough by now. Better than anyone, he'd guess. And he knew her enough to know she wasn't shy or timid, or even embarrassed. She met things head-on and accepted her feelings as genuine. Well, hell! So did he. Wasn't that one of the things about her that attracted him? The way she was so damn honest about how she felt, what she said? He had sworn he'd never feel this way about a woman again. But he did. And he thought she probably felt the same way about him. But she didn't want to burden him with it, not as new as it was for her. She was private that way.

He watched her for another minute or so, until she took a swipe at her eyes again and looked around in the near darkness with that bewildered expression on her face, and as it always did, that wide-eyed, innocent look brought him to his knees. He waited until she tucked the ribbons inside her blouse and lay down, then he rose and came to her. He knew she heard him, knew he was there. And he knew it would have to be his doing.

He dropped to his knees, then lay down beside her. "Jenny . . ." he said, opening his arms as she turned into them.

"I love you, Jay," she said, crying against his shirt.

"I know you do, sweetheart. I know."

"I don't want to be in love with you. I don't want to be in love with anyone right now."

"I know, but it isn't something we can plan. It happens whether we cooperate or not."

"I'm not—"

"Jennifer," he whispered, "you talk too much." He found her mouth, and undoing her clothing, his hands found her breasts—her perfect, beautiful breasts—and he expelled a sigh of release. Her hair, against which he pressed his face, was silky and cool; but her throat was damp and warm. He kissed it.

Damp and warm was the way he remembered her best.

He kissed her, almost in apology at first, then feeling his own hunger answered, he lost himself in the warmth of her. He wanted her now, just as she was. He closed his eyes, imagining what it would be like to have her, to see her watching him with those wide lavender eyes of hers as he came into her. He groaned as he visualized how they would close when she wrapped those long, coltish legs around his waist.

"Jay?" she whispered.

"What?"

"Why didn't you tell me you were married?"

"I'm not married."

He felt her stiffen. He was amused, because he had known what to expect now that he was getting to know her, and his heart lifted at the thought.

"But you said . . ."

"I know what I said. I said the woman you asked about was my wife. *Was,* Jennifer. Was."

"Was," repeated Jennifer.

"Right," said Jay.

He was still thinking about her—what she had said. It came as no surprise to him that she loved him. He had suspected as much for some time. But she was a proud woman. He knew what it had cost her to tell him, to declare her feelings. And that made him ask himself, *What are my feelings for her?*

It couldn't be love, of course, he was smart enough to know that—grateful to be spared the spreading of that castrating disease. No, he didn't love her, but many of love's facets were there—just a little weaker in intensity. A brilliant instead of a diamond of the first water.

He jumped when she pinched him, a deep, rumbling rush of laughter filling his ear. He looked at her, loving the laughter banked in her eyes, the words that bubbled from her like a happy chuckle. "For a moment I thought you were dead. I just wanted to see if I could get a rise out of you."

"Keep looking at me like you are and you'll get one, all right."

"Oh?" she said, going for him again.

"So that's the way you want to play, huh?" He rolled over her, pinning her beneath him, his hand going down to her rump and giving it a pinch. She squealed and started laughing as she tried to pinch him back, but he caught her and pinned her to the blanket. She grew quiet suddenly, lying still under his searching gaze, the laughter slowly fading from her face.

"Tell me about yourself . . . your past . . . your wife . . . your family."

Jay closed his eyes. He had been prepared for this question for some time. In fact, he was a little surprised she had waited this long to spring it on him. He knew she was watching him, waiting for him to tell her what she wanted to know. "There isn't much to tell."

"Then it won't take you very long."

He didn't say anything for some time. She was becoming accustomed to that in him, and it didn't bother her as much as it had in the beginning. She waited a moment longer, and when he remained silent, she did as she often did around him: started one of those one-sided conversations that drove him insane. If she couldn't motivate him to talk, she could drive him.

"You weren't born of sea foam, and you didn't spring full-grown from the head of Zeus, so you had parents, Jay. What was your mother's name?"

"What difference does that make?"

"Tell me . . . please."

Please. He could never remember her saying that to him before.

"Please, Jay."

"Jessamine."

She smiled triumphantly. "Jessamine . . . it's lovely."

"As she was."

He had turned now and was looking straight at her with

that strange look he sometimes gave her; weary, amused, irritated, a look that was both intense and impersonal, as if he were warning her that no matter how much of himself he gave to her, there would always be something of himself that he held back.

She went on chattering about what she imagined his parents were like, asking questions, waiting for his silence, then baiting him with her verbal seduction until he told her what she wanted to know. The girl was tempting beyond belief, witty, captivating, beguiling with her own brand of charm —a chatty flirt, a sultry-voiced enchantress. Everything about her ate at him like a nagging chorus that replaced his enforced celibacy with the intense need for frantic rutting. She was as provocative, disturbing, and arousing as a candid look at a naked woman.

"Tell me about your wife."

His body tightened like a coiled spring. "Leave it alone, Jennifer."

"Talk to me, Jay."

He closed his eyes. When he opened them, it hurt her that he looked away. She gently laid her hand on his arm. "Please."

He put his hands flat on each side of her face, covering her ears, the pressure firm, dragging her to him, and kissed her. Her hand tightened and curled, digging into his arm. It wasn't a kiss of submission but one of authority, almost punishing in its intensity. It hurt to feel him kiss her in such a cool, technical way, with no expression of feeling—none of the throbbing warmth she had learned to expect. She pushed against him, struggling to break his hold, wanting nothing more at this moment than to get away.

He jerked his head back, speaking in a hard, uncaring way. "That should help you remember what your mouth is for."

She slapped him. "And that should help you remember what my hand is for!"

He released her abruptly and rolled away, coming

quickly to his feet. He walked to the fire, dropping to his haunches to stir the coals to more vivid life, then tossing on a few more pieces of wood. He turned toward her, and she had a glimpse of the gunfighter in him. Her mouth went dry. For a moment she felt what it would be like to face him on the street.

He watched her for a long time, and she was determined not to be the first to look away. She wondered how much longer she could look at him like this without screaming when, the fire glow behind him, he stepped forward like Satan from the flames. A knot forming in her throat, Jennifer watched him approach.

He moved toward her slowly, steadily, without the graceless movement of a man long accustomed to the saddle. His face was impassive, his mouth grim and taut, his lips no more than a hard slash across a masculine face so arresting that it was disturbing.

He was a man who radiated seductive charm like a flower gave off fragrance, sweet and strong. He was destructive, lethal poison with his brand of breathless virility and tolerant charm. Men like him, with their inexhaustible potency, went from conquest to conquest—in the traditional sense of promiscuity—and once the seduction was accomplished, moved on.

She could see it now, something about him, the inexhaustible potency that women didn't want to miss. He came toward her, stopping close, then dropped down beside her.

"I'm—" she began.

"Be quiet."

"But—"

"Do you want to kiss or talk?"

She shut her mouth.

"I always did like a smart woman," he said. He rolled over, bringing her up to lie on top of him, her hair falling like a waterfall over his face. Threading his fingers and lifting the heavy mass, he pulled her closer, kissing her mouth open, his hands stroking her back, kneading, pressing.

"Whenever I touch you, I find part of myself. Don't be afraid of me, Jenny."

"I'm not," she said, pushing him back to the blanket, covering his face in a rush of kisses. It was the first time she had allowed herself this freedom, to kiss, to touch, to take the lead, to be free and uninhibited with him. He lifted his hand to take one inky curl in his hand. "A man can't win," he said with an exaggerated tiredness. "If the devil doesn't get him, a woman will."

A devilish twinkle came into her eyes as she mimicked his action by twirling a lock of his own hair with her finger. "Have you lost, then?"

"A little setback, nothing more." He rolled, reversing their positions, then heaved himself up into a sitting position, and the loss she felt was as immediate as the cool rush of air where his warm weight had been a moment ago.

"Go to sleep."

"I'm not sleepy."

"Don't ask any more questions."

"Every time we make a little progress with civil conversation, you have to quash it."

He turned toward her. "Quash?"

"Quash."

He grunted. "Then leave it *quashed.*"

"I'll think about it," she said, getting comfortable and closing her eyes. He watched the fire for some time, thinking, almost to the point of forgetting she was still next to him. He looked down and found her asleep. She was lying on her back, one hand curled beneath her ear, while long, sable strands of hair swirled around a face that had the texture of fine porcelain. She looked delicate and soft and fragile like this.

And quiet.

It was almost dawn when he awoke to find her rooted up against him like a kitten, soft, warm, purring. A long strand of her hair tangled in her lashes and he lifted it away. He had never seen such lashes, black and curved and flirty, even when closed. And that mouth, full and ripe, ready for kissing. The sight of her like this . . . it could not let him be, and he felt the pull of it, intense and tormenting, like a storm building. He could feel it clawing at him, something soft and penetrating about her that seeped into his heart and passed into his blood. Like an obsession, she surrounded him, controlling all thought, all action, possessing his head, his heart, his senses.

"Little seductress," he whispered, touching the curve of her face with the back of his hand. Before he knew he was doing it, he rolled over her and threaded his fingers through her hair, tilting her face up toward his. He lightly traced the shape of her mouth with his tongue, feeling the quickening of his body at her sleepy sigh, the slight shift of her body beneath him. Shafts of fire consumed him; the blood in his veins burned. He lowered his head to her, unable to pull back, unable to ease the madness that gripped him, drawn, compelled, driven, feeling the mysterious force of his desire to know her. The quickening of wild impatience drove him to search the tender curve of her neck, pressing forward, lost somewhere between damply placed kisses and the scent of warm, firm flesh. Passion worked toward its conclusion, satisfying with a kind of deep silence and intensity, a wild struggle with himself as he felt the throbbing in her throat, the blood swell in his loins. He placed his face between her breasts and touched the soft, warm weight of her, then parted her blouse and pulled the ribbons of her chemise apart.

He kissed nothing but softness, where she was as sweet and fresh as the night air, sweet with the pendulous weight of sleep. Blood rushed to his head and pounded against his temples, the rhythm of it pulsed into his kisses. Overcome with the wonder of it, to have her in his arms now after wanting her for so long, he trembled in triumph, his desire white-hot. He felt the keenness of it, the essence of her flowing into him like a madness. He wanted to touch her everywhere, to discover each rapturous place, to touch her again and again until she was damp and begging.

She had always seemed just a little ahead of him, a sunbeam dancing upon the water, teasing and tempting, just out of reach. Until now. Now everything was sharp and intense, his whole body alive and burning, pierced with the urge to mate with her that flared like a spark when she whimpered and opened her eyes.

"Jay," she whispered, and he knew in that moment there was only one Jenny and only one kind of love. But, oh, he had had a thousand imitations. The reality of it came into him like a pistol shot. She was watching him. He could not move, as if his very being were trapped, his soul greedy and hungry. And still those eyes of hers, the color of rainwashed violets, were upon him.

The look he gave her was heartbreakingly tender.

She suddenly felt all flushed with loving and being in love. She loved; she felt the first shy flutterings of it beating within her heart. She had always wondered what it would feel like and had imagined it coming with the violence of a thunderstorm, striking with the intensity of lightning. But that was all wrong. Love was a softer thing, a kind emotion that came as easily as breathing and felt just as natural. As the perfect peace of it welled like a fountain within her, her lips began to tremble. She nuzzled closer, feeling no caution within her, no reserve. "I like sleeping with you."

Jay felt her words like a blast. Soft words. The soft words of a woman. It was the thing he feared most. Words spoken like that could kick the soda out of a biscuit. He didn't want to think about what they did to a man. He had no time for a woman in his life, no matter how badly he wanted her. There was no place in his life for softness.

16

The next day they rode into Stephenville, wet, tired, and mud-splattered. It had stopped raining about an hour ago, and the sun was out, but it was too humid to have much effect on their wet clothing. They rode past the Methodist church on the left, where three young men were hammering new shingles on the steeple. Lining the street on both sides were a few houses, some of them limestone, but most of them neatly painted clapboards with big, wide porches and neat yards.

The street was drying faster than their clothing, hardening only at the highest peaks left by wagons cutting the street into deep ruts that crisscrossed like tangled ribbons. It was difficult for the horses to make their way in the narrow ruts, but it was worse between the tracks where the teams had trampled and slithered in the mud. They passed one hotel, and Jennifer wondered where they were going, but she had learned that when Jay was in one of his quiet moods, she might as well save her breath. She didn't have the energy to dismount, anyway. As they passed the saloon and a few horses that were switching their tails at the hitch rail, one ill-tempered blue roan let fly with a hind leg, catching Jennifer's bay in the flank. The bay let out a squeal that a stuck hog couldn't top. And then all hell broke loose.

Every horse within twenty feet laid back his ears and rolled his eyes, and then they started snapping reins and bucking and kicking all over the place. Jennifer, of course, wasn't seeing much of that action because her horse took off, crow-hopping and snorting, hell-bent for breakfast.

She was hanging on for dear life, too terrified to release the saddle horn, even when Jay's arm whipped around her waist. "Let go, for chrissake!" he shouted, and she felt herself pulled from the saddle, her feet dangling as he rode close to the sidewalk and dropped her on her feet.

"I'll be right back," he said, looking mad enough to bite. He rode off, catching her horse and leading it to the livery, where he dismounted. Jennifer turned and went inside the dimly lit hotel. She found a lumpy horsehair chair and collapsed into it, closing her eyes.

Two hours later Jennifer was lying on a squeaky bed in a rather sparsely furnished hotel room, trying to go to sleep. She had been feeling wretched all day, with dull, throbbing pains low in her abdomen. Halfway through her bath they had gotten worse. By the time she had her gown on, she had started her bleeding. She knew what that meant. The next five days were going to be miserable. She closed her eyes.

A pounding on the door woke her up. "Go away."

"Jennifer, open the door."

"I'm resting."

"Open this goddamn door or I'll break it down," he roared.

Wearily she dragged herself from the bed, walked to the door, threw the latch, and hurried back to the four-poster bed, almost diving in, pulling the sheet up under her chin. The door opened. Jay stepped inside. The door closed.

"I have been waiting on you for one solid hour. We were supposed to meet downstairs for dinner, in case you've forgotten. And from the looks of things, I would say that you have."

"I gave the maid a note to give you when she came after my bathwater. I'm sorry you didn't get it."

"So am I. Now get up and get dressed. We've only an hour left to eat before they close."

"I'm not hungry."

"Jennifer . . ."

"Jay, I don't feel well. Please. Just leave me alone. I'm sorry about dinner. Really." She rolled over, hugging the other pillow. "I did send you a note."

His weight lowered the mattress as he sat down beside her, then his hand cupped her shoulder. "What's wrong? Do you need a doctor?"

Without turning toward him, she answered, "No. It's not a matter of life or death. I'll be all right. I just feel wretched right now. A good night's rest and I'll be fit as a fiddle tomorrow."

He turned her over to lie flat on her back, placing his arms on either side of her, looking down into her pale face. He felt her forehead. No fever. "Does your head hurt?"

"No."

"Feel like you're going to throw up?"

"No."

"You don't have a fever."

"That's nice."

"Where do you hurt?"

She tried to turn away but he held her. She closed her eyes. "Jay . . . take my word for it. I don't feel well. Please. No more questions. Let me rest."

Her face was rosy now, and he wondered if she would start running a fever. She didn't look too bad, but he'd seen things creep up on people before. For his own peace of mind he decided to get the doctor.

"I'll send for the doctor."

"No!"

"Jennifer . . ."

"I don't need a doctor."

He smiled, rubbing the backs of his knuckles against her

cheek. "All right. I'll get the doctor for me. I'd feel better if he checked you."

"Why can't you understand? Are you dense?" Her chest was rising and falling rapidly, her face a darker red.

He pulled back and sat up straight beside her. "I'll be back in a minute with the doctor." He stood and walked to the door.

"Jay! Please don't." He opened the door. She couldn't believe anyone could be so thick-skulled. "Please," she croaked, feeling the heat exploding on her face. She groaned in frustration and called softly after him. "It's my time. Please . . ."

Jay froze, his hand on the doorknob, then he dropped his forehead against the door, thumping it against the wood three or four times. Thick-wit! He should have guessed. He should have known. A gush of tenderness rose in him and he closed the door softly and turned back to the bed. She was lying on her side again, facing the opposite wall, her face buried in the pillow she hugged against her. He came down on the bed beside her, his hand on her shoulder once again. "Jennifer . . ."

Fearing she would strangle on her humiliation, she whispered, "Please go. I want to be alone."

"Is there anything I can get you?"

"No."

He pulled the sheet up a little more, tucking it around her shoulders. "Do you need a blanket?"

"No. I'm fine."

"Are you chilled? Want me to close the window?"

"No. Everything is fine."

"Some warm milk?" She almost gagged.

"No. Thank you. Please leave." She heard him sigh. His hand left her shoulder. The bed rose when he stood. She counted his footsteps to the door. Silence. She waited to hear the door open and shut. Silence. At last she lifted her head and looked. Jay was standing with his back to her, his arms braced against the door, his head dropped low. Before she could say anything, he turned, seeing her wide eyes staring at him. Her eyes narrowed, then closed against a wincing grimace that twisted her lovely features in pain. When the pain eased, she opened her eyes, and knowing he had seen, the color came rushing to her face once more. She looked so lost and helpless, almost desperate. It was the first time he had seen her unable to strike back. He felt like his insides had shattered.

She groaned and turned away. "Can't I have any privacy? Isn't there anything you won't do? Can't you see what this is doing to me? Get out!"

"I can't," he whispered brokenly.

She heard him move, felt the bed give, flinched when he touched her arm, "I can't leave you like this . . . hurting. Tell me what I can do."

She didn't say anything.

"Has this happened before?"

Dear God! Why can't he leave me alone? "Yes, you fool. It happens to every woman . . . *frequently.*"

"I mean the pain. Does it occur often . . . that is, regularly?"

"No. Not every time," she said with a moan.

"When it does, what do you usually do . . . for the pain, I mean?"

"The usual . . . probably the same thing your wife did."

"My wife never . . . that is, if she did . . . I wasn't married all that long," he said.

Her sigh sounded tired. "Sometimes whiskey helps. A little whiskey with honey and lemon juice."

His sigh sounded relieved. "I'll be back in a minute."

True to his word, it seemed she'd hardly closed her eyes when he was rolling her onto her back and spooning the whiskey mixture into her mouth. After five or six spoonfuls she said, "That's enough."

He put the spoon down and picked up a damp cloth,

running it over her face. "You don't need to do this," she said, feeling her face get warm. "I'm not dying."

He smiled. "I know. But I . . . can't you humor me a little? I'm here, Jennifer, because I want to be."

She rolled away from him and closed her eyes. He kept rubbing his hand across her back, feeling disarmed and helpless. He wondered if other men felt this way. This and childbirth, he thought, were part of a woman's mystery, that strange link between her sexuality and motherhood, a time when a man is a total outcast, when the woman turns a blind, and sometimes embarrassed, eye to him. He might have taken Jennifer's virginity, but this was a part of herself, her badge of womanhood, that no man could touch; more the mystery because there was no male counterpart.

The room was darker when she heard him call her name, felt him lift her head, bringing the spoon toward her. "You slept for a while, but you're getting more restless now. Are you feeling any better?"

She nodded because she couldn't talk with the spoon in her mouth. She swallowed, making a face, and he smiled down at her.

"I want you to take a little more this time. So you'll rest better."

Finally she pushed his hand away. "I don't want any more."

"Can I get you—"

"I don't want anything. No warm milk. No more whiskey. No blankets. I just want . . ." She turned away, clutching the pillow. He didn't know what else to do, so he rubbed her back for a long time. Then he stood and removed his boots. He lay down beside her, close to her back, his arm going around her waist. Some time later he had just drifted off to sleep when her voice reached him.

"Will you hold me?"

"I am holding you."

"Under the covers."

He started to tell her he didn't think that was a very good

idea. But he was already pulling the sheet back. "Come here," he said, and she rolled against him, feeling his arms enfold her, his hand coming up to the back of her head and pushing it against his chest. He stroked her hair, his lips pressing softly against her head.

"I think I'm drunk."

"Do you feel much pain?"

"No."

"Then I'm glad you're drunk."

"Me too. This feels infinitely better," she said with a soft sigh.

"I'm glad you think so," he said. "As for myself, I'm a complete physical wreck."

"I don't think honey and whiskey would help that," she said.

"Nor do I."

They didn't say anything else for some time.

"Are you asleep?"

He chuckled. "Not anymore."

"Do you think I'm pretty?"

"Is that you or the whiskey talking?"

"Both of us, I think."

"Yes," he said, releasing a breath. "You're pretty. Beautiful, in fact. I've told you so before, I think."

"Was your wife pretty?"

Silence. Then, raggedly, "Yes."

"Prettier than me?"

He was still stroking her hair. "Not prettier. Different." He paused. "But even then, considering the difference, there's no question. You are prettier than Milly. But what is beauty anyway? Just something in the eye of the beholder. 'Ask a toad what is beauty . . . he will answer that it is a female with two great round eyes coming out of her little head, a large flat mouth, a yellow belly, and a brown back.' "

She hit him lightly on the chest. "You shouldn't say such things to a sick woman."

"I didn't say them, Voltaire did."

Even in the dimness she could see the teasing curve of his fine mouth. "You're a handsome man, Culhane, but I think you and the devil drink through the same quill."

"You can't find me too handsome if you're comparing me to the devil," he said.

"You compared me to a toad."

"That was different. I was quoting poetry."

"Oh." She thought for a moment, then whispered, " 'His jacket was red and his breeches were blue, and there was a hole in the back where his tail came through.' "

He laughed heartily, kissing the top of her head as he said, "That was quick thinking for a drunk woman, but it isn't poetry."

"It's Coleridge."

"You like poetry, I gather."

"Um-hm."

He pushed her head back, looking down at her, and she asked, "What are you doing?"

"Something you probably won't like, since you'd rather drink whiskey and quote poetry." He rubbed his cheek against hers, the short whiskers scraping lightly.

With a shaky breath she whispered, "We poets have a variety of interests."

He chuckled and lowered his head. Just as his lips brushed hers, she whispered in a near frantic way, "Jay . . . please. I can't . . ."

"Shhhh. I know. Trust me, Jenny." He kissed her, his lips warm and sweet as they parted hers. Gentle. So gentle. His tongue inside her mouth. His fingers caressing her scalp. Then she felt his hand at her waist, stroking, massaging, then dropping lower, kneading, pressing her stomach, where the pain had dulled to an ache.

"Jay . . ."

"Let me. Don't be embarrassed. It's part of being a woman. You aren't ashamed of being a woman, are you?"

"No." But she buried her face between his chest and his arm, her hand spreading flat against his chest.

He used the heel of his hand to press deep. "Relax, angel. Close your eyes."

"Is this where it hurts? Here? Or here?"

"There . . . all over."

"Does this help?"

"If I said no, would you quit?"

He kissed her again. "What do you think?"

"Jay, I can't do anything. Don't—"

He kissed her to shut her mouth. "I'm not always an animal, Jenny. I can hold you, sweetheart, just like I'm doing, without making love to you."

She relaxed. She had already decided that in some ways Jay was a lot like her father: fairly easygoing, basically kind, strong-willed, opinionated. She now added *gentle* to the list.

He was two men, really, one with the rough exterior he showed to the world—a killer of killers, a cool individual, even when the chips were down, and that gave him a definite edge when facing a hot-blooded lawbreaker. He played a harsh game with death, living a life that had little romance, in spite of a gunfighter's mysterious appeal. The other was a man she had only seen occasional glimpses of, a man he kept buried inside. Was the weight he lugged behind him a self-imposed punishment he wore like a hair shirt?

Her days with him had taught her something. She had always seen a gunfighter as he was presented in a two-bit novel, a two-gunned Galahad—a knight in dusty boots with a faraway look to his gaze—a larger-than-life figure with eyes like polished steel and a draw that was lightning fast. But she had learned Jay was simply a man, one with a past, and like the others of his ilk, he shared their failings, fears, and weaknesses.

She lay there thinking and wondering about him. She was lying close to him now, but she wanted to be closer. Something between them had broken open that night, something warm and natural. She had let him share a very personal thing. Couldn't she ask the same of him?

"Will you tell me about your family . . . what you were before, before something happened . . . what made you give it all up?"

"Some things a man doesn't like to talk about; some things a lady shouldn't ask."

"That's the way I felt when you came in here tonight."

"It's not the same thing."

"It's close."

Her hand was rubbing absently across his chest. "Why do you try to drive away everyone who tries to get close to you?"

"Some people I don't want close to me."

"Me, for instance?"

"I don't want to fight, Jenny. Not tonight."

"I know you better now. You're not cold and ruthless, even if you try to make me think you're a tough piece of shoe leather, hard and without mercy. But you are too brittle . . . you can't bend . . . and that's sad. What doesn't bend, breaks."

"I don't bend. And I suppose you do?"

"Women bend. Being held in submission has made us flexible. Never being allowed to make decisions, we learned to react to those that had been made for us. We learned to bend—the reasons are unimportant; some out of fear or duty or necessity—but in spite of it all, we've learned to adapt."

"Just like the cockroach."

"Who was probably seen as inferior by the mighty dinosaur."

Who got his ass kicked out of creation and got lost somewhere in the book of Genesis. Jay had the urge to pull off his socks and stuff them in her mouth.

"Tell me about Milly and Jessamine."

He sighed, not really an angry sound but more one of

resignation, as if he knew she would ask that question sooner or later. "What do you want to know?"

"What happened between you and Milly? Is she dead?"

"Yes, she's dead." Jay watched her, his eyes narrowing as he contemplated the reason for her prying and the wisdom of trusting her. She had been curious about him since the beginning, but now, since he had bedded her, she would feel entitled to know, and in a way she was. Once he started, he might as well give a full accounting, because she wouldn't give up until she had it all, anyway.

"I might as well tell you everything. You'll keep hounding me until I do. I met Milly when I was a midshipman at the naval academy in Maryland. Her father was a doctor. They lived just a few blocks from the academy, on Cornhill Street. I met her at a dance, surrounded by every available male in Anne Arundel County. I thought it was love at first sight. I was young . . . she was beautiful. We married shortly after my graduation. I took her home and introduced her to my family. I was a naval officer with a ship assignment. After we'd been married just a few months, I had to leave. I was at sea for six months, and Milly was living with my family, virtual strangers to her, and yet I was expecting her to cope . . . cope as best she could and still remain the same.

"By the time I came back, we had been married only eight months, but Milly was different . . . she'd changed. It was the first time I noticed just how young she was, how little depth there was to her. Still, we were married, and we tried to make a go of it. For three weeks we tried. But whatever we had before was gone, and we couldn't seem to find it. After a disastrous three weeks, Milly told me why. She was in love with my brother, Pierce, and she wanted a divorce." He stopped talking, his eyes focused straight ahead as if he were seeing a vision. Then, as if the trance had suddenly passed, he blinked and looked at her.

"Of course, a divorce was possible, but there were so many reasons why I thought it wasn't. The obvious things, like social stigma, religion, family—none of those were my main considerations. I told myself it was because I still loved her, because I was convinced I could ignite the same old flame that had once burned between us. But it was all a sham. She no longer wanted what I could give her . . . what I was giving her . . . but I couldn't seem to stop. Looking back, I think it was because I didn't want my brother to have her."

"So you refused?"

"Yes. We moved out of my parents' home, got our own place. Things were shaky between us from the beginning. I wanted Milly to conform to my way of thinking, to want the same things I wanted. I was so foolish, thinking I saw in her things that didn't really exist, virtues she had never possessed. And I trusted her and Pierce. When they told me they had never slept together, I believed them . . . until I came home one day and caught them."

"Oh, Jay . . ."

"I'll never forget the expression on her face. Her beauty, her virtue, seemed to fade before my eyes. She laughed and asked me what I expected, that I could force her to remain my wife but I couldn't keep her out of Pierce's bed." He shook his head, a grim smile on his face.

"The divorce was set in motion. A month before it was final, they were both killed in a boating accident. I had just come into port a couple of days before it happened. People began to talk . . . pure speculation, but after a while the story was circulating that I had something to do with it, that it was the perfect crime because of my sailing background. Enough interest was generated that there was an inquest. Thankfully, due to our just having arrived in port, I still spent most of my time on ship. We were able to document that I was on board when they died. It was ruled an accident." His voice was shaky now. He pulled her close and buried his face in her hair. "You can't imagine what it was like for those few weeks until the inquest. It was worse than if I had had leprosy. For a while I thought my own parents were afraid I'd had something to do with it. It was so hard for them. Seeing me was a constant reminder. After the inquest they tried to help me put my life back together, but it just wouldn't work. I was dead inside. I resigned my commission and left Savannah. Both my parents died within two years after I left. My mother's heart was broken. My father died a year later, of the same affliction. They were very close, very much in love. He couldn't live without her. As for my brothers and sisters, I receive letters now and then, but none of them seem to be itching to see me."

Her hand slipped inside his shirt, between the buttons. He inhaled sharply when she touched his bare skin. He kissed the top of her head.

"Enough talk. Go to sleep, or I'll have to dose you with more whiskey."

When her hand stopped making circles on his chest, he knew she was asleep. He lay awake for a long time, holding her, wondering what it was that made a woman the way she was. When one of them got the act-funnies like this, he always felt like he was holding a dead man's hand. Life was nothing more than a game of numbers: aces and eights; sixes and sevens. It didn't vary much.

Jennifer had finally managed to extract the story from him. But why not? She'd been hounding him about it long enough. He remembered the night she had asked if he was married. He had wondered what difference it made. He hadn't asked for her hand, and that was the *only* situation he could think of where marital status would make a difference. Are you married? Do you love me?—the two most over-asked, pointless questions in the world.

Jennifer was like any other woman, he guessed—a fly in the ointment, never content to let well enough alone, always asking questions, extracting answers like pulled teeth. Milly had been like that. Getting her mind headed in one direction, Milly would take off like a runaway boxcar, sparks flying. Simple, logical answers weren't enough for her. She wanted details. And she would pester him until he gave them to her. He remembered one time when he had casually mentioned to Milly that he'd run into one of her old friends who had moved away when he stopped in at the bank.

"How did she look?

"Good."

"But *how* good? Is she still slim?"

"About the same as she always was."

"What was she wearing?"

"A dress."

"Jay, give me more details than that. What color was it?"

"Some light color, I think."

"Blue?"

"Maybe. I really don't remember."

"It wasn't yellow, was it? Julia always hated yellow."

"I don't think so. Seems I would've remembered if it was yellow, since that's your favorite color."

"How did she fix her hair?"

"It was up."

"But how was it fixed? Curls? Braided? Coiled? Was she wearing a rat?"

"Christ, Milly. It was just up, under a hat.

For a moment Jay closed his eyes, trying to pull the memory of Milly's face into view, but it was like looking into a cloudy mirror. The image was there but lacking detail.

Jennifer stirred in her sleep. Jay lay his head next to hers and closed his eyes. He felt more relaxed than he had in a long time—almost the same feeling he had after sex. Sated and strangely satisfied. Yes, Jennifer was like any other woman in a lot of ways, and he couldn't really hold that against her. "You're the damnedest woman I've ever had the fortune or misfortune—I'm not sure which—to come across," he whispered, then closed his eyes to sleep.

* * *

He insisted they stay one more night in Stephenville. Jennifer hadn't awakened in one of her best moods, and Jay, seeing the faint circles under her eyes, thought she needed more rest. Jennifer thought Jay needed to mind his own business. She wanted to go home.

"Home?" repeated Jay.

"Home," said Jennifer, hoping he wouldn't ask any more questions. How could she explain what the tenderness he had shown her the night before had done to her? How could she explain that she was falling more and more in love with him each passing moment? The euphoria she had enjoyed when she first discovered she loved him had vanished. The reality of loving and not being loved in return crept in unexpectedly. To prolong her time with him would only serve to make her more miserable in the end. He did not love her. He would take her home and leave. She would never see him again. Those were the facts she could no longer ignore. They were facts she could not change. Her only choice was to protect herself as much as possible at this late date. She couldn't stop loving him, but she could prevent falling any further under his spell.

But it was hard.

His face was before her constantly, even when her eyes were closed. The fact that he cared nothing for her—that he would be leaving without a backward glance—lingered, robbing her of her usual exuberance and joy, leaving her life dull and clouded with melancholy.

"I've just spent half of my summer dragging your reluctant carcass back here by the heels, and now . . . *now* you say you want to go home? Tell me, angel. What took you so long to decide?"

"I haven't the faintest idea. I just decided, that's all. And I don't want to stay here another day. I want to go home."

"Tomorrow."

"You can leave tomorrow. I'm leaving today."

"And how will you do that? You don't know the way to Weatherford."

"I don't have to. I can take the stage."

"So that's how it is? War has been declared?"

"You said that, I didn't."

His eyes narrowed. "I've got some business to attend to. I'll be back in time to take you to dinner." He paused, so furious with her, he could hardly think straight. He had never seen anyone so stubborn. "I expect you to be here when I return."

"We don't always get what we want in this world. Haven't you learned that by now?"

His face was storm-cloud dark. "Tell me one thing. Do you, or do you not, intend to be here this evening when I return?"

"I've already told you my plans."

"That you're taking the stage?"

"If you don't intend to leave until tomorrow, yes."

"We'll see about that, lady. We'll see about that." Jay turned on his heels and stormed from the room, locking the door behind him.

Half an hour later when he returned, Jennifer was hoarse and her hands were numb. The door, of course, wasn't harmed.

"What are you doing back?" she asked, moving away from the door and glaring at him.

"I've brought you a tray so you won't starve until I return." He stepped out of the doorway to make room for a tub and water being delivered. "Your bath and lunch. Is there anything else I can do to make your stay here a more pleasant one?"

"Yes," she said sweetly. "You can leave."

The three maids delivering the tub and water fled from the room. Jay turned and walked to the door. "Until this evening, then."

"Jay . . . you aren't going to leave me locked in here all day?"

"I am."

"You wouldn't dare!"

"Watch me."

"I'll find some way to get out."

"I've taken care of that little job as well. Even you wouldn't be foolish enough to climb from a third-floor window. Your food and bath are here, so there's no chance of you pulling a fast one on any of the maids. They have been instructed not to clean this room today, or to come near it, no matter how big a fuss you throw . . . unless, of course, there is a fire. And don't think of starting one yourself. I've already removed all the matches from the room."

"Go ahead! Have your fun! I'm sorry I ever laid eyes on you. I'd rather be dead than to have to go one more foot in your company. Is this how your wife felt? Is that why she preferred your brother?" The minute the words were said, she would have given ten years of her life to call them back. But they were gone, like feathers tossed in the wind.

Jay froze. And it was probably a good thing, because if he could have moved at that instant, he would have put those long fingers of his around that small white throat of hers and shut her up permanently. An insult from Jennifer stung more than from any other. "If you can manage to have your fanny downstairs at daybreak, we'll shove off. As for the rest of this journey . . . you keep your goddamn mouth shut and stay the hell out of my way. And I can promise you, lady, I'll do my damnedest to keep clear of you." He opened the door, the expression on his face cold and hard. "I'll be back before dark to light your lamps." He closed the door behind him.

She ran to the door, pounding on it. "Jay Culhane, don't you dare do this to me. You can't lock me in here like some animal. If you leave me in here . . . Oh, I hate you." She slumped and slid down to the floor, calling him everything she could think of, knowing he couldn't hear her.

Jennifer hadn't meant for things to go as they had, and she felt horrible about what she had said. That was a spitefully mean thing for her to do—throwing that comment about his wife in his face like she had. Yet in spite of her caustic words, she didn't think she deserved to be locked in her room. She simply could not believe he would leave her in there all day.

But she knew he would.

Stunned, she sat on the floor for a long time. Then she prowled the room like a caged animal, opening every drawer, searching every inch to see if there was anything to help her get out. She went to the window. It was three floors down to the street, just as he'd said. When she had exhausted every avenue and herself as well, she fell across the bed and raged until she was too tired to do anything but sleep.

It was late afternoon when Jennifer ate the food Jay had left for her, such as it was. A sausage roll, a hard loaf of bread, and a jug of water not exactly being her idea of elegant dining. She put the tray back on the table and tested the bathwater. It was cold. But it was a warm day, and she didn't have anything else to do. She bathed, washed her hair, and dressed. And then she sat down to wait.

Jay was later than he had said. It was almost dark when she heard the key slip into the lock. When he opened the door, a water jug smashed on the wall next to him. The second time, it was a drinking glass. Then a plate. Silverware. Half a loaf of hard bread. A hairbrush. Two shoes. He made it through the door just in time to wrestle the lamp from her hands.

"It's been a real day for outbursts, hasn't it? I do hope you feel better after that one, because there won't be any more. I've had it up to here." And he showed her just how far that was.

"Let me lock you in here for the day and see how you're acting when I return."

"I didn't come in here to argue. I promised I'd take you to dinner. That's what I intend to do. I'm starved."

"Good. Then you go eat. I've eaten."

"I want you to come to dinner with me."

"Thank you, no."

"This has to end sometime, you know. We can't go on like this indefinitely."

Her heart wrenched at his words. *But I want to go on indefinitely,* she thought. But what she said was "We don't have indefinitely."

It took him a minute to recover from that reminder. "This is the last time I will ask you. Are you coming to dinner with me."

"No."

"Very well. Good night, then."

"You aren't going to lock it again, are you?"

"Of course."

"But I can't go anywhere. The stage isn't running this late."

"I don't trust you, Jennifer, any farther than I could throw you."

"How can I go anywhere this late in the day?"

"You could always steal a broom."

She didn't even yell after him this time. She wasn't going to give him the satisfaction. But she did spend the next fifteen minutes moving all the furniture in the room she could move, stacking it against the door. Then she sat down to wait.

Hours later she changed into her gown. The room was dark, and although the window that opened onto the street was open, there weren't any sounds drifting through it. She climbed out of bed and went to the window, poking her head through. The street was dark; a few squares of yellow light coming from several saloons patchworked on the street. A dozen or so horses were tied to the posts; other than that, the street was deserted. *It must be late,* she thought. The clanky notes of a terribly off-key piano made her wonder if that was where Jay was now. Or had he simply gone to his room after dinner?

It was her fault he was gone. Wasn't that what she

wanted? To be away from him? It wasn't as if he'd locked
her in her room and deserted her to go out for a night on
the town. She had a strong suspicion that he was being such
a cad because she had hurt him by being so snappish and
crabby that morning. Well, didn't everyone expect a woman
to be snappish and crabby when it was her time? Just because she'd made a fool of herself by cutting off her nose to
spite her face was no reason for Culhane to do the same.

While Jennifer was thinking about him, Jay was swirling
whiskey around in his glass—trying to understand Jennifer
—his mind half on his desire for her and half on the brutal
words she had hurled at him earlier. The pain from her
words still stung. The recall of it hadn't done much to subdue the desire he felt for her, but as far as trusting her, he
didn't. She had killed any chance for that. The Jennifers of
the world were all alike. They would wheedle and pry and
plot and scheme to get what they wanted, and then, when
they did, they would turn on a man. Men might be stronger
and more privileged, but it was the women who held the
real power. A woman could break a man in a way physical
labor, or even war could not. He had been right to think he
had no need for a lady in his life. What he needed was a
whore—a good, honest whore—no strings attached. One he
could walk away from in the morning. No more fancy ladies. He'd had his fill of them. They were all the same, once
you got them naked and sprawled in your bed. A vivid
image of Jennifer the night he had first seen her came into
his mind, then melted into a thousand mental pictures he
carried of her. She haunted him in a way that whiskey
couldn't erase. Milly had bothered him like that once. But
he had been fool enough to marry Milly.

Milly. He tried to bring her face to mind, but the image
was distorted and warped, like the tintypes that got wet the
time the Savannah River flooded and soaked the photograph albums in the front parlor of his home when he was
just a boy. Jessamine had cried for days because the pictures were ruined beyond repair, and they were the only

ones she had of her family. He tried to recall Milly's face again, but the image was still blurred. He tried harder and it came into focus, only it wasn't just Milly. It was Milly and his brother, the way they were when he came home and found them in his bed. They hadn't even heard him open the bedroom door, and for the longest time he stood in the doorway, unable to move, unable to believe what he was seeing.

"Love me, Pierce."

"I will, darling. I will."

Pierce had rolled them both over, he on top. The sheet had fallen away and they were both naked. It was easy to see Pierce's dark hand as it moved up Milly's white thigh to disappear between them, but when Milly moaned deep in her throat, Jay knew where his brother's hand was, and he knew how Milly would feel right now; warm and wet and slick.

"That's it, baby. Let it come. Let me show you where the stars are born."

He finished the last of the whiskey in his glass, then poured another. He pushed his chair back, crossing his legs on the table in front of him, and lit a cigar. The redhead at the bar was giving him the eye. He lifted his glass toward her, then tossed the whiskey down.

By the time he walked from the saloon, the redhead on his arm, Jennifer had the furniture stacked in front of the door. By the time he decided to be honest with himself, that he didn't want any other woman, Jennifer was in bed. By the time he sent the redhead packing and headed for the hotel, Jennifer was asleep.

Bump! Thump! Screech! Jennifer sat up in bed. Whatever was that noise? There it was again. Her eyes flew to the door, just in time to see the furniture slide back and Jay squeeze through the small opening. She got up and walked angrily to the door. "Those things were put there for a purpose," she said.

"It'll take more than a few sticks of furniture to keep me out of here."

"Go to bed, Culhane. I'm trying to sleep."

He followed her to her bed. When she crawled between the sheets, he followed her there too. And found himself promptly shoved to the floor. "What in hell was that for?"

"Go sleep in your own room."

"I'm sleeping here."

"Where have you been? You smell like cigar smoke and too much whiskey." And something else Jennifer couldn't quite place. Perfume? "Have you been out with a woman?"

"In what sense do you mean?"

"The only sense you know anything about."

"Then suffice it to say that I sure as hell haven't been out with a man!"

"You're drunk."

"Not completely, just enough to dull your harping."

"Get out. Then you won't have to listen or get drunk."

"I'm not leaving. Now move your fanny over. I'm coming to bed."

"Go peddle your peanuts somewhere else." She eyed him critically. "I swear, you've got more nerve than a toothache . . . coming back here after some other woman . . . Don't you think for one minute you can come crawling in my bed after you've been in *hers.*"

"I haven't been in any goddamn bed but yours."

"Now that's sad enough to bring a tear to a glass eye."

"Jennifer—"

"Don't you dare say 'I'm warning you,' because *I'm warning you!*"

"Of what? What can you do now? You've already broken everything in this room, called me every name under the sun, made so much racket that no one will stay on this floor. You've screamed your head off all day and no one has come to help. Tell me, sweetheart, just what other options do you have?"

"I refuse to talk to you."

"Not one of the options I expected but one I'm glad to hear," he said. Then, softly, "Now come here Jenny, my love, and show me what that mouth of yours is really for."

"Forget it."

Smiling slightly, he said, "Come here."

"When two Sundays come together."

He laughed, not knowing if it was from amusement or resignation. "How am I going to apologize if you won't come here? I was wrong to react to you as I did. I wasn't very understanding and I'm sorry."

"Did you sleep with her?"

"Who, for crying out loud?"

"The owner of that cheap perfume!"

"No . . ." He grinned. "Although she seemed mighty willing. But every time she got close, I kept thinking of what I left back at the hotel."

"And what was that? Your money?"

Jay threw back his head and laughed. He acted before Jennifer could think, coming quickly to the bed, pushing her back in it as he sprawled over her, pinning her beneath him. Kisses roamed over her face and throat.

"Before you get all amorous and carried away, I think you're forgetting something," she said.

He looked down at her flushed face, the downcast eyes, the resigned set to her mouth. "I'm forgetting something? Like what?"

"Like last night."

"I remember everything about last night."

"Then you remember that I can't . . . that is, I won't be able to . . . blast it all! You know what I mean!"

"Yes, I think I do. But why are you reminding me of that?"

"I thought you needed to be reminded so you wouldn't . . . that is, if you had forgotten that it's not possible . . . I didn't want to embarrass you, you know."

Jay tried to keep a straight face. He clenched his jaw so hard, he thought his teeth would shatter. There were times when she seemed to have stepped from the pages of a fairy tale, a mysterious princess—tempting, tantalizing—always just a little beyond his reach. But it was the almost comical expression on her face as she struggled with the right words that did him in. He caught her in his arms, unable to stop laughing even when he was smothering her with kisses. When she doubled up her fist and pounded him, he only laughed harder.

"Jennifer, my angel," he said between gasps for breath, "who do you think I am? Ivan the Terrible?" She beat him harder, throwing in a few choice expressions as she went along, and he laughed harder, his wildly placed kisses getting wilder and farther off target. Before long she was laughing, too, and he gathered her close, bringing her surprised lips to his for a slow, searching kiss. He saw her through a sun-sparkled daze, her mouth moist from his kisses and still open to him, her skin soft and supple beneath his fingers. "I can hold you in my arms, you know, without making love to you. There are always ways to compromise almost any situation. What's happening to you is something secret and unknown to me, something I can't understand or share, just as it's something personal and private for you. But I can hold you in my arms and kiss your sweet mouth and, by so doing, feel I've drawn just a little closer to sharing it with you, just as I would hope my holding you would help you understand I have never been more aware of you as a woman or more in awe of you than I am right now."

Her extended fingers came up slowly to trace the fullness of his mouth. "This mouth," she said softly, "is the most seductive thing about you."

He picked up her fingers and kissed them one by one before lacing them with his own and bringing their hands to lie at their sides. "I can't make love to you, sweet Jenny, but there's no reason on earth why you can't make love to me."

He rolled to his side, bringing her with him, then he

opened the fastenings of his pants, reaching out for her hand and guiding it to him. Shy at first, she hesitated. He encouraged her with a kiss, then words softly spoken against her ear. A strange, trembling excitement fluttered over her. Her fingers closed over him, his heat transferred to her. His breath came in long, ragged swells; his eyes taking on a drowsy look just before they closed. "Touch me, Jenny. Touch me and I'll show you what to do."

17

"I'd sooner face a firing squad," Jennifer said as they pulled up and took their first look at the Baxter house, which seemed to rise up before her like an object of terrifying size.

"Perhaps it won't be too bad," Jay said. "As the saying goes, the dog is a lion in his own house."

Feeling more dog than lion, she reluctantly followed him through the gate. She was so accustomed to seeing him like this, riding just ahead of her, her eyes on the blue shirt that stretched across his broad back. She had stopped seeing him as her antagonist, learning to see him as a protector, then later as a friend, and at last as a lover. But she could not suppress what she was feeling now: that he was deserting her.

It could well be their last evening together, for Jay had made no mention of when he planned to leave. Soon she would be drawn into the bosom of her family and he would go away. Would he go to the trouble of getting her alone to tell her good-bye?

Like an answer to her question, Jay turned around and rode back to her, coming up beside her, his hand resting on the horn. "You're awfully grave. Are you feeling all right?"

Her face burned. "Although it's no concern of yours, I'm feeling fine."

He laughed at her and kicked Brady into a gallop.

When she stopped in front of the house, Jay was standing on the porch talking to her father, but he came down the steps and lifted her from her horse before she had a chance to dismount. Their eyes caught and held, then she was wrapped in her father's embrace.

"Papa," she whispered against his broad, comforting chest.

"I had planned," Rand said, "on giving you a very severe dressing-down, but seeing you home and in one piece—" His voice broke.

The front door opened and minutes later the rest of the Baxters surrounded her. But even then, surrounded by those who loved her most, she felt bereft, and her eyes went searching. She saw him through the haze of faces and questions, watching her, his hands tucked in his back pockets, one knee slightly bent, the butts of his pistols protruding like hipbones from the holsters. She remembered the night he told her his guns were weighted, and that was the reason they lay heavy against his thighs, tied with rawhide strips. And for just a moment she saw him as he had been in Mexico, standing against the backdrop of a desert campfire, his cartridge belt with its neat row of looped leather filled with brass-cased cartridges crossed over his chest.

Her father must have overcome his emotional upset and recovered his voice, because in the next instant it boomed. "Jennifer, you hammerheaded little idiot, what in the hell possessed you to endanger your life and hightail it across the border like an avenging angel? Saints preserve us, didn't you inherit anything from your mother and me that resembles intelligence? Stop looking at your toes, dammit! Do you think I sent you to college so you could go gallivanting around the country in total disregard for your own safety? You can thank your lucky stars—if you have any left—that Culhane was able to find you and get you home safely. If

you didn't look like you'd been run through the mill, I
swear I'd lock you in your room and throw away the key."
He turned toward Susanna. "Yes, I can see that she is tired.
But what, by God, do you think we are? Yes, love, I can
talk to her about all this later. All right. Take her upstairs,
then. But see that she makes it up the stairs without breaking her fool neck." He looked at Jay. "You and I can have a
talk in the library over a glass of port . . . as soon as this
honking gaggle is cleared out of the way."

"Randolph Baxter!" Susanna wailed. "How could you
possibly think of grilling either one of them at a time like
this?" Her arm went around Jennifer. "Just look at her!"
Susanna put both hands on each side of Jennifer's
face. "You poor darling. You're exhausted. And Mr. Culhane . . ." Her eyes went to Jay. "You," she said with a
twinkle in her eye, "look as good as you did the last time
you were here."

"Travel agrees with me," he said.

Susanna's eyes went over him again. With a laugh she
said, "It must, Mr. Culhane. It certainly must."

Rand said, "Don't you think we should—"

"No, Rand, I don't. Not right now." She was walking
toward the staircase now, her arm still around Jennifer.
"Come along, Mr. Culhane. I've got a room ready for you
as well. I know you must be tired, and even if you aren't, a
nice rest would serve you better than a question-and-answer
session with Rand."

As they went up the stairs Clara was telling Jennifer how
her other sisters had returned to their homes, all except
herself and Abbey and Faith, who were "in town shopping
for a big dinner party Papa is giving next week." Clara
grabbed Jennifer's hand. "Oh, you poor dear. Your hands
are rough as cobs! And your face is terribly tanned. And
your clothes . . . come on, we'll have you all pretty and
sweet in no time." She began pulling Jennifer behind her.
"What an adventure you must've had. Oh, Jenny, I do envy
you. Do tell me all about it." Clara took one last look at Jay

before he disappeared through a doorway with Susanna. "However did you keep your maidenhead intact around a man who looks like that?" She turned back to Jennifer, saying, "I'm afraid I would have—" Clara froze in mid-sentence, seeing the look on Jennifer's face.

Jennifer figured she was fated to spend the rest of her life never knowing just what it was that Clara would have done, because Susanna came through her bedroom door in a rustle of black silk and hugged Jennifer again. "Dear me!" she exclaimed, breaking away. "You two look like I've just interrupted something." She looked from Clara to Jennifer. "You might as well tell me now. . . ."

And then Jennifer Leigh Baxter did something neither her mother nor her sister could ever remember her doing. She burst into tears. "There, there," Susanna said, stroking Jennifer's head. "It can't be as bad as all that."

"Oh, yes, it can," Jennifer said, sobbing. "It's worse."

"Well, whatever it is that's happened, I'm sure we can fix it."

"If it's what I think it is," Clara said, "it can't be fixed. Once broken, always broken, as they say in China."

Susanna was patting her hand. "Don't take on so, Jenny. If we can't fix it . . . we'll get you another one."

"That option is out as well, I'm afraid," said Clara. "You're only allowed one. After that it's rather open-ended."

"Now," Susanna said, taking Jennifer's hand in hers and giving it a pat. "Tell me all about it. You know there's nothing in this world I loathe more than being left in the dark."

At that Jennifer wiped her eyes, let out what could only be called a groan, and proceeded with the story.

Jennifer was put to bed by her mother and sister and slept like the dead all the next day. Faith and Abbey came in to wake her in time to bathe for dinner, both of them perched next to the tub like two openmouthed sparrows waiting for each tidbit Jennifer would feed them and asking question after question. *It would have been easier to deliver a speech in the library . . . at least I could have gotten by with telling this tale only once.*

With her sister's help Jennifer squirmed and wiggled her way into her best haircloth bustle and her black sateen corset, wondering how she was going to stand such confining clothes after becoming accustomed to the skirt and blouse she had worn for so long. But the corset gave her the hourglass figure that was fashionable. She almost fainted from lack of oxygen when she leaned over to draw on a pair of black silk stockings, swearing her feet had grown a foot wider when she thrust them into a pair of magnolia satin slippers with buckles of rubies and diamonds—fake ones, of course.

A full hour before dinner was to be served, Jennifer stood before the oval floor mirror in her bedroom and looked at herself in a willowy creation of magnolia satin embroidered with beads of many colors, elegantly shimmering with soft, rosy tints.

The dress was one Susanna had bought for her the summer before in Paris, and she had seen nothing like it before or since. From any angle it was stunning, the back having two bouffant puffs below the waist that flowed into two rows of satin pleats and double-shirred ruching to form a long train. The tablier was richly embroidered with beads and silk all the way to the floor, where it ended with two satin pleats. The corsage was short on the hips and laced behind, ornamented with embroidery like the tablier. Embroidered epaulets rested on the satin-and-lisse pleats that formed the sleeves, and a jardiniere of roses rested on one shoulder. The bodice was low enough to get attention and just high enough to keep Jennifer's bosom covered, meeting with a daring dip in the center where a satin bow rested like a dare to be untied. Her hair went up in a chignon with pale sweetheart roses.

Too agitated to stand around in her room, and too sensible to spend any more time on her person once she had declared herself ready, she decided it might be to her advantage, anyway, to be the first one down for dinner. Coming down the stairs and bumping into the butler, she said, "Hector, have my parents come down?"

"Your father is in the library, miss . . . and might I add, it's jolly good to have you home."

"You might indeed, Hector. And thank you," she said, twirling around for him when he complimented her dress. Then she blew him a kiss, not waiting to see that it had turned his face red.

But she did stop just outside the library door when she saw Rand's face turn as red as General Lee's feathers. "Female intuition, my backside! It's female, all right, but I wouldn't go so far as to call it intuition. It's nothing more than feminine drivel from the female side of the family. That must be why they call it the spindle side—because a woman's mind is full of loose threads."

"Better thread than sawdust," Clara said, then threw up her hands. "Think what you please, Papa, but I agree with Mama. It's Jenny's sharp reasoning that makes her so sensitive to what is going on around her."

"It's her damn-fool female understanding. *That's* what motivates all that altruistic nonsense. A man would be that way, too, if he listened to all that melodramatic sob-stuff. Your sister," he said, "has more damn crusades than the age of chivalry."

"And just what are you calling melodramatic sob-stuff?"

"Sentimental hogwash. Female brainwashing and cheap feminine tricks. Jennifer's logic runs from illogical to irrational. Thank God a man was spared all that emotional handwringing and tear-jerking pathos. It would have made sob-sisters of us all. Can't understand for the life of me why a woman would turn away from all her domestic bliss for a bunch of tub-thumping, demagogic utterances that amount to nothing more than soap bubbles—all full of air and gone before you know it."

Jennifer declared in so many hushed words that the visit

to the library could wait. Rand was always in a better mood after dinner; he could even be called jovial after a glass or two of brandy. She hurried on down the hall, catching sight of her mother standing before the huge window in the music room as she passed.

"Oh, Mother, we had such a time getting me dressed. While I bathed, Abbey and Faith sat on the tub so we could talk, but Abbey had a little too much hanging over and got her bustle soaked. And you should have seen the three of us trying to stuff me into my corset, and then Abbey laced it way too tight, so I almost fainted when I leaned over to put on my shoes. Well, what's your opinion? Do you think I'm laced too tight? Faith said yes and Abbey said no." She looked down at herself. "It *does* make my bosom seem a trifle large. Don't you think it's a little too . . ."

Jennifer noticed her mother's brows were raised to a scandalized height, and there was the oddest twinkle in her eye that did not go with the tightly held mouth. Susanna turned away from the window and came toward Jennifer, placing her hands on Jennifer's shoulders and turning her around as she said, "I think your father may have been right when he said you needed finishing school much more than you needed a college education. I must have neglected to tell you there are certain subjects a lady should never discuss in front of a gentleman. But since you've already brought the subject up in front of one, we might as well ask his opinion on . . ."

But Jennifer was no longer listening. She had already turned enough to see Jay. Over her horrified gasp Susanna said, "Well? What do you think? Do you think she will prove too much of a distraction at dinner tonight? Should I send her up to change?"

He had been leaning against the piano, but when Jennifer turned to face him, he straightened, as if he'd been called to attention. She stood there in a golden bath of afternoon light that came through the window, staring blankly at Jay, feeling all funny inside. "I didn't realize you were here, because if I had, you can be assured that I would—"

Jay cut her off smoothly. "Personally I think Jennifer would cause a distraction at dinner wearing a towsack. The dress, I think, is exquisite just as it is." He watched the clash of emotions so obvious in her expression, wondering what in hell he was going to do about everything. He hadn't expected ever to see her dressed as she was, nor looking more beautiful than she had before. How was he going to deal with being separated from her when just having her out of his sight for one day was eating holes in him? He couldn't think straight around her, he knew that, and he needed some time to think clearly, for a change. But he couldn't seem to find much pulling him to go back to the life he'd known before. He only knew that the longer he stayed, the harder it would be to leave her.

Her embarrassment was slowly being replaced by a new irritation. Just what had her mother and Culhane been discussing? She wasn't such a fool to think it didn't concern her. Jennifer leveled her gaze on him. He was up to something, the devil. . . .

Appropriately, the devil was wearing black—trousers, that is—and a bottle-green jacket with a velvet collar. And the pants—Mary, Joseph, and Jesus!—they were indecently snug, outlining the longest length of well-muscled leg she'd ever seen. Jennifer's heart began to throb, and her breathing was such that made her think she had indeed laced her corset too tight.

She had seen Jay many times, but never like this. His lean face seemed so much more deeply tanned against the stark white shirt. Even dressed as a gentleman, he was, as always, terribly handsome in a barbaric way. Even a gold earring would not have been out of place on him. The glimmer of lights overhead danced like moonbeams on water, across the golden highlights of his hair. She could not fault in the slightest the way he was dressed, but he looked, and was, a man of hearty, lustful appetites—unashamed and unconcealed.

Caught gaping and seeing the spark of interest in his eye made her open her Louis XV fan with a snap and try to fan the fire from her face.

"Dear me," Susanna said, "The temperature in this room is rising faster than my yeast rolls, which reminds me that I need to check on a few things." She smiled as she crossed the room, saying as she went through the doorway, "If you two should happen to snap out of it before I send someone to call you to dinner, I'll expect you in the dining room at eight."

Jennifer didn't snap. And neither did Jay.

She was thinking that without a doubt Jay Culhane had the most wicked eyes, the proudest nose, and the most arrogantly sensual mouth that she had ever seen. He also had absolutely no manners. For no man had *ever* stared at her as he had in front of her mother, his eyes boldly stripping every thread and bead, one by one.

But he wasn't in love with her, she had to remind herself. Love and lust were two four-letter words that began with the letter *L,* but the similarity ended there. Where had she gotten the flyblown idea that he might be in love with her? The look Jay gave her wasn't love. He had a wolf in his eye. Nothing more.

How stupid of her to think he might ever love her. It came creeping back to her, the time she had asked him why he'd never remarried. Her heart sank like a stone when she remembered his cold reply: "Why should I keep a cow when I can buy milk?"

With a soft, strangled cry Jennifer whirled and ran for the door. He caught her before she made it, slamming the door shut in front of her. She fought him like a crazy woman, but he subdued her easily, both of them slamming against the wall yet feeling nothing, neither of them, but the sudden freeing of so much emotion that blind intuition took over.

His arms went around her as he turned her, his mouth groping blindly for hers. She bit him and pushed him away.

"You can't maul me in my parents' home!" she said between gasps, fighting and straining to break his hold. "Let me go before someone sees us!"

"When you calm down you beautiful little wildcat. Uh-uh! Don't bite. I'll bite you back . . . and I promise you, you won't like the places I would pick."

"You degenerate!"

"And here I thought I was being articulate. Ouch! Damn you, you little viper! Let go of my finger!" He gripped her wrist, squeezing tightly, increasing the pressure until she began to loosen her bite. Then he twisted her in a half circle, catching her against him, both of her hands held in one of his own. She was breathing heavily now, and from where he stood over her, her pale, lovely breasts looked about ready to spill over the floodgates.

She kicked him and he jerked her more firmly against him, his hand going up to the back of her neck. "You have quite a few buttons back here, don't you, beautiful? Let's see how many of them we can undo before someone comes in."

"You bastard! You would strip me in my own house!"

"You better believe every word of it, you temperamental little shrew. I'd like to strip you of every stitch and keep you naked and flat on your back for a solid month."

She fought him again. "You won't be here long enough for that," she snapped as he pinned her back against the wall. She went suddenly still under his long gaze, the anger fading slowly from her face. His breath was coming hard and fast against the sensitive skin below her ear, but his words were soft and low. "Someone ought to teach you not to look at a man that way. . . . Aww, Jenny, let's don't fight. Not now. Not ever."

His hand curved over the side of her neck, his thumb stroking her with agonizing slowness. Then he applied pressure, drawing her to him, meeting her halfway, his lips brushing hers, nibbling, teasing with light promise, then, with a groan, covering her completely. "Jenny . . . I can't think when I'm with you. You tie me up inside. Help me. Tell me to get the hell out of your life."

"And if I won't?"

He groaned, whispering against her throat. "Then I'll—"

"Jennifer? Are you in there?"

"Clara!" Jennifer said as Jay released her and stepped back.

Jay groaned. "I never should have brought you home."

"I tried to tell you that," she said.

"Jennifer?"

"Yes, I'm here."

The door opened, and Clara peered around the opening, her face flaming red. "Sorry . . . Mother told me to knock before I came in. It's five past eight and Papa's roaring like a hungry old bear."

She looked at the two of them. "Get yourself composed. I'll hold Papa off for a while. A good argument before dinner always helps his indigestion." Clara closed the door.

Jay's arms went around her, drawing her against his chest. "I've got to be in Fort Smith by next Friday. Leaving now, I'll have to ride like hell to make it." He drew back, rubbing his finger along the hollow of her cheek. "I want some time with you . . . alone . . . where we won't be disturbed. I'll wait until day after tomorrow to leave." He reached for her hand, his eyes never leaving hers. "You're so damn beautiful. It's difficult to breathe when I look at you." He drew her hand through his arm and led her to the dining room.

Jennifer looked up to see her mother standing in the dining room, looking at Jennifer and Jay as they walked into the room, her eyes round and owlish with knowledge. Well, let her think what she would.

As she passed, Susanna looped her arm through Jennifer's and gave it a squeeze just as she said, "Mr. Culhane, don't stand there like a block of wood. Come along now.

I've at least two hundred questions I want to put to you, and I promise to be hanging on your every word."

Rand and Clara were across the room, nose to nose, in what looked like a bombardment of heavy artillery, both of them red in the face. Abbey and Faith rushed over to greet her with hugs, Abbey immediately giving what Jennifer thought was her most devoted attention to Jay.

"You have certainly made a transformation, Mr. Culhane . . . not that you didn't look good before."

Jay laughed. "Why, thank you. And you are looking every bit as lovely as you did the first time I saw you."

"How kind of you to say that. Flattery like that . . . well, I am simply speechless!"

Liar! thought Jennifer. Sometimes Abbey could be downright nauseating. And now Faith was acting like she had just been struck by lightning. There wouldn't be much conversation out of the two of them for the remainder of the evening. Of that she was certain. Taking one last look at her simpering sisters seated on each side of Jay, Jennifer felt like she was going to throw up.

All in all, she would rather be tarred and feathered in the Weatherford courthouse square than spend the next two hours at dinner, with Abbey making a fool of herself over Jay Culhane and Clara acting too dim-witted to be mistaken for one. If they only knew, Jennifer thought, but somehow even that wasn't comforting. She hated to admit it, but it simply amazed Jennifer that she, a woman who had always withstood the most charming and seductive men, would fall for a man like Jay Culhane, a man women everywhere would always be falling all over themselves to get to.

Jennifer decided to stop acting jealous and eat her soup. At about that point in time she got a blast of her father's hot air.

"The other girls were married by the time they were her age," Rand said.

"There are some things you can't rush, Randolph," replied Susanna. "Jennifer will marry when she finds the right man."

"I'd come nearer to believing that if she were looking."

"Love is where you find it, darling. Remember how we met." Susanna patted his hand.

"You know duels have been outlawed for years," Rand growled.

"That wasn't exactly what I meant, dear."

"That's one of the thing that irritates me most. Why can't a woman say what she means?"

"Because you wouldn't understand it, even if we did," Clara said.

"Clara," Rand said, "I can see why that husband of yours agreed to let you stay another week."

"Don't get upset while you're eating," said Susanna.

"I'm not upset. I just think it's time for Jennifer to settle down."

"You've got to be patient, Rand. Jenny is the baby."

"Jenny is a headache!"

"Papa, please," Jennifer said, "can't we talk about something else? I just got home. I don't want to start on this the minute I walk in the door."

"When will we talk about it, then? The last time I mentioned it, you took off to visit your crazy aunt. And she's never been married, either. You keep on messing around her and you'll end up an old maid, just like she did."

"Papa, I'm not exactly a spinster."

"You're not exactly looking around, either." Rand paused, buttering half his roll. "I've decided to throw a big shindig next weekend . . . invite all the eligible men in the area and—"

"Papa, I don't want or need your help. Last time you intervened, you dragged home that horrible old man who didn't have any teeth," Jennifer said.

"A girl that's waited as long as you can't be too choosy. Besides, Jeremy Crankstaff owns half the state of Texas. You want teeth, marry a barracuda."

"May I be excused?" said Jennifer.

"You may not," said Rand. He buttered the other half of his roll.

"What about Herb Foley's oldest boy?" Abbey said. "He's young and attractive."

"I don't like Herb Foley or his son," snapped Rand.

"Okay. So you don't have to marry him," said Clara.

"Will you stop it!" Jennifer shouted, slamming her hands down on the table and rising to her feet. "You're all acting as if I'm not even here. Stop talking about me as if I'm some cow you're trying to get to auction."

"We're only trying to help, Jenny," Abbey explained.

Jenny silenced her with one look. "I'll do my own choosing, thank you. Just like *you* did."

"Well, I'm speechless," Abbey said, her face turning red, "I'll admit it's a bit unusual in this day and age for the family to pick a husband—"

"Unusual?" Jennifer shouted. "It's lunatic!"

"Sit down, Jennifer," Rand said.

"Not unless you drop this ridiculous subject."

"It so happens I've just said all I wanted to," Rand said, giving Abbey a wink. "How about you?"

"Papa, you know she's *speechless,*" said Jennifer.

Abbey laughed. "I can't think of a thing to say."

"Humph!" Jennifer said. "That will be the day!"

Dear God! Would this evening never end? Would dinner never be over? Would she never be free of the torment of seeing Jay like this and knowing he would leave, and she would never again feel his arms around her, never know the feel of that warm mouth against hers? She couldn't bear it any longer. She had to get out of this room. Away . . . far, far away from Jay Culhane.

Thankfully dinner didn't last all night. But Jennifer didn't get to escape as she had hoped, for she had no more risen from the table when her mother said, "Jenny, do come into the music room and play something for us."

Something about that settled heavily in Jay's heart. In

fact, Jay's line of thinking would have staggered Jennifer. For the first time in his life he was totally dumbfounded at what he was feeling. And it wasn't all feelings for Jennifer. More so, it was his reaction to that idiotic conversation her family had had at dinner. He had never before felt angry enough to throttle an entire family, nor had he ever considered kidnapping a woman. Yet at dinner, listening to all that nonsense about finding her a husband, he was considering both, and that left him on edge and more than a little angry.

Women had always played an important role in Jay's life —due, he supposed, to the close bond between him and his mother and the affection he had always felt for his sisters and the other female members of his extended family. And he had loved Milly, at least in the beginning. But something had gone wrong, and now Jessamine and Milly were dead, and he hadn't seen his sisters in over five years. And during that time he had meticulously cut any affection or need for a woman from his heart—save the physical need only a woman could sate. But that, he knew, was only the unattached, physical pumping of his loins and had nothing to do with the feelings that lodged within the heart. For this reason he had preferred to keep all his encounters with women impersonal, not returning to the same woman often enough that she could ever mistake herself for his mistress or go so far as to think he cared.

His almost violent reaction to the conversation at dinner unsettled him. Whenever he heard anyone mention the word *marriage* in connection with Jenny, he wanted to shove the words back down their throats. He couldn't think of Jennifer as belonging to this family, and certainly not to any other man. Over the past weeks he had grown to think of Jenny as his. The thought of some unknown man doing the things with her that he had done filled him with such rage that he felt a white-hot pain sear his insides. He couldn't forget that black-haired little imp with those damn purple eyes and a mind that whirled faster than a windmill. Her and her independent spirit.

And just what in the name of heaven was he going to do about it? She fought him every inch of the way, and he knew she would never, absolutely never, be brought to heel by any man, himself included. But something about that pleased him. He didn't like to think that that beautiful, defiant, headstrong, yet loving, generous heart of hers would be squeezed lifeless by any man. Jenny was bred to run. Keeping her hitched to a buggy would break her.

It surprised him to admit that he understood her, knew how she would have to be given a lot of rein, never snubbed short to the post. Was he, then, the man for her? Is that what he had known from the beginning, from the moment he had seen that wide-eyed look in the picture on the piano?

But it was neither her wild spirit nor her passion that made him feel the painful leap of his heart. It was the desire to preserve her wild spirit in its naturalness, to protect her from those who would try to crush her and break her to their will. And that discovery angered him further. For then he knew beyond a doubt that he wanted Jennifer Baxter more than he had ever wanted anything—Milly . . . his commission . . . anything. He was dangerously close to being angry when he followed Rand into the music room.

Jennifer was already seated at the piano playing Chopin when he entered, and that angered him further. He wanted her to himself, dammit. He didn't want to share her with anyone.

She played three pieces—Jay couldn't have told you which ones if someone had held a gun to his head. His thoughts were too much centered on Jennifer, hands moving gracefully over the keys, the trailing coils of the blackest hair this side of midnight hugging her lovely neck. He watched her brow furrow in concentration, remembering the many times on the trail he had seen her look just that way, and then he made the mistake of looking at her mouth and remembering the way it felt against his.

Rand and Susanna went up to bed shortly after Jennifer finished her last piece. After they were gone, Clara suggested they play cards—poker. Faith, after having reminded them that poker was a form of gambling and not appropriate for ladies to play, went to bed. So Clara, Abbey, Jennifer, and Jay played poker.

An hour or so later Jennifer went to the kitchen to refill the wine decanter. When she came back a few minutes later, only Jay remained in the room. Jennifer set the decanter on the table. "Did Clara and Abbey go to bed?"

"They did."

Jennifer looked uncomfortable. She glanced at the door. "I wish they had waited until—"

"Sit down, Jennifer."

"I don't think I should—"

"I know what you think, goddammit! I'm not going to toss your skirts right this minute." His voice softened. "If I feel the urge coming on, I'll give you fair warning. All right?" She nodded, but he could tell by the way she stared that she didn't have any idea what she was agreeing to. "I just want to have a glass of wine with you. Then I'll walk you upstairs." She sat down uneasily, parked on the edge of her chair.

Jenny was under his skin. He wanted her. And he was a man who took what he wanted. But with her, it never seemed to be enough. He had meant to act the gentleman, to court and woo her with soft words and ply her with enough red wine to make her receptive; he intended to wait for the right moment to tell her how he felt—nothing more. He only wanted to be alone with her, to talk to her, to tell her how he could not bear the thought of riding out of her life and leaving something he considered to be his to another man.

He looked at her sitting across the table from him, wide-eyed, her rosy lips trembling. She was looking at him the way a man looks when he first realizes he's been shot. It tore at his guts to see it in her lovely violet eyes. The shock of reality.

Get out of here, Jennifer. Run! Quickly! Before he fully understands. She leapt up, her chair clattering to the floor as she fled through the door.

He let her go.

18

❧ ❧

Jennifer avoided him all the next day.

At least that was how it looked to Jay. It really wasn't something she consciously planned. It just happened because she was absorbed with her family, and he began to see this absorption as proof of her female inconsistency, feeling just a little betrayed by the smooth way she went on with her life, ignoring him. She was like part of his past coming back to haunt him.

Jennifer barely had time to catch her breath all day. Between getting her sisters off, undergoing another grilling by her father, and acting casually polite to Jay throughout dinner, she was mentally exhausted. She would go to bed early. At least that was the excuse she gave immediately after dinner, when she shot from the dining room as if the back of her dress was on fire.

By the time she reached her room, she was positively glowing with nervous energy. She put on her gown and went to bed. Half an hour later she got up. She took a warm bath, put on another gown, and got into bed. Half an hour later she got up again, tiptoed down to the kitchen, and warmed a glass of milk. After drinking it she returned to her room, crawled into her bed, and closed her eyes. Half an hour later she threw the covers back. "Damn. Damn. Damn!" This wasn't working. No matter what she did, she couldn't get that blue-eyed devil out of her mind.

A change of scene was what she needed. As she had always done as a child, Jennifer slipped out of the house and headed for the barn, where she sat on a feed sack and debated the issue of Jay Culhane while she stroked Castor's soft fur. Pollux walked in and out between her legs, his tail in a question mark. Two hours later, all talked out, her throat dry and her eyelids growing heavy, she deposited Castor on the floor next to Pollux, who had by this time given up on the question, curled up into a ball, and gone to sleep.

Walking down the stone pathway, making her way through flower beds and clumps of shrubbery, Jennifer found she was thinking more and more about the fact that Jay was upstairs asleep in one of their beds. It was a very frustrating thing for her to be thinking, she knew, but she couldn't seem to get him out of her mind. *Jay . . . Jay . . . Jay . . .*

She opened a gate and closed it behind her, following the curve of the walk around a clump of yellow daffodils that looked more white than yellow, bleached by the full light of the moon. The wind rustled through the trees overhead, and all around her crickets were busy doing whatever it is that crickets do to make that irritating noise.

"Where are you going, little girl?" said a deep, masculine voice from somewhere behind her. She screamed and jumped a country mile.

The body that belonged to the voice stepped out of the shadows, and she whispered, "Culhane, you idiot! You scared the living daylights out of me."

He looked magnificent standing there just a few feet from her, his eyes on her nightgown. She looked down at herself; finding that everything vital was covered, she was immediately grateful that she had had enough sense to put on a modest gown, even if she didn't have the brains to know better than to come outside dressed in one. What she didn't realize was that its very simple construction and smooth lines were far more seductive than another, more revealing one might have been.

She didn't think to question his presence out here at this time of night. She simply counted her blessings. For Jennifer was in love—hopelessly in love—a love that was not returned, but nonetheless fierce because of it. She was hurting tonight, hurting from the fact that he didn't feel as she did, hurting because he would go on without her. Crazy with love, it was a struggle to keep from hurling herself in his arms. He had asked where she was going. *Get your mind off throwing yourself at him,* she thought. "I'm going to the house."

"From where? Where have you been, Jenny? This time of night . . . dressed like that . . . meeting your lover on the sly?"

She wanted him to take her in his arms, but all he wanted to do was talk. She felt the pain of his rejection so intensely, she could feel the scars left upon her heart. It was so hard to concentrate upon her thought processes, trying to act lighthearted and glib when she wanted to cry. Her hands flew to her face, ready to hide her tears as she drank in the sight of him for what would probably be the last time—the honey-gold tones of his hair, the unbelievable blue of his eyes, the sensuous mouth, the sun-worshipped color of his skin. "You're the only—" She caught herself. She had been about to say he was the only lover she'd ever had.

"I'm the only what?"

"The only one obnoxious enough to ask me a foolheaded question like that." *The only one I'll ever love . . .*

"Where have you been?"

Do you know how hard it is for me to talk to you like this? "Clementine had her kittens today, if you must know," she said, which was a lie. Clementine had had them the day before, and Jennifer hadn't bothered to look in on them at all that night. But still, it made a good story. Much better than the truth.

He stepped farther out of the shadows into the full moonlight, and her heart grew still. "Clementine, I take it, is a cat," he said.

She laughed, nervously. *Surely he knows. Surely he can see . . .* "She'd be a strange one, having kittens if she wasn't." She met his teasing grin and tried to laugh again. But then, overcome by the warmth she felt just being near him, the intimacy of being with him out here like this, the pain of his rejection, she stopped and looked abruptly away, her arms crossing at her waist as if hugging herself.

"Are you cold?"

"No."

He studied her a moment. "What are you thinking about that's putting a frown on such a beautiful face?" he asked softly.

A shiver rippled across her. Her voice was husky when she replied, "Do you think I'd tell you?" She laughed, hoping that betraying emotion would not trap her. "I know what happens to foolish women who tell all their secrets." She paused when her voice broke. After a second she took a deep breath and went on. "But if you must know . . . I was thinking the stars are awfully bright tonight. Brighter than usual. There isn't a cloud in the sky. And the moon . . ."

"Do you have such dark secrets that they must be kept hidden?"

No. I love you. And it's no secret. I want the world to know. "I didn't before . . . but I do now."

He winced at that. Their eyes met and held. "And the telling of your secrets? What happens then?"

She avoided his eyes, wondering if she should continue standing out here with him like this, how much longer she could remain cool and casual before she lost control completely and groveled like a fool at his feet.

"What happens when you tell your secrets, Jenny?"

She was trembling now, but not from the touch of cool night air upon her painfully heated skin. "They turn into weapons."

"The same as people."

She looked at him warily, her heartbeat coming on too strong, too fast. "What do you mean?"

"You've been avoiding me all day."

Another struggle for words. "I've been busy. There have been so many . . . demands upon my time."

"But not so much as to prevent an hour or two in the barn, leisurely spent with . . . Clementine the cat."

"I was with Castor and Pollux most of the time." She turned away, keeping her arms crossed in front of her, afraid she might throw them around his neck if she didn't. She looked down at the pathway, kicking a rock back into the flower bed.

"Jenny," he said softly. "Look at me."

I can't. I can't look at you without being reminded of what I'm losing. She raised her head but did not turn around, hearing him chuckle.

"Still the stubborn one," he said.

She didn't want to be called stubborn. She wanted to be called a hundred things other than stubborn. She wanted him to take her in his arms and tell her all the things she wanted to hear him say, beginning each one with *beloved, darling,* or *sweetheart.*

She looked straight into his eyes, hoping by this show of aggression that he wouldn't be able to see in them all the things she was feeling. The air around them was cool. The night sky was liberally dusted with stars. It reminded Jennifer of a night in the desert when she had watched him standing naked by the fire. She looked at his face, wondering what questions were forming behind those beautiful eyes, what words she would hear from those lips she longed so to kiss. She looked at his gentleman's clothing, still seeing a bit of the gunfighter in him. They had fought well and loved well—she and her gunslinger. She regretted coming across him out here like this. Her heart was breaking. She loved him so much. *How will I ever get over him?*

"Don't look at me like that," he said. "Have your feelings for me changed so much that you cannot spare me one soft look, one kind word? Has something happened since you've come home? Something to make you change your mind about me?"

She shook her head, unable to talk, unprepared for the effect of his words upon her. She couldn't answer him. Words didn't seem to be capable of connecting with her feelings tonight. Nothing seemed to go right, nothing seemed to exist in her world anymore, except her desire to have him lie with her, to take her in his arms, to have his warm hand stroking her bare hip, to hear the husky tones of his voice softening her down to the very marrow of her bones.

For a long while he stood gazing down at her, breathing in her scent, which mingled with the wild honeysuckle that drooped from the branches of an old elm tree. She was different tonight. Subdued. His time with her had provided no experience with the expressions he was now seeing upon her lovely face. He had expected she would be glad to see him, or at least angry that he had been so brazen to intrude. Instead she looked barely composed, her eyes shimmering a little too brightly, her face a shade too pale. Her breathing was erratic, her posture stiff, as if each bodily movement required deep concentration. Disappointment rose in him. "Have I done something to make you angry with me?"

"No," she croaked. "Nothing."

"Then if nothing has happened, if your feelings have not changed, why have you been avoiding me?"

"If you can't figure that one out for yourself, it would do no good to tell you." She wanted desperately to tell him all the things she was feeling right now. She wanted to tell him that when she was in his arms, there was no right or wrong, no rules to follow but those of the heart. But she could not. She could not tell him how his nearness made her blood sing in her veins until she thought her love indestructible. What were the words that would tell how beautiful it felt to sleep with him under a thin blanket on the hard ground under a stardusted desert sky, with the cold ashes from the fire settling in her hair and the morning dew touching her lashes?

"I can see you aren't going to make this easy for me," he said. "And I can't stay here drinking Gilbert and Parson's Hygienic Whiskey with your father until you soften. You are the most beautiful creature I've ever seen. I never grow tired of looking at you. Your colors are so pure . . . hair as black as midnight . . . skin of the whitest white . . . eyes the color of violets." He shook his head, a sign of his disbelief. "Dear God, Jenny . . . I've never wanted anything in my life as much as I want you right now. I'm not sure I can retain any semblance of sanity if I wait much longer."

All the distance she had put between them was suddenly gone. Vanished, as if the sun had come out suddenly after a long and dreary rain, spreading its warmth and painting the world with the softest tones of molten gold. "I don't know why you worry so," she said so softly, he had to step closer to hear. "I'm so softened now, my muscles are all turned to pudding."

He stood looking at her in that quiet way he had that drove her insane. "It's a dangerous game you're playing, little girl. Out here in your nightdress, your hair falling soft and seductive around your shoulders, saying things a man wants to hear. Aren't you afraid of me? Of what might happen? Don't you know what the night can do?"

Her eyes widened. Her heart thumped in anticipation. But he said nothing more. His face was authoritative and unsmiling. He was a man of indomitable will and liked to have his own way. He went to her, standing wonderfully close, his hands resting lightly on her shoulders, his thumbs making the softest ripples of gooseflesh along the skin of her neck. She shivered, and he wrapped her in his arms, content to hold her there for a moment, as if he could feel the wild, frantic beating of her heart and had granted her this time to allow it to quieten before his mouth came down swiftly upon hers, hard and searching. After the initial surprise of it she lost the desire to talk. She couldn't muster up any resistance, no misplaced will could she call upon to come to her defense. Nothing would help her resist the urgent demand of his lips, the hard arousal of his body, the unsteady rhythm of his breathing against her flesh, the unbridled thrill that leapt to life like a spark when he touched her.

Suddenly he was unbearably close and he swept her into his arms. "What are you doing?" she asked. "Are you crazy? Put me down! Jay, let me go."

"I've been trying to let you go ever since the day I met you. But I can't." He carried her to a stone bench beneath a sweeping oak tree. He held her against him, his chin resting on the top of her head. She could feel every detail of his body against hers through her thin gown. She looked up at him. His face was so close to hers, she couldn't see him distinctly. But his breath ruffled across her hair. And his arms were warm and strong around her. And his kiss . . . when it came . . . so gentle upon her lips.

She felt her heart race, then lurch. For a moment she thought it had stopped beating completely. She was floating, held only by his strong, comforting arms. Then he was looking at her, his pupils dilated, the blueness swallowed up by black. She was looking at him as if she had never seen him, never really looked at him before this moment. The arched curve of his brow; the strong clip of his jaw; the silky thickness of his hair, a little long, and terribly masculine because it was. She wanted to touch him everywhere, to hold him to her until she absorbed him completely. How had she spent so much time with him and never seen him as he really was: the perfect cheekbones; the widow's peak at his forehead; the warm, honeylike scent of his skin. She could spend the rest of her life looking at him like this, watching the expressions change in his eyes, learning the movement of his mouth.

"Is this something you planned? Coming out here dressed as you are, knowing it would make me think about things I had no business being reminded of. Did you plan to meet me out here like this? One last chance at seduction, avoiding me all day to make it somehow sweeter?" He sounded angry and tired, his eyes were drilling into hers.

"No."

"I think it is." She could feel the tension and anger in him leap across the distance between them. "Since the day I was given the job of coming after you, you've been nothing but trouble. From the moment I found you in Mexico, you have gone out of your way to endanger my life, dig into my past, and tempt me beyond reason. And for what reason? Because your father asked me to find you? What in the name of all that's decent did I ever do to have the likes of you thrust upon my shoulders, to have my life invaded and my guts twisted in knots? I've tried to help you . . . I've protected you with my life . . . I've given you comfort . . . I've made excuses for you . . . gone out of my way for you . . . Well, by God, it stops. No more. It is finished."

She tried to dig deep within her resources to fire her anger, but she was so stunned, she could only whisper, "What do you mean? What are you going to do?"

"I am tossing in the chips, Jenny."

"I don't understand."

"I want you. It's that simple. I want you. So much that I'll do anything to have you."

Jennifer flinched like she'd been stabbed in the back. Never, never would she have expected this. *Come be my lover, yes. Or my mistress. But wife?* "Are you trying to say you love me?"

"I wish to hell I knew. I'm not a sane man anymore. Not since I met you. I adore you. I lust for you. I can't bear the thought of leaving here without you. But is it love?" He laughed, his hand raking his hair. "I honestly have no idea."

"You've come to tell me good-bye?"

"No," he said. "I've come to ask you to marry me."

For a moment she was silenced by shock. But then, in a delirium of need and response, she yanked his head down and kissed him hard. "Yes," she whispered. "Yes . . . yes . . . *yes!*" And the old sweet insanity swept over them both until they were half crazed from wanting. Then slowly the obsession began to ease, and he lifted his lips from hers. "I'll make you a good wife, Jay. I know I will. I love you too much not to. When do you want to get married? Can it be soon? Can I wake my parents? Where do you want to live . . . here or maybe in Savannah . . . would you like that? Or would you rather find someplace new? Do you want to go back into the Navy? Of course, that's out if we stay here . . . I know you could learn to ranch . . ." Her exuberance flowed out of her as she suddenly realized that Jay had pulled away and now stood stiffly before her, an odd expression on his face.

"What's wrong, Jay?"

"Don't start getting a lot of big ideas, Jennifer. With me you won't have the rich life you're accustomed to. I'm a deputy marshal. The hours are long, the pay inadequate. I'll be on the road a great deal. It isn't much to offer you, but it's my life and I'm asking you to share it with me."

Hope. Joy. Expectation. They all died within her at that moment. How could he expect her to live like that? What kind of life would it be? How long would they have before she was a widow, left to raise their children alone? "I can't, Jay. As much as I love you . . . I can't."

"Yes, you can. You can do anything you want . . . just as you've always done."

But Jennifer was shaking her head.

"Jennifer, why?"

She came to him, her arms going around him as she buried her face against his chest, feeling as if she were bleeding from every pore in her body. "I'm not a loner like you." Her words were shaky and frightened, each breath a painful struggle. "I can't exist alone. I've always lived in close association with my family, with those I love. If I was married to you, I would want you with me. I never knew who I would marry, or even when, but I've always known what my marriage would be like—filled with loving and giving, a time to raise children together and provide the example for their maturing."

"You can't love me very much and talk like that," he said.

"It's because I love you that I can. I love you, Jay. So much that I want to be honest and fair—for your sake as well as mine."

"Don't try to placate me."

"I'm not." She waved him away when he started to say something else. "I've prayed and prayed that you would grow to love me, that you would ask me to marry you." Her voice grew hard. "He answered my prayer but in a way that hurts more than it would have, had you never asked. I may never know if I've made the right decision—God knows I'll grieve over it for years to come. But I'll have to learn to live with it, even if it means being an old maid. But you . . . what will you do, Jay? Will you keep living by your gun? Jumping at shadows to stay alive? Keep punishing yourself for your past until it's more real to you than the present?" A choking sob, full of anguish, rose in her, and she almost screamed at him, her fists pounding on his chest. "How long, Jay? How long will you live like that before you're shot in the back and left to bleed to death in some manure-trampled street?"

His hands plunged into her hair and twisted until her face was lifted to his, and then he stopped the brutal flow of words with a kiss that was just as brutal. He kissed her until she gasped for breath, until the corner of her lip was split and seeped blood. His kisses were crazed with longing, lust, anger—and the despair of what he had lost. "Damn you," he whispered into her mouth. "Damn you for making me care." He kissed her again, the fury of need and passion driving him beyond himself. Ill-fated wanting. Destructive need. Desperation beyond the bounds of what was normal. *No. Not now. Not like this.*

His hands were on her breasts, the hardness of his groin painful against the bone of her hip. Nearing panic, she shoved and clawed at him, driving him more insane each time she moved. With a final bid for sanity she slammed her knee against his groin, striking him a little too far off-center to drive him to his knees but close enough that he jerked back from her and leaned over from his waist, gasping for breath. "Go in the house, then," he said, "if you don't want to be raped. For God's sake, don't stand out here any longer, half dressed as you are, and tempt fate."

She stepped back a few feet and watched him gasp for breath, until the pain subsided and he straightened. "I thought I told you to leave."

"I know." She gave him a weak smile. "But then, I never was very good at taking orders, was I?"

"Why? Why are you still here? Why are you doing this to both of us? I've offered you what you wanted. You've admitted that. What else do you want? My head on a goddamn platter?"

"I want you free, Jay."

"Free? *Free?* What does that mean? Free. Jesus! You're crazy."

"I'm in love. And if that makes me crazy . . . I guess I must be. I love you so much, it makes me feel like the world has tilted and I might slide off. I didn't want to love you. I tried not to."

"Don't love me."

"Tell this tree to scoot over twenty feet; that would be far simpler."

"Of all the reactions I expected . . ." He laughed dryly and shook his head. "That you might refuse . . . it's the only one I hadn't counted on."

"I couldn't marry you, Jay. Not now. Not like this. You're still pulling too much weight behind you. You're dragging such a heavy load from your past. I can't fight that . . . I won't. Tagging along behind you as your lover or your wife, it would always be the same. I would always wonder, each time I watched you ride away, if that would be the time you'd meet someone just a little faster, if I would ever see you again, except with your cold, stiff body slung over the back of a horse. I want more than to stand over your coffin at a five-dollar funeral. There's nothing in your life for me, Jay. Not like it is now."

"More conditions?"

She turned away from him. "Call it what you like."

He was silent for some time. "What are they, these conditions of yours?" He sighed. "What do I have to do to prove myself?"

"You've already done that. It's part of the reason why I love you."

"Then what's missing?

"Have you ever considered going back, trying to come to grips with what happened back in Savannah?"

"Don't start harping at me about that," he warned. "I've got more important things to do."

"More important things than clearing your name, laying old ghosts to rest?"

"Don't peck at me, Jenny! There is nothing in Savannah but cold ashes." He looked at her, his hands digging into her arms. "What could possibly be there for me now?"

"Your freedom. The best way out is through the door. You can't hide in the attic forever." She knew he would probably explode now, and their talk would be over. He wasn't a man to take being called a coward with a grain of salt. But as he often did, Jay surprised her.

"The darkness hides a lot of things, Jenny. Ugly things. Things that are best left in the dark."

"That's not true. You . . ."

"Enough!" he said, pulling away from her, pushing her away when she tried to come to him.

She sat down on the stone bench and pulled her legs up beneath her, resting her head on her knees. She sat there for some time, until her feet were getting cold and she decided to go into the house. As if sensing she was about to leave, Jay came to her, dropped down beside her, and took her in his arms. "Jenny . . ."

"I won't ever feel about anyone the way I feel about you," she said, her hand cupping the strong line of his cheek. She put her arms around his neck. "But I can't come with you. I just can't."

His hair looked dusted with stars, and his eyes glittered like sapphires in the dark as he stared at her exquisite face. Aware of her as he was, taking her in his arms wasn't the wisest thing he could have done. Instantly, his body began to rouse and harden, inundated with desire that was neither disciplined nor flexible. Rigid with need, his eyes dark with passion, he gave in to the madness of it. With a softly sworn curse of surrender he brought his mouth down hard on hers.

Jennifer knew the moment his feelings changed. She had no desire to resist him, for she wanted this as much as he. Meeting his kiss with all the fire and passion within her, she heard Jay groan and for a moment lost herself completely. Reality closed in when he swung her up into his arms. She knew something wonderful was about to happen.

The breeze caught in her skirts and fluttered them around her ankles as he carried her across the lawn and through a narrow wicket gate into an orchard. The trees stood silvered by moonlight, still and quiet, except for the familiar sounds of the night. They were alone now, just the two of them surrounded by the wonders of God's creation. Garden of Eden.

Jay's steps were whisper-quiet as he walked over soft orchard grass and garden clover, and down a stone path that led to the orchard house. He carried her inside, where

lofty walls of lattice and glass protected fruit trees too delicate to be grown in the orchard, as well as hundreds of
blooming plants. Tonight the windows and doors were open
to welcome the cool evening breezes, and everywhere orange trees and myrtles were planted in pots, while flowers
filled wickers and wooden troughs. Along the glass walls,
palms and baskets draped with trailing vines and leafy ferns
were silhouetted against a backdrop of scattered stars. And
still he did not stop. They passed a stand of garden tools
and a bench where a dented old watering can rested, stopping just beyond, where a cluster of garden chairs and sofas
rested upon a rich Persian rug, stacks of pillows covered in
exotic Eastern fabrics scattered about.

There, he lowered her to her feet, still holding her close
and she searched his face. Moonlight picked out his features; the familiar sounds around her gave way to the un-
even rhythm of his breath. The air was cool, but where his
hands caressed her back she was unbelievably warm. She
closed her eyes and leaned her head against his chest, inhaling the scent of all that was dear to her: the scents of the
orchard outside, and within, the rich humus riding on
flower-fragrant air, and closer and dearer still, the warm,
tangy scent of his skin and clothing.

Her desire for him came in an open, honest way, possessing a wholesome cleanliness, an earthy quality that was
neither sordid nor shameful. He was so warm, so male, so
solid, so close. And she loved him so much. The need for
him was something she could not deny, something she
could not hide, and the revealing of it came not at all
gently, but like a shower of peach blossoms driven before
the wind, beautiful and fragrant, borne along by a current
too strong to resist, severed from the bough forever. She
wanted him.

She wanted him, wanted the feel of his mouth upon hers,
wanted the weight of his body pressing her down, wanted
the warmth of his thighs cradled against hers, the strength
of his arms around her, the hard impact of his desire. She

loved him. She wanted him. She needed him. But she could never have him. And the finality of it filled her with such desperation she felt both wanton and out of control. She wanted him one last time, wanted to be loved with such intensity and power that the memory of it would last, but even as she thought it, she knew one time with him would never be enough.

His arms tightened around her, making her wonder if he knew her weakness for him, if he could feel her body tremble with desire. "Are you cold?"

"Yes and no. Everything seems to be in extremes. My flesh is covered with goose bumps, but everywhere you touch . . . you raise blisters." He touched her mouth with his, her body absorbing the tremors of his laughter.

"I'm feeling a little scorched myself," he said as she wiggled against him, trying to find the way she fitted against him most perfectly, the way she could be touching him in the most places. He began to draw her down with him, down to a bed of scattered pillows upon a Persian rug. After their clothes had fallen away, the realization that they were naked, alone, and about to make love for the last time held them motionless for a moment. His weight resting on his elbow, Jay's eyes gazed at her face before dropping lower to her perfectly shaped breasts, his head lowering to nuzzle the smooth skin as his hand came up to caress the soft flesh of her belly and dropping lower.

By the time he brought his lips to her mouth, she was wild beneath his fingers and he kissed her with maddening slowness; something leapt through her like a shaft of fire, arousing all the passion that had been building within her. "Jenny . . ." he whispered thickly. "Sweetheart, I can't wait any longer." With a gentleness she had never before seen in him, he brought his lips to hers, enclosing the front of her in a cocoon of warm male flesh, her back resting upon the richly woven fabrics of the mystical East. All she knew were the dear and familiar sounds and smells around her, the luxurious seduction of opulent fabrics and the worship of Jay's hands and mouth.

"You're driving me crazy," she whispered in a raw, urgent way.

"As you have driven me for countless weeks."

He pressed himself against her, and she felt the throb of him against the naked flesh of her thighs and gasped.

"Tell me," he said. "Tell me you want this as much as I do." His hand went between them, touching her. "You want me; there's no denying that. You're crying for me now."

She didn't tell him, she couldn't find the words, and the thought that he would be leaving in the morning hovered like a teardrop ready to fall. No, she couldn't tell him. But she could show him. Her mouth touched him with a melting sweetness that was irresistible, her hands moving across the smooth muscles of his body, exploring with such eager brazenness that he groaned softly, kissing her with a possessive cry. "You didn't tell me you believed in surprise attacks."

"I don't. I believe in winning."

His fair hair glistened. His brow was drawn together, his eyes glazed with desire. She lifted her hand to stroke his cheek, her eyes on his beautiful wide mouth. The sudden realization that there really would never be another time like this between them struck savagely. Never had she wanted him more. Never had she realized there were so many things about him she wanted to know and learn. The heated desire for him in her loins she could deal with, but how would she ever be reconciled to not having him in her life?

"You're taking unfair advantage," he said, "looking at me like that."

"I do what's necessary when I'm playing for keeps."

"I wish you were playing for keeps," he said softly. "I wish to hell you were."

Suddenly everything was unbearable—loving him, being with him, losing him—and she rolled away from him, sobbing out the unfairness of it all. And he was there, just as he had always been, turning her back to him, his arms coming warm and strong around her and holding her close. She burrowed closer and cried harder, seeing herself spending the rest of her life with a neat little garden and a cantankerous old billy goat just like Pearl and Aunt Winny.

"Crying won't solve anything," he said.

"Neither will leaving, but you're going to go ahead and do it, so don't tell me not to cry."

His hands plunged into her hair and he kissed her. "Kiss me, Jenny. Kiss me and love me and make me forget. Love me like you could never let me go." He spread her legs with his body and drove into her, feeling the clinging heat of her surround him. Crazed and wild with desperation and longing, he sank his soul in her, deeper and deeper, demanding that she come with him. Stroke after stroke he brought her closer and closer to the edge, then with one final stroke he hurled them both into a mindless void. And even then she arched against him, her legs clutching him, her hands against his buttocks driving him deeper, until he touched her as deeply as he could and she cried out his name. "Dear merciful God," he said, stunned at the convulsion that drove his seed from him in scalding spurts and twisted his guts. "This," he whispered hoarsely, "is what you're going to remember all the days of your life. Whenever another man makes love to you, you will remember how it was with us. This is what being loved feels like, Jenny. You won't forget it . . . because you won't ever feel this way again."

She closed her eyes. In this orchard bower she had tasted the forbidden fruit and eaten of the tree of knowledge. Enchanted with garden poppy and bewitched, she fell into a deep sleep.

Jay woke her with a kiss. His eyes searched her face

before his mouth sought hers, his words coming soft and husky, a warm murmur riding on his breath. "Love me, Jenny . . . one last time," he whispered. "One last time before I go."

PART IV

Destiny grants our wishes
but in its own way in order to give us
something beyond our wishes.

Goethe, *Effective Affinities*

19

❦ ❦

Whoever had said, "Prospect is often better than possession" knew what he was talking about. By the time summer had passed, Jennifer was realizing that those who live on expectations are often disappointed. She began to reflect upon her emotionally sterile existence and ask herself a few questions. It was obvious she had lain dormant, waiting for the passage of summer. Waiting and existing. But for what? And why?

"Get on with your life," Rand Baxter said.

She felt a little ashamed to admit it, but if she was going to be totally honest with herself, she would have to confess that she had persisted in thinking she would hear from Jay. A letter, a telegram—some word from him telling her that he missed her, that he was as miserable without her as she was without him. It wasn't that Jay had given her any particular reason to believe he would ever try to contact her, or that he had, in some covert way, given her any false hope. It was simply because she felt, deep down within the very marrow of her bones, that Jay Culhane loved her enough to put things right in his life.

"Give it a little more time, Jenny," Susanna had said. "Why don't you go on back to Brownsville? Get involved in your teaching. Time will pass much faster that way."

So she had returned to Brownsville at the end of summer to take up her teaching position. And for four months she had gone about her day-to-day existence, running here and there, forming plots and subplots, her mind racing and planning, only to discover in the end that the only plotting she had done had been against her very self.

He isn't coming back.

So why had she waited? Why had she persisted for so long at this lunatic sport, spending herself like a racehorse, all because of the persistent, amorous feeling for a man who hadn't cared as much as she'd hoped. Because she thought something might change; because she wanted it to change. But even as his name crossed her mind she knew Jay Culhane would never change, and she, Jennifer Leigh Baxter, had wasted the last bit of summer and early fall waiting for the impossible, when all she had gotten from her patience was unreasonable silence.

Jay Culhane never thought about her anymore.

And she wasn't going to give him any more of her thoughts, either. As Aunt Winny had told her the night before over supper, "It's time to get down to where the water hits the wheel. It's beginning to look like he isn't coming back. Start accepting some of the invitations you've been getting. I know you won't forget him, but you *can* get over him."

"I know I should, but my heart isn't in it. And you know there isn't anyone that compares with him," said Jennifer.

"You're hankering for the earth and the moon with two strands of barbed wire around it—and expecting it to be whitewashed."

Aunt Winny was right. No longer would she allow thoughts of Jay to dominate her existence. Never again would she devote so much of herself, consciously or unconsciously, giving up opportunities and even friendships in order to remain true to a man who had never been hers. She realized now that by keeping this hopeless and quite fruitless commitment to Jay alive, she was losing herself.

Winter came and stayed, one crisp, cold day following another, most of them dry and filled with sunshine, often appearing, from inside the house, much warmer than it actually was. In December Jennifer had a date with Johnny Rayburn, for a New Year's celebration. In February Kip Carter gave her the biggest box of heart-shaped candy she had ever seen, and three dozen of the reddest roses. In March the world outside was warming up, and she began to spade her garden, careful not to disturb the daffodils, cannas, tulips, and hyacinths that had been planted earlier and now bloomed in profusion. On Texas Independence Day, Hardy Steinway took her to a barbecue and dance at the schoolhouse.

In April Jennifer decided it was no use. There wasn't a man alive who could replace Jay Culhane, or even come close. If she was destined to be a spinster, she might as well spend it teaching school. On April 5, she signed a contract to teach school the following year.

On April 9, a telegram arrived from Susanna. Her brother, who lived between Savannah and Charleston, had written that Jennifer's cousin, Marilla Claiborne, was getting married in July and wanted Jennifer to be her maid of honor.

She showed the telegram to Aunt Winny. "So she finally landed a fish," Winny said. "Lord knows she's baited her hook enough. Guess this one was too big to throw back."

"Either that or it was the last minnow in the bucket," said Pearl.

"Me, maid of honor at Marilla's wedding," said Jennifer. "I haven't seen Marilla in three years."

"Count your blessings."

Jennifer couldn't keep the heaviness out of her words. "What blessings? If I was honest, I'd have to say I'm just a little jealous of her."

"Whatever for?"

"Because she's getting married and I'm not."

"Don't put yourself in the same pickle jar with that girl. You two don't piss through the same quill."

"Are you going?" she asked her aunt.

"I haven't decided yet. I'll let you know."

"How about you, Pearl?"

"Nope. I wouldn't walk across the street to see a wedding. Besides, I don't like to be gone anywhere for very long. I have to get back to my rat killing." Pearl looked at Jennifer. "I can see you're going."

"How's that?" said Jennifer, giving Pearl a grin.

"You're hopping like cold water in a hot skillet." Pearl eyed her critically. "I still think you've got worms."

Jennifer laughed. "Pearl, sometimes you are meaner than a two-stingered wasp."

"Naah, I ain't," said Pearl. "I'm as mild as a moonbeam."

It was the middle of May before Aunt Winny made up her mind to go.

The month of June was a busy one. Between closing down the school for the summer, putting up as many vegetables from her garden as she could, and making several trips into Brownsville for fittings for her bridesmaid dress and a new traveling suit, Jennifer still managed to find time to think about Culhane.

She also thought a lot about Savannah, because Marilla's future husband was a Savannah man, and since Marilla's family lived almost as close to Savannah as they did to Charleston, the wedding was to be held in Savannah. What would it be like to go there, to be in the same town where Jay grew up? She was bound to meet people who knew him, men he had played with as a child, perhaps an old teacher or former minister, merchants who had sold him cinnamon sticks on Saturday afternoons, women who had known the thrill of his touch. She might even meet one of his brothers or sisters. But no matter who she met, or how many people she came across who knew Jay Culhane, the one person in the world she wanted to see most would not be there.

The third week in May, Jennifer and Winny took the stage to Weatherford. A week after that Jennifer, Winny, and Susanna, weary and sick of trains, stepped onto the platform at Charleston, their legs rubbery and unsteady after a week on a rocking train. They barely had time to straighten their hats and look around when Preston Claiborne, affectionately known as Claib, came rushing across the wooden platform, looking as splendid and youthful as he had the last time Jennifer had seen him. Jennifer couldn't help laughing at the way Susanna squealed with delight when Claib picked her up and whirled her around, her Manila Longchamps hat sailing from her head, the cluster of roses going in one direction, the long ostrich plume in the other, catching on a gust of wind and floating off the platform—much to the delight of a shrieking group of children, who immediately gave chase. Aunt Winny held Claib off with her parasol when he came after her.

Soon they were clipping down the shady, moss-draped streets of Charleston, behind a smart pair of matched bays that pranced with flashy precision, on their way to Uncle Preston and Aunt Sassy's town house. While Claib rode on ahead on a chestnut mare, inside the carriage Aunt Sassy was bursting to tell her sisters-in-law and niece all about Marilla's wedding, her stout bosom swelling from the effort.

"Four months? She didn't have a very long engagement, did she? You didn't mind?" Susanna asked.

"Personally I do not think it's a good idea to plan a wedding in such a slapdash fashion," Sassy replied.

To which Winny responded, " 'Marry in haste, repent at leisure' is what I always say."

Jennifer gazed at her aunt. If ever there was a person who could endear herself through wit alone, it was Aunt Winny.

Jennifer loved her mother for having given her her start in life, for the strong foundation that was laid during her formative years, for her love and devotion, her tremendous capacity for understanding. Just how many mothers would have taken the news that her daughter had given herself to a man without the sanction of marriage, in the same loving, supportive vein in which Susanna had? And she adored her father for his blustery, old-bear ways, his supportive strength, his judgment, his ability to cope—ten women would try the patience of a saint—for the model of what a husband and lover could be.

But it was her Aunt Winny whom Jenny loved for no reason in particular, and yet for every reason under the sun. She looked at the slim, impeccably dressed woman, with her erect bearing and almost haughty pride, thinking her unruly carroty hair was the only clue to the woman inside. It was Aunt Winny who made her think.

"Has Marilla known the young man long?" Susanna was asking Sassy as she opened her lace-and-ivory fan, having a go at her face.

Aunt Sassy mopped the sweat from her forehead with an embroidered linen handkerchief. "The whole thing is such a mess," Sassy exclaimed, fanning herself with her handkerchief, the fat on her plump arms swinging to and fro from the effort. "I simply don't know where to start."

"Try the beginning," said Winny.

"Yes, well, Marilla and Stephen—Stephen Tattnall, that is—have known each other for about four years now. Of course, both families have long suspected they would marry, and in fact, Stephen made it official in January, when he formally asked Preston for Marilla's hand. They originally decided to be married next Christmas."

"What happened to change their mind?" Jennifer asked.

"Stephen's mother, Eula, has been in ill health for some time. Last week she went into a sudden—and I do mean sudden—decline. The family doctor doesn't give her more than a few weeks. Eula knows her death will throw the family into a year of mourning and she doesn't want that to happen. She wants to see Marilla and Stephen married before she dies. It's her last wish, you might say. So, after discussing this with her doctor, it was decided things needed to be rushed as much as possible."

"That's why you're having the wedding in Savannah?"

"Luckily for us, living almost equal distance from the two, it didn't really make much difference. Preston probably does more business in Charleston, and that's why we keep a town house here, but I would say our social life leans a little more toward Savannah."

"Tell me about Marilla's young man," Susanna said, but Jennifer didn't hear Aunt Sassy's reply, lost as she was in her own thoughts.

Preston Claiborne was waiting for them when they arrived. Aunt Winny told him just how wise he'd been to ride his chestnut instead of taking the carriage with them, and Uncle Preston laughed. "My mama didn't raise no fools," he said, handing the reins to the groom and taking Winny's arm. "So, dear sister, what news have you from that most wretched of all places in the universe, Brownsville?"

Jennifer lost interest in what they were saying as they were given a quick tour of the stuccoed brick town house near the Ashley River—a stately mansion with the most beautiful formal English garden Jennifer had ever seen. She was given a room that was bright and airy, fortunately on the third floor, with a magnificent view of the harbor formed by the meeting of the Ashley and the Cooper rivers —thankfully high enough to admit the cooler breezes that came across the water. But Jenny didn't get to spend much time in the well-appointed room, the next few days being taken up with final dress fittings and parties before they moved to the Claibornes' large estate in the country.

They spent three days spoiling themselves with gracious country living before the entire Claiborne clan transported themselves to Savannah, the last week before the wedding.

They arrived in Savannah late in the evening, and as they drove along the streets where silver-gray skeins of moss draped the trees and hundreds of dogwoods and azaleas lined the avenues, Jennifer decided no city in the world could be more beautiful than Savannah, with its parks and squares and homes scattered between that sparkled like crown jewels. Everywhere she looked, it was breathtaking. And it was Jay's home.

But Jay would probably never come back here again. He would finish out his life alone, with nothing to call his own except his horse, his saddle, and whatever meager belongings he could carry with him. And he would die in much the same way he lived: alone, friendless, and on the move. It broke her heart to see him throw away so much potential.

They proceeded over the cobblestone streets, arriving at the Ballastone Inn on Oglethorpe Avenue, just as Preston finished telling them that the stones were brought to Savannah as ballast in the holds of sailing ships and were dumped on arrival, then used to pave the streets. Hot, tired, and ready for a bath, Jennifer was the first to poke her head out of the carriage.

After dinner Susanna came into Jennifer's room. "Lord, I'm close to busting my stays! I've never eaten so much," Susanna said. "I shouldn't have eaten such a large bowl of black turtle bean soup."

"And I shouldn't have had so much praline coffee," Jennifer said, giving her own tummy a pat. "But it was so good."

"You didn't eat much, I noticed. Are you all right, Jenny?" Susanna crossed the room, placing her hands at strategic points around Jennifer's face. "You feel a little warm."

"It's the heat, that's all," Jennifer said.

"Either that or too many mint juleps."

Weddings are exciting events, and everyone in Savannah knew of the upcoming nuptials. That meant guests, and gifts, parties, and meeting new people. One of these new people was Stephen's friend, Christopher Warren. Mrs. Fishpeck, the parson's wife, was the first to say Jenny and Kit went together like two peas in a pod. Kit was the rogue of five counties in Georgia and three in South Carolina, as Mrs. Fishpeck, who had been around long enough to know, could tell just by looking.

The night before the wedding, the Claibornes hosted a big party in the hotel. The punch was flowing freely, quite a bit of it through Jennifer's cup. At half past nine Winny said to Jennifer, who was by this time looking quite pale, "You better go outside and get some air. You're looking as pale as a gutted fish."

Jennifer fled from the room. A laughing Kit found her a few minutes later, her face turned to receive the benefit from a wonderfully cool breeze blowing up from the Savannah River. She was sitting on a stone bench on the veranda. "Jennifer, my pet. Are you all right?"

"I think I'm drunk."

He laughed. "Well, that's nothing to be terribly upset about. It isn't the end of the world."

"That's easy for you to say. You aren't the one that's going to wake up with a head the size of Bald Mountain."

"On you it would be lovely. Don't be so despondent. You're only a little bit drunk. You haven't had that much to drink. You just aren't used to it."

Aunt Sassy had enough foresight to put Jennifer and Marilla in the same large corner room at the hotel, which made it easy for them to strengthen the friendship they had maintained since they were children by letters and the occasional exchange of visits. To be such good friends, Jennifer and Marilla were complete opposites—Marilla being very petite with china-blue eyes and hair the color of old gold. But they got along well together, and because of this, they stayed up a little later than they should have.

They overslept the next morning, which left them little time to dress. Part of the problem was solved by having two tubs delivered so they could bathe and wash their hair at the same time. By the time they had finished dressing, the room was in complete disorder, something Aunt Sassy noted by saying she hadn't seen such a disaster "since those dreadful Yankees fired on Fort Sumter."

Aunt Winny, of course, set her straight by informing her, "It was the darling Rebels that fired the shot that started the war, and it just happened to be aimed toward Fort Sumter."

Aunt Sassy, being a woman of great compromise, altered her statement somewhat by saying, "Since those dreadful Yankees burned Atlanta."

They arrived at Christ Episcopal Church at half past six and hurried into the bride's waiting area, where they put on the last-minute touches that seemed so important but changed little. As people began to arrive, Jennifer felt her palms perspiring. By the time the organ music reached her ears, her breathing was short and shallow. When she heard the quick knock on the door, a voice calling out, "Ceremony starts in five minutes," she felt dizzy.

Marilla, wearing a lovely Parisian gown of ivory satin, draped with Brussels lace and trimmed with orange blossoms, turned away from the window and looked at Jennifer. As the maid of honor, Jennifer wore a dress of pale *ciel*-blue satin with bead embroidery. Short, puffed sleeves of dotted mousseline de soie covered her shoulders. A jabot fell between branches of embroidery that covered her breasts. "You look so beautiful," said Marilla. "I'm glad your dress is blue."

"Why is that?"

"If it was white, they might mistake you for the bride."

"No, they wouldn't," Jennifer said. "They could tell the difference by looking at your face."

"Jenny," she said, taking a deep breath, "I'm so nervous. You don't know how happy I am that you're here. It makes me think we're just playing dress-up, like we used to do when we were little."

"Except this time I get to wear a pretty dress too," Jennifer said, helping Marilla drape the long tulle veil and securing the cluster of orange blossoms to Marilla's pompadour roll of hair.

"I was a spoilsport, wasn't I? Always having to have my way . . . always the bride."

Jenny smiled weakly. "It was good practice," she said, hugging Marilla. "You're still the bride."

"Oh, pooh! You'll be one soon, just you wait and see."

"I don't think so."

Jenny opened her mouth to say something else, but a sharp rap on the door interrupted her thought. The door opened and a small-framed woman poked her head into the room. "It's time," she said. "Take your places."

Eight attendants preceded Jennifer, who was the last to walk down the aisle before Marilla. As she took her place at the back of the church, over the confusion of feathered and festooned hats and ornately coiffed hairdos, Jennifer could see the groom and his best man standing to the minister's left. The aisle seemed a hundred miles long. She was feeling just a little nervous. She had never been in a wedding before. The last bridesmaid was in place now, and Jennifer began her slow-paced stroll, smiling as she passed dozens of unknown faces that turned to stare at her. But as she passed the pews that were marked by satin ribbons for the family of the groom, there was one face that turned to look at her, and it wasn't the face of a stranger.

Jay Culhane.

Jennifer's breath caught in her throat, and she almost stumbled, catching herself just in time. Tension stretched like vibrating wire and she prayed that God wouldn't be so heartless as to let her faint or burst into tears before the wedding was over. She had never been so thankful for the bouquet of flowers she was holding, and she could only hope they hid the trembling of her hands. She couldn't take her eyes off him as she kept walking, staring in a transfixed sort of way, like a person who sees a runaway wagon bearing down but is unable to move out of the way. His eyes were locked upon her, just as hers were upon him, until she saw the rosy-cheeked blonde next to him lift his hand and bring it to her lips. Jennifer looked away, breaking the contact, and then, as if the break had released the paralyzed cells in her brain, her mind screamed, *Jay . . . Jay . . . Jay.*

Overcoming his shock at seeing Jennifer, Jay Culhane sat up a little straighter. He knew she saw him now, and her recoil hurt. He had never thought that seeing him would be distasteful to her, that the laughter and softness he had known so well would go suddenly cold and stiff in recognition. A darkness settled over the very spirit of him, heavier than any he had ever known. All this time away from her, all the ways he imagined her, not once had he ever suspected she would hate him. She was close enough to him now to reach out and touch. His eyes lifted from the bouquet that trembled in her hands to those beautiful violet eyes of hers, those unforgettable eyes.

When she reached the front of the church, she took her place at the side of the altar. She lifted her head slowly, catching Stephen's brown eyes upon her, returning his wink with a weak smile as she looked toward the back of the church. Marilla was walking toward her, down a candlelit aisle, Uncle Preston at her side. For just a moment she allowed her eyes to seek him once again, feeling her eyes burn at the look of sad regret that shadowed his beautiful face, the stab of pain she saw there as she jerked her eyes away.

Dearly beloved . . .

Jennifer wanted to throw her bouquet and run screaming from the church; she wanted to go to him, scratching the eyes out of the pasty blonde next to him; she wanted to hurt him and make him suffer for all the pain she had felt. Marilla handed her bouquet to Jennifer, and she took it mechanically, feeling all hard and wooden inside as she watched them repeat their vows; the throbbing reminder that he had once asked this of her pounding like a cannon within her heart.

Do you take this woman . . .

He realized then that without her he would never have any peace. He kept his eyes on her face, willing her to look at him: *Look at me, Jenny. See my heart in my eyes.* She looked, and his heart gave a wild and frantic lurch, then her lashes lowered and for a moment he was stunned, not really believing what he'd seen in her eyes but overwhelmed and elated at the thought of it. No woman, absolutely *no* woman, looked at a man like that and felt cold and indifferent. *Like me, she is hurt.* His heart soared, he felt elated— and hurt. It was something he knew well, something he had lived with for so long. Hurt, he knew how to handle.

To love, honor, and obey . . .

The blonde next to him said something, but Jay didn't hear. He was under a spell, bewitched by the shock of seeing Jenny at all, stunned to see her in Stephen's wedding, being maid of honor when she should have been his bride. Never had he seen her look so lovely. As she stood at the altar, he watched the rise and fall of those lovely breasts, and the agony of subsequent denial was more than he could bear. His eyes dropped lower, remembering the delicate ribs that climbed like stairs across the milky whiteness of her midriff.

You may now kiss the bride . . .

The blast from the organ nearly drove him from his seat, his eyes skimming over Marilla and Stephen as they began their long walk back up the aisle. He shifted his position and closed his eyes, seeing her now the way he remembered her best: the amethyst clarity of her eyes, huge with the wonder of her first arousal; the perfect way her mouth went round with surprise when she discovered the hardness of his own. He blinked, then looked away, her form taking shape before him once again, this time calling to mind firm thighs the texture of heavy cream, soft as down, and, higher up, the shocking contrast of their stark whiteness against the thick, curling blackness she wore like a crown.

Jenny . . .

Their gazes met, and for a moment he thought she might drop the bouquet and rush into his arms. But her ironlike will gained control and he watched the lovely, pale face freeze. She looked at him coolly, holding his gaze longer than necessary, as if by doing so, she was telling him that she didn't care enough to hurt. Then she looked away, calm and easy, with total indifference, as she passed, and walked out of the door into the warm Georgia sunshine.

Marilla and Stephen were already in the carriage when Jay stepped through the doorway. He returned Stephen's wave, seeing Jennifer standing beside the carriage, sparkling beautifully as she talked to one of the bridesmaids. He excused himself from his clinging friend and headed her way.

"Hello, angel eyes."

That voice. Jennifer froze. She didn't want to look into his eyes, which could melt her like butter. She didn't want him to know . . . His hand on her shoulder. Dear God, how familiar that aching touch. She turned, looking up at him, and felt her insides twist.

"Leave me alone, Jay."

"I want to see you."

"No!" She looked around to see if anyone had heard. "I can't. They're waiting in the carriage for me now. I've got to go."

"At the party, then."

"Jay—"

"At the party, or by God, I'll embarrass the hell out of you."

"You already have."

"It can be much worse, I promise you."

How can it be worse? her mind screamed. "I want nothing from you. Especially your promises."

"Yes, I seem to remember you saying something like that once before."

Jennifer turned away and began picking rice from her bouquet. A minute later the leech was back, hanging on

Jay's arm. His hands clenched into fists. A moment later Jennifer walked away.

It was a short ride by carriage from the church to the reception afterward, held at the home of the groom. As the carriage turned down the pebbled driveway the well-manicured lawn came into view. Everywhere she looked, the grass was sprinkled with clothed tables. Softly glowing lanterns strung in the trees, crisscrossing the yard.

At the Tattnalls', Jennifer attached herself to the ample-bosomed matrons at the reception, thinking their dowdy midst was the perfect place to hide, unaware that her lovely, dark sleekness made her stand out.

Kit rescued her, taking Jennifer's arm and leading her on a weaving path beneath the softly swaying lanterns. Near the raised dancing platform that had been built especially for the wedding, Kit took two cups of punch from a maid as she passed by, handing one to Jennifer. Across the green, Jennifer saw Jay and the blonde. Beneath lowered lashes, she watched them approach the dance floor, Jay taking the woman in his arms. Jennifer's body jerked in recoil.

"You're awfully pale. Do you feel all right?"

"I'm fine. It's just the heat."

"Do you want to dance?"

"Not right now."

"Dear me," Kit said, "I was hoping you would."

"Why?" Jennifer was watching the dancers; her eyes kept going to Jay and the blonde.

"Because that was the only way I could think of to hold you in my arms without getting my face slapped. Who is he?"

"Just someone I knew."

"Knew? As in past tense?"

"Yes. It's over."

"That's a relief. He's a big, mean-looking brute."

"His disposition is as nasty as it looks."

Kit laughed and chucked her under the chin. "It must *really* be over. I do hope, pet, that we will remain friends."

Jennifer frowned. Jay and that woman were walking along the dark fringe of trees across the green. They disappeared into the shadows.

"Are you sure it's over?"

"I thought you wanted to dance," she said, changing the subject.

"I did. I do."

Jennifer only danced three dances with Kit because Stephen's father drafted him to drive one of the carriages to take some early-departing guests into town. After Kit left, she wandered among the tables looking for her mother and Aunt Winny.

She spotted Winny's glowing orange halo, which looked like a second sun, and headed in her direction. Winny was talking to Mr. Fishpeck, the parson.

"Politics and religion change. Women don't."

"Aunt Winny, have you seen Mother?"

Winny turned toward Jennifer, and Mr. Fishpeck gave Jennifer a grateful look, then bolted.

Winny looked Jennifer over from head to foot. "That dress ought to do it," she said. "It's perfect."

"Perfect for what?"

"Bait."

"Bait?"

"He's here, you know." Jennifer's face darkened with sudden understanding. Winny's eyes were warm and reassuring. "I figured you'd seen him. Hard to miss, that one is."

"I saw him . . . and the suckerfish with him . . ."

"You don't need to worry. You've got just the dress to catch Culhane's eye."

"I couldn't catch his eye buck naked!"

Up went Winny's brows.

"You know what I meant!" Jennifer snapped.

Winny's eyes went back to Jennifer's dress. "I still say that dress is good bait. You look like a turned-down bed with two pillows."

"He's had a whole year to show me how interested he is." Jennifer gave Winny a reproving look. "Don't you go meddling. Leave well enough alone."

Winny looked like she was considering that, then she said, "This party is as dull as a hoe. I wonder where they keep the whiskey? Have you tried the punch?"

"Yes. There isn't any liquor in it, though."

"Never is. We need to find the men's supply. They always put out one punch for the ladies and tea sippers and another for the men. That's the one we want."

"I had enough of that stuff last night."

"That's probably why you're so pale. Where'd you park your young man?"

"Kit? Stephen's father asked him to drive one of the carriages to town."

"That's nice to hear." Jennifer looked up, her eyes narrowing when she met Jay's gaze. "If he knows what's good for him, he'll stay there."

"Culhane! If you aren't a sight for sore eyes." Winny looked him over. And he did look good in those black evening clothes of his. "You're looking fit enough to wrestle a couple of mountain lions. Still sweet on me?"

Jay grinned. "Does a bear sleep in the woods?" His eyes were on Jennifer. Winny, a woman who hadn't been born yesterday, followed his gaze.

"Culhane, if you lean any farther, you're gonna fall flat on your face." said Winny.

Jay laughed, grabbing Winny and whirling her around in his arms. As he put her down he planted a good one right on her startled mouth. If it had been any other man, Jennifer would have collapsed with laughter at the look on Winny's face. Never had she seen her aunt speechless; her face was turning red.

"What are you doing here?" Jennifer asked, giving him a disgusted look.

Jay didn't get a chance to answer because Susanna walked up to them. "Mr. Culhane, hello."

Jennifer's eyes went from Jay to her mother, then to her aunt.

"Is this your doing? Is that why he's here?" Jennifer asked accusingly.

"I haven't the faintest idea why he's here. I would imagine he came for the wedding, like the rest of us," Susanna said. "Jennifer, are you feeling well?"

"Don't tell me how pale I am!" Jennifer looked at the three of them, thick as flies in August. She loved her mother. She loved her aunt. But neither of them had any right to interfere in her personal life. She would have Jay Culhane on her own terms or not at all. Mother and Aunt Winny and their meddling be damned. How could they shame her like this by being in cahoots with him? She saw how Jay seemed to be enjoying all of this, and she rounded on him. "Why are you here?"

"I've been waiting around to talk to you."

"Is that what you and the woman were doing slinking around in the shadows at the edge of the trees? Waiting on me?"

His heart soared. She had noticed. He grinned. "If I'd known you were so anxious . . ."

"Where's your anemic friend?"

"I think I lost her in the shadows."

"Jennifer, I've never seen you act like this. What is wrong with you?" asked Susanna.

"Nothing's wrong," Winny replied. "She's just overcome with joy."

"Yes, I can see that she is," said Susanna.

Jay wasn't saying anything. He was observing Jennifer, who was too preoccupied to notice what he was doing. It wasn't hard. He couldn't keep his eyes off her. He wanted to drag her behind the nearest tree and make love to her until she squealed with delight. And when he finished doing that, he wanted to throttle her.

Jennifer was still talking to her mother, but she had her eye on him. Then she threw up her hands and said, "I think you're all against me on this." She looked off. "There's Kit. At least he doesn't treat me like I had two heads." She whirled and ran to meet Kit. And Kit looked pretty happy to see her headed in his direction.

And Jay was none too pleased about that. He scowled, watching the young pup slide his arm possessively around Jennifer, his hand just a little too high over her waist to sit right with him. Jay clenched his fists. Jennifer and Kit were on the dance floor, and he was taking her in his arms.

"Jay . . . yoo-hoo . . . Jay!"

Jay cringed as he, Susanna, and Winny all turned in unison to see where the dreadful noise was coming from. He groaned.

"Looks like she found her way out," said Winny.

"Regrettably, it looks like you're right." Jay turned toward the blonde. "Excuse me, ladies."

"Where you off to, Culhane?" asked Winny.

"I'm going to take Blanche back into the trees and choke her."

"Need any help?" asked Winny.

"No," said Jay. "I want to enjoy this by myself."

An hour later Winny found the men's punch, then set off to find her niece. By this time Jennifer was alone—Kit having been captured by a group of Stephen's friends to plan a surprise for Marilla and Stephen when they got into their buggy. Taking Jennifer by the arm, the two of them defected to the enemy's camp. An hour after that, Susanna found Jennifer and Winny huddled together, laughing over a cup of punch. Susanna collapsed next to them. After a while her mother whispered something and Jennifer nodded.

A short time later Jennifer made her way toward the house, careful to stay along the fringe of trees that lined the yard, and slipped quietly into the library, closing the door behind her. She took a few steps to bring her farther into the dimly lit interior, then paused, her eyes scanning the perimeter of the room when a voice from the vicinity of the sofa said, "What are you looking for?"

Jennifer jumped three feet. Never in all her twenty-two years had she been so startled. Her knees buckling beneath her, Jenny reached for the back of a chair to give her much-needed support. Jay rose from the depths of the sofa in front of her.

"A bluebird, flightless and afraid, a shimmering vision that clouds my memory and sings the saddest tune of what might have been. How are you doing, sweet Jennifer?"

Jennifer frowned, trying to bring Culhane into clearer focus. "Tolerable, as they say here in Savannah. And yourself?" Jay's smile made her insides warmer than the punch had.

"Tol'ble, as the *natives* say here in Savannah."

Jennifer was scanning the room, the memory of his devastating smile flowing warm and thick in her blood. He came around the sofa, standing no more than three feet from her. "Are you nervous, or are you looking for something? A place to sit, perhaps?"

Her hand came up to her throat. "No . . . that is, I'm looking for Mother's silk shawl. She thought she left it in here."

"I don't think so."

"She must have been mistaken, then." She turned toward the door.

"No! Jenny, wait."

She paused, her eyes resting lightly upon him, but she said nothing.

"I asked your mother to arrange a few minutes of privacy for us. I want to talk to you."

"I think not. I believe we said more than enough in Weatherford."

"We didn't say shit in Weatherford. *I'm* the one who did the talking in Weatherford. All you did was turn your nose up and your thumb down. Well, things are different now."

"I doubt anything has changed since that time, certainly not you."

"You know me so well?"

"As well as anyone, I think."

"You don't know me at all."

"All right! I don't know you! But I will always cherish my misconceptions about you."

"Ah, sweet little Jenny, there is so much you don't understand."

"I understand more than I'd like to."

"I'm not sure that's true, my love."

"I don't care what you think. You need to understand one thing: I have no interest in becoming involved with anything that concerns you." *My love?*

"You might be surprised."

"As I have been countless times before."

"You were interested once."

"Once does not a lifetime make."

"Is that a quote?"

"No. Stop laughing, Culhane. Things have changed between us."

"Have they? Darling, I hope not. That would make you sound like a shallow flirt."

She shrugged. "Perhaps that's what I am. But name me a woman that doesn't have a little of the flirt in her, or one you would be interested in if she didn't. It's part of our charm, Culhane." *Darling?*

"To a certain degree, when a man doesn't get an overdose."

She turned, then caught herself, turning back toward him. "Before I go, I have just one thing to ask you. What are you doing here?"

His white teeth gleamed against his tanned face, his bold, blue eyes enjoying her. "I've come for the wedding, of course. The same as you."

"But why? What are these people to you that you would

come back for . . . to a place you professed so violently to loathe?"

He understood now why she looked so hurt, what she was asking. Why had he come back to Savannah when he wouldn't do it for her? "The Tattnalls are old family friends. Stephen and I went to school together. His brother, Brian, is married to my cousin, Bethany. I believe, further back, we have a grandfather or two in common."

"Is that all?"

"Perceptive, aren't you?" He looked thoughtful, as if he were weighing something. Then he sighed. "No. That isn't all. Stephen and Brian are . . . were my wife's first cousins."

"Strange," Jennifer said, gazing over his shoulder to the oil painting above the fireplace. "What strange twists and turns there are in life's little mazes. What tricks fate likes to play on us." She looked away. "I need to get back."

"Just give me a few minutes. That's all I ask." He wasn't sure if that was a nod or not. "Jennifer, love—"

"Don't call me that!"

"Why? That's what you are, you know."

"Liar! What are you trying to do? Soften me up so you'll have someone to warm your bed while you're here?"

"I don't have to go to those extremes."

"No, I'm sure you don't. There are probably a dozen women right now with hounds out on your trail."

"Not any more than you've got sniffing after you, I would imagine."

"You can leave Kit out of this."

"Oh, it's Kit, is it? The boy isn't even dry behind the ears."

"Maybe I'm not interested in his ears."

"It won't work, my love. You aren't going to provoke me. The boy isn't for you. He isn't man enough to run you a close second, let alone hold his own."

"And you are, I suppose?"

"I try," he said, watching her closely.

She was getting edgy now. She didn't know what she wanted.

He didn't know what she wanted, either. He knew what she needed. He came to her, reaching for her, his hands touching her shoulders. She slapped at him and jerked free. Jay walked to the door and threw the lock.

"Are you crazy? What are you doing?"

"Giving us some privacy." She took a step back.

"I don't want privacy!"

"Jennifer, you don't know *what* in the hell you want." He came forward.

"Someone might come in here." She retreated.

"They can't. I just locked the door."

"They might . . . knock." She looked over her shoulder, seeing her way clear.

"I've taken care of that as well. Barham is watching the door."

She slammed to a halt. "Who the hell is Barham?"

Jay threw back his head and laughed. "Ah, Jenny, Jenny, Jenny. There will never be another woman like you. At least not for me. I can tell you've been around your Aunt Winny. That's one of the things I love about you, one of the things I missed the most. You're no lightweight, my angel. You've got a lot of substance. Something firm to take hold of. You're the kind of woman a man likes." He had a wicked gleam in his eye now. "You're especially the kind I like." He grinned. "Barham is the Tattnalls' butler."

"Well, you aren't my type at all."

"What's wrong, love?"

"Just get away from me. Leave me alone."

He wrapped his arms around her and pulled her down on the sofa with him. "Ohh! I don't understand any of this. Why don't you leave me alone? Why can't you take no for an answer?"

"Jennifer, shut up."

"Culhane—"

"Shut up, my darling girl, and kiss me."

She didn't know why he asked; he certainly didn't wait for her to kiss him. She pushed him away, drawing her head back. When he tried to kiss her again, she turned her head away.

"Jenny. Look at me. Please?" She did, and his heart leapt, as it always did when her eyes touched him.

She knew that look, knew what was to follow. Some of the hardness seemed to have rubbed off him. He was the same and yet he wasn't. He leaned closer. "Jay," she said sharply when she realized his intention, "I don't want this."

"You may not want it but you sure as hell need it."

"Have you no shame? My *mother* is out there."

He laughed. "Now *that's* a compelling thought."

"Jay, I'm warning you—"

He yanked her against him. "Ahh, Jenny . . . Jenny . . . Jenny. Sweetheart, to feel you in my arms again, after so long. . . ."

She fought and twisted, resisting until she finally wrenched away. But he let her go only as far as his powerful muscles would allow. Tired and breathless, feeling the punch and tightly laced corset working against her, she felt betrayed and strangely bereft of will. He pulled her against him, his heart thudding madly against her breast.

"Dear God, Jenny," he said hoarsely against her throat, "I want you." He had her backed up against the sofa now, bringing his thigh between hers. "I want you," he said, "so damn much. You're driving me mad." It all came back to him in a heated rush: the way it had been between them; how it felt to hold her like this; the unique scent of her; the wild-honey taste of her mouth; the throaty purr deep in her throat when she wanted him as badly as he wanted her.

He wanted to take her right now, here, in the library, and he was mindless with the thrill of it. She arched against him, whispering his name, as she had done so many times before. His hand came up, between them, and found the solace of her breast, caressing until she groaned, and then sliding beneath the bodice to surround the warm, sweet flesh of her exquisite breast. He tried to remember where they were. In the library. The forbidden nature of it, the risk—and, yes, the lustiness of it—drove him insane with excitement. He slid down to the floor with her, drinking in the breathy heat of her that surrounded him.

He kissed her nose, her mouth, her eyes, her cheek, then his hands touched her forehead and curled around her ears before settling into the warm nestling of hair at her nape. And she liked it. Heaven help her, she liked it.

And he knew she liked it. He could tell by the way she squirmed beneath him like she couldn't get close enough. His hand dropped lower, coming up under layers of petticoats, seeking and finding a warm length of leg, then following the line of it, rubbing and caressing, now circling her knee, and higher, to caress the contour of her thigh. She moaned, low and deep, her legs parting for him, his hand groping, seeking, knowing what to do, then sliding with trembling devotion into the wet velvet of her. Her breaths came in quick little pants and she shuddered in wrenching release the moment he touched her. "Jesus!" he said, kissing the dampness of her throat, her face.

Jay began fumbling with the buttons on his trousers, giving Jennifer a moment of time, and a moment was all it took for the distant sounds of music to filter into her consciousness. Through the blissful fog she began to hear the movement of feet in the hallway outside the door, the echo of voices carrying down the empty corridors. Slow awareness flooded her. With a gasp of earth-slamming reality, she pushed him off her and sat up, rearranging her clothing and smoothing her hair as she came to her feet. She reached out and gripped the back of the sofa to keep from falling, her other hand clenched in a fist and pressing against her stomach. The thought of what she had done, where she had done it, and how easily she had played into his hands made her feel cheap and common, something Jennifer had never felt before. And the self-disgust of it made her sick.

Jay followed her up, his body still screaming with need, and for a moment he just stood there looking at her, his breathing ragged, his fists clenched at his sides. He read clearly the revulsion on her face. *Bitch!* She would squirm and wiggle for him until he gave her what she wanted, but when it came to putting out the fire in him, she was all scruples. For a split second he was afraid he might resort to rape. As he brought that under control he began to fight the urge to put his hands around her slender white neck and squeeze. He hated her. He loved her. He could kill her right now with his bare hands. He could spend the rest of his life making love to her.

When he was able to speak at last, his tone was low but loaded with anger. "Since you obviously enjoyed the service I just performed, I can only surmise the nauseating disgust you radiate so well must be for me. That's biting the hand that stimulates, wouldn't you say?"

"You're too cruel to be called an animal," she said bitterly, fighting back tears. He saw the shattered look in her eyes as she said, "I loved you too much ever to feel those things, except when they were directed toward myself. How blind you are, Jay Culhane. How totally blind—and utterly stupid."

"Come here. We need to talk. I won't touch you."

She laughed and shook her head. "You don't even understand, do you?" Tears were rolling down her cheeks. "I feel sad for you, you know that? In spite of it all, I really and truly feel sad. Her lips trembled so that for a second she couldn't speak. Then, with a shuddering breath, her voice so low he could barely hear, she said, "You have taken possession of me, and I hate you for it."

She turned and ran for the door.

"Jenny!" he called after her. She threw the lock.

Bewildered, angry, and confused, Jay was at a complete loss. Before he could respond, Jennifer slipped out the door. A few minutes later she found her mother and aunt, who by this time were as ready to depart as Jennifer was.

At daybreak the next morning the Claiborne party, with Susanna and Winny in tow, left for their country home. Jennifer had decided not to go. At eight o'clock the following morning, Jennifer took a carriage from the hotel to the train station. At nine-thirty she was on the westbound train. She was going to put as much distance as she could between herself and Jay Culhane. She was going back to Weatherford and then on to Brownsville. She was going home, and none too quickly to suit her taste.

At eleven forty-five that same morning, the brass lion on the massive front door of the Claibornes' country estate banged long and loud, causing the butler to drop the silver tea set he was carrying to the dining room. Leaving the mess to the maid to clean, the butler wore his frostiest look as he opened the front door. But Jay Culhane, standing on the other side of the door, didn't even notice.

Jay removed his hat, stepping around the butler into the foyer. "I'd like to see Miss Jennifer Baxter, if you would be so kind as to tell her Jay Culhane is here."

"I'm afraid that's an impossibility, sir. Miss Baxter didn't come back with the family."

"She didn't? Where is she?"

"I'm not at liberty to reveal that, sir. If you would like to speak to her uncle or her mother . . ."

"Susanna's here?"

"In the drawing room, sir. With Miss Winny. If you'll step in here, I'll tell her you're waiting in the parlor."

Jay handed the butler his hat and walked into the parlor, not taking a seat but pacing back and forth in front of the window. A few minutes later Susanna swept into the room wearing a green-and-white-striped dress.

"Mr. Culhane, this is a surprise," she said, trying to look surprised.

Jay took her hand. "Mrs. Baxter. You are looking younger all the time."

"It must be the humidity, plumps out the wrinkles, I'm told," she said, giving her chin a pat.

Jay laughed at that. Susanna Baxter didn't have too many worries as far as wrinkles were concerned. She was a very attractive woman and remarkably well preserved. But seeing her made him think of Jenny and why he had come. "The butler tells me Jennifer didn't come back with you last night."

"Yes, I'm afraid she cut her stay short. She took the nine-o'clock train this morning."

"The train? To Texas?"

"Yes."

"She's traveling alone? Do you think that was a good idea?"

"I was assured it was quite safe. And besides, you probably know her as well as I do. Can you really see *anyone* telling Jenny what she can or can't do?"

Jay, angry as he was, had to smile at that. "No, of course I can't."

"I'm sorry you rode all the way out here for nothing."

Jay nodded. "Well, I've taken up enough of your time. I'll be getting on back. When you see Jennifer, tell her . . . oh, never mind," he said, taking Susanna's hand once more, then leaving with a very determined stride. "I'll tell her myself."

"You've got your work cut out for you, Mr. Culhane. You know that, don't you?"

Jay stopped, then turned. A smile stretched across his face, and Susanna could see what her daughter saw in him. "Yes, ma'am, I reckon I do."

Susanna moved to the window, parting the curtain with her left hand and watching Jay mount a glossy blood bay. He spurred the spirited animal into a full gallop, and Susanna shook her head. "Love never made a man wise," she said, dropping the curtain back into place.

20

"Comfort and speed" is what her one-hundred-dollar first-class ticket stub read, but after seven hours of rocking back and forth to the hum of *click-click, click-click, click-click,* Jennifer felt she was not only going mad but also was inclined to agree with the famous author of *Ramona*, Helen Hunt Jackson, who'd said, "It is impossible to be just to a person or a thing disliked. I dislike the sleeping-car sections more than I have ever disliked, ever shall dislike, or ever can dislike anything in the world."

As she stood to one side, watching the porter ready her sleeping berth, Jennifer wondered just why it was that she found this train, which was practically identical to the one she'd ridden the week before with her mother, so much more uncomfortable and irritating than the one she had ridden from Fort Worth to Savannah. Two reasons, she decided.

First, she didn't have Aunt Winny's wit and Susanna's whimsical chatter to listen to, and second, on the trip to Savannah, she hadn't as yet had that distressing encounter with Jay Culhane.

"There you go, miss, she's all ready," the porter said proudly, stepping back from the sleeping berth.

Eyeing the berth, Jennifer thanked him and handed him two bits. Heretofore she had thought all sleeping cars were the same. But now, studying the contraption in which she was to spend the next eight hours or so, she wasn't so sure. On the trip out, their train had been equipped with that ingenious device for sleeping created and designed by George Pullman, the Pullman car.

This more prehistoric version of the sleeper was rather dismal-looking, and Jennifer wondered just how she was going to go about getting a night's rest in a contrivance that looked like it had been designed by a lunatic contortionist. But suddenly remembering the crowded misery in the second-class cars she had passed through, she decided this torture rack she had been assigned for the next five nights wasn't so bad. Still, she couldn't help thinking that this was going to prove to be a very long night.

Jennifer yanked the berth's curtains closed and sat down, drawing her legs up Indian-style. Sitting on her berth and catching her breath, she began to unbutton her jacket, stripping down to her chemise and drawers, when she looked up, noticing that the wooden panels above her were so highly polished that she could see clearly into the berth above her. She breathed a sigh of relief, however, because thankfully that berth was empty.

It was at that moment that she realized she needed her hairbrush and nightgown and that they were stowed under her berth. Sticking her head out, she looked first to the right, then to the left. Seeing the hallway deserted, Jenny opted to go for it in her chemise and drawers. She had no more gotten prone on her belly and inched her way forward than the door at the end of the compartment opened and the conductor entered, followed by three robust men. Amid catcalls and whistles, Jennifer grabbed her gown and brush and dived between the curtains, striking her knee painfully in the process.

After several attempts to pin the curtains together, Jennifer was about to give up when she hit upon the idea of pinning her drawers at one end, which didn't add enough material to allow the ends to meet but did narrow the opening considerably. At last she was gowned, brushed, and ready to lie down. But no sooner was she settled in—falling asleep after what seemed such a long time—than the train took a sharp curve, lurched, and hurled her out of her berth and into the passageway, where she joined other horrified passengers in various stages of dress or undress, slamming against one another in burlesque fashion. She had an even harder time going to sleep the second time, but eventually fatigue claimed her.

At daybreak the next morning, her body in rack and ruin, Jennifer decided she would not spend one more night like this. She dressed and went searching for the porter, who directed her to the conductor. Once she had located him, Jennifer, taking on all the attributes of her Aunt Winny, began to relate the unfortunate events of the previous night, adding a little embellishment as she went along. When she had almost finished, she stopped suddenly. The conductor was regarding her with a fascinated air.

"Back up there a minute, little lady." His hands shot out. "Whoa! I mean, figuratively. Repeat more slowly what you just said."

"The *whole* thing?" Jennifer asked with a disgruntled look.

"Just back up to the part about the man."

"I woke up once during the night with a man's foot in my face . . . the man in the berth next to mine."

He was looking more fascinated by the minute. "I got that part. Now tell me about the other man."

"That was the second time I was awakened. This time a strange man had his head poked through the curtain and was staring at me . . . while I was asleep."

"And?"

"I boxed him with my hairbrush."

He was smiling now. "Go on."

"The third time I was awakened by a man trying to

climb into bed with me, and as I am sure you know, those sleeping berths are severely restrictive and small for one person, let alone two." She saw his amused look. "Not that that would have made any difference, of course, but the point is . . . dang blast it, man! I could have had my person assaulted or been robbed or murdered."

"I understand," he said a in genuinely sympathetic way, "but I don't know what I can do about it."

"What about a private car? I know you have them. I've ridden in Mr. Gould's car before."

The conductor looked surprised. "You know Mr. Gould?"

Jennifer nodded.

"Jay Gould?"

"Him too," said Jennifer. "And I know his son George and his daughter Anna. Mr. Gould and my father have done a lot of business together. I know Mr. Gould owns this railroad!"

"Yes, he does." He was considering something, Jennifer could tell that much.

"Give me your berth number, Miss Baxter. I'll have the porter collect your things."

Fifteen minutes later the conductor opened the door to a sumptuous private car. He didn't tell her whose car it was, and Jennifer wasn't about to ask—that would be putting too much stress on her good fortune. After her baggage was delivered, Jennifer put her things in order, then reclined on a luxurious velvet sofa and inspected her new home. This car had it all: costly upholstery, rare paintings, marble plumbing fixtures, and a big brass bed with a ceiling mural above it.

After a sudsy bath, her first in a real marble tub, and elegantly served dinner, Jennifer parked her person in the middle of the brass bed and turned off the lamp. Supremely comfortable and very sleepy, she still couldn't believe her luck—bless Jay Gould's heart. She smiled, thinking she could just hear Aunt Winny's say, "Now, wouldn't that blow your dress up?" when she told her.

Well past midnight, a slow-walking stranger dressed in black paused at the door of the last car on the train. After a few maneuvers with a pocketknife the door opened, and he stepped into a sumptuous private car. He moved quietly. His legs were long, and his spurs shined dully in the dim light, their ring silenced by thick carpeting and the sound of metal wheels rolling along miles and miles of metal track.

The train lurched, its mournful whistle crying out into the night. The stranger approached the brass bed and paused, a smile stretching across his shadowed face. He saw her hair, sleek as black satin, trailing like a cast-off gown over the side of the bed, so long that it touched the floor. He lifted a heavy section of it in his hands and let it sift through his fingers, closing his eyes, as if that would help him retain the memory of it, as cool and silky as the desert sand at night. Quietly he removed his boots, then put his weight upon her bed.

Jennifer stirred in her sleep, turning over, tangled up in bedding and gown and coal-black hair. He stretched out beside her, studying the perfect oval of her face, her courtesan's lashes and rosy mouth. Carefully he lifted the first satin tie at her throat and pulled it through the knot; once, twice . . . ten times, until they all lay open, then one finger came up to trace the valley between her breasts and push the sides away and down, past her navel and the soft roundness of her belly, then lower, where the dark shadow between her milky thighs lay. He parted her thighs and touched her drowsy warmth. She groaned and shifted in her sleep, giving him better access, the sleepy flesh yielding.

Four buttons on his pants and he was free. He entered her and covered her mouth with his own. Groggy and sleepily aware of a slow pleasure building like a dark, swirling current through her body, Jennifer floated with it. With a groan Jay melted into the core of her, knew for one moment frozen in time how it would be between them if she were truly his. By slow degrees Jennifer awoke to the awareness of a hard, sleek body, smooth and powerful, moving in perfect rhythm with her own.

Her eyes flew open, knowing the hard, powerful body, the iron-banded arms, the brilliant blue eyes that watched the result of passion on her face. She bucked against him, clawing his back and thrashing wildly, like a fish trying to throw a hook. He felt the despair of it sinking into the depths of his soul, knowing he had come so close, only to watch it slip away again. He was beyond himself now, emptying himself within her, but the pleasure of it had already leached away, and he knew how she must feel, hollow and empty and afraid.

He kissed her with a tenderness he had never felt before, nuzzling the exquisite velvet of her throat. "Jenny," he whispered, "love me. Please love me." But when he lowered his mouth to hers, she turned her face away, and he felt a painful fluttering as he kissed her ear.

He held the gauzy warmth of her, even now, when completely spent, feeling a slow, erotic ache that could be heard in his moan. How empty it seemed now; he felt exposed and somehow helpless, knowing the magic had gone, that the moment in time when he should have been closest to her, he had gone on alone. When he lifted his head, she was watching him, a bewildered expression on her face. His hand slid along the side of her neck, his thumb stroking the fullness of her bottom lip. "No one, sweet Jenny, can obey two masters. Not for long. Sooner or later you're going to have to decide. Who will win, I wonder? Your heart, or your foolish pride?" Then, with a groan of agony, his arms were around her, as sure and steady as the heart that beat beneath her breast.

"I won't let you do this." It sounded like a cry. She almost got away from him, but he jerked her by the hair and twisted her beneath him, stopping her cry brutally with his mouth, kissing her, devouring, until she lay exhausted and breathing heavily beneath him, knowing she had driven him to the point of desperation, feeling the pain of his anger, desire, and despair, as if they were her own.

"Goddamn you," he whispered brokenly against the sudden dryness in her mouth. "Damn you to hell." His forehead rested against hers, his breathing hard, his eyes closed. Wanting. Always this wanting. Dear God, will it never end? His face was moving over hers, kissing, seeking; past control, he was hard and fierce against her.

"You rutting bastard, leave me alone!" His head flew up. He jerked his arm to bring the back of his hand down to slap the resistance from her face . . . until he saw the fear in her eyes and realized what he had almost done. He shoved himself away from her, rolling away. She watched the agony gripping his face, heard the words drawn raggedly from his lungs. "Give me a minute . . . I'll get out of your way."

Her heart sinking with wretchedness, unable to watch him hurting, she touched his arm. "Jay . . ."

"Leave me alone, damn you! If you don't want me, then stay the hell away."

With a low, painful wail, she rolled against him, locking her arms around his neck. Feeling him stiffen in resistance, she squeezed tighter, placing wild, frantic kisses along his neck, knowing the sinking weight of failure until his hand drove into the hair at the back of her head. "Aw, Christ," he said. "I must be crazy . . . or dead."

He kissed her so sweetly, she was overcome with the sudden rush of helplessness, the feeling that she was slowly sinking into him, losing herself in a surging gush of warmth that left her trembling and limp. And all the reasons she had to hate him melted like vapor in the sun. His arm slipped behind her head and he kissed her with such intensity, such power, such passion, that her arms came up to grip him to keep from floating away. He was strong and solid and warm—a strength to cling to in a crazy world turned upside down. His strength, his passion—and yes, his insistence and determination—sent tremors streaking wildly across her heated skin. He kissed her like he had never kissed her before, and she felt dizzy, like the world was spinning, and long before it steadied, she was kissing him back.

"I still want you to marry me, you know," he said, holding her against him after making love to her a second time.

She didn't say anything.

"I take it that means no."

She kissed his mouth softly, in answer, then released a sigh. "It's still the same, isn't it? Just as it was before. Nothing has changed at all. Except that we're both a year older."

"I guess not even telling you I love you would matter, then, not at this point."

"It matters . . . but it won't change anything. I can't live the way you do, Jay. I can't and I won't. How long will you be the fastest? How long before he comes along . . . the young hothead who's just a fraction faster with a gun? How many times will those chambers fire before you make a mistake, one tiny slipup that leaves you bleeding to death in some miserable hole? Every time I see you, I'm reminded that this might be the last time. You'll come to your end quickly, but me . . . I'll die a little each day."

She looked at him, holding her gaze steady, until at last he saw the pain of finality. She looked away. When he tried to draw her back to him, she struggled, writhing, pushing at him, until he brought his hands up and tangled them in the long skeins of her hair, holding her head immobile as he tried to kiss the resistance from her mouth. "It's no good, Jay. You're fighting the wrong thing. I'm not the source of the pain in your life." His kiss was pleading, and yet held a hint of sadness. The warm pressure was suddenly gone. His eyes glittered dark and angry above her. "Jennifer, you're a fool."

The look on his face frightened her. Had she gone too far? Said too much? Pushed him to the edge? She tried to pull away from him, but he jerked her back against him, leaving her giddy from the impact. "You're crushing the breath from me."

"I hope to God I do. I hope I leave you breathless. I hope I draw the last measure of life from you. I want it all, Jenny —your body, your heart, your very soul. I won't settle for anything less. And I'll have it. I'll have it all, because I'm as strong as you are, and by God, you won't turn me away. I'm going to kiss you, and keep on kissing you, until you faint. I'm going to draw the very life and breath from you. And when I do, I'll ask for more and more and more. You've needed this for a long time. You've never had a man that was strong enough for you, one you couldn't worm and wheedle and twist around your little finger. I may not be what you think you want, but by God, I'm what you're going to get. I know you, Jenny."

"You don't know anything!"

His mouth slammed against hers and she submitted without a whimper, too stunned to push him away, having no desire, really, even to try. Her heart thundered in her chest and she felt her body shudder with the sudden appearance of fear, fear of his power, fear of his strength against the mounting weakness that defeated her. And still he kissed her. Would he never stop? *I'm going to kiss you and keep on kissing you until you faint.* Her heart pounded in her temples, the blood rushed thickly to her head. Around and around his words swirled in her head—*until you faint . . . until you faint . . . until you faint.* And her own mind screaming, *Please stop . . . don't ever stop*—until she felt she was going crazy and she let out a whimper.

"Tell me you love me!" he said, his face hovering over hers like a flapping hawk. He shook her. "Say it," he said, "or by God, I'll kiss you until they have to pry us apart." She opened her mouth but was so stunned by what was happening, nothing came out. He shook her again. "Tell me, damn you! You can't betray your heart any more than I can. You were made for me, Jenny, from the very beginning. And you're going to tell me, or so help me—"

"I love you," she said. "I love you. I love you. I love you." She was pounding him with her fists now. "I love you but I despise you. You loved me the first time you made love to me, but you wouldn't admit it. You loved me then, you love me now, but what good does it do? Well, listen to me. I can see you are hurting, and that you suffer. But I don't feel sorry for you. I have no words of comfort. I'm glad you hurt. Do you hear me? I'm glad. I want you to hurt like I hurt. I want you to feel the hopeless agony of loving and being denied that which you would gladly die for. What right did you have to deny us what we could have had? We had something beautiful, and you took it away. And I hate you for it. I hate you for teaching me to love, then hurting me. I hate you for leaving, for turning your back and walking away. I hate you for being in Savannah when you had no right to come back into my life. And most of all, I despise you for being with the pasty-faced straw-for-brains who couldn't keep her sticky fingers off you. If I were a man . . . if I were stronger . . . I think I could kill you for it."

"I never would have pegged you for the jealous type. Still, it pleases me."

"I don't give a fig for what pleases you."

"Yes, you do, and for your information, that rattle-head was just an old family friend, a girl I grew up with. I was her escort, nothing more," he said, sitting up on the side of the bed and pulling on his boots.

"How did you find me?"

"I went to your uncle's house. Your mother told me."

"Remind me to thank her."

"She had no way of knowing what I planned."

"What did you plan, Jay? What was the reason for going to this much trouble to catch me?"

"I'm glad you realize it was trouble. I had to ride like hell. If it hadn't been for that two-hour stop you made . . ." He paused and looked at her, his expression suddenly serious. "Nothing has changed for me. I still want you, Jenny. Even more than I did before. I love you." He was looking at her strangely. "I don't know what to do about you."

"Maybe that's because you still haven't decided what it is you want. Sometimes I wish it was another woman. That's something I could understand. But this?" She threw up her hands. "This is something I can't deal with. How do you fight someone's past, the road to destruction they've chosen for the present? You're like a man in love with two women. You can't seem to decide which of us you want. You're going to have to choose. You can't have both. I told you that before."

She saw that her words had cut into him, but he didn't say anything. The old angry, dark look was back, etched deeply upon his brow.

"You can't seem to put a stop to your own pain; you keep yourself locked into something that will eventually destroy you. You want everything on your terms. You never once have considered me. I have a good life—it's productive and satisfying—and I'm happy. I love you, Jay. But I can live without you."

He was listening to her, she knew, but his look was still dark and angry, his back to her as he stared out the window, seeing nothing but endless, dark night.

"You need to get your life together. Decide just what it is that you want. But leave me alone. If you ever come back, if you bother me in any way, I'll have you arrested."

He turned toward her. "I'll see you whenever I feel like it."

She watched him; the hope that had so newly sprouted within her withered and died. Thinking Jay had come to his senses and come after her to set things right . . . she suddenly saw how foolish she had been. Nothing had changed. Nothing. He had come back into her life, but only for a moment, and for all the wrong reasons. It was too late for them. The reality of it was much sharper now, much more so than before. This time she wouldn't go home to lick her wounds and wait, thinking he would come back to her. This night had been sort of a parting gift, both in being with him one last time and in knowing that after tonight she would never see him again. There was a sense of finality here that had been missing when he'd left her in Fort Worth.

He came up behind her, slipping his arms around her waist. "Come with me."

"Don't." She pulled his hands apart and stepped away. "It won't work. Not for us. Not this way."

"How can you be so sure?" His voice was relaxed, calm.

"What are you going to do for the rest of your life? How will you support a wife and family? Do you still intend to keep your job as a marshal?"

"Yes. I told you that before. The territorial judge, Isaac Parker, wants me to take on a full marshal's position instead of a deputy's. It would mean more money."

"But the time away from home . . . the risk to your life . . . they would be the same, wouldn't they?"

"Yes."

"Then you see, it's the same as it was before. I can't live like that, Jay. I told you that before: It's not the lack of money. I don't want to raise my children alone. I don't want to be a widow."

"You're still saying no?"

"Yes, the answer is still no."

"The job . . . that's what you object to?"

"Yes."

"Are you saying you'll marry me if I give up my job as a marshal?"

"I don't want to use something like that to manipulate you. I would hope you would quit because you want more for yourself, for the family you might have."

"Still, the incentive is there. To marshal or not to marshal, that is the question."

She simply stared at him, knowing clearly what she had always wanted whenever she met the right man: marriage, children, a lifetime with the man she loved. But what did she have with Jay? Nothing more than a fermenting mixture of doubt; a shaky foundation teetering at the precipice that would eventually tilt too far, hurling her into an endless void. Was that why they called it falling in love?

"Why are you so stubborn? Why do you persist in throwing it all away? Why don't you give it a try? You have nothing to lose." *Nothing more than my heart, my reason to live, the hope for any future happiness. And you? Why are you so stubborn, so proud . . . so damn stupid? Why can't you extract yourself from your past? Why can't you give me the same chance you gave Milly? Why can't you see that I'm nothing like her, that I could no more turn away from you than I could stop breathing?*

There must have been something final in the way she was looking at him, because his whole countenance seemed to change as he stood there, looking at her. And then, without a word, he turned and walked toward the door.

"Good-bye," she said, but he didn't reply. *Good-bye, my love.*

Five days later the train pulled into Fort Worth. Rand was there with the buggy to pick her up. After loading her trunk he climbed in the buggy beside her and patted her hands with one of his big ones, picking up the reins with the other. "It's good to have you home, sugar."

Jennifer scooted closer and dropped her head to her father's shoulder. "It's good to be back home."

"I was surprised when I got your wire, that you were coming home, while Susanna and Winny decided to stay longer. What happened?"

"It's a long story. I'll tell you later."

"How long can you stay?"

"Just until Mother and Aunt Winny return, then we'll go on back. I've got school coming up, and there are a million things I need to do before then. I can't believe my summer is almost gone."

She grinned at him, pushing the black feather that trailed

from the brim of her hat back from her face, but that did little good. The moment she released it, the feather flipped right back. "Blast and double blast," Jennifer said, reaching up and giving the feather a twist. With a snap, about four inches of it broke off in her hand. She held it in her palm, a gust of wind catching it, and she laughed as it floated forward and landed on the broad back of the carriage horse.

Rand laughed, giving her a hug. "That's my girl," he said. "You always were a funny little thing. Never could predict how you were going to turn out."

She wrinkled her nose at him. "What do you mean, funny?"

"The other girls, well, I always had a picture in the back of my mind . . . Abbey and her mothering ways, I knew she'd end up with a houseful. And Clara, loving to cook like she does, I wasn't at all surprised to see her going a little plump. Even Heddy running off with that cowhand didn't really surprise me. Heddy never did think about anything before she did it, and she always did exactly as she pleased."

"And me?"

"You were the puzzle. Not bigger than a minute, three quarters of you hair. Never saw so much hair on a little girl. Dainty and feminine you were, but there was always some disparity there, like they didn't have enough of everything to go around when they created you, so they had to scrape you together, taking a little out of this bucket and a little out of that, until they came up with a whole being."

Jenny laughed. "That's the oddest story of creation I ever heard. You better not let Reverend Thatcher hear you talking like that. He thinks our family is strange enough as it is."

"He's probably right, but I've never seen another one I'd trade mine for. We've just got a lot of distinct personalities in our bunch . . ."

"And I'm the most distinct, I take it."

"I would use the word *complex*." He slapped the reins

against the gelding's back, picking up the pace, then looked at her. "You always looked like a little painted china doll with your white skin and black, black hair. And that tiny little head of yours seemed much too little to bear the weight of all that hair. One look and you'd think you were frail and delicate, but you were the most robust and energetic of the bunch. Wild as a March hare you were, but you always looked neat as a pin. I found it hard to discipline you. I remember so many times when you stood before me in the library, with those big, round eyes on me, looking as sweet and innocent as a cherub, your little white apron stiff and spotless, your patent-leather shoes shiny as a button. And I'd be hearing the worst stories about what you had just done. So I'd hem and haw and try to work around it, and you'd look me in the eye and say, 'I did it, Papa.' "

Rand took out his handkerchief and wiped his eyes. "Damnation, it was hard to spank you. And after I did, you would climb into my lap and hug my neck and tell me how sorry you were and how you'd try to be a good girl. You were the only one of the girls who would do that. The others would stay mad at me for days, pouting and giving me plenty of space." He shook his head. "You were as stubborn as they come, yet the easiest child to get along with. I finally figured you were only stubborn about those things you really and truly believed in. And when you believed in something, you were a little scrapper, but other times you were the softest, most gentle-natured one of the bunch. Your mind was always going in fifty directions, yet you always took note of the little things. You were smart, pretty, and had more friends than you could shake a stick at. At times you looked like the haughty little rich girl, only to turn around and befriend the scraggliest kids in school, giving them your lunch. . . . Once you gave your brand-new Easter dress away two days before Easter." He looked at her again. "You remember the time you blackened that little Nethercutt girl's eye?"

Jennifer's hands came up to her mouth with a gasp, and

then she laughed. "Yes. She stole the silver bracelet you'd brought me from Paris."

"You remember what you did after you beat the socks off her?"

"Yes. I gave her the bracelet and told her that the next time she wanted something to ask for it, that it was a sin to steal."

He reached over and cuffed her lightly on the chin. "It's a difficult thing to do, you know that?"

"What is, Papa?"

"To let the last one go." He looked off for a moment. "Never bothered me this much to see the other girls leave, but watching you grow up, I just never seemed to think there would ever be a time that little Jenny would pack up and leave. There's a finality to it, like it triggers something in a man and makes him grow old all of a sudden."

Jennifer squeezed his arm, dropping her head against his shoulder once more. "I'm sorry I grew up, Papa, but I couldn't stay a little girl forever."

"No, I wouldn't ask that of you." He slapped the reins to pick up their pace a little. "What are you going to do with your life, Jenny? Do you think you'll ever consider getting married?"

"I do sometimes, but most of the time I feel like there's something wrong with me. Men don't stay around me very long."

"It's because you scare the hell out of them, that's why."

"Scare them? Why would you say that?"

"It'll take one hell of a man to balance the scales with you. You're just a little too pretty, a little too smart, a little too talented, and too opinionated and confident. On top of that, you have more money than most men make, and if anyone made it past all that, our family would give him second thoughts."

She reached for her parasol and opened it with a snap. "So what am I supposed to do? Act like a dolt?"

"No. Just keep being yourself, sugar. One of these days

the right man will come along, a man as determined and stubborn and smart and good-looking as you are. And he'll be strong . . . God help him, he'll have to be. And he will be. He'll be strong enough to challenge you and man enough to love you, and he'll prove it to you without smothering you or crushing you beneath his foot. You may not think he's the one, and it may anger you to have someone you can't push around, but you'll admire the hell out of him for it." He looked at her. "And he won't settle for half a loaf, either. He'll want it all, Jenny. And he won't stop until he gets it." He shook his head. "Damn it all! I hope I'm still around when that day comes. I want to shake the man's hand that can hold a lightning bolt and not get burned."

By the time Rand said his last sentence, Jennifer wasn't listening. What he was saying was coming home to roost, sounding too much like something she had heard before. *I hope to God I leave you breathless. I hope I draw the last measure of life from you. I want it all, Jenny. Your body. Your heart. Your very soul. I won't settle for anything less. And I'll have it, little girl. I'll have it all, because I'm as strong as you are, and by God, you won't turn me away. You can fight me all you want, deny your feelings until you're blue in the face, but it won't do you any good. I'll have you. . . .*

The following Monday, Susanna and Winny returned. Later that night Rand was propped up in the big four-poster bed, watching Susanna brush out her long auburn hair, something he had done almost every night for over half of his life, and he never tired of it.

"Rand?"

"Hmm?"

"Jennifer is in love."

Rand's head came up off the pillow. "In love? Our Jenny? With a man?"

Susanna stopped brushing and turned to look at him. "Of course it's a man. What else would she be in love with?"

"One of her damn causes."

"No. This is a different kind of love. Serious."

"Who is he? Someone she met in Savannah? Awfully short notice, if you ask me. I believe in knowing someone a long time. And being engaged for at least a couple of years."

"Is that why we married six months after our engagement?"

"That was different. We knew what we were doing."

"The man is perfect for her, Rand."

"Perfect?"

"Perfect. A perfect fit."

"A perfect fit?"

"Like a glove."

Rand frowned. "Are we talking about the same thing? That bastard hasn't had his way with her, has he?"

"That isn't the kind of fit I was talking about."

"It's a damn good thing. I'd hate to kill the bastard before his wedding."

"That makes sense, Rand. There wouldn't be a wedding if you killed him."

"Who is he?"

"Jay Culhane."

"Jay Culhane? The marshal, the one—"

"The same."

"Our Jenny and Jay Culhane? The marshal? She must be out of her mind. In love with a gunslinger. A drifter. A man running away from his past. It's ridiculous. He's too old for her. He's been married before."

"I thought you liked him."

"I like him but that doesn't mean I want to marry him."

"He hasn't asked you. I think it's Jenny he wants."

"How do you know? Has he written her? Why wasn't I told? Why haven't I heard anything about it all these months? Why didn't you tell me?"

"I didn't know until we went to Savannah. He was there, Rand. At the wedding. A blind man could have seen they were in love with each other. I wish you could have seen the way he looked at her when she walked down the aisle."

"Like she was a prime cut of beef and he was coming off a forty-day fast, I would imagine."

"That's why she left before I did. She wanted to get away."

"I thought you said she loved him."

"Rand, stop and think. She does love him. And he loves her. They both haven't realized it yet. He followed her, came to see her, her first night on the train. She was in her berth, asleep. He woke her up."

"And?"

"They're in love, Rand. Don't you remember what that was like?"

"My baby," he said, shaking his head. Then, louder, "My baby! That worthless bastard raped my baby!"

"It wasn't rape, Rand, and it wasn't the first time."

"He took her virginity when he had no goddamn right!"

"He may not have had any right, Rand, but he had plenty of cooperation." She laid the brush down. "Will you be sensible?"

He stared at the yellow roses in the wallpaper, talking to himself.

The man's been married before, and he's much too old.
> *But she loves him.*
It doesn't make sense. She doesn't know what she's doing.
> *But she loves him.*
He compromised her, took her to his bed.
> *And she let him.*
Who do they think they are, taking carts before horses?
> *But they're in love.*
And how do I know that, when nothing's been said?
> *Susanna told you.*
What difference does that make? How does she know?
> *Because she was young once.*
So was I. But I don't understand.
> *But you understood once.*

I did? When was that?

         When you took carts before horses.

That was different. We were in love.

"So when is the wedding?" Rand asked.

"I don't know if there'll be a wedding."

"I thought you said they were in love . . . in love and made love. In my book that equals a wedding!"

"This is a different book, Rand. There won't be a wedding."

"Why the hell not?"

"They're both way too stubborn; each of them wants it their way. They can't reach a compromise."

"This doesn't make any damn sense. What do you think I should do? Go beat some sense into his head?"

"Of course. That would be perfect. Just what they would need. More reasons to stay apart. Just try to be a little understanding. Jenny isn't herself right now. I thought it would help if you knew why."

"She's pregnant?"

Susanna threw up her hands in exasperation. "No! Of course not." She paused, then said, "At least I don't *think* she is."

"Think?" he repeated. *"Think!* We'd best be finding out in a damn hurry. If she is, we'll have to find that galloping Galahad and inform him he's fixing to be a husband and a papa in very short notice." He looked at his wife. "You go talk to her. Tell her we've got to know one way or the other."

"I will, just as soon as you tell me just how I'm going to go about rushing Mother Nature along. There's only one way of knowing for sure, and that's a few weeks off."

"Oh," said Rand Baxter. "Right."

Susanna removed her wrapper and climbed into bed, looking from the lamp burning beside her to her husband. "Are you ready for me to turn the light out?" she asked.

"You know, love is a funny thing," Rand replied. "I remember my father told me there was never a problem too big in a marriage that you couldn't let the sheets decide."

"That sounds like something your father would have said," Susanna replied, "but it doesn't have anything to do with my question. Do you want the light on or off?"

Rand rolled over and put his arms around his wife, hauling her against his chest. "Why don't we let the sheets decide?" he said, doing the most delicious things in the vicinity of her ear.

A slender, lace-covered arm slipped from the sheets and snapped off the light.

21

"If this miserable feeling is love," Jennifer told her mother the next morning, "then I don't want any part of it."

"There's a certain amount of suffering that always seems to come with being in love," Susanna said. "At one time or another every person that has ever been in love goes through periods of rapture, only to suffer occasional emotional upheavals. You want what you don't have, or if you have it, you want more of it. If your feelings are returned, you float on clouds. If unrequited, you sink in the mire of misery. At best it can only be called a sweet mystery."

" 'Sweet misery' is more like it."

"So what are you going to do about it, Jenny? You can't sit around moping forever. It isn't like you."

"I don't know. I *hate* this feeling. I've never felt this way before—so . . . so out of control. I thought I had more self-discipline than that. But these feelings . . . oh, I don't know, it's just that my love for Jay seems to persevere, even when faced with complete rejection. I don't understand why I continue to seek love from a man who has abandoned me."

Susanna smiled, patting Jennifer's hand. "It's only been a little over week, Jenny."

"But if he loved me like he said—"

Susanna put her finger over Jennifer's lips to silence her. "Don't you dare, Jennifer Leigh. You weren't raised to be emotionally fixed on having your own desires met." Susanna grew silent. "I suppose that is more our fault, mine and Rand's. You were the baby, and that always places a burden on a child. That, coupled with the fact that you were born just a month after Irene died, I'm afraid we both spoiled you. Perhaps that is why you expect Jay to behave the way you think he should. You're two different people, Jenny, from different backgrounds, different families. You're different sexes."

Jennifer looked at her mother as if she thought she were crazy. "I'm not a drooling imbecile! I haven't lost all touch with reality. I can still tell the difference between men and women."

"I didn't mean that. I'm only trying to point out your differences. Because of them, you can't expect Jay to act and feel like you would do if you were him."

"I know that. I know I don't like the way he acts. I don't even like the way *I'm* acting. I never thought I'd see the day that I moped over anything. I'm just a mass of confusion. Sometimes I wonder if I love him at all. Maybe I don't even know what love is."

"Love can't be measured or defined. It's not a single concept, and it's different things to different people. You can only define what you think love is."

"Well, don't ask *me!* I think it's impossible, absurd, and insane. I don't know why anyone with average intelligence would choose to live like this. You're a complete ass the whole time. When you're together, you act like a mindless fool. When you're apart, you're so foul that you can't stand yourself. I ask you, just what are the benefits?"

Susanna raised one brow and smiled.

"Besides *that,*" Jennifer snapped.

The next week Jennifer and Winny returned to Brownsville. Unable to forget Jay and needing a cause to keep her from "going stark raving mad," as she told her mother, Jennifer returned to the life she had known before Jay came so fiercely into hers.

September came, and, with it, the beginning of the school year and the feeling of being needed, which was always important to her. Throwing herself into her work had helped her regain some semblance of sanity, retrieving her from her ever-present sadness, leaving her to feel like she walked a tightrope—one slip and she would plunge back into the pit of despair. So she pushed herself, taking up more causes, hoping that by giving to others she might be given some measure of peace in return. But physical exhaustion doesn't reach all the way into the mind, and often, after a grueling day of teaching, then missing the evening meal, devoting her time to taking notes for a meeting she would attend later that evening, she would return home late, totally exhausted. Often, at times like this, times when she was weary beyond belief, the memory of him would come and she would burst into tears and cry herself to sleep.

Aunt Winny dropped by with a bushel of corn. They sat on the porch shucking the ears. "Thad Carpenter's oldest boy came by the other day."

"Luke? How's he doing?"

"Fine. He was asking about you."

"Hmm."

"He wanted to know what I thought about his asking you out."

Jennifer stopped shucking to look up. "What did you tell him?"

"I said it wouldn't hurt none to ask."

Jennifer shrugged. "Luke Carpenter . . . I don't know."

"You can't keep comparing them all to him, you know."

"I know, but it's just so hard not to. Once you've tasted champagne, it's hard to settle for water."

Winter came, cold and bleak, the coldest on record for

many years. Already there had been a couple of hard
freezes and ice storms. And, in between, arctic winds and
gloomy, overcast days, as if the whole world had suddenly
gone melancholy, as she was feeling. Yet its very bleakness
was a refuge for survival, a place of solitude and sanctuary.
Often Jennifer would find a moment of quiet—when her
students were bent over their work—and she would find
herself standing in front of the window staring at the frozen
yaupon that grew beneath the window, seeing its ice-en-
cased berries and feeling as if she were looking into a mirror. Would the warm, thawing sun ever come back into her
life? Would she ever again feel joy and exuberance? Was she
to be denied for all time the feeling she used to have about
life—that it was a paint box filled with vivid colors?

It had been eighteen months since he had returned her to
her parents and ridden out of her life, four months since
that night on the train. If things had turned out differently
that night, she could have been expecting Jay's baby. Jay's
baby. She leaned her head against the cold pane of glass
and closed her eyes, trying to imagine what Jay's child
would look like—blond and fair like him, or stamped with
her own darkness? Often her thoughts would run along this
vein and she would feel relieved that he hadn't saddled her
with that burden. Other times she would feel cheated and
angry, denied the love of her life, and unable to understand
why she had been denied his child as well. Often the vision
of herself with Jay's child was so strong, she could almost
smell the sweetness of mother's milk and baby powder and
fresh-washed clothes. It confused her that the vision
seemed so realistic at times. A gust of wind whistled around
the corner, shaking the yaupon, rattling its stiff branches
against the schoolhouse, chasing away the tender smells
and reminding her of her own frozen barrenness. She wondered if Jay thought about her anymore.

The first time Luke Carpenter asked her out, Jennifer
went. The second time she turned him down.

"I don't think one short evening at a church social is a very good test of compatibility," Winny said.

"Aunt Winny, it wasn't short. It went on forever . . . or so it seemed."

"Hmm," Winny said. "Maybe Luke isn't the one. Maybe you're just not ready."

"Maybe I won't ever be."

"You will, when you let go of Culhane."

"I don't know. . . ."

"When you want it bad enough, you will. Hunger will lead the fox out of the forest."

There were so many times she would be busy inside her small house, bent over the papers she was grading or easing her aching body between cold sheets, and she would start, suddenly sensing a presence, feeling so keenly Jay's vitality and warmth. She had only to think of him like this—sense his presence or recall a past memory, the touch of a too warm palm sliding across her naked hip, a hot look of possession—and she would feel that explicit pain tighten her breasts, spiraling downward to her thighs and softening her knees, leaving her with that buttery feeling that only his memory could evoke. It angered her to know that the vagueness of his presence could throw her into delirium so abruptly.

Many times she thought about going back to Weatherford and taking up the life of the wealthy rancher's daughter, filling her life with laughter, gay parties, and courtship. She knew it wouldn't be hard to find a husband. She was still blessed with her beauty—she could be thankful the destruction wrought by Jay's rejection had all been internal —knowing that whenever she went into town or attended church, men would follow her with their eyes, just as they did here in Brownsville. Yes, even in Weatherford the looks would be the same: hot, lustful looks of hunger, or the warm and proper looks of possession and ownership.

A handsome, wealthy rancher in his thirties began to drop by, under the pretext of being neighborly, offering her the use of a hand or two to help with chores, the use of a buggy or a faster-gaited horse. He was warm and cordial, a gentleman like her father, and she let him take her out a few times, to a church social or a community dance, even visiting Winny and Pearl on a few occasions. That very afternoon he had dropped by, leaving her a choice cut of beef, lingering a little longer than necessary, and asking her, just before he mounted, if she would go with him to the next community dance. Her heart wasn't in it, but she was tired. Tired of being alone. Tired of feeling old. He gave her the most loving of looks and kissed her hand when she finally agreed.

She had been right, she was sure, to isolate herself while she battled Jay's memory, waiting until she could obliterate every shred of feeling for him. And she found, as time went by, that she could go for longer and longer periods without the tormenting memory of him, and her body began to settle into a state of sleepy dullness, her mind responding to the discipline of forgetting.

The night was well advanced and bright with moonlight by the time Jennifer finished the last report card and yawned, thinking it was time to go to bed. She stacked the cards and clicked off the lamp. An anxious wind stirred in the black fringe of trees that edged the perimeter of the yard, moaning restlessly among the eaves and swirling like an aching groan around the chimney. But inside the small house, everything was silent.

Weary, yet feeling a strange, quiet peacefulness, she washed her face. After unbraiding the coil of hair at her neck, she brushed it out and reached for her gown, pulling it over her head, only to discover it wouldn't go. Yanking it off again, she saw that the satin bow at the neck had slipped into a knot. After several minutes and no success with the bow, she felt a sudden urge to cut the knot and be done with it.

She reached for a pair of scissors lying on the dressing table. She paused, listening to the sound of the wind howling around the house, and had a sudden memory of another night such as this, a night in a tiny little house in Mexico, when the wind drove a breathtakingly handsome rogue through her doorway in a swirl of fury. She shook her head to chase away the unwelcome thought but was soon distracted by the banging of a loose board somewhere in the night. It sounded as if someone was walking across her porch. She laid the scissors down and turned around.

A splintering crash. A sudden rush of dust and debris into her room. Shielding her eyes, she looked toward the door.

It couldn't be.

But it was.

No! her mind screamed. He was a thousand miles away, wearing a sheepskin jacket and a U.S. deputy marshal badge, hunting down some outlaw or renegade Indian, a gunslinger, a lawman in the Nations, hardened and running from his past.

But there was no mistaking that face, those eyes, the eaglelike cast to his bearing, the quick watchfulness of a gunman: Jay Culhane.

Jay Culhane as she had known him. Cold. Ruthless. Arrogant. "What are you doing here?"

"Do you really have to ask?" he said softly.

This was Jay Culhane as she had never seen him before. Jay, with a mocking fire in his eyes, the shiny gold buttons of his dark uniform flashing brilliantly against the lantern's light. But it couldn't be. This tall, handsome man, resplendent in his dress uniform, polished brass buttons, and gold braid, his captain's bars jumping out at her. She blinked her eyes, but he was still there, looking magnificent in his naval officer's uniform, the look in his eyes telling her it was all for her. That uniform . . . Suddenly the significance of it struck her.

For her.

It had all been for her.

A sob caught in her throat as he closed the door behind

him and took a step toward her. "I came back," he said, "because I couldn't live without you. I still want you, Jenny . . . on your terms . . . if you'll have me."

"Oh, Jay . . ." It was too much, more than she could bear. She hardly knew what to say or do when he crossed the room quickly, drawing her into the warmth of his arms, taking her breath away with the thirsty nature of one long kiss. Blinded by the threat of tears, she whispered, "Dear God, is it you? Is it really you?"

"It's me," he said, and he kissed her again, feeling the old, sweet insanity he always felt around her. "I came back because I was a heartless, driven bastard who thought everything in the world was his for the taking . . . until I found something I wanted more than anything and couldn't have."

"When?" she said, standing back to look at him in his splendid uniform. "When did you do this? When did you decide to do this?"

"That's why I was in Savannah."

"When I saw you at the wedding? You didn't go back just for the wedding?"

"Lord, no! I went back for you, Jenny. Only for you . . . and in the end, for myself as well." He shook his head, drawing her against him, pressing the side of her face against his chest. She spread her hands wide and rubbed the thick wool of his jacket, feeling the hard muscles below. "You know, my love, it was so simple. I couldn't believe it. All these years I had been running from what happened in Savannah, thinking I could never go back. And then, when I did, I found there wasn't anything there to run from. My life picked up right where it had been. I was accepted, welcomed, even admired. It was like nothing had happened. Even getting my commission to go back into the Navy . . . so simple. All this time," he said, a touch of wonder in his voice. "All this time I've been running. . . ." He tilted her face up to his. "It was me, Jenny. I was running from myself."

Her thoughts whirled around and around, spinning into a restless blur. She was hardly aware that he had stopped talking until his mouth returned to hers, the kiss as soft as the breath that rushed from her lungs. "I love you, Jenny. I love you so much." His voice faded to a ragged whisper, his lips moving over her face, sending her senses up in smoke as his hand came up to cover her breast. He knelt down before her, and Jennifer groaned when he rested the side of his head against her belly. "I want you to bear my children. I want to see you big with my child." He took her hand in his. "Marry me, Jennifer. Please. I'll spend all the days of my life loving you and making you happy. Say yes, my heart. Say yes."

"I said that the minute you walked in the door." She dropped to the floor beside him. "I love you, Jay. You and only you. Forever."

His arms came around to encircle her in love. His tenderness, his gentleness, his understanding—all as much a part of him as his arrogance and ruthlessness. He was two men, really. One he showed to the world. The other he showed to her, to the woman he loved. It was part of the magic, the way he had about him that so charmed her, making her forget everything but him. She snuggled closer to him, feeling drowsy and deliciously happy. He stroked her hair, her head under his chin, pressed against his throat. She closed her eyes, listening to the wind blowing around the house, hearing the sound of Jay's heart tapping out a message to her beneath all those layers of beloved bone and muscle. Three times he had come to her like this, three times he had stepped out of the darkness and the wind of the night. He would not come again, because this time she would not let him go.

He stood, drawing her to her feet, content just to hold her against him. Slowly she became conscious of his body shaking against her. Thinking he was overcome with emotion and feeling such intense pain for him, she pulled away and looked at him, which was Jay's undoing. Laughter was imminent.

"What . . . ?"

"I know there isn't a damn thing funny about all of this, but there's something else I didn't tell you. About two months ago I received a package from that crazy aunt of yours."

"From Aunt Winny? She never mentioned it to me. What did she send you?"

"A book of verse."

There must have been something funny about the way she was looking at him, because Jay laughed. "It was a book of Robert Burns's poetry . . . with a note attached that directed me to page twenty-seven." Jennifer was obviously waiting for him to go on, and he couldn't keep from laughing.

"What did she want you to see on that page? Which poem was it?"

"An appropriate one, I'm afraid." He looked on the verge of laughing again. " 'To a Louse,' " he said, grinning at her. "Jenny, my heart . . . my love, if you would but stop laughing, I might impress you with my best Scots burr."

> *O wad some Power the giftie gie us*
> *To see oursels as ithers see us!*
> *It wad frae monie a blunder free us,*
> *An' foolish notion.*

His mouth came down on hers, his grip so strong that his hands felt bruising against her shoulders. He was done with talking and with teasing. There would be no laughter now. With the ease and skill that came so easily to him, he spoke certain soft words against her throat, then shifted her adroitly in his arms, taking her intimately into him as he did every time they touched.

She threaded her hands through the soft layers of his

hair, recalling the feel and smell and nearness of him, thinking how she had never thought to feel again the breathtaking touch of his quiet words against her throat. She had fully expected to go to the end of her days, never again to share a laugh with him—that wild, frolicsome laughter that comes when passion is spent, or to know once more the heady feeling of hilarity that comes with the casual banter of words, the soft sharing of wit. But most of all, she had expected never to delight in the sunny pleasure of loving and being perfectly loved in return.

But that was all in the past now. Jay was here, standing before her, warm and living, flesh and blood. A memory that had come to life, a vital pulsing awareness with energy and an urgency quite its own.

The flame in the lantern burned low, then went out. The room faded into darkness. From out of that darkness came a hand, warm and infinitely tender, closing over her own and leading her to the bed, and when they reached it, Jay scooped her into his arms and placed her on the quilt, covering her softness with its counterpart, his own hard body. He lowered his mouth to her and everywhere he touched scalded like dancing flames, growing and building, spreading like wildfire. She was mindless, wanting to touch him everywhere, dying a little inside each time he kissed her. His hand caressed her belly and the top of her legs and they opened for him. She whimpered as he slid his fingers deep inside her, his breath rushing outward as he did.

Everywhere he caressed her, kissed her, touched her with his mouth and body. Again she whimpered, this time when he withdrew his fingers from her, only to moan softly when he put them in his mouth. "I love the taste of you . . . you're sweet as a baby's breath everywhere I touch you. I love you. I adore you. I can't get enough of you." And slowly he filled her.

A lifetime with him . . . will it be enough? She looked up into the face of her love. He rose before her like a vision out of the pages of mythology, a golden god, his smile burning into her soul. Love filled her like the swelling waves of the ocean, coming one after the other, running together, and stretching into infinity. It was enough.

He was smiling at her as he looked down into her face, her violet eyes black in the moonlight. For just a moment he felt consumed by those eyes, swimming in their bottomless depths, as if he were looking into the future. He saw himself in the vision and he recognized Jenny, too, both of them happy, yet older than they were now. But the other faces in the revelation he did not know. They were young faces, female, a half dozen or more—faces he had never seen before, faces that were strangely familiar to him.

For the flickering of a moment he thought they were the faces of his children.

EPILOGUE

There is repetition everywhere, and nothing is found only once in the world.

Goethe

Weatherford, Texas

Jess stood beside the piano in the parlor, staring at the enraged face of her father.

"What do you mean you've been learning how to fly? Fly what?" asked Jay Culhane, his face darkening with sudden understanding. "Don't you stand there and tell me you've been learning how to fly an airplane!"

"But I have, Papa."

"I refuse to let you. I will not give you permission, Jess. Is that clear?"

Jessamine sighed. "I wasn't asking for permission, Papa."

"Then why are we having this asinine conversation?"

"I wanted you to know that I know how to fly before I told you that I'm going to England tomorrow."

"To England? What on earth for?"

"To fly across the English Channel."

"Have you lost your mind?" Jay paused for control. "I won't allow it."

"I'm going, Papa. I've already made the arrangements. I'm twenty-three years old. I'm old enough to make my own decisions."

"That's another questionable issue for debate, but we'll push it aside for now," Jay said. "What is this obsession to fly over the English Channel? If you have to fly over something, why not the Trinity River?"

"There's no challenge in that. I want to be the first woman to fly over the English Channel."

"What makes you think you can do something like that? I'm not sure it's possible."

"But it is. Louis Blériot just flew from Calais to Dover in thirty-seven minutes."

"Jess, why don't you take a trip . . . travel . . . see the world?"

"Papa, you know the last time I traveled I couldn't find my way out of Chinatown."

"And you want to fly over the English Channel? No. Absolutely not. I refuse to let you go. Haven't I told you a thousand times that a young woman doesn't go traipsing into strange places alone?"

"Mama did."

"Oh," said Jay. "Who told you that?"

"Aunt Winny. She told me to remind you that Mama had done the same thing when she went to Mexico almost thirty years ago."

Jay shook his head. "I guess this is all my fault. We should have stayed in Savannah." He shook his head again. "My first mistake was coming back to Texas after I retired. My second mistake was letting your great-aunt come live with us."

"Papa, I'd like to have your understanding."

"Have you written to Tyler about this?"

"No."

"I don't know why, but I find it a little strange that you would deem it necessary to tell your father when you have decided to keep your husband uninformed."

"I'll be back before Tyler would get my letter. I don't want him to worry. I'll tell him when he returns."

"It will be months before Tyler's ship is back. You know that."

"Yes, but I've decided to wait until then to tell him."

"And your daughter? What do you plan to do with little Laurie while you're gone." Jay scowled. "You'll take her with you over my dead body!"

"I thought I'd leave her here until I return. Aunt Winny thought that would be best."

"Aunt Winny again," said Jay. "Doesn't that woman know how to act old?" He looked from Jess to Jennifer, who had been quietly listening until just moments ago, when she suddenly found herself distracted by an arrangement of flowers next to her. Jay, his eyes on his wife, said, "My love, did you hear what your daughter just said?"

It was the second time today that Jess had been *her* daughter, but Jennifer was used to that. Whenever things got a little shaky in the Culhane household, Jay denied having anything to do with the birth of his seven daughters. "Yes, dear. I heard."

"Well?"

Jennifer paused, a lily in her hand. "Well, what? Do you mean Aunt Winny or the airplane?"

"Both."

"Well, as for the airplane, I think Jess is right. She's old enough to make up her own mind."

"Never mind that," Jay snapped. "What about your aunt?"

"What about her?"

"She's stirring up trouble again."

"She's just speaking her mind."

"Because she has nothing to lose," said Jay. "But that's beside the point. What about your daughter?"

"I understand how Jess feels. She has always been stimulated by a challenge."

"Then she can find another challenge."

"I want to fly the Channel, Papa."

"Jay, you told me once that everyone should believe in something," Jennifer said.

Jay looked at his daughter. He looked at his wife. Then he threw up his hands.

"Where are you going?" asked Jennifer.

"You said everyone should believe in something. Well, believe I'm going to have a good, stiff drink."

Jay had his drink. In fact, he had two. Then he left the house. When he opened the back door, the sun was setting over the henhouse, and General Lee XV—Jay's prized old English black-breasted game rooster—was sitting on the back fence preening. Seeing the door open, General Lee ruffled his breast feathers, then stretched his neck, letting go with a loud crow. He was just flapping his wings and readying himself for another majestic blast when Jay stepped off the porch.

"Good morning, Grandpa. Where are you going?"

Jay looked across the porch, his gaze resting on his five-year-old granddaughter, Laurie. She was waiting for him on the front steps, a little bisque doll with her hands folded primly across her starched yellow dress, her face radiant as she turned the full light of her eyes upon him. Jay paused, looking into Laurie's delicate little face, surrounded by an abundance of long hair as thick and straight and black as an Indian's, and skin as fair and white as lamb's-lettuce when it bloomed. And those eyes, just like her grandmother's they were, the color of cornflowers, looking more lavender than blue, and so big that they didn't seem to belong on such a tiny face.

"I thought I'd meander on down to the creek for a spell," Jay said. He ambled down the steps and walked a few feet before pausing, then he turned to watch Laurie pop up like a cork and follow him.

"I'll come with you," she said as she thrust her hand into her grandfather's. When they had almost reached the creek, Laurie broke away from Jay with an excited shriek and ran up the path ahead of him.

Jay watched her go, feeling a pain wedge itself into his consciousness. Laurie. His youngest granddaughter, Laurie, the daughter of his youngest daughter, Jessamine. Jessamine, the last of seven girls. He looked at Laurie. She was the apple of his eye—and the spitting image of her grandmother, her child's brow furrowed under the weight of youthful curiosities. It all passed before him as he watched her head up the same path her grandmother had skipped over so many years ago. Dear God, how old it made him feel.

Back at the house, Great-aunt Winny was peeking out the window. "You might as well come on in. I ain't dead yet," Winny said, her voice crackling as she turned to watch Jennifer tiptoe into her bedroom. "I'll swan! You couldn't sneak up on the blind side of a flounder."

Jennifer joined Winny at the window just in time to see Laurie and Jay walk across the yard. "You have a special fondness for Laurie, don't you?"

"Did I say something?"

"No, Aunt. You didn't have to. I've known it for a long time. Of all our girls, Jess was the one who captured your heart, and now it seems her daughter has done the same. Papa was the same way. You remind me of him sometimes."

"Humph! Don't go lumping me into the same ball of dough with Randolph Baxter. We never did have a compatible bone in our body."

"I don't know about that," Jennifer said. "I always thought you were very compatible. Neither one of you liked the other. How can you get more compatible than that?"

"You're right," Winny said. "Jess is the only one of your girls who's worth hanging around for. The others—all six of them, mind you—I wouldn't give you a plug nickel for the lot. And now little Laurie . . . I've never put too many requests before the Lord Almighty, but I'd sure like to see that one grown. Just a few more years to see her to the age you were when you came to Brownsville to teach, your head crammed full of ideas."

"Oh, Aunt Winny . . ."

"Don't you Aunt Winny me! There ain't no need to be dragging out your black dress. I'm still good for a few more miles yet. I've said I want to see Laurie grow to womanhood, and I will—Lord willin' and the creek don't rise." She looked at Jennifer. "Jess told him about flying?"

"Yes. He didn't take it too well."

Winny stared out the window again, her sharp little eyes on Jay and Laurie. "He'll come around," she said.

Jay, Jennifer thought, watching him hold his granddaughter's hand—Jay, still tall and youthfully slender, his golden good looks now lightened to silver, but even so, he was still devastatingly handsome. She watched until they disappeared into the trees that lined the creek.

"He looks as lost as a July snow," Winny said. But when she turned, Jennifer was gone.

He was teaching Laurie to skip stones when Jennifer quietly came up behind them. Without taking his eyes off Laurie, he held out his arm to her, and Jennifer joined him, sighing as he drew her against him, and she tilted her head to rest against his chest.

The sky above them looked a mile high, the softest shade of blue, turning pink where the sun was beginning to set, not a cloud in sight. And all around them the earth wore the rich, varied shades of summer green while the smell of new-cut hay hung heavy in the air. Over on the opposite bank, an old bullfrog was tuning up, and when Laurie's stone went skipping, a school of silver-black minnows darted out of sight.

When it was time to go, Laurie skipped up the path ahead of them, and Jay, his hand going around Jennifer's waist, pulled her against him, kissing the top of her head when it came to rest on his shoulder. At the end of the path Laurie turned three cartwheels and then waved at them before hiking up her skirts and running back to them, stopping when she thumped against them.

"Guess what I want to be when I grow up!"

Jennifer pulled a leaf out of Laurie's dark, glossy curls. "What do you want to be, my angel?"

"A schoolteacher!"

"That sounds like something your Aunt Winny would say." Jay studied Laurie's face. "Is that what she told you?"

"No, she just said I could be a schoolteacher anywhere I wanted to. Even Africa!"

"Oh, dear," Jennifer said.

"*Oh dear* is right," said Jay.

"He sure is walking fast. Where is Grandpa going?" asked Laurie, taking Jennifer's hand and watching her grandpa hurry up the path.

"I think he's going into the house to throttle Aunt Winny."

"Uh-oh," said Laurie. "He better watch out. Mama said Aunt Winny was as sharp as a weasel."

"And you're as bright as a head of cabbage in a pumpkin field," Jennifer said, taking her granddaughter by the hand and walking toward the house.

The last shaft of daylight slanted across the wide front porch, striking Jay and Jennifer as they sat in the porch swing. Jay was holding Jennifer's hand, twirling her wedding ring around and around. Then he kissed her fingers.

"What did Aunt Winny say when you told her you were going to put a stop to her meddling once and for all?"

"She said, 'You're a good man, Culhane. But you're a beginner.' "

The sun slipped behind the horizon, giving way to the gentle hush of evening. In her upstairs bedroom, Winny Claiborne was telling Laurie about Africa, while farther down the hall, Jess was packing her flight suit in her satchel. On the front porch, Jennifer Culhane was watching a firefly in the oleander bush, feeling the gentle caress of her husband's hand as he laced his fingers through hers. Closing her eyes with a satisfied sigh, she rested her head against his shoulder. As his arm came around her she was thinking that happiness might not stretch very long, but truly, it was of infinite height.

FREE FROM DELL

with purchase plus postage and handling

Congratulations! You have just purchased one or more titles featured in Dell's Romance 1990 Promotion. Our goal is to provide you with quality reading and entertainment, so we are pleased to extend to you a limited offer to receive a selected Dell romance title(s) *free* (plus $1.00 postage and handling per title) for each romance title purchased. Please read and follow all instructions carefully to avoid delays in your order.

1) Fill in your name and address on the coupon printed below. No facsimiles or copies of the coupon allowed.

2) The Dell Romance books are the only books featured in Dell's Romance 1990 Promotion. Any other Dell titles are not eligible for this offer.

3) Enclose your original cash register receipt with the price of the book(s) circled plus $1.00 **per book** for postage and handling, payable in check or money order to: Dell Romance 1990 Offer. Please do not send cash in the mail.
Canadian customers: Enclose your original cash register receipt with the price of the book(s) circled plus $1.00 **per book** for postage and handling in U.S. funds.

4) This offer is only in effect until March 29, 1991. Free Dell Romance requests postmarked after March 22, 1991 will not be honored, but your check for postage and handling will be returned.

5) Please allow 6-8 weeks for processing. Void where taxed or prohibited.

Mail to: Dell Romance 1990 Offer
       P.O. Box 2088
       Young America, MN 55399-2088

NAME_____

ADDRESS_____

CITY_____STATE_____ZIP_____

BOOKS PURCHASED AT_____

AGE_____

(Continued)

Book(s) purchased:_____

_____

_____

I understand I may choose one free book for each Dell Romance book purchased
(plus applicable postage and handling). Please send me the following:

(Write the number of copies of each title selected next to that title.)

MY ENEMY, MY LOVE
Elaine Coffman
From an award-winning author comes this
compelling historical novel that pits a
spirited beauty against a hard-nosed
gunslinger hired to forcibly bring her home
to her father. But the gunslinger finds
himself unable to resist his captive.

AVENGING ANGEL
Lori Copeland
Jilted by her thieving fianceé, a woman
rides west seeking revenge, only to wind up
in the arms of her enemy's brother.

A WOMAN'S ESTATE
Roberta Gellis
An American woman in the early 1800s
finds herself ensnared in a web of family
intrigue and dangerous passions when her
English nobleman husband passes away.

THE RAVEN AND THE ROSE
Virginia Henley
A fast-paced, sexy novel of the 15th century
that tells a tale of royal intrigue, spirited
love, and reckless abandon.

THE WINDFLOWER
Laura London
She longed for a pirate's kisses. . . even
though she was kidnapped in error and
forced to sail the seas on his pirate ship,
forever a prisoner of her own reckless
desire.

TO LOVE AN EAGLE
Joanne Redd
Winner of the 1987 *Romantic Times*
Reviewer's Choice Award for Best Western
Romance by a New Author.

SAVAGE HEAT
Nan Ryan
The spoiled young daughter of a U.S. Army
General is kidnapped by a Sioux chieftain
out of revenge and is at first terrified, then
infuriated, and finally hopelessly aroused by
him.

BLIND CHANCE
Meryl Sawyer
Every woman wants to be a star, but what
happens when the one nude scene she'd
performed in front of the cameras haunts
her, turning her into an underground sex
symbol?

DIAMOND FIRE
Helen Mittermeyer
A gorgeous and stubborn young woman
must choose between protecting the
dangerous secrets of her past or trusting
and loving a mysterious millionaire who has
secrets of his own.

LOVERS AND LIARS
Brenda Joyce
She loved him for love's sake, he seduced
her for the sake of sweet revenge. This is a
story set in Hollywood, where there are two
types of people—lovers and liars.

MY WICKED ENCHANTRESS
Meagan McKinney
Set in 18th-century Louisiana, this is the
tempestous and sensuous story of an
impoverished Scottish heiress and the
handsome American plantation owner who
saves her life, then uses her in a dangerous
game of revenge.

EVERY TIME I LOVE YOU
Heather Graham
A bestselling romance of a rebel Colonist
and a beautiful Tory loyalist who
reincarnate their fiery affair 200 years later
through the lives of two lovers.

TOTAL NUMBER OF FREE BOOKS SELECTED ____ X $1.00
= $_____ (Amount Enclosed)

Dell has other great books in print by these authors. If you enjoy them, check
your local book outlets for other titles.